FALL

Candice Fox is the middle child of a large, eccentric family from Sydney's western suburbs. The daughter of a parole officer and an enthusiastic foster-carer, Candice spent her childhood listening around corners to tales of violence, madness and evil as her father relayed his work stories to her mother and older brothers.

Candice won back-to-back Ned Kelly awards for her first two novels, *Hades* and *Eden*, and her third novel, *Fall*, was shortlisted for the Ned Kelly and Davitt awards. She is also the author of the critically acclaimed *Crimson Lake* and co-writer with James Patterson of the *Sunday Times* No.1 bestsellers *Never Never* and *Fifty Fifty* set in the Australian outback.

Praise for Candice Fox

'Definitely a writer to watch.' Harlan Coben

'A bright new star of crime fiction.' James Patterson

'A fast-paced, expertly crafted read with a cast of colourful characters.' *Guardian*

D0263331

FALL

Candice

FOX

arrow books

1 3 5 7 9 10 8 6 4 2

Arrow Books
20 Vauxhall Bridge Road
London SW1V 2SA

Arrow Books is part of the Penguin Random House group of companies
whose addresses can be found at global.penguinrandomhouse.com.

Penguin
Random House
UK

First published in Great Britain by Arrow Books in 2019
(First published in Australia by Bantam in 2015)

www.penguin.co.uk

A CIP catalogue record for this book is available from the British Library

ISBN 9781784758363

Printed and bound in Great Britain by Clays Ltd, Elcograf S.p.A.

For Danny, Adam and Jess

Prologue

Before the blood, before the screaming, the only sound that reached the car park of the Black Mutt Inn was the gentle murmur of the jukebox inside. It was set on autoplay, tumbling out a cheerful line-up of greatest pub hits one after another, but there was none of the growly sing-alongs of usual pubs, no thrusting of schooner glasses, no stomping of heels on the reeking carpet. The jukebox played in the stale emptiness of the building, and by the time it reached the car park it was no more than a ghoulish moan. It was windy out there and the stars were gone.

The Black Mutt Inn attracted bad men, and had been doing so for almost as long as anyone could remember, as though the ground beneath it had somehow hollowed a vent to hell, the men who frequented it drawn in by the familiar heat of home. Nightly, at least, a bone was broken on its shadowy back porch over some insult or breach or another, or a promise was made there beneath the moth-crowded lamps for some violence that would occur on another night. Sometimes a plot was hatched there – the corners of the inn's undecorated interior were very good for whispering, and the walls seemed to grow poisonous ideas like vines, spreading and creeping around minds and down necks and along legs to the rotting floorboards.

The staff at the Black Mutt saw nothing, said nothing, but they absorbed secrets and requests, their ears and palms always open, their lips always sealed. They were loyal to no one and this earned them respect.

On this night, Sunny Burke and Clara McKinnie entered the Black Mutt with their laptops and bags of chilli jerky and bright, suntanned smiles. The man behind the bar said nothing, saw nothing. He just served the drinks.

Sunny and Clara brought their smiles into the Black Mutt, and though their Macleans glimmer didn't reach any farther than the murky light above the door, the two carried this weak glow to the bar and set up shop there under the mirrors. Three men sat against the wall whispering, and another two stood at the pool tables watching the two travellers fresh from Byron, stamped with its optimism and cheap weed stink. Clara ordered a champagne and orange juice and downed it quickly, and Sunny nursed a James Squire and rubbed her legs.

Into the dim halo of light stepped a man from the pool tables, and from that very second, although the bleach-white smiles remained, things in the world of Sunny and Clara began to get very dark.

'G'day, mate,' the man said, thumping Sunny between the shoulder blades. The man was tall and square and roped with veins, and the two hands hanging from his extra-long arms looked all-encompassing. Sunny looked up, appreciated the density of the man's beard and smiled, swallowing envy.

'Hey.'

'Just down from Byron, are we?'

'We've been there a week,' Clara beamed.

'I can see, I can see.' The man brushed the backs of his fingers against the top of Clara's shoulder, a brief brotherly pat. 'Sun's had its way with you, beauty.'

'We're just on our way back to the big smoke,' Sunny said.

'If you ask me, you've just come from the big smoke,' the stranger jibed, and nudged Sunny in the ribs, hard. 'Tell me you've got some grass for sale. *Please* tell me.'

Sunny laughed. 'Sure, mate.' He glanced at the other figure in the shadows, the man by the table leaning on his cue. 'No problem.'

'I don't get up to Byron often enough. Me back's no good for the drive.'

Sunny nodded sympathetically. The stranger threw out a hand and Sunny gripped it, felt its concrete calluses against his palm. 'No probs, no probs. How much are you after?'

'Aw, we'll do all that later. Hamish is the name, mate. Can I invite you to a game?'

'Yeah! Shit, yeah. This is Clara. I'm Sunny.'

'Me mate over there's Braaaadley, but don't you worry about him. He don't talk much. Plays a rubbish game of pool, too, don't you, Brad? Ay? Wake up, shithead.' The man squawked back towards the pool table but roused nothing in his partner. 'Excuse me, miss, excuse me, but me old Bradley's prone to leaning on that pool cue till he drifts off and no amount of slapping can get him back, if you know what I mean.'

'Right,' she laughed.

'You want some jerky?' Sunny asked.

'Nah, mate, nah. I'm all good. Me chompers ain't no good, as well as me back. I'm falling apart at the seams here, mate.'

They racked the balls while Clara and the silent one watched, now and then letting their eyes drift to each other, the hairy man in the dark struggling beneath the weight of his frown, the young woman rocking awkwardly, swinging her hips, holding onto the cue. She finished her second champagne and wanted another, but the men were talking and laughing and making friends, and Sunny always had trouble making friends, so she didn't interrupt.

'How about a little wager, just to make things interesting?' Hamish asked.

'Yeah, sure.' Sunny puffed out his chest, ignoring a warning look from Clara. 'Where do you, I mean, what do you usually –?'

'Five bucks?'

'Five bucks?' Sunny laughed, coughed. 'Sure, mate, sounds great.'

They played. Clara was the most excitable, howling when she sunk the white ball, cheering when Sunny scored. There was plenty of kissing. Rubbing of backsides. The men in the booths watched them. The happy group at the table were cut off from the rest of the world by the cones of light that fell upon them.

'Very good, young sir,' Hamish said, offering his big hard hand again. 'How about another?'

'Twenty bucks this time,' Sunny said. 'You can pay me in labour, if you like. The van needs a wash.'

'Sunny!' Clara gasped.

'Listen to this guy, would you?' Hamish laughed. He squeezed the young woman on the shoulder, made Clara's face burn red. 'What a cocky little shit. You're lucky you're so goddamn beautiful, Sunny me old mate. No one's gonna knock that gorgeous block off no matter what you say.'

They laughed and played again. Hamish was hard on Bradley. The balls cracked and crashed and rolled in the pockets. Clara was good. She'd always been good. Her daddy had taught her the game young, bent over the felt, his hips pinning her against the side of the table. But she knew when to sacrifice a shot so that she didn't lean over too far and give Bradley a view of her breasts, her arse.

The man looked at her funny. Made her ache inside.

'One more?' Sunny said. The bar was empty now but for the bartender, who was motionless in the shadows. Sunny won, and won again.

'One more, little matey, and then it's off to bed with you. What say we make it interesting, huh? Everything you've won, you give me the chance to win it back. We go even. I lose, you take the notes right outta my hand, no hard feelings.'

'Mate,' Sunny drawled, 'you win this and I'll give you double what you owe me.'

'Sunny!'

'Oh ho. Just listen to this guy,' Hamish laughed.

'Sunny, no.'

'Cla,' the boy drew her close, 'they haven't won a game all night. It's fine. I'm just having a laugh.'

'Sunny –'

'Just shut up, would you?' Sunny snapped, giving her that look. 'I'm only having a bit of fucking fun.'

Clara shut up because she knew what men could do, and it began with that look. She watched the men shake hands, rack the balls. When the game began, it was all Clara could do to keep those lips shut as Hamish leaned down, took aim and began sinking balls.

The table was empty of Hamish's balls in less than two minutes. And then he sunk the black in a single shot. Sunny never got a turn.

'Mate,' Hamish said when it was done, straightening and leaning on his cue, the smile and the charm and the humour forgotten now, his eyes lazy as they wandered over Clara. 'Seems you owe me quite a bit of cash.'

In the car park, Bradley walked behind them, glancing now and then towards the Black Mutt, although no such careful eye was needed. Not here, not where a hidden hole drilled straight to hell warmed the air as it breezed across the asphalt and ruffled Clara's thick dark curls. Hamish's hand on the back of her neck was like a steel clamp. They approached the Kombi van, the only one in the lot. It was parked out in the middle of a huge barren wasteland so that the young couple would be safe from whatever might be lurking in the towering wall of dark woods when they returned. Clara put her hands out to stop Hamish slamming her into the side of the van and turned. Bradley had let a steel pipe slide down from where it was hidden high up inside his sleeve.

'Give me an inventory,' Hamish said.

'There's the CD player, some cash, and Clara has some jewellery,' Sunny was saying, fumbling with his keys. 'There's the weed, too. You can take it. Please, please, I'm asking you now not to hurt us.'

'You go ahead and ask whatever you like, you snotty-nosed little prick,' Hamish said. 'You bring out whatever you can from in there and we'll see if it's enough, and if it's not, I'll decide if anyone gets hurt.'

'Take them up to the ATM,' Bradley grunted. Clara jolted at the sound of the silent man's voice. She turned and found him staring at her, eyes pinpoints of light in the dark.

'Sunny,' Clara croaked, tried to ease words from her swollen throat. 'Sunny. Sunny!'

'Shut up and hurry up,' Hamish snarled.

'I'm going. Please. Please!' Sunny was pleading with anyone now. Clara heard the pleas continuing inside the van, heard the rattling of boxes and drawers. As soon as the boy was out of sight she felt the man with the concrete hands slip his fingers beneath her skirt. Hamish smiled at her with his big cracked teeth and pressed her into the van.

'All this excitement getting you wet, is it, baby?'

'Sunny! God! Please!'

'Your pretty boyfriend better come up with something very special, very soon, baby cakes, or I'm afraid you're footing the bill on this one.'

'How about this?' Sunny said as he emerged from the van, hands full, thrusting the items at Hamish. 'Will this do?'

The knife made Hamish stiffen, made his eyes widen slightly as they dropped to the items in Sunny's hands, which all fell away and clattered to the ground, revealing the leather handle they concealed, the leather handle attached to the long hunting blade that was now buried deep in Hamish's belly.

Sunny, as always, didn't give the man a moment to appreciate the surprise of the attack. He pulled the knife out of his stomach and plunged it in again, pushed it upwards into the tenderness of Hamish's diaphragm and felt the familiar clench of shocked muscles. Clara slid away as the young man went for a third blow, took her own knife, the one she kept flush against her body between her breasts, and went for Bradley. The hairy man backed away but Clara's aim was immaculate. She set her feet, pulled back, breathed, swung and let go. The knife embedded in Bradley's back with a thunk right between the shoulder blades, and he fell and rolled like roadkill on the tarmac.

She went to the silent man and pulled out the knife, wiping it on the hem of her soft white skirt. Bradley was still alive, and she was happy because it would be a long time until she was finished with him. Clara liked to play, and though it wasn't really Sunny's thing, she thought maybe because they were on holiday he would indulge her just once with some games. She turned and looked at him, Bradley still gurgling against the asphalt under his cheek.

'Baby.' She turned on her sweet voice for her killer partner. 'What if we took this one home and –'

A whistle and a shlunk.

At first it seemed to Clara that Sunny had fallen, until she felt the wet spray of his blood on her face. She tried to process the noise she'd heard, the whistle and the shlunk, but none of it made sense. She crawled, shaking, and with her hands tried to piece back together the split halves of her boyfriend's skull, grabbing at the bits of brain and meat sprayed across the asphalt around him. There was no putting Sunny back together again.

She kneeled in the blood, both his and Hamish's, and tried to understand, little whimpers coming out of her like coughs. Hamish was sitting up beside the van, his hands still gripping at the knife wounds in his belly.

A whistle and a shlunk, and the top of his head came off. He slid to the ground.

Clara looked around at the tree line behind her, a hundred metres or so away, and then looked at the trees in front, the same distance, dark as ink and depthless. The silence rang, and under its terrifying weight she crawled, tried to get to her feet, heading towards the bar. Another whistle, another shlunk, and her foot was gone. Clara fell on her face and gripped at the stump of her leg. She didn't scream or cry out because there was only terror in her, and terror made no sound.

Clara lay and breathed, and then after some time began crawling again. She heard the sound of uneven footsteps, punctuated by a metallic clop, and looked up to see a figure coming towards her slowly, barely distinguishable against the dark of the trees from which it had emerged. The sounds kept coming out of Clara, the shuddering breaths through her lips, but through them the metallic clopping kept coming. A woman moved into the light of the van. Clara could see she was leaning on an enormous rifle, using the gun like a crutch.

The woman stepped quietly between the bodies of the men, and Clara lay in the blood and looked up at her. She thought, even as shock began to take her, about the woman's black hair, how it seemed to steal some blue out of the night and hold it, like the shimmer woven through the feather of a crow. The woman with the gun bent down, used the enormous weapon to lower herself into a crouch. Clara wondered what wounds she was carrying, what gave the other killer such trouble as she settled herself beside the dying girl.

Eden looked at the trees, the bar, finally at the girl on the ground.

'Just when you think you're the deadliest fish in the water,' Eden said to the girl.

Clara gasped. Her fingers fumbled at the wet stump where her foot had been. Eden sighed.

'I admire the game,' Eden said. 'I really do. It's clever. Two naïve little travellers just waiting to be picked on. You flounder around like you're just drowning in your own idiocy, and you see which predators come to investigate the splashing. Who could resist you? You're adorable. You lure them out into the deep, dark waters and then you surge up from below. Pull them down.'

Clara fell back against the asphalt, her mouth sucking at the cold night air, throat blocked by shock.

'If I was well, this would have been more personal,' Eden said, her leather-gloved hand gripping the rifle tight. 'But I haven't been at my best lately, so I'm afraid there's no time for play.'

Clara tried to speak, but she couldn't force words up through the whimpers. They came out of her like hiccups. The woman with the long dark hair rose up slowly, pushing the rifle into the ground, and when she'd risen fully she actioned the great thing with effort, once-strong hands betraying her as the bullet slid into the chamber.

'I'm the only shark in this tank,' Eden said.

The last gunshot could be heard inside the Black Mutt Inn. But no one listened to it.

The Victims of Crime support group of Surry Hills meets every fortnight. The only reason I started going is because my old friend from North Sydney Homicide, Anthony Charters, goes there. If I didn't have a friend there, I'd have never bowed to my girlfriend Imogen's demands that I get counselling for the 'stuff that has been going on with me' the last few months. That vague collections of terms, the 'stuff' and its propensity to 'go on with me', frequently came between the beautiful psychologist and me in our first few weeks of dating, when she realised she'd never seen me completely sober. She said she couldn't imagine me 'relaxed'. Privately, I argued I was a lot more relaxed than Imogen herself. Imogen takes an hour and a half to get ready in the morning, and the first time I farted near her she just about called the police. That, ladies and gentlemen, is not 'relaxed'.

But, you know. You don't tell them these things. They don't listen.

I'd started courting Dr Imogen Stone in the dangerous and electric place between my previous girlfriend being slaughtered by a serial killer and my partner detective almost getting herself disembowelled by a pair of outback monsters. Imogen liked me, but she was dealing with the psychological aftermath of both events. I was by all accounts an unpredictable, volatile and difficult-to-manage boyfriend. She couldn't count on me to turn up on time, say appropriate things when I met her friends, drive her places without her having to worry that I was about to career the car into the nearest telegraph pole. She couldn't be sure when I ducked out of the cinema that I wasn't going to knock back six painkillers in the glorious solitude of the men's room stall, or lose myself in thought and just wander off, turning up back at her apartment at midnight drunk and stinking. I was a bad beau, but I had potential, so she didn't give up on me. Ironically, I understand that the 'fixer-upper boyfriend' that I seemed to be is just about the perfect model for the worst type of man you can be attracted to – according to the psychology textbooks I'd perused in her office, it was the cute, broken bad boys who became abusers.

Nevertheless, Imogen took me on, and Imogen started nagging me to get help. So I started trudging with all the huffing melancholy of a teenager at church to a basement room of the Surry Hills police station every Sunday to sit under the fluorescent lights and listen to tales of horror and fear. It made Imogen happy. It made Anthony happy. I considered it my community service.

Somewhere, sometime, somebody set up a support group in a particular way and now all support groups are set up like that, whether you're trying to get over being sexually assaulted in a public toilet or you're addicted to crack. You've got the grey plastic fold-out tables pushed against one wall, the veneer pulling away from the corners and the top stained by the rims of coffee cups set down meaningfully, mid-conversation, to indicate concern. You've got the two large steel urns full of boiling water for coffee and tea, the ones that will, if you go anywhere near them, even so much as to fill in your name on the sign-in sheet, mercilessly burn some part of you. There's no avoiding the coffee-urn burn. To this you add a collection of uncomfortable plastic fold-out chairs forming a circle just tight enough to inspire that quiet kind of social terror made of things like accidental knee-touching, airborne germs and unavoidable eye contact. And voilà! You've got a support group.

There were fifteen chairs set out on the industrial grey carpet and Anthony was sitting in one when I arrived. I responded to his presence with a wave of paralysing nausea. Getting over a painkiller and alcohol addiction makes you respond to everything with nausea. You get nausea in the middle of sex. It lasts for months.

I'd worked with the bald-headed, cleft-chinned Detective Charters and his partner for about two weeks when my former partner committed suicide and the bigwigs were trying to find me someone else as a playmate. I'd have liked to have stayed with him. He was inspiring – not in the cheesy internet quote way, but in a real way, a way that gets you out of bed. He was somehow still enthusiastic about justice and the rule of law and collaring crims like it was a calling, even though his own seventeen-year-old son was in prison for five years for accidentally leaving a mate with brain damage from a one-punch hit at a New Year's Eve party. I figured if Anthony could get out of bed after that, I could get out of bed after Martina being killed (me allowing her to be killed) and Eden almost dying (me standing there doing nothing while Eden almost died). If Anthony could keep on keeping on after everything that had happened to him, maybe I could get over all the women I'd failed in my life, eventually. Maybe I could get over not doing anything about my father's long, slow emotional abuse of my mother. Not saving Martina. Not saving Eden. Not being there when my ex-wife had a stillborn child.

Anthony had been as powerless to save his own son. And yet here he was, smiling at me as I came to sit by his side. Maybe being powerless was okay.

When I'd asked him, Anthony put his unshakeable spirit down to the support groups. He attended one for drug addiction, one for victims of crime and one for anxiety. I thought I'd give it a whirl. It would shut Imogen up.

'Francis,' he said. I cradled my coffee and licked my scalded pinky.

'Anthony.'

'How's the comedown?'

'I think I'm past the shakes.' I held out my hand for him to see, flat in the air before us. My thumb was twitching slightly. 'I'd still murder you for a scotch, though, old mate.'

'I reckon scotch might be on your trigger words list, mate.'

'Probably. It's a big list.'

Some recovery groups don't let you say particular words, 'trigger words', because some members are getting over a level of addiction so great that even the sound of the name of their drug of choice can send them into a relapse spiral. Even if you're not an addict, but you're in a support group parallel to addiction groups such as Victims of Crime or After Domestic Violence or Incest Survivors, you have to acknowledge that some members of the group might also be enrolled in addiction groups, so for their benefit you don't say the words.

The first rule of Drug Recovery Group is that you do not talk about drugs at recovery group.

It sounded like a whole lot of bullshit to me. I wasn't sure all the tiptoeing around really helped anyone. I'd tested my trigger-happiness, said 'Endone' loudly and slowly alone in my car, like a little kid whispering a swearword at the back of class. I had not gone and started popping pills. But I was a rule-follower by nature, so I didn't say 'Endone' in or anywhere near the meetings I attended. I didn't say 'scotch', or 'bourbon', or 'cocaine', or 'ecstasy', or 'Valium', or 'oxy', all guilty pleasures of mine at some time over the previous months. I mentioned that I had a variety of 'drugs of choice' at my first meeting when I introduced myself, but I hadn't shared since.

In fact, I hadn't said anything. Imogen had told me to 'go' to the meetings. She hadn't told me to 'participate'.

People stopped milling around the treacherous urns when the facilitator, a hard-edged little blonde woman named Megan, came into the room with her large folder of notes and handouts. About twenty-five of her photocopied handouts were in the bottom of my car, boot-printed and crumpled, hidden in the undergrowth of a forest of takeaway containers and paper bags. Their titles peer at me from beneath old newspapers and cardboard boxes. *Six ways to beat negative thoughts. How to tell your friends you're in danger of self-harm. When 'no' means 'no'.* Sometime after the first meeting, I lost my eight-step grief diary. I hadn't even put my name on it. Diaries are for little girls.

When Megan was in place the people around me joined in the opening mantra in a badly timed monotone reminiscent of the obligatory and dispassionate 'good morning' we used to give Mrs Towers in the third grade.

'I am on my way to a place beyond vengeance, a place beyond anger, a place beyond fear. I am on my way to a place of healing, and I take a new step every day.'

I didn't say the Victims of Crime mantra. It was way too cuddly for me. I didn't know what Megan's story was, but if she'd made up the mantra herself it sounded to me like she was making a big deal of being bag-snatched or something. There is no place beyond anger. Everybody's angry to some degree. Nuns are angry at sinners. Kindergarten teachers are angry at the government. When you've come up against violence, real violence – you get punched by your husband for the first time, or someone pulls a knife on you in the regular, sunny traffic of a Thursday morning commute – you realise there is no place beyond anger. It's in there. In everyone. No matter what you put on top of it, no matter how long you starve it or lock it up or deny it. Anger is primal. It's in our DNA.

'We've got a couple of new members with us tonight,' Megan said as Justin, the group kiss-ass, brought her a paper cup of green tea. Justin had been gay-bashed to within an inch of his life on Mardi Gras night when he was twenty-one. Victims of Crime was his life. 'This is Aamir and Reema.'

The Muslim couple with their backs to the door nodded. Reema was looking deep into her empty paper cup like she'd found a window out of the room. I was jealous. She adjusted the shoulders of her dress nervously, and her husband sat forward in his seat, a big man, his hands clasped between his knees.

'Hi, Aamir,' everyone said. 'Hi, Reema.'

'Now you don't have to share,' Megan assured them. 'No one has to share in these groups. Sometimes it can be healing just to listen to the stories from those around us and to recognise that the trauma we have experienced in the wake of serious crime is not unique, and neither is the journey to wellness. Sometimes we like to start the meeting with some "triumphs of the week" or with some readings. But it's a pretty fluid structure here.'

'We don't mind sharing,' Aamir said. He shrugged. The anger tight in his shoulders and jaw. I could see it. Anthony, beside me, could see it. You get to know the look of a man on the edge of punching someone when you're a young cop wandering among groups of homeless in the Cross, Blacktown, Parramatta. Bopping around the clubs on George Street while groups of men hoot and holler at women from cars. It becomes like a flag.

'Well, good.' Megan smiled. 'That's great. Like I said, there's no pressure. Some of our members have never shared.' She glanced at me. I felt nauseated. 'This is a supportive environment where we have attendee-centric mechanisms –'

'I'll share.' Aamir stood up suddenly. He was even bigger standing. No one bothered telling the huge man that standing wasn't part of the group dynamic, that in fact it intimidated some of the rape survivors. He rubbed his hands up and down the front of his polo shirt, leaving light sweat stains. 'I'll start by asking if anyone here in the group knows me? If you know my wife?'

I was confused. It was great. I hadn't felt anything but nausea and boredom in all the sessions I'd attended, so this was a novel start to the night. The group members looked at each other. Looked at Aamir. Aamir shrugged again.

'No? No? You don't know me? You've never seen me before?' Aamir's stark black eyebrows were high on his sweating brow. He did a little half-turn, as though members might recognise his back, the little tendrils of black hair curling on the nape of his thick neck. His wife wiped her face with her hand. No one spoke. Anthony examined the man's face.

'I don't think they underst–' Megan chanced.

'My son Ehan was abducted one hundred and forty-one days ago,' Aamir said. He went to his chair and sat down. 'One hundred and forty-one days ago two men in a blue car took my eight-year-old son from a bus stop on Prairie Vale Road, Wetherill Park. He has not been seen since.'

He paused. We all waited.

'You don't know me, or my wife, because there has been little or no coverage of this abduction in the media. We've had one nationally televised press conference and one newspaper feature article. That's it.'

Aamir was a lion wrapped in a man. The woman across the circle from him, who'd been in a bank hold-up and now suffered panic attacks, was cowering in her seat, pulling at her ponytail. Megan opened her mouth to offer something, some condolence, some segue back into the normality of group sharing, but Aamir raged on, a spewing of well-practised words with which he had assaulted anyone who would listen since his son disappeared.

'If Ehan was a little blond-haired white boy named Ian and we lived in Potts Point, we'd still be all over the national news.'

'Oh, um.' Megan looked at me for help.

'We'd have a two hundred thousand dollar reward and Dick Smith flying a fucking banner from a fucking blimp some-where. But we've had nothing. Two days the phone rang off the hook, and then silence. I forget sometimes that he's gone. Every night at eight o'clock, no matter where I am, no matter what I'm doing, I think, *It's Ehan's bedtime. I have to go say goodnight.'*

Megan widened her eyes at me.

'What are you looking at me for?' I said. The sickness swirled in me.

'Oh, I wasn't.' Megan snapped her head back to Aamir. 'I wasn't. Sorry, Frank, I was just thinking and you were in my line of sight and –'

'Are you a journalist?' Aamir turned on me. I didn't know how I'd been brought into the exchange until Megan buried her face in her notebook. The same thing she'd done when I signed on to the group.

'No,' I said. I looked at Aamir. 'No, I'm not a journalist. My girlfriend was murdered. I'm the only other person in the group who's here for murder-victim support. That's why she's staring at me. She wants me to say something hopeful to you.'

'Our son wasn't murdered,' Reema said.

'Well, Megan sure seems to think he was.'

'I never said that!' Megan gasped.

'Your girlfriend was murdered.' Aamir sunk back down to his seat. He was so far on the edge of it I didn't know how he was upright. He hovered, legs bent, inches from me. His huge black eyes were locked on mine. He knew his son was dead. And he was angry. White-hot-flame angry at everyone he laid eyes on.

'She was murdered. Yes,' I said.

'What was her name?'

'Martina.'

'And what happened after she was murdered?' Aamir asked.

'What do you mean?'

'What happened?' he insisted. 'What happened then?'

'Nothing,' I shrugged. Everyone was looking at me. I licked my lips. Shrugged again. 'Nothing. She was murdered. She's gone. There's nothing . . . afterwards, if that's what you mean.'

Aamir watched me. We could have been the only people in the room.

'Nothing happens afterwards,' I said. 'There's no . . . resolution. You go to work. You come home. You come to these groups and you –' I gestured to the coffee machine. 'You drink coffee. You say the mantra. There's no afterwards.'

Everyone looked at Megan to deny or confirm my assessment. She opened her folder, shuffled the papers, collected her thoughts. One of the urns started reboiling itself in the taut seconds of silence and I heard the spitting of its droplets on the plastic table top.

'Let's look at some handouts,' Megan said.

Anthony was waiting for me by the vending machine after the meeting. We walked up the stairs and onto the street.

'That was a bit harsh,' he said.

'What?'

'The whole "there's no afterwards" thing.'

'Reality is often harsh,' I said. We paused to watch Aamir and Reema walking to their car. The big angry man glanced back at me as he opened the passenger door for his wife. His expression was unreadable. It was the first time that his expression had been unreadable since I had laid eyes on him an hour earlier. The rage was gone, replaced by something else. His shoulders were inches lower. I didn't know what had taken over from the boiling hot fury that I saw in the meeting room, but whatever it was, it was cold.

'Do you really believe that?' Anthony asked me. 'That it means nothing?'

'Murder?'

'Yes.'

'Yes,' I said, 'I do. You don't get over it. You don't realise the mystical fucking meaning in it. You don't accept that it, like everything, happens for a reason. Come on, Tone,' I scoffed at him. He exhaled smoke from his cigarette.

'Every night at eight o'clock that guy tries to say goodnight to his dead kid.' I nodded at Aamir's car as it pulled into the street. 'And he'll be doing it until the day he dies.'

She always felt better when night was falling. The darkness folded over her like a blanket, protective. Light had never been a friend to Tara. It seemed to fall on all of her at once, seemed to wriggle into her creases and folds and dance around her curves, to expose her every surface. Tara always had plenty of surface. She'd never been able to keep track of all there was of her, and Joanie was there to point out the parts she forgot, those bulges and bubbles and handles of flesh that slipped and slid from under hems and over belts.

Pull your shirt down, Tara. Pull your pants up, Tara. Pull your sleeves down, Tara. Jesus. Everyone can see you.

Everyone can see you.

At the dinner table Joanie would grab and pinch and twist a slab of flesh Tara didn't know was exposed, a roll above her jeans or the tender white flesh on the backs of her arms. You couldn't cover Tara with a tent, Joanie said. She could feed an African village. Getting downstairs to dinner became a journey she couldn't take, so she began to take her meals up in her attic bedroom, staring at the park, the runners going round and round between the trees. Sometimes getting from the bed to the computer was too much. Tara simply lay between the sheets and dreamed about African people cutting her up and sharing her, carving down her thighs in neat slices like a Christmas ham until there was only bone – gorgeous, strong, light bone. Bone that shone, redemptive and clean. Tara lost herself dreaming.

The girls at school giggled at her bulges, the blue bruises that peppered them. Though decades had passed, their voices still bumped and butted around the attic room, red balloons of hate floating.

Why do you call your mum 'Joanie', Tara?

Doesn't she love you?

Tonight Tara stood by the windows looking over the park and watched the night falling, the bats rising, and remembered her mother. It was nine months since Tara had woken from her coma, nine months since Joanie had gone, but Tara could still hear her voice sometimes, hear her footsteps in the hall as she readied herself for some party or dinner or charity function, as she pulled on her silk-lined coat and checked herself in the hall mirror. Joanie with her elegant ash-blonde hair falling everywhere in filigree curls.

In time, all the light of the warm day dissipated, replaced by a wonderful darkness. Tara stood by the window and watched the runners on the paths in Centennial Park recede into shadows, only blinking lights indicating their jolting journeys as they continued, round and round, round and round. Then rolled away.

The Tara who watched them now was very different from the one who had watched them when her parents were still alive. Tara hugged herself in the little window, let her fingers wander over the new landscape of her body. Bumps and ridges and flaps of flesh as hard as stone, lines of scars running up her arms where the fatty flesh had been sucked dry, cut, pulled taut, stapled. Bones poked through the mess at her hips and ribs and collarbones. Her face was a mystery. She hadn't looked at herself since that first glimpse as she was waking from the coma. She spent the first month in the hospital in silence, lying, feeling herself. Neurologists came and played with her, confirmed that she could, indeed, understand them. Then a nurse had emerged from the fog and quietly told her what she'd done to herself. Tara had looked at her new self in the mirror. Touched the glass, made sounds. To her it had been laughter, but to the nurse it had sounded like snarls.

I stood in the kitchen of my house in Paddington and looked at the burned walls, the fingers of blackness reaching up the bricks to the charred roof beams. The tiles had fallen and disappeared, revealing blue sky and orange leaves. I smiled. The oven had been cleared away, the cupboards stripped off, the sink unscrewed and discarded, leaving black eyeholes in the wall. The flames had warped the floorboards leading down to the bathroom and tiny courtyard. I folded my arms and looked at it all, smelled the plasticky taint of melted things.

I'm well aware that traditionally first houses are purchased by people much younger than me, and in much better condition than this one. The terrace in William Street was a write-off, advertised to attract developers who might be tempted to buy the row, knock it over, put in a flashy deli and be done with it. The kitchen was a bombshell, the backyard a wreck and the upper floor wasn't safe for human habitation. The elderly owner had let the place go for decades, and the floorboards had taken it the worst. By order of the City of Sydney Council, I wasn't even supposed to be sleeping in the building, and I was supposed to be working on it wearing protective gear. But I ignored that. My home base was the front bedroom, where I'd dragged a mattress and a few laundry baskets of clothes, my phone and some snack food. The bathroom worked. I still had the apartment in Kensington and there was always Imogen's place. But for a couple of nights a week I had been sleeping in my new house, just so I could drift off listening to the creaking and cracking of the building, the unfamiliar noises of the neighbours coming home from work, their kids playing in the street. City ambulances racing for St Vincent's and drunks singing as they wandered home. Rats scuttling somewhere close. It was dingy, but I owned it. I'd committed to something. That was big for me.

Committing to things. Listening to my girlfriend. Getting off the drugs and the booze. Yes, I was going somewhere, even if it wasn't some mystical place beyond anger that couldn't possibly exist. Because I wholeheartedly believed what I'd said to Aamir. There is no 'after murder'. There is no reasoning, bargaining or manipulating with murder – when someone close to you has been slain, something enters your life that will always be there, a little black blur at the corner of your vision that you learn to ignore as naturally as you do your own nose. But, stained as you are, you have to go on and learn to see again. Build things. Change things. Own things. Martina wasn't coming back. It was time to return to life.

As I was standing in the morning sunshine from the informal skylight, I heard the front door open and close, and Eden's uneven gait on the unpolished boards. She was walking with a single aluminium crutch with an arm cuff and a handle. She'd worked her way down from two of them. I'd seen her at the station gym a couple of days earlier trotting awkwardly on the treadmill, somewhere between a jog and a walk, now and then reaching for the console to steady herself. The problem was her core strength, I thought, but I wasn't sure. A pair of serial killers had slit her open from sternum to navel on their way to cutting her right in half. She'd lost most of the hearing in her left ear from having a gun fired in her face, and her nose wasn't straight anymore. But despite all her new little imperfections, to look at her now it was hard to imagine how close she'd come to dying in my arms. When I found her on that farm she had been a red mess.

'Oh look, it's the invalid,' I said. Eden had to be the world's most beautiful cripple, but I knew that underneath her whippet-lean frame and deep gothic eyes hid a creature who was far from anything like beauty. I had no doubt, standing in her presence, that though Eden couldn't run yet, that she was easily wearied and had lost some of the sharpness of her brutally dry wit, there was a very dark power residing in her still, and she was as much a threat to me as she was to the killers, rapists and evildoers she spent her nights hunting. She came up beside me and took in the black walls, raised her head slowly and looked at a pigeon as it landed on the edge of the roof hole.

'Why didn't you just tell Hades to keep the money?' she asked, sighing. 'He'd have been smarter with it.'

Eden's father, Hades Archer, ex-criminal overlord and the world's cleverest body disposal expert, had given me a hundred thousand dollars to find out what had happened to the love of his life. Sunday White had gone missing before I was born, and Hades had hired me as much to get one of her relatives off his back as to find out himself what had become of the lost young woman. I put the cash together with my inheritance and bought the terrace on William Street. Eden shifted papers around on the floor with one of her fine leather boots, shook her head.

'I can't believe you, of all people, fail to see the potential in this place. Things of beauty are made of forgotten places like this, Eden.' I started mapping the kitchen with my hands. 'Stove there, stainless steel benches here, big kitchen island with one of those cutting board tops. You know the ones? Drawers underneath. Rip all this out and put a big window in. Fucking brilliant.'

'Stainless steel is so 1990.'

'Marble then. Wine rack over here.'

'You're a recovering alcoholic.'

'My cooking wine, Eden. My cooking wine.'

'Who do you think's going to do all this?' She squinted at me.

'Me.'

'You can't change a light bulb without adult supervision and a stackhat.'

'You, then. Come help me. You're handy.'

'No.'

'You're just jealous.' I shook my head. 'There's no need to be cranky, Eden. You can come and visit my brilliant new house whenever you want. Take photos of yourself in it to show your friends.'

The pigeon sitting on one of the roof beams ruffled its feathers and crapped on my floor. We both looked up at it.

'We'll have dinner parties,' I said.

'Look at you. Less than a year ago your plates were getting dusty from disuse and the local Indian takeaway guy had invited you to his wedding. Now you're planning soirées.'

'I like the word "soirée". I like soirée and nostalgia.'

'It's a commitment, I guess, even if it is a shithole,' she sighed. 'That's a big deal. Congratulations.'

'I've been a big deal for a while now, Eden. You just haven't noticed.'

'You could go on a commitment streak. Marry that mind-quack and have freckly children with abandonment issues.'

'Let's not get ahead of ourselves.'

As though she'd heard herself being spoken about, my girl-friend Imogen opened the front door and clopped into the hall in her second-favourite lavender velvet heels, her upturned nose already wrinkled at the smell. She had an Ikea bag in each hand. What a sweetheart.

'Sorry, Frank, I didn't realise you had company,' she beamed. 'How are you, Eden?'

'Dr Stone,' Eden said. The tone had no warmth in it, I noted, and then reminded myself that, like an old gas heater, Eden took hours just to get to room temperature. Still, something passed between them. Eden's eyes fell to my missing kitchen cupboards and Imogen's stayed on her, searching, almost, for something. I coughed, because I'm like most men – completely ignorant of women and their looks and tones and inferences and what they really mean. The two could have been about to launch into a mid-air kung fu battle or hurl each other to the ground in a passionate embrace. I didn't know. I hoped the cough would delay whatever was going on until it made itself obvious or went away. Imogen excused herself to wash her hands. There was something sticky on the front doorknob. I didn't know what.

Eden stood playing with a live wire hanging from the ceiling, twisting the plastic casing around her finger.

'What's wrong with you?' I jutted my chin at her. 'Someone asks how you are, you don't say their name and qualification.'

'Oh, I'm sorry. Should I have responded with a list of neurotic compulsions I may or may not exhibit?'

'You've been colder since Rye Farm, Eden. I've noticed it. You're weirder, if that's possible.'

'It's always possible.'

'I don't want you to get any weirder than you already are.'

'What a chauvinistic thing to say. Want to tell me how to wear my hair too?'

'Up.'

'I did my mandatory counselling.' She shrugged. 'I don't need to be shrinked in my free time. If Imogen wants to shrink someone, she's got more than enough mental dysfunction going on here without starting on me.' She gestured at me with an open hand. All of me.

'She's not shrinking you. She's my girlfriend. She's saying hello.'

'Shrinks never stop shrinking. They shrink all day long until everyone around them is shrunk.'

'You don't like her,' I concluded. 'Of course you don't.'

'She's a shrink.'

'Stop saying shrink.'

'While you're here, Eden,' Imogen said, emerging from the stairs, flicking water off her fingers – I have no hand towels – 'I've been telling Frank for a while now that it'd be nice if the three of us got together for dinner sometime, maybe? I'm sure he hasn't passed that on to you. I thought it'd be nice to get to know you a bit. You know. Because Frank and I . . . Now that we're –'

'Fucking?' Eden said. I threw my head back and laughed at the ceiling. The pigeon flew away.

'In a relationship,' Imogen sighed.

Eden's phone buzzed and she took it out of her pocket. Looked at it, slid it back in.

'We need to go, Frank,' she said. 'Now.'

'All weeknights are fine with me.' Imogen followed us to the door. I grabbed my jacket from the edge of the mattress in the front room and turned to hear Eden's response, but she was already heading through the front gate. I kissed Imogen and fondled her ponytail in a way that I guessed was conciliatory before running out the door.

Ruben was pretty sure he had the cruisiest job in Sydney. He'd been caretaking the three-storey monster of a house on the edge of Centennial Park for three weeks and he hadn't seen the owner, or anyone associated with the building, once. He'd been translating job advertisements from the *Telegraph* using his phone while sitting at the arrivals terminal at Sydney airport, waiting for his bus. He had begun with the briefest one. Cleaner wanted, twice weekly. He emailed the agency advertising the job, which hired him and explained that he was to let himself in, make sure the place was dust-, insect- and mould-free, and leave.

He'd been in the country ten minutes and already had a job – great pay, zero human interaction and completely self-directed. Too good to be true. It was like the start to an old horror film.

The only catch was that Ruben wasn't the best cleaner on earth. He'd never got over his teenage habit of shedding clothes and letting them drop wherever he stood, which had bothered a lot of travellers in the dozens of hostels he'd stayed in across Europe, down through Asia and finally along the coast of Australia. He also loved tissues, gum, elastic bands – he'd use them and fling them, telling himself he'd pick them up later.

He was a flicker of toothpaste onto clean mirrors and a leaver of stubble in sinks. Getting a job as a caretaker was a bit of a stretch for Ruben, but he was up for the challenge.

He was posted a key and emailed a map to the house on Lang Road, across the street from Centennial Park. He was to go through the house from top to bottom and alleviate the damages of disuse. Fight back the dust. Fluff the pillows. Spray bleach on the creeping mould. The emails didn't mention anyone living in the house. Nor did they mention when the occupants would return. Ruben didn't ask any questions. The pay was too good.

He spent the first day showing himself around, gathering the things he'd need for the job from the places they were hidden all over the gigantic house. There were cleaning products in the kitchen, but everything was covered in dust and mould. He'd need a new vacuum just to clear it off the floors. Ruben guessed his being hired was a reluctant measure from someone who didn't want the house to fall apart – he arrived at the very moment dampness and mould threatened to cause permanent structural damage. The precise moment when vermin had begun to colonise the ground floor but hadn't begun to destroy it.

The overgrown back garden was a haven for spiders, who made their homes in the corners of every downstairs window. But, strangely, the front garden, which might attract the scrutiny of passers-by, was perfectly manicured. The house was dark and creaked a lot, and Ruben had to play music all day long just to stop himself getting the creeps. He spent as little time as he could in the many bathrooms. Horror-film ghosts always appeared in the bathroom mirrors first.

It took him until the very end of the first day to realise there was someone in the attic room. At the beginning he'd ignored the creaking of floorboards that followed him every-where, but as he rose through the levels of the house towards the loft he heard a television playing. At first he thought it must be outside, next door perhaps, but when he stopped to listen he realised it was upstairs. Something was being played on it, an advertisement run through in full, then rewound to certain spots and played again. Over and over the words and the theme music rolled. He shook the dust from the covers in the rooms below, mentally translating the words in his poor English.

My ten-week program gives you everything you need to escape the you that you've become and find the person you should be. Take up the challenge today! It's easy.

The words replayed over and over.

. . . escape the you that you've become . . .

. . . escape . . . you . . .

. . . find the person you should be . . .

. . . find the person . . .

It's easy.

Ruben listened for a voice, a movement, anything to indicate that a person was playing the advertisement. There was nothing. It was as though whoever was up there was a ghost.

I didn't get to the crime scene straight away. I was following Eden up the gentle green slope towards the tree where the body had been found when I spotted little Amy Hooku standing nearby with her arms folded, staring at the grass in that little-girl-lost way she sometimes got about her. Amy was barely seventeen years old and not afraid to show it. She wore a blazing red top covered in dancing pandas, heavy black jeans and glittery silver Doc Martens. The extreme buzz cut of bleached blonde prickles jarred against her Vietnamese features. Complicated electronic gear hung all around her like vines on a small thin tree: huge earphones at her neck, things clipped to her belt, two phones bulging in her back pockets – one personal, one police department. She was the only teenager in the country with a standard-issue cop phone, and it was only because she'd earned it. I came up behind her and grabbed the back of her skinny neck.

'I've got her. Backup! I need backup! I've caught Sydney's greatest liar.'

'Get your hands off me, asshole.'

She tried to swing at me and I grabbed her wrist, put a leg into the back of her knee. I let her hang helpless for a second. The face was all teenage exhaustion at my incredible lameness. The crowd at the edge of the police tape gave us confused looks – the wild-faced white guy manhandling the stringy Asian girl.

'What is wrong with you?'

'I'm excited to see you. You must have grown a foot and a half.' I pulled her up and grinned at her, punched her in her hard shoulder. She had grown taller, but not filled out at all. She was a miniature replica of the tall, lanky and incredibly beautiful woman I knew she would grow into. Her parents had been absolutely stunning people – he a broad-shouldered football-player type and his wife one of those bony models who always seem to glow gold. I knew Mrs Hooku from the autopsy photos, the *60 Minutes* special on the murders. I'd seen her father around the North Sydney Metro office, a quiet shadowy figure who walked too fast.

'What are you doing here, Hooky Bird?'

'I'm on my way to class, actually. Saw Simmons.' She nodded towards another officer we both knew, a bald crime-scene photographer from North Sydney Metro. 'Knew it must be a good one.'

Amy 'Hooky' Hooku was a genius, but I tried not to think about that. Beyond the punk-Japanese-rocker angry Hello Kitty thing she had going on – or whatever the hell it was – she possessed a rare kind of superintelligence that had seen her drop out of high school like it was child's play and sail into top university courses in computer science with an engineering major. At seventeen. I'd met her in North Sydney Metro when I was there working in Asian Gangs. My work had been mainly chasing up big drug crime families warring over territory, but they'd brought me in to consult on the Hooku family murders under the misconception that I could speak Vietnamese.

I was the one to sit Amy down in her school principal's office a year and a bit earlier and tell her that her younger sister had murdered her parents that morning. It had been a violent bloodbath that Amy only escaped because she'd unexpectedly spent the night at a friend's house and gone straight to school the next day.

I was a poor choice for the role. I was just about as situationally and experientially alien to an Asian teenage girl as a person could get. But with counsellors running late and the principal blubbering like a lunatic in the hall, it was down to me to tell Amy what had happened. Somehow, together, we'd worked through it.

I guess from that moment in the principal's office I'd managed to be separated from the rest of the world in Amy's mind. So she treated me like a human being and, however begrudgingly, put up with my childish bullshit, my roughhousing and my teasing. From what I heard from other people, though, she was very difficult to get to know. Pulled the 'Me no speak Engrish' act whenever she was approached by strangers, no matter how friendly they were. All that was crap, of course. She'd grown up in Wollstonecraft. When she couldn't back out of interactions by playing the voiceless migrant, she could be openly aggressive, so the rumours went.

After her family was killed, the North Sydney bigwigs had approved her for a few low-profile administrative jobs here and there just to give her something to do while she hung around the station. She was a constant presence there after the murders, in the same clothes for weeks, just sitting in the waiting rooms staring at the crims or, if she could manage it, creeping into her dad's office to sit in his big leather chair.

People understood her obsession with the office – her father had been rooted to that chair in his glass cubicle, a silent figure tapping away at a computer, chasing down internet frauds, as rigid as a tree. I didn't know him but I'd been aware of him, the way someone will be aware of a chair or a desk without really taking notice until it disappears or is moved. Detective Hooku didn't move, though, until he disappeared, and all that remained of him was in that office. The office smelled like his cologne. It was covered in his used coffee cups. The laptop screen was marked with his prints.

Amy wanted to be close to her dead dad, so she kept sneaking into the headquarters.

They'd chase her out, the other cops, but she'd get back in through the fire escape doors. Once they had front and back door staff on the lookout for her, she stopped with the doors and started climbing in through a tiny window in the men's room. After a while the North Sydney superintendent let her file incident reports as part of unofficial 'work experience', quietly, trying to avoid the scandal of a kid having access to sensitive criminal information. I avoided Amy as much as I could in those days, though I wasn't around the station a lot anyway. I felt uncomfortable around her. I'd seen her family's crime scene and didn't know how to not think about that when I spoke to her.

Amy thrived in admin, but she was hard to entertain. She started messing around with the station computers, installing new programs, making things easier, better, fixing bugs none of us technologically illiterate dinosaurs had any idea about. When the Major Crimes Unit assembled a task force to combat online grooming of teenagers for underage sex, Amy watched while our out-of-touch middle-aged divorcees pretended to be young girls and boys in online chat rooms, and failed dismally. She knew all the language, the symbols. The cybercrime section of Major Crimes started letting Amy be in the room during online chat sessions, consulting verbally only. Then they let her sit in one of the chairs near a screen, still only verbally interacting with the crims, her words and advice translated through the police officer at the computer. Then, when someone got up to get a coffee one day, Amy slid into the driver's seat and controlled the conversations with the online pedophiles, 'supervised stringently' by cybercrime officers. Amy's 'work experience' had become work. She was still so young that had the papers got wind of what she was doing, the kinds of people she was talking to, there would have been a national scandal. Somehow the news never got out. It was because Amy was good. No one wanted to lose her.

She baited them, reeled them in, landed three major rock spiders in her first week officially on the job – one of them a cop at another station. She was a ruthless fisherman, an incredibly convincing liar. She could be a sexually confused fourteen-year-old boy in one chat window, and a nerdy, love-starved twelve-year-old girl in another. Her words were full of the misguided romantic fantasies so many normal young people her age brought to the online hunting grounds. She was fast and she was convincing. She set up names, family members, school grades, hobbies for her aliases. She could remember that the thirteen-year-old girl she was playing named Alice from Redfern had a cat called Stanley that'd been hit by a car and sprained its left back leg, at the same time as remembering that eleven-year-old Jessica from Mosman didn't have pets because she got allergies. She had photographs for these people – multiple ones. I had no idea how she did it. Amy could lie like some of the worst sociopaths I'd ever met. Without hesitation. She was a hooker of bad men.

'So what's the story?' I motioned towards the crowd under the tree.

'Looks like a jogger copped it. Bashed, I think. I heard them saying she got it last night and someone's called it in this morning.'

'That's no good.'

'Nope.'

'How's your aunt?'

'Oh Jesus. How's *your* aunt?'

'Alright, alright.' I raised my hands in surrender. Amy had a real aversion to being treated like a child, even though she clearly was one. She let me get away with it most of the time, but when other people tried to mother her, she snapped. You couldn't ask her how she was doing at uni or if she was seeing anybody or whether or not she was eating right. I wondered sometimes if she did eat right. She was all bones and sharp edges.

'What's your partner up to?' she asked.

'You know Eden?'

'No. But I guessed she's your partner.'

'How?'

'She's giving you the stink eye.'

I looked over and saw Eden at the edge of the huddle, her eyebrows raised at me. I nudged Hooky off balance and ruffled her spikes.

'See you round, punk.'

'Yeah,' she said.

Things were not good over by the tree. There was never any glamour to it. From what was left of the body I guessed she'd been a beautiful woman. Long muscular legs in torn purple nylon tights, matching top, one sleeve of a green jacket hanging from the left arm. No shoes. Sporty socks. Eden held the tarpaulin up and I peered in. The onlookers shuffled to get a glimpse. The blue light falling through the tarp onto the girl's mashed face turned the bloody meat it had become purple, like she was wearing some melted Halloween mask. I looked for eye sockets but found none.

'Someone's angry,' I said.

'Mmm-hmm,' Eden agreed.

Immediately, things start to pop and sizzle in your mind. Academy training in the psychological patterns of killers. An angry perp, someone capable of this kind of brutality, is usually known to the victim. Pretty difficult to get this aggressive, this violent, with a stranger. Facial injuries, in particular, are usually personal. The positioning of her body, lying on her back, hidden from view of the road – was the killer ashamed of his act? It was a bit confusing on that score. According to the textbook, a victim positioned on her back and uncovered suggested a willingness for the body to be found. Usually killers who are ashamed of what they've done curl the body on its side, suggesting peacefulness, sleep. Or they turn her over, hide the face and injuries in the grass. On the back, face up, is probably how the victim fell out of the guy's arms, carried fireman-style and then flopped down, arms out. So the killer wasn't displaying any shame in the positioning of the body. But leaving the victim off behind the bushes – that was strange. In the right circumstances, it could have been days before one of the joggers pumping along the road at the bottom of the hill smelled her, before someone let a dog off the leash and the beast came up here. A mixed display. Not ashamed, but not exhibitionist. There was an uncertainty about it.

This was probably a first kill.

I looked around at the paperbarks surrounding us, pale and spotted trunks that had stood watch over the girl's final seconds. Or had they? There was no indication that the brutality had occurred here. No blood spatter. But the victim looked like a Centennial Park jogger. I'd been one myself once. Centennial Park is a great starting ground for weight-losers rather than serious runners – it's mostly flat, and the familiarity of landmarks helps you control the panic that you'll never make it to the end. The main obstacles are old people, dogs, kids on push scooters. I shifted the girl's shoulder up a fraction and looked at the lividity, the dark purple on her back and hips where the blood had begun to pool. There were carpet patterns in the blood on the backs of her arms.

So if the runner was picked up from here, but wasn't killed here, why was she brought back here? Why risk returning a victim to the place where you abducted her? Was the location important to the killer? Maybe she wasn't taken far. Maybe the whole thing happened in the park. I looked towards the road, at the cars parked under the trees.

'Let's set up a tent before we move her. I want to catch any fibres.'

Eden rose and directed a nearby tech to bring in a tent so we could examine the body without onlookers gawking at us. I instructed another to go down and get a video of all the cars in the immediate vicinity.

42

I heard a noise. I reached under the tarp and unclipped a mobile phone from the girl's waist. Wires ran up through her shirt, under her bra, to her collar. I pulled the headphones clear and looked at the screen. Her running music was still playing. 'Hazard' by Richard Marx. Ominous. I scrolled through the songs and found the girl had a weird compilation going. Plenty of 1980s love ballads and murder songs. Depressed taste. A recent break-up? Was she pounding the pavement to lose the kilos gained during a now-dead relationship? I sat back on my haunches and realised it was the first personal thing I knew about the girl. Her current music taste. More personal details would follow, and they would all be sad to learn. Sometimes the stupidity of it hit me suddenly, right in the middle of the job. Everything she had been, whoever she was going to be – it was all over now.

'Hey, dickhead,' Hooky called. I looked over. She was standing closer now but still off and away from the centre of the crime scene, not wanting to contaminate any of it with her DNA. It's shockingly easy to leave pieces of yourself at a crime scene. Just by standing there, flaking skin and dropping hairs like a tree shedding its winter leaves.

'Did she have an app going?' Hooky asked.

'A what?'

'An app.'

I looked at her blankly. Hooky beckoned me and I took the phone. I let her direct me around it. As a kid, there would be no handling evidence for her.

'There are programs you can download onto your phone specifically for running,' Hooky said. 'They play your music, track your progress, time you, mark your distance and elevation.'

She gave me a bunch of very quick instructions. I stopped the music and brought up a screen full of numbers and images.

'How the hell do they do that?'

'GPS.' She rolled her eyes. Eden looked over my shoulder. Hooky made me bring up a green and grey map crisscrossed with colourful lines and numbers in flashing bubbles.

'See here?' Hooky pointed with her pinky finger. 'She did two laps of the park yesterday afternoon, 5.14 pm. Then she went off track . . . through the bushland over there, Queens Park Road. There was a pause of . . . three minutes. Then we're onto a road. Her pulse goes up from 180 to 210 beats per minute.'

'This thing can do heartbeats?' I looked at Eden. She was deadpan. I guessed this kind of technology had been around for a while. I felt old.

'Then she's off again.' Hooky frowned at the phone. 'She speeds up to forty, then sixty kilometres an hour. Either the chick was running like the Terminator or she's been put in a car.'

'Fuck me!' I said. 'We can follow this right to the crime scene?'

Hooky tugged my arm back down so she could see the phone. 'Yup. Looks like the killer drove her out to . . . Mangrove Road, Ashfield. Stopped for fifteen minutes. Then drove her back here.'

I pressed the bubble on Mangrove Road tentatively, not sure what would happen. A window opened marked with a small red X.

Heart rate error. Connection lost.

'We're going to need a secondary team to follow us and

a third to check out the pick-up point by Queens Park Road.' Eden turned and began walking towards the car. She beckoned for the head crime-scene tech and gave him instructions as she hobbled down the slope, her aluminium crutch making holes in the wet grass. 'Frank, give me that phone. We need to get screen shots of the map and send them to headquarters.'

I glanced back at Hooky as I ran towards the car. She was at the top of the hill smiling to herself.

Eden gets this look about her when she's on the hunt. She always has. Pointed. Cold. I like to try to keep things light and casual, especially when I'm a passenger with no way to control how fast the car's going or which route we take. If I can't keep a lid on my excitement, I start chewing my nails, my knuckles, my collar. My stomach starts churning.

Since her run-in with a killer, Eden's pointed look has developed a really deadly edge. She drives like she's handling a getaway car, sailing through gaps she has no cause to be confident about. I hung on to the seatbelt and tried to remember if you're supposed to go stiff or limp in a crash. We headed across the city towards Ashfield with people leaping from crossings and holding their children as the sirens announced our approach. The radio was playing, and as news broke on the hour Eden glanced at it.

'. . . the remains of at least four people in a burned-out Kombi van outside the Black Mutt Inn near Suffolk Park, just south of tourist hotspot Byron Bay. It is believed at least some of the victims suffered gunshot wounds. Police are asking –'

Eden switched the radio off.

'Ashfield,' I said, glancing at the phone now and then, trying to avoid making myself sick. 'Why Ashfield?'

'I don't know,' Eden said.

'Bit of a horrible name for a place. Ashfield.'

'You should pen a stern letter to the mayor.'

'Maybe I will. The bus!'

'I can see the fucking bus, Frank.' Eden swerved.

'Jesus Christ, we're both gonna die.'

'Would you shut up?'

'Would you look at the road?'

Eden tossed a glance my way just as we blasted through a massive intersection, a half a second's worth of gap between us and a removal van passing across our bonnet. Silence lingered in the car, my words pulsing. It's always very present between us, the fact that Eden could at any time, and rightfully so, decide that killing me is the best thing for her future. As far as I could tell, it was only me and her father who knew what she really was, what she had done. People wonder, I'm sure. Our colleagues, our clients, some of the journalists who have covered her career. They wonder about that hard look, about her incredible instinct for catching killers, her seemingly biological ease at physical combat. She's a natural chaser, hunter, fighter. Once a man in my very position got too close to discovering who Eden really was and her brother put a bullet in his head. Her brother was gone now. Eden had killed him to save my life. But I didn't feel any safer. I couldn't afford to.

Arriving at the scene was anticlimactic. In an alley between two warehouses in Ashfield's industrial wasteland, the path the murdered girl had taken came to a point. Sandy black earth and bricks that hadn't seen sunlight in years. Eden parked and we walked into the gap and looked ahead to the wire fencing at the end, the dead grass. There were a couple of boot prints beside a pair of tyre tracks. The tracks showed the vehicle had come into the gap, where the driver exited, walked around the vehicle, got in the back, exited again and got in the front. The GPS showed the van was stationary here for a mere fifteen minutes. Fifteen minutes to leave the victim totally unrecognisable.

Eden and I stood close enough, but not too close, waiting for the crime-scene techs. There were plenty of cigarette butts and bits of paper around for collecting. I don't know about Eden, but I stood there still and silent because I wanted to be sad for a little moment at the sight of the footprints, the reading on the phone in my hand. The heartbeat rose. Then the heartbeat was lost. It was a lonely place to die.

'Kill van,' Eden said suddenly, nodding. I looked at her. Her arms were folded across her chest, her eyes squinting in the dim light, following the footprints back and forth. 'It's a good move. Mobile, so you can grab and go at any time. Easy to acquire. Don't need to clean it. Just light it up and leave it. Ted Bundy had one for a while there.'

She sniffed and took her jacket off, crouched low with difficulty to look at the tyre prints. I felt a little ill and went back to the car to wait.

Hades Archer was starting to feel things were getting too quiet around the house when he noticed the men gathered at the bottom of the hill. He'd been told men his age became restless towards their twilight years and sought the company of people who didn't necessarily want to hear their stories or drink their coffee. Men his age became a burden on people when they got bored. So the trick, it seemed, was not to get bored. Always have something brewing. A project. A purpose.

The average man took up golf in his retirement years. But Hades had never been close to average.

He kept this restlessness at bay by focusing on his work. His legitimate work, mostly. Waste rates in the city were always increasing, which meant he was constantly facing the challenge of finding space in his landfill for non-recoverable garbage. He spent the months carefully considering which technology upgrades he could get government funding for, how to make use of the non-recoverables, whether there were charities that could benefit from some of the items he couldn't find buyers for – the thousands and thousands of bags of clothes, the old but still operational appliances, the building materials. He considered which landfill plots to turn over, knowing it took six or seven months for the bodies he hid beneath the layers of waste to degrade to the point that they wouldn't be decipherable among the sludge and decay when the plots were dug up and relined for fresh garbage. He remembered where and when he'd buried people, and around about what their body type and fat content had been. He wasn't dumb enough to write this down anywhere, so it was a purely mental game. A memory puzzle. He'd heard men his age were advised to play them to keep the brain ticking.

It was an entertaining little test. Hades would stand on the doorstep of his little shack on the hill and look out over the fields, the trucks bumbling along in the distance spewing their black smoke into the air, and try to remember where he had buried this body or that one – and how deep. Ah yes, over there, by the fence behind the car shed, he'd buried the skinny rapist Denny 'the Preacher' Mills. East of the Sorting Centre, he'd planted Sharon the black widow. And just last week, in the north quadrant, he'd sunk some junkie punk whose name he never learned. He had felt a twinge in his back as he loaded the boy's body onto the front of the digger.

In a way, what Hades did was a lot like gardening. He'd heard gardening was good for retirees.

That evening, as the old man watched the sun falling behind the round grey mountains of trash, he felt a certain pulling in his chest which told him that for all his activities, his gardening and his memory games, there was still something lacking in his life. There was only so much organising a man could do before there was nothing left to arrange. His nightly meals were cooked and frozen – hearty containers of lamb stew and shepherd's pies and soy chicken stir-frys in their dozens. He was well into his next artistic project – a mighty wolf assembled out of hundreds of discarded black Singer sewing machines. Lots of welding work. Time-consuming and dangerous. But when he'd done all that, there was an unsettling stillness left behind. It was then that Hades let his eyes wander from the horizon and spied the men gathered down the hill beside the last truck to come in.

As the old man reached the bottom of the hill, one of the men turned away from the gathering and walked by Hades swiftly. Hades was surprised to see the grimy character had tears in his eyes. His fluorescent orange vest was spattered with all manner of tip muck – garbage juice, ink, paint, grease. Hades said nothing to the young man. You didn't acknowledge a man in his weak moments. Hades edged his way into the gathering.

All heads were bowed. At first Hades thought the object of their attention was a young kangaroo. The dog had the bony, elongated figure of a gangly joey. But the colour was wrong and so was the size. The animal was the sunburned caramel of ice-cream topping and milk-chested, a mixed-breed thing with a long snout and a pink nose. It was far too thin for how long it was. In fact, it was starved beyond anything Hades had ever seen, and he'd seen the dingoes that frequented the tip get down to bones and leather during the wintertime when the tip seagulls went back to the shores and wild cats were hard to come by.

The dog's lips were puckered inwards, and its hips were a collection of intricate spikes and ridges pushing up against skin. It was lying lifeless, white eyes bugging from its skull. An open garbage bag lay beside it, spewing its contents onto the ground.

A second man in the gathering walked away.

'There's got to be something in here,' one of the men said. Hades looked up and saw him rummaging through a garbage bag identical to the one the dog had obviously been pulled from. 'There'll be a bill with an address. A piece of paper. Something.'

Hades looked around as the men started rifling through the bags. Three of them remained, staring down at the dog.

'You do it,' one of them said to another.

'I can't fucking do it.'

Hades bent down. He heard his knees pop and crack as he lowered himself beside the animal. To his surprise, the chain of furry bone links jutting from the dog's hindquarters began to quiver, then to wag. Hades put his hand on the animal's cheek, smoothed its hairless leather ear back over its bony head. The dog was colder than a live animal should have been. Its tail continued wagging.

'Someone's gotta do it,' a man said. 'We can't just leave it like this. It's cruel.'

'Here. Here. Look. An address. I've got a fucking address in Lavender Bay. Let's go. Let's get the fucking pricks.'

'It might come good,' Hades said, more to himself than to the men around him. 'You never know.'

The men watched as Hades eased his big hands under the dog's hips and shoulders, gathered the thing into his arms. It weighed less than a child might. The dog was long. Its impossibly narrow legs dangled limply over his arm, its head lolling. Hades looked at the faces of his workers as he got to his feet, each wavering helplessly between fury and despair, then he turned and laboured up the hill towards his shack.

That night Hades sat on the floor of his tiny kitchen, his favourite things from the tip adorning the walls all around him. Taxidermied birds and framed dried flowers. Ten pocket watches hanging from their chains in one corner of the ceiling. Polished, renewed, ticking with life again, their engraved tributes reflecting in the light of several mismatched lamps. *To Sam, On Your Graduation.*

The dog lay in Hades' arms in a bundle of blankets and looked at all the things above him, not having expected, Hades imagined, to see anything again after the inside of the garbage bag.

Plenty of things had come good for Hades out of the bottom of garbage bags over the years. The secret, he always believed, was seeing the potential when all was apparently lost. Potential was a sly thing. It hid in the darkest of places. When the dog wagged its tail at the centre of the circle of men gathered at the bottom of the hill, Hades had seen that potential. He'd smiled to himself. Now he held the dog to his chest, looked at his watch and decided it could have more water. He took the plastic syringe he'd found in his medical cabinet, filled it with water from the glass sitting on the linoleum beside him and squirted a little on the dog's hairy lips. Slowly, weakly, the beast awakened from its half-delirium and began to lap.

It would be a long night, but Hades had nothing better to do.

Imogen Stone liked money, and she liked murder, and there was nothing wrong with that. If she'd been able to pass the intake for the police academy, she'd happily have been a homicide detective, like her boyfriend, the murder-police poster boy Detective Frank Bennett. But she'd been young all those times she applied, and once the stain of her late teenage 'narcissistic tendencies' and 'lack of life experience' had been recognised in the personality test, they stayed with her through all her subsequent applications. She'd outperformed on the aptitude tests, but this couldn't shadow what the psychological report called her 'grandiose sense of self'. It was ridiculous.

At the time, eighteen years old and quick to anger, she hadn't known what these terms meant. So she started researching how they were applied in psychology, and then started working towards disguising them, so that never again would they stand in the way of what she wanted. She became more reserved. More studied. She cultivated 'shy' and 'sweet'. She played down the apparent 'overconfidence' she'd displayed in the academy interviews. She got so good at understanding her own psychological dysfunctions that she fell in love with the science of it. Being a cop psychologist was as close as she could get to that old dream of being the crime fighter, of rubbing shoulders with truly dangerous people, both in and out of the job – not just pretenders – and she'd whizzed through the interviews for that role. But sitting there day after day in her leather armchair under the city windows, putting the pieces of broken cops back together, had done nothing for her narcissism.

Imogen loved herself.

In the end, it was impossible not to. Imogen had taken her one and only failure in life and turned it into a thriving success. Sydney's boys in blue looked to her as their saviour. They itched and twitched for her wisdom. It was Imogen they thought of deep in the night when sleep evaded them, sitting in the icy light of the bathroom, more comfortable among the razors and scissors than they were in their own beds next to their wives. It was Imogen they called. She was their triple-O. The first time she counselled one of the old boys who'd rejected her application as a young woman, she'd truly known what power was. Sitting there listening to him cry, she burned silently with hateful pleasure.

And then her first murder case. The missing Cherry boy.

George Cherry, eight, had gone missing as so many little angels go missing, on a walk home from school, the shark-infested waters between the classroom and home where the number of kids getting into cars and walking hand in hand with adults masks the hunt of society's nastiest. At first it was assumed the boy's estranged father had him. As happens so often, the critical first hours focused on the wrong man. Hours in the interrogation tank. More hours turning over the family home. Panic after the first lead failed, scrambling, stupid moves, roughing up the town's resident kiddie-fiddlers and the cultivation of myths in the media. More interviews.

More rummaging through drawers and leading dogs around tiny yards. Little George Cherry tumbled through the cracks. But he landed in the minds of his three pursuing detectives and they never forgot him, no matter how hard they tried. Imogen had been counselling the detectives for four years before her curiosity was piqued. Home alone one night and bored out of her mind, she went online on a sheer whim and the first thing her eyes beheld on FindGeorgie.com was blazing red lettering announcing a two hundred thousand dollar reward.

Imogen had taken on the case. And Imogen didn't lose.

She also didn't follow the rules. She didn't fill in reports. She didn't respect privacy. Imogen was all about winning, and in some dark corner of her mind she knew this was because all her life she'd been terrified of ending up like her father. A thirty-year veteran of the same security firm. A pencil-thin, hopeless man, the butt of his friends' jokes. Imogen's father was all she had, and she'd spent too many childhood afternoons watching him clearing up paper plates and empty beer bottles while his mates stood around the fire pit in the backyard of their suburban rental, munching damp bread and laughing globs of it into the grass. When he died, Imogen discovered a funeral plan for the old man that provided funds for a ceremony so lavish, so extravagant, it appeared he'd been contributing to it all his working life. Imogen hadn't accessed even half the funds for the ceremony she organised. As she'd predicted, only eight people attended.

Imogen was her own crime-fighting superhero. She didn't mind bending the law to get what she wanted, and that was what made Imogen so good at the armchair-detective game. Dr Stone put herself on the Cherry case and eight months later was leading a squad down an embankment on the Murray River to the child's bones. She didn't let them mention her name in the paper. That would have been narcissistic. Grandiose.

Imogen had found something better than public recognition. She'd found murder money.

After the first case, she was hooked. She began hunting across the internet for cold cases she could conceivably solve, or at least contribute to, gaining a tasty share of the reward money. Sometimes it required her to do some unethical things. She wandered around in restricted-access police archive rooms. Now and then she carefully plugged her clients for details on their cases, making them reveal things that wouldn't necessarily be therapeutic in their revealing. She cultivated a network of administrative assistants, lab technicians and secretaries who now and then slipped her the information she needed. It wasn't ethical – but it wasn't hurting anybody. She told herself that all good detectives bent the rules.

Imogen was far more powerful as an armchair detective than she might ever have been as a cop. Sometimes it made her feel sorry for people like Frank, with his constant phone calls about reports, warrants, codes, legislations – crime-scene handling and the endless, endless discussion of contamination. Contamination of crime scenes. Contamination of impartiality. Contamination of witnesses. Frank's work in homicide had turned him into a physical and metaphorical germophobe. He wrapped the tasteless chicken and mayo sandwiches he took to work like they were radioactive. He wouldn't talk about anything related to his cases, wouldn't give her those tasty little tidbits she needed to fuel the hungry, voyeuristic thing inside her. Not until she begged him, anyway.

Imogen was no germophobe. She got as dirty as she could in her perfect hobby. She loved the feel of grit beneath her nails from digging and digging for truth, like a happy little mole.

After the Cherry boy, there'd been a few other half- and quarter-reward jobs, but nothing that had excited her like seeing the forensics team break earth above the boy's grave, the dig marked out on her coordinates, on her intelligence. She solved the mystery. She caught the bad guy. She hadn't felt that same exhilaration since. But now, sitting outside Maggie Harold's house, Imogen believed she could feel that rush again.

She folded the map in her lap and looked at the dusty windows of the little hovel outside Scone. Mynah birds tussled over territory on the lawn, hopping angrily in the grass, kicking up dust. It was dry out here. A nowhere place dotted with tiny towns where everyone knew everyone, punctuating huge distances where no one knew anyone at all. The house had been difficult to find, but now that she had, Imogen wasn't leaving until she was certain the woman calling herself Eden's biological grandmother was revealed as a fraud. One at a time, slowly but surely, Imogen would tick off all the lies of Frank's partner, reveal her for what she really was. The missing Tanner girl.

By the time she dropped this on the homicide department, there would be no keeping Imogen's name out of the paper. Eden Archer would be her greatest catch.

Eden's mistakes at Rye Farm had left her with much more than a slit belly, though that was the worst of her physical injuries by far. The incision the killer made began just above her belly button and travelled upwards, deep enough to completely ruin all core strength she had previously possessed but blessedly not deep enough to spill her guts. In the violence before this injury, she had her nose broken, four teeth cracked, tendons permanently ruined in her neck and her left eye socket fractured. She compressed a disc in her lower back falling from the twine that had suspended her in the pig kill sheds.

All of these things took time, and money, to fix. Some things Eden knew would never be right, not in the days in the hospital, or the weeks in the rehab clinic, or the hours she spent on massage tables trying to repair ruined bits of herself. Eden had trusted one of her attackers, a foolish young girl she thought she might be able to help. It would be the last time Eden let the human part of her grow through the cement cracks – that struggling, pesky weed had almost got her killed.

She had let herself enjoy the company of another human being, feel genuinely connected. The girl's laughter, her touch, her big, trusting eyes. Eden was shocked how easily she'd accepted the lies of another monster. It was frightening to realise that there were hunters out there even more skilled at killing than she was. Masters of disguise even she couldn't pick.

Never again. She would trust no one. She would let no one in. One person, and one person alone would touch her, and it would be Merri, her massage therapist. That was it.

By the time Eden arrived at Pearl Massage in Vaucluse that evening she'd reverted to using both her aluminium crutches. The day had been nothing but waiting, but it had weighed on her shoulders so hard that she now walked bent in the torso, her neck twisted slightly to the side. Her eye socket throbbed. She and Frank had stood by the secondary crime scene for four hours while tyre tracks and footprints were cast, photographed and collected. Slowly, details about the girl at the park began to flood through their mobiles as forensics, photographers, beat cops and secondary detectives phoned in. They sat side by side, taking down details in their notebooks, pointing with their pens when something relevant came up. Ivana Lyon. Twenty-three. Flight attendant. Strangulation. Blunt force. Single. No bad relationships. No kids. Apartment. Coogee. No indications of SA.

No indications of sexual assault. Eden paused at that one and tapped the paper a few times with her pen. She waved at Frank, the phone hot and wet with sweat in her fingers, and underlined the words. He frowned, but no time had presented itself throughout the day to discuss what that meant.

Eden thumped into Merri's brightly lit salon and received silent glances from three of the nail artists grinding at the fingernails of their middle-aged clients. Merri came out from the back room and smiled at her, all dazzling white teeth. She was a short woman, Thai, the hard, high shoulder pads of her black jacket making her look like a tiny war general, a Napoleon with painted eyebrows far too long and square to appear even close to real. Merri was a brutal woman. Her words to the young nail girls were short, sharp and loud. One of the girls flew from her client, dropping her tools on the white towel on the table, and began making Eden a herbal tea.

'Darl-eeng,' Merri said, taking Eden's arm in her cold, hard hands. 'You need help. You come. You come now.'

'I do. Thanks.'

Eden followed the little woman into the candlelit back room. She stripped to her underpants in the warm glow, breathed in the lavender incense choking the oxygen out of the room. She lay on the towels and sighed, trying to control the physical twitches that always began when she knew she was about to be touched, the quivering in her calves, the chemical desire to flee. Merri gathered her long black hair, rolled it and tucked it into a towel. Merri was a small woman, but she was strong. It had taken Eden a long time to find someone who would push her as hard as she needed to find relief. She needed to go well beyond a normal client's pain barrier. Far enough that the pain cancelled out all else – the worry and confusion over Ivana Lyon, the image of her ruined face on the grass.

'Afterwards, we talk, darl-eeng,' Merri said lowly, positioning Eden's feet at the end of the bench.

'Talk?' Eden lifted her head from the towel. 'About what?'

'Not now. We talk after. We fix you first.'

'No, tell me. What are we talking about?'

'You quiet,' Merri said and forced her knuckle into Eden's sole. Eden felt the heavy air rush into her, let it ease out as she relaxed back onto the bench. It was never long enough. She needed to focus on every second.

Afterwards Eden lay in a half-sleep, listening to the meditation album playing on the old CD player in the corner, the bird sounds and rolling waves, the gentle pipe music. The extraordinary pain Merri forced on her had receded into an intoxicating warmth, a pleasurable ache in her muscles. She turned her head and found the little woman sitting on a plastic chair beside her, pouring her second cup of tea. Eden propped herself up, took the little china cup and sipped from it, felt the steam on her damp upper lip.

'Someone come here for you,' Merri said, holding her own tea. Eden felt like she was pulling herself out of a drunken stupor, though it had been years since she had been drunk. She lay and looked at Merri, let the tea rest in her hand on the top of the bench. The older woman seemed worried. Eden frowned.

'What do you mean?'

'Two day ago. Someone come here, for you,' Merri said. 'They want give me money for photo of you.'

Eden pushed herself up, her body slowly becoming colder in the warmth of the room. Merri stood and the two women stared at each other in the dark.

'A woman,' Merri said.

'A woman asked you for a photograph of me?' Eden pointed at her chest.

'Yes.'

'You're . . . you're not making any sense.'

'She come here, a lady. Pretty lady. She has picture of you.' Merri illustrated with her hands, held up an imaginary photograph. 'She tell me, "Get picture of Eden Archer. I give you five thousand dollars. I give you five thousand – one picture."'

Eden felt her heartbeat quickening. She felt it all over her body, her fingers pulsing as though being squeezed by invisible hands.

'When was this? What kind of picture did this woman want?'

'She want picture of this,' Merri said. The little woman reached out and touched Eden on the bright pink birthmark beside her left breast. Eden lifted her arm and looked at the mark, at Merri's white fingers pressed gently into the coloured flesh. She felt her stomach plummet. All the muscles in her back tensed at once, tugging her straight spine crooked once more in one huge simultaneous spasm of terror.

'Get me my phone,' Eden said. 'Now.'

In the old days, the Raymond Chandler days, homicide detectives used to spend the first forty-eight hours of a case running up leads themselves without eating, sleeping or shitting, without consulting anybody or writing reports or logging every goddamn sneeze in an incident log. Those days are gone. In the initial flurry after a murder, in between reporting to management every time someone swings their dick anywhere near the case, you field eight thousand phone calls. They're half organisational, half procedural. You assign everybody a place on the case – make sure no one you're working with has a conflict of interest, knew the victim or anyone related to the victim. You get your secondary detectives and their assistants all in a row, give them jobs and make sure they do them. You make contact with all the relevant medical bodies. The pathologist, his or her assistants, and various organisations that will take charge of and then pass the body on its way through the hospital, down through the morgue, into the freezer, back out again. It's kind of like organising a gigantic, gruesome surprise party – the details need to be managed in their millions, and it's all got to be kept secret from the press. Dozens of journalists call while you're putting things together, and you have to fend them off one by one with convincing lies and warnings so they don't get in the middle and blow the whole thing.

In general, I hate being on the phone. Unidentified numbers. The awkward silences. Trying to decide when the conversation is over or how to end it in an appropriate manner. The terror that someone's going to ring and they're going to remember me and I'm not going to remember them. I know. It's weird. My mother had it. The stuff I've done. I've chased guys with guns into dark warehouses. I took a crowbar to the head in an airport loading dock and then nearly got shot in the face. A German shepherd took a chunk out of my calf the size of a lemon on the way into a drug dealer's house. But none of that is as uncomfortable as when you're on the phone, particularly if it's to someone in authority, and you can't hear them clearly. And you have to say so, and then the person on the other end speaks louder and you still can't hear properly.

I found that the best way to deal with my phone phobia is to make sure I'm doing something else at the same time. So I invested in a hands-free set. I hooked the phone up while I worked on my house that evening. I cleared the kitchen of dust and hair and fluff with a broom and then started chipping out the burned bricks from where the oven had caught fire. The roofing guys had been in during the day and closed up the hole above me, but the ceiling was still incomplete, exposing wires and lightly charred beams. I put the bricks in a pile and sat looking at the hole I'd left with a tired satisfaction, fielding calls from the younger detectives and sucking a non-alcoholic beer.

In the first few hours, the minion detectives didn't know much more about Ivana Lyon that could help the case. The autopsy was being done overnight and I could view her in the morning. Apparently there were no leads in the family – no one was acting weird, they were all horrified and the mother was in a Valium-induced coma. Ivana had been a mild-mannered, hard-working girl who was popular. She liked to party but wasn't a tweaker. We had plenty of friends and ex-boyfriends to sort through for potential suspects. Everything was fine at her job. Her colleagues were all your garden-variety flight attendant types – clean, neatly dressed people with lots of Tupperware.

I wasn't too enthusiastic about there being leads among Ivana's friends. If the attacker knew her, it seemed a strangely risky move to grab her off the side of the Centennial Park jogging track in front of dozens of potential witnesses. He'd have had a much easier time grabbing her in her apartment, or at her car, or a million other less populated places she probably frequented. My guess was that the murderer didn't know her, that she'd been a random pick. But then again, that didn't fit with the brutality, the obvious fury of the attack. Who gets that angry at a perfect stranger? I sat on the floor and looked at the black bricks and felt confused.

Imogen walked in at nine carrying takeaway boxes. The smell of curry preceded her. I tried to shake away the cerebral impulses that started zapping at the sight of her, those mental flashes that put my girlfriend and the murdered girl I'd spent all afternoon staring at together and transposed the images before my eyes, my police brain trying to terrify me.

'It's my baby!'

'Hi, baby.' She looked around, looked at me, looked at the three empty beers by my hand. Her pretty upper lip curled. 'You know you're filthy, right?'

'Give me a kiss.'

'No.' She stepped awkwardly around the pile of dust and stuff I'd swept from the floor, pulled a plastic step ladder from the wall and brushed it off before sitting on it. 'You're drinking again?'

'They're virgins.'

'Still.'

'I know,' I sighed. 'I'll start again tomorrow.'

'We should really go to my place. Get you a shower.'

'I thought women liked men who worked,' I said. I flexed my biceps. She missed it.

'Women like men who can afford other men to work for them.'

I pointed at the ceiling. She looked up at the newly patched roof.

'Impressed?'

She said nothing. A call came through in my ears and I answered it with the button on the cord at my chest.

'Frank Bennett.'

'What's up, dickhead?'

'Well, well. What's up, Hooky baby?'

'I called to see what's happening with that girl,' Hooky said. 'The park girl.'

'Piqued your curiosity, has it?' I laughed. Imogen was watching me carefully. I made an apologetic motion and got up, heard both my knees crack. I moved down the hall.

'I like to keep abreast of these things,' Hooky said. I could hear a train in the background. 'North Sydney's not letting me have any fun while my exams are on. My life has become very pedestrian very quickly.'

I walked out the front of my terrace and told Hooky what I knew so far about Ivana Lyon's murder. It was a cool night, but nice. Next door, the young family was getting ready for bed, bath-damp little kids around the couch, and mother brushing hair out of eyes, getting her sleep-time promises. A little fairy-tale behind glass, like those robotic Christmas displays they used to put up in shopping centres. Mum perpetually smiling, nodding. Shiny boxes around a pipe-cleaner tree. I watched a possum clamber along the guttering above the upper-floor windows of my terrace and slip silently through the broken front window into the empty upstairs bedroom. I updated Hooky on everything I had. When my eyes fell I saw Imogen standing in the doorway. I made another apologetic wave and finished up with Amy, grabbed Imogen and kissed her as I walked inside.

'Who was that?'

'Girl who works for my old station,' I said, half-dreaming at the sound of my feet on my own floorboards.

'Woman who works for your old station,' Imogen corrected.

'No, actually,' I laughed. 'Girl. She's seventeen. Does some consulting work for us.' I could hear the possum on the upstairs floor. I banged on the wall and listened to it scurry in terror. Imogen followed me back into the kitchen, where I retrieved the curry boxes, snuck a forkful of massaman from one. 'We can go to yours now, if you like. I'm done here.'

'Great.' She slapped my butt when I bent to get my backpack. She stood in the doorway as I gathered up bits and pieces I needed – mostly paperwork.

'What's a seventeen-year-old girl doing calling a middle-aged man on his mobile?' she said suddenly. The words tumbled out of her fast, as though she'd spent the last couple of minutes holding them back, trying to talk herself out of them.

'Huh?'

'It's just a little bit slutty, isn't it?'

I laughed. It was a half-humoured laugh, half-shocked one. I wasn't used to Imogen using dirty words. And the thought of Hooky being anything close to warranting the term 'slut' was absurd. I thought of her as something like an oddball little sister, or a niece. A little bird I'd seen take a big hit once, but I was now happy to see flying again.

'Slutty? Oh my god! She was just calling for an update on the case.'

'An update on the case,' Imogen scoffed. It wasn't a pleasant sound. It was half sneer.

'She was.'

'Is it her case?'

'No.'

'Uh-huh,' Imogen folded her arms. 'You called her "baby".'

'Holy crap, you're jealous. This is hilarious.'

'Is it?'

'I've always called her "baby". It's not baby like . . . baby. Amy is a baby. She's like . . . a little girl.'

'You call me baby.'

'Ah. Well, I use the term with a different intention.' This conversation was getting weird.

'Uh-huh,' Imogen said.

She looked at me standing there with the curry boxes in my hands and my backpack on my shoulder. It was almost as though I'd been caught out on something. Guilt churned in the pit of my stomach. Once again, I felt the sting of being unable to understand the ways of women, their secret codes and inferences. We'd slipped into another language. I didn't even have a basic grasp of what was being said here, what I'd done wrong. I bit my lip and replayed the conversation with Hooky, tried to decide if anything untoward had been said by either party. But it hadn't. It really hadn't. There'd been work stuff only and a bit of the bantering that we always did. I couldn't even begin to conceive of there ever being anything else to it.

'Baby,' I said, reaching for Imogen, 'don't be silly.'

'Come on.' She jerked her head towards the front door. 'Let's go. It smells in here.'

Tara remembered. The memories came as tides, slowly rising, hitting their peak, and when they did she would sit on the bed and indulge them because she'd never had the strength to fight. She never knew which one would come. When she was at her most vulnerable the memories were of her youth – a Tara just starting to adapt to her pudginess, a Tara just beginning to assume her role as class reject. A short Tara, wide and soft, fleshy like a piglet, her little belly swelling and stretching the front of her sports polo as she panted. Cross-country day. That memory was always close at hand. The smell of freshly cut grass. The dread of the barbecue smoke in the school playground, the creamy fluorescent zinc being smeared on noses as the count-down to the afternoon session began. Tara the fat child rotating through as many excuses to Mrs Emmonds as she should muster, trying to find what would work, what would make the woman ignore her mother's threats. *My child will participate.* Tara heard the warning every year from the cordless phone in the kitchen, Joanie stabbing the countertop with a finger as house staff swirled and ebbed around her, preparing lunch. *Don't take any of her shit.*

It wasn't shit today. Tara really did feel sick. She tucked herself into the dark corner of mouldy bricks where the kindergarten block met the sports shed and breathed, listening to the big kids unloading the plastic markers and streamers with Mr Tolson. Tara held her belly and breathed. She was just learning to swallow the crying. She'd always been a crier, but she was beginning to relish in the hard, hot lump in her throat, the power she exerted in keeping it down, in keeping the tears at bay. Tara didn't have power over many things. But she was beginning to understand, at eight, that she could control her own emotions. She could bring on or suppress rage like it was connected to a switch. She could make herself shake and sweat with fury, or make herself cold and fatigued with calm.

As the day wound down towards the big race, Tara watched the other girls weaving ribbons into their hair and painting zinc dots on their cheeks. She went into the girls' toilets and did the same, worked the colourful cream into her plump face.

At the start line, no one noticed her. She kept to the back, the horizon ahead dominated by the shoulders of the enormous Year Six boys. Peter Anderson was wearing a Native American ceremonial chief's headdress, his freckled cheeks lined with zinc. The colourful tails of the feathers fluttered madly in the wind. The boy started up a chant for Stuart House and it grew so loud that it almost drowned out the crack of the starting gun.

Tara moved with the jostling bodies, and then she was on her own, little girls she'd remembered cowering in the playground on their first days in kindergarten rushing past her. She tried to befriend them once and for a few days had held a little posse of younger children as friends. But as they passed now they seemed not to recognise her. Their class clans had fused together and shut Tara out. By the time she rounded the first quarter marker, Peter Anderson was rushing past her, his huge legs striking out, hitting the grass with thuds. Boys from Flinders and Cook houses followed, grabbing at the feathers. They were still chanting their house songs. Tara could hardly breathe.

Run, run, boys and girls,
Try to get away,
We won't stop, can't stop,
Gonna make you pay!

For the next quarter, all she did was wait for the bigger boys to lap her again. When they did they came in silence, the game on now, the home stretch in sight. Tara huffed and struggled through the bush at the bottom of the school, following the rustling pink streamers over rocky ground, her thick ankles rolling over sharp stones in the clay. Small helpless sounds came out of her. In the rocking, bouncing world she spotted Mr Lillington standing among the trees, a carpentry magazine in his hands, his heavy brow furrowed. The older man heard Tara bumbling along well before he saw her. Tara hung her head, burned as he watched her slowly approach.

'Hey,' the man said, jutting his chin. 'Harper. Harper. Down there and around to the right.'

Tara wheezed, looked, tried to control her whimpering. Sweat rolled down her calves. The teacher pointed, raising his furry brows.

'Down there, girl,' he said.

He said 'girl' the way Joanie said 'stupid'. But when Tara looked, she saw the trail leading off towards the quadrangle and nodded. A shortcut. The music teacher watched her go, his lined face softened by pity.

She heard other children laughing as she cut away. But Tara only wanted it to be over. She emerged at the edge of the field as Peter Anderson sailed through the finish ribbon, his arms outstretched and shirt gone. Girls visiting from the high school pelted his hard, pale body with water bombs. Tara clambered up the rise and headed for the lines of teachers and parents.

Her mother would be there among the crowd somewhere. Tara sucked air and forced herself on. She was so slow that she could measure individual expressions as she passed, heard snippets of words from the parents.

Whose kid is that? Harper. Harper girl . . . chubby little . . . rolls . . . kid's gonna have herself a heart attack.

'That girl's snorting like a piggy,' a girl at the edge of the crowd said, pointing at Tara as she passed. 'Piggy, piggy, piggy.'

Tara felt sweat in her eyes. She pounded towards the finish line. A crowd of her classmates was waiting for her there, stretching their thin, strong limbs, zinc rubbed from noses and dribbling from wet chins. She could smell the barbecue.

Oranges. Tubs of quartered oranges. Tara headed up the straight and it was Craig Dune who threw the first slice.

'The food's up here, fatty-boom-bah! Run, run, run.'

Tara felt an orange slice bump against her chest. Then another. Suddenly a rain of them, boys and girls from older grades hurling the slices at her legs, her face. Teachers shouting, reaching for little wrists. She caught a rind in the eye and slid in the wet grass. She fell hard on her side before the finish line. She could see the balloons, the girl with the broken leg and the timer sitting on the stool.

In the crowd, Joanie had her arms folded, eyes on the horizon. Tara scrambled to her feet and pushed through the bodies of the adults, the forest of hips and stomachs, until she reached her. Her mother stood beside a woman who might have been her twin – both caramel goddesses wrapped in strips of fine grey silk. Joanie's ringlets were pulled tight in a ponytail on her square shoulder, the curls cascading down her chest.

'Mum,' Tara gasped through the tears. 'Mum.'

'Is this your little one?' The woman beside Joanie looked down at Tara with a mixture of concern and humour, her crooked smile faltering when she noted the orange juice dripping from the girl's hair.

'Mum,' Tara pleaded, tugging at Joanie's elbow. 'Joanie.'

'No, my one's out there.' Joanie shrugged Tara's hand away, laughing uneasily, pointing towards the curve in the track and the bushland beyond. 'My Tara's out there somewhere.'

'Joan–'

'Go find your mother,' Joanie said, pushing Tara's face away. She turned her hip, blocking the child from the woman beside her. 'Jeez. Weird kid. Anyway, so you were saying?'

Tara waited, but her mother didn't turn back around. In time she walked through the crowds towards the school.

They try to tell you that if you've got a couple of observers at the autopsy, it's because they need experience for their forensic medicine degrees, but . . . I don't know. I've had so many young observers hanging over my shoulder through the years, I just can't get next to the idea that studying to be a ghoul is so popular. When we arrived to view the autopsy on Ivana Lyon there were two young men already there, guiltily fumbling with their notebooks, surgical masks pulled tight like the shoelaces of kids on their first day of school. I gave them a fiery look as I waited for the tech to set up. I'm convinced a certain percentage of these kids are just too curious about murder corpses to stay away.

Beyond the glass, someone from Ivana's family was watching. An older brother or something it looked like. I've only seen parents attend once. I don't know why family would come at all. It's not how I'd like to remember someone I loved. I guess in murder cases they like to see that nothing goes awry. The liver isn't dropped on the floor or accidentally swapped with the patient on the next table. It's pretty grim.

Eden was unusually fazed. It was by all accounts her bread and butter, but she was restless, sighing, looking at her watch. She'd ditched the crutch for the morning, but I expected her to be back to it by midday. Leaning against the table, her ponytail pulling up the corners of her eyes and her blouse pressed to within an inch of its life, she might have been the old Eden, the one I knew before her brush with death. Except that she was chewing a thumbnail. Her eyes were hard. I nudged her in the side and she jumped.

'What's wrong with you?'

'Too much coffee.' She stretched her neck so that it cracked on either side. I knew that was a lie but I didn't push it. Eden could have snorted coffee like cocaine and not got the jitters. She absorbed chemicals like a sponge. I'd never seen her so much as tipsy.

'You've got to come to dinner with Imogen.'

'No,' she said.

'What makes you think you can put her off forever? She gets what she wants. She'll start turning up at your house, I'm telling you.'

'I would strongly suggest she doesn't do that.' Eden looked into my eyes. I felt a cold splinter in my chest, sweat prickle at the back of my neck. I cleared my throat, tried to focus on the technician laying out the tools like some kind of slow, methodical sadist. The brother behind the glass was watching the ceiling, fighting tears.

'What's your beef with Imogen?'

'I think you can do better.'

I scoffed. She was serious. I hadn't expected the comment. It was kind of sweet. Strangely, bizarrely sweet, coming from a complete sociopath and ruthless serial killer who I'm sure got up every morning and looked at herself in the mirror and wondered whether today was the day she should kill me and dump my corpse in a mangrove somewhere, watch crabs pluck out my eyeballs.

'Imogen is –'

'Imogen's an owner, Frank,' Eden said. 'She's going to own you and train you like a newborn pup until you either bend to her command or snap her hand off one day, and it's probably going to be the latter before the former.'

That hurt. She was referring to the time I'd hit my first wife in a drug-fuelled brawl at our cheap fibro bomb of a rental house in the Western suburbs. It was more than a decade ago, but Eden's brother had brought it out into the light and Eden was never going to forget it. She didn't forget things she knew about people. It was probably just a stab in the guts to cover for the compliment, to balance the universe, but in any case it seemed unfair.

'And then when you do snap at her, boy,' she said, 'then she's really going to own you.'

'This conversation is getting far too deep,' I said. 'Come to dinner. Please. I'm asking you nicely. Stave off your jealousy of Imogen for an hour or so.'

'My what?' She squinted.

'Your barely contained jealousy of Imogen.'

'Jealousy over what? What could Imogen possibly ever have that I would want?'

I tapped my chest and nodded knowingly, gave her a happy wink.

'One of these days you're going to wake up to yourself.'

'Hopefully not,' I said.

I jostled her in the ribs again with my elbow and she jumped, swiped at me. Her flesh felt weird under my skin. I reached out and grabbed at her ribs, and heard a crackling sound under the fabric that was very familiar to me. Something I'd heard many times.

'What is that?'

'Get your fucking mitts off me.'

'Is that a tattoo?'

I was certain I'd heard the crackling of sticky tape and the squish of damp plastic wrap, which is the kind of dressing only applied to a freshly inked tattoo. I'd stopped counting how many tatts I had myself. I was proudest of the gigantic traditional-style eagle, wings spread, that dominated my chest. My first. It was tough to go big on your first ink, and that's basically all the image stood for. My young, stupid toughness. The design could have been anything.

'Do not touch me, Frank. Ever.'

'We're about to get going here, people,' the head technician said. He lifted the sheet from Ivana's body and pulled it down over her naked figure, folded it at her feet. I looked up and saw that the brother was gone.

Ruben tried not to snoop but he couldn't help himself. Something was very wrong in the house by the park, but he couldn't fit the clues together, could not make any kind of sense out of what he saw. The path he took vacuuming from the ground-floor kitchen to the stairs outside the attic room was like a morbid tour of the moment things went wrong, the last days of joy before the hellish fall.

The previous summer he'd been in the States and stopped in Dallas to take the tour of the preserved Book Depository from where Lee Harvey Oswald had shot President Kennedy. He'd stood behind the glass and looked at the spot where the killer had perched, saw the scuff marks in the dust, the boxes still sitting unpacked as they had been that fatal day, forever to remain as they were, as though the moment could be returned to, changed somehow, if nothing was touched. He'd heard the haunting shots ring out over the little speaker in the corner, punctuating the commentary of the virtual tour guide. The house on the park was like the Texas School Book Depository. A frozen moment of terror and pain.

The wrongness of it all had struck him as he entered the bedroom the first day, puffed the pillows and shook the dust off the bed covers. The bedroom belonged to a man and a woman.

History books on his side of the bed, business management books on hers. Ruben's written English comprehension was terrible, but he flicked through the pages and found a shopping list bookmark in one. Then he spied the man's heavy Omega watch sitting by the lamp. He glanced behind him at the door. Felt a tingle in his palms. Why had the master of the house left his watch there? It was obviously his daily watch. No case or box to speak of. Why wasn't he wearing it when he left? Why hadn't they tucked it away, knowing that a foreign student with no paperwork and barely enough cash to make rent would be walking around the house? Ruben thought it was odd. His own parents trusted no one, and they hardly had anything to call precious. When they'd had viewings to sell their house in Perugia the old man had taken everything and stashed it at his mother's – even a set of crystal wine glasses from the back of the kitchen cupboard, as though people at the viewing could possibly manage to smuggle the set out in a bag or under a jacket, clinking and chiming as they ran towards their car.

There was more strangeness the more Ruben looked. The watch and the history books on the man's side of the bed were far dustier than the items on the woman's side. The pages were yellowed from the sun. So they had lain untouched longer. Wherever he'd gone, she'd left his things just as they were, gathering dust. There was something sad about it.

When Ruben entered the downstairs living room he found an empty wine bottle and a packet of sleeping pills on the little table beside the couch. There were three pills missing. On the floor was an empty sterile needle packet, the kind his brother carried in the pocket of his paramedic's uniform. It was stamped Prince of Wales Hospital. The needle packaging, the wine bottle and the pill packet were all covered in dust. Whatever had happened, the evidence was right here where it had fallen.

Ruben stood in the doorway, feeling cold all over. According to the job advertisement, the family who owned the house had gone away to spend some months setting up a business abroad. He heard a creak in the floorboards above him and went back to vacuuming. On his way out, he ducked through the couple's bedroom to look at the en suite. All the toiletries were still there. The toothbrushes leaning, waiting, in their ceramic stands.

I was the first to arrive at dinner, so I kept the obsessive Indian waitresses at bay by flipping through my notes on Ivana Lyon's autopsy, my notepad on the empty plate in front of me. It was busy at Malabar South Indian Cuisine on Darlinghurst Road even though it was a Wednesday. I'd never seen the place quiet and I was there a lot. Malabar was helped enormously by how many bad Indian takeaway joints there were in the area, peppered all the way up Oxford and William streets, the hopeful guilty pleasure of city workers on their way home. These same workers, disappointed enough times in front of their televisions, found joy and bliss when they discovered Malabar. Groups stood outside the windows smoking and jostling in the growing cold, leaping forward when their numbers were called and darting away into the night, plastic bags trailing steam.

I tried to keep my mind on the job, but at the table next to me a strange kind of group had gathered. I couldn't keep my eyes off them. It was the woman who attracted my attention first. I'm a red-blooded Australian male, so I notice women. I understand it's good practice to try to train yourself out of this tendency – especially if you're attached. You're supposed to forget about women, each with her own distinct kind of magic, never the same as the one you saw before, a dimple in a perfect smile or a raspy laugh you can imagine cutting the dark of a warm bedroom. This one was very eye-catching and not in the traditional way.

She looked apocalypse-ready. She was muscled all over, the way survivors are muscled – a woman whose body was prepared both for running and fighting, for climbing and hiding and sliding down hills. She was more than 'sporty'. She looked dangerous. Three huge guys sat at the table with her, talking in low voices, passing bits of paper around and signing things. The woman turned her head and showed me her sharp profile, and as she did I watched all the muscles in her neck move, some loosening, some tightening – the wires and chains of a great machine working. This is what women were becoming these days. Beautiful machines. Softness and curves and fat were things of the past. Everything was skin-tight and rock hard. It was exciting and kind of scary. I'm not sure it was really my thing.

Get your mind back on the job, Frank.

We knew plenty about Ivana Lyon from the autopsy. The body holds no secrets when you're dead. The autopsy told us she'd been exercising for some time, lifting weights as well as cardio, and she liked upper body exercises. Her triceps were well defined, and she had strong hands and the nice little calluses you get on the upper pad of your palm from not bothering with gym gloves. She wasn't pregnant, a smoker or a big drinker. She'd had braces once. She suffered mild psoriasis on her elbows.

I tried to take note of all these little bits and pieces and then forget them. I didn't like knowing the victim too well. As I got older it was harder to keep the murders impersonal. You start relating to them and you're in big trouble. Suddenly you think, oh yeah, I get the occasional spot of psoriasis on my elbows.

I had braces too for a while. I've had that callus on my hands. Next thing you know, you and the dead girl are best friends in your mind and you're willing to arrest the waitress for the murder just to cure your own broken heart. The justice system doesn't work like that. You can't cry over all of them.

Ivana Lyon had been dragged somewhere, knocked about a little on the journey. She'd had her wrists taped for a long time after death – probably right up until she was dumped back at the park at around 7 pm. She'd put up a little bit of a fight but not much of one – there'd been no scratching or biting, which indicated to me that she'd probably been drugged. How do you drug someone while she's jogging around a public path in view of hundreds of witnesses?

Her water might have been spiked before or during the run. That wasn't the likeliest option – but it was possible. The killer would have had to get hold of her water bottle before taking her, but if you knew her why bother letting her go out for the run in the first place? If it was someone she didn't know, the killer would have had to access the bottle she took on the run somehow – which might have occurred, if Ivana had stopped and put it down at any point. A bit of a gamble, though, following a runner around waiting for her to put her water bottle down. What if she never stopped for a break during the run? What if she stopped but she didn't let the bottle out of her sight? It was a bad plan.

Ivana Lyon's autopsy revealed a strange injury to the back of her left thigh, right below her buttock. It was bruised like a track mark and still open when she died. I didn't like the idea that there might be a killer out there with a tranquilliser gun putting down runners like jaguars on the plain, but I couldn't think of another way around it. I had to wait until midnight for the toxicology report, but I was pretty sure it would back me up. Someone had hunted Ivana like an animal. Tracked her, caught her, barrelled her into a van like a lion on its way to the circus. I was sure of it.

My phone vibrated in my pocket, a text. Imogen saying she was late, probably. She was the only person who texted me. When I opened it up, however, there was a message from Hooky. I felt my nose wrinkle involuntarily. Imogen in my ear like she was sitting beside me.

What's a seventeen-year-old girl doing texting a middle-aged man? Slut. Slut. Slut.

The text read: *Tranquilliser gun, right?*

I smiled and texted back: *You're in pedos, girl. Not homicide.*

She replied before I had time to put the phone away: *I want in!*

When I looked up from my phone, Eden was settling into a chair beside me. She poured herself a glass of water, glancing ruefully towards the door without saying hello.

'You didn't change?' I frowned.

'Don't start.'

'You attended an autopsy in that outfit, Eden. You think you could have slapped on a different shirt to come to dinner?'

'You're murder police, Frank. Not fashion police.'

'Imogen's going to come through that door in a second, desperately overdressed now.' I pointed towards the front of the restaurant. 'It's going to be awkward.'

'Frank,' Eden smiled at me, patted my hand, 'Imogen's always desperately overdressed.'

We engaged in a long, uncomfortable silence, looking at the tablecloth. Imogen walked through the door eventually, offering no relief at all in her foxy orange dress, little pearl earrings and the pride of her collection: the eight hundred dollar Jimmy Choos. She only wore orange when she really meant it – I understood it was a difficult colour to pull off – and as she approached the table I saw her face harden. When had my life become this way? I wondered. When had I begun to sweat over what women were wearing? Imogen bent to kiss me and clouded me with Chanel.

'Eden, thanks so much for coming.' She grinned and kissed Eden on the cheek. Eden hadn't seen the gesture coming and stiffened as though electrified. My phone flashed on the table – another text from Hooky – and Imogen's eyes fell on it just as my hand did. I tucked it away and she gave me a look. The look a woman gives you when she's cataloguing something in her mind, putting something away to burn you about later.

'Shall we order?' Eden asked.

'Imogen just sat down.'

'I know what I want,' Eden shrugged, jutting her chin at the nearest waiter. He came to the table and Imogen scrambled for her menu.

'We'll order wine now.' I kicked Eden under the table. 'The Malbec, please.'

The waiter nodded and retreated and Eden looked satisfied with herself. She picked up her knife and turned it by its point on the table.

'Well, what a crazy week,' Imogen said brightly. 'First that Byron Bay thing and now this.'

'What Byron Bay thing?' I asked.

'A couple of young travellers and a couple of scumbags from some backwater hole behind Byron,' Imogen said. 'Police found them all stuffed in a burned-out van. Can't seem to figure out the connection between the two parties. It's all over the news.'

'How weird,' I said.

'Do we have to talk shop at the table?' Eden snapped.

'Tough week, Eden?' Imogen smiled.

'I'm fine.'

'Oh, I just mean –'

'She's not counselling you, Eden,' I said. 'She's just asking how you are.'

'They never stop, Frank,' Eden raised her eyebrows at me, widened her eyes. 'They never stop.'

'Who never stops?' Imogen frowned.

'Let's order.' I waved for the waiter.

Eden settled after a while. The balance seemed to have been tipped between punishing Imogen for being an 'owner' and making me uncomfortable, which she didn't seem to want to do, possibly for the first time ever. Eden appeared to have a bit on her mind, which was unusual. She was pretty good at compartmentalising. Dropping the job when she couldn't do anything with it, picking it back up again when she could. She kept looking off towards the front doors, letting Imogen and I talk. She hardly ate, though what she ordered was by far the best choice on the table. She waved distractedly at me when I asked her if I could finish it. Imogen didn't seem to get the hang of Eden's closed personality. Kept plugging her with personal questions and getting nothing in return, though she spent plenty of time offering up examples from her own personal life as encouragement – stupid ex-boyfriends and her loser father and a nightmare boss who had come down on her too hard.

'Are you dating right now, Eden?'

'No.'

'Single for a while?'

'Yes.'

'I used to work with this guy named Nick who I think would be just perfect for you,' Imogen grinned and glanced at me. 'He's an anxiety specialist. I met him for the first time when –'

Now it was my turn to drift off. I like to tune out when Imogen talks about other men, in case I catch tales about guys with better jobs, bigger dicks, houses without possums in their upper floors. I don't know why women insist on talking about their ex-boyfriends and crushes in front of you, but over the years I've learned to ignore it. All impotent angst over guys I'd never met had ever given me was grey hair and restless nights. When I drifted back in it was because Eden was kicking me under the table.

'What does it matter what my parents do?'

'Oh, I don't know. It doesn't matter. That's not what I mean.' Imogen laughed uncomfortably. 'It's just, I don't know. My dad inspired me to do what I do. He was a very clever man but he never really fulfilled his potential. He could have been so much more than he was. When I decided I wanted to be a psychologist . . . I mean, maybe your father –'

I got out my phone, glanced at the time.

'We're going to have to wrap this up, ladies. I've got calls to make tonight.' I put my arms around both of them. 'Not that I'd rather be anywhere but sandwiched between you two gorgeous creatures.'

Eden peeled my hand off her and got up, started sifting through her wallet with the hard-edged face of a john looking for money to pay a prostitute. Somehow it seemed appropriate.

When I got back from the bathroom, Imogen was still sitting at the table, staring at the lone fork left over from the swift clearing the waiters had done. There's something sad about a freshly cleared restaurant table. The stains of a party attended, enjoyed, finished. Imogen didn't look sad, though. She looked cold. I sat down and went to grab my phone from where it sat in front of her but her hand was over it before I could.

'What the fuck is this?' she asked. She pushed the button at the bottom of the phone and the screen lit up, flashing a preview of a message from Hooky. *Hook me up!*

'She's talking about the Lyon case. The jogger. She wants some part in it. I don't know. She's hungry.'

I shrugged. Imogen stared at me.

'What?'

No response.

I opened the message stream and showed her.

'See?'

'Why isn't she texting Eden?'

'She doesn't know Eden.'

'Why isn't she texting Command?'

'She doesn't know anyone in Command,' I laughed. 'Jesus, they wouldn't want her kept in the loop anyway. It's not her case.'

'So you'd be doing her a favour.' Imogen licked her painted lips. 'You and some hungry little girl texting back and forth, doing each other favours.'

'Fuck me, Imogen. This thing you've got going with Hooky is just . . . it's madness. She's a child. She's texting me in a wholly and completely work-related capacity. That's it.'

'Oh, I'm sure.'

'Babe, I don't know why I'm sitting here defending myself. I don't have to explain this to you. It's nothing, and I'm telling you it's nothing and you're ignoring me. What you're insinuating is kind of sick. She's seventeen years old.'

'I'm not insinuating that you're trying to interact inappropriately with a seventeen-year-old, Frank. Open your ears. I'm insinuating that a seventeen-year-old is trying to interact inappropriately with you.'

'And that I'm doing nothing about it.'

'I'm trying to help you realise what's going on, so that you can do something about it.'

'Well, thank you, Imogen. Thank you very much. You're such a giving person.'

'Fuck you.'

'Fuck me?' I scoffed.

'Yes. You're being rude. And mean.'

'You're being rude. You don't know this girl. Her sister bludgeoned her parents to death. She sprayed their brains all over their pretty pink bedroom.'

'That's terrible.'

'You're right. It was terrible. In fact you have no fucking idea how terrible it was,' I said.

'I'm sure it was the kind of terrible life event that might reorient a person's whole perception of the world. Of people. Of relationships. Of appropriateness.'

'Oh lord,' I sighed. 'Stop.'

She shrugged. My face felt hot. I sipped the water nearest to me, tried to back down the angry stairs I was slowly ascending. 'What are you doing going through my phone in the first place?'

You'll either bend to her command or snap her hand off one day.

'Why shouldn't I be able to go through your phone? Going through your phone shouldn't worry you, Frank, because you should have nothing on there that you wouldn't be happy for me to see.'

Imogen rifled violently through her handbag, threw her phone onto the table so that it bounced dully on the cloth. People turned in their chairs.

'You want to see my phone?' she snarled. 'Go ahead.'

'I don't want to examine your phone, Imogen. I'm not that fucking needy.'

And then when you do snap at her, boy, then she's really going to own you.

Imogen looked at me, broken. Then she got up and left. I tried to chase her, but she slipped through tiny gaps between the chairs of other patrons I just couldn't fit through. She was gone before I could see which way she went.

Tara liked Violet the moment she saw her standing there in the doorway of her bedroom, twirling a piece of her long white hair around a willowy finger. She didn't know how long the girl had been watching her at the desk, playing with her dolls.

Well, she wasn't sure 'playing' was the right word. She was sure playing wouldn't have upset Joanie so much. When Joanie had found Tara's Barbies, with their cropped hair and their burned eyes, the hundreds of holes she'd dug into their breasts and crotches and stomachs with the heated needle, she had begun to scream. But to Tara, indeed, it was playing. Toying. She couldn't seem to leave the Barbies alone, the way she couldn't seem to leave a sore alone. Her father kept bringing them in their beautiful pink cardboard boxes, and they would sit on the shelves staring out at her from behind the clear plastic windows begging her to unwind the wire from around their wrists. Then once she had them free, Tara would feel the urge to play. The needles she found in the housekeeper's closet. The matches she found in the kitchen.

The way the Barbie's big, glossy blue eyes blackened and bubbled and sunk as Tara slowly inserted the needle made her mouth wet. She cleared her throat and shoved the dolls aside. Violet came right into the room and sat on the bed.

'Hi,' the girl said. 'I'm Vi.'

Sometimes, after that first day, Tara sat alone in her room and smiled to herself and whispered, *Hi, I'm Vi*, in the soft and lilting way the girl did, like a birdsong on a clear morning. Years later Tara would wonder if she had been in love with Violet then. Her first crush.

'My mum's downstairs with your mum.'

'Oh. Okay.'

'She says we've got to hang out together.' Violet raked her fingers through her hair. 'But I don't mind. This is a cool room.'

The girl reached out and jangled the string of Nepalese bells hanging above Tara's bed. Tara hadn't heard the word 'cool' regarding anything to do with her ever before, whether it was her room, her things, her clothes, her self. She was the very definition of uncool. She caught a flash of herself in the mirror and twisted quickly in the chair, the wire back cutting into her flesh in a cross-hash pattern. It made her look like a rolled brisket. She pulled her cardigan over herself and locked her eyes on the Violet girl's impossibly thin ankles.

'How old are you?'

'Thirteen,' Tara mumbled.

'I'm thirteen too.'

She said it like it was an achievement. She'd made it to thirteen. Tara smiled at the floor, scratched at her neck, leaving red marks she tried not to stare at in the mirror.

'So what do you do?' the girl asked. Tara noticed that she was still touching her hair. Always touching her hair – raking it, pulling it, twisting it into ringlets that unrolled and fell impossibly straight, refusing to be manipulated. While the girl toured the room, Tara gathered a small ball of fallen hairs in her fingers and rolled and rolled it in her palm, making it tight, a tiny snowy creature that she tucked into the pocket of her cardigan.

'Do? Um.'

'Yeah, like, what's your thing? What do you do?'

Tara scratched hard at her neck, felt her face flush. She clenched one fist, just one, by the side of the chair, feeling her knuckles crack.

'Um. Um.'

What are you doing here? Why did she send you here? What do you mean 'do'? I don't know what other kids do. I don't do anything. I hide. I hide. I don't know. I don't know. I don't want to look stupid. I don't want –

'I'm a ballerina,' Violet announced. Tara exhaled hard.

'Oh.'

'It's my career. Do you have a career?'

Tara breathed.

'You've got to take care of a career like it's a baby,' Violet said, shooting up onto the bed, standing in the centre of the room suddenly like curtains had opened before a mattressed stage, like an audience had been revealed, had demanded her presence. She looked at herself in the mirror, did a series of little rises and falls, flattened her hands on her ribcage and pushed, hard, inwards until the whole upper section of her torso collapsed like a balloon, the air expelled neatly. She was like a fold-out. An origami girl of crisp white paper. She slid her hands down, did the same with her waist, seemed to want to squeeze herself dry like a sponge.

'Your career is a little life that belongs to you. You love it. You care for it. You think about it every minute. You do your duty to it, because if you don't, it'll die. And you'll have killed something. Killed a baby. You'll never forgive yourself. You know?'

Tara did know. Her own mother spoke of such things. Not of careers, but of killing.

You're killing me, Tara. You're killing me with this. Look at you.

Tara got up, stood looking at Violet squeezing herself in the mirror, and wanted to join in, but didn't know how. She loved Violet already. Loved her milky smooth skin and white hair and the smell of milk all about her like a newborn animal, pure and untainted. Tara thought if she touched her the girl would probably be cold, might feel like condensation on a bottle left on the counter in the kitchen. Violet turned to Tara and grabbed her forearms. The bigger girl felt a rush of electricity run through her, right into her chest, like stepping on a stair that wasn't there, the terror followed by the blessed relief. Violet squeezed her fleshy elbows, slid her fingers along until they were holding hands, the two of them, just standing there in the room where no one dared enter, where her own mother hadn't been in years. Tara wasn't alone. For a moment, she was wholly and distinctly not alone.

'You've got to make sacrifices if you want a career,' Violet said.

'Okay.' Tara nodded eagerly.

'I'll show you my trick, if you want.'

'Yeah. Great!'

'Have you got a toothbrush?' The girl grinned.

Tara sat on the stairs afterwards while Violet brushed her teeth, gripping the banister with both hands. It was only when Violet had begun her routine that Tara realised how many bones the girl had, and how very close they were to the skin. The girl gagged. She became, for a few minutes, a spiny forest creature, a thing filled with venom, expelling it, expelling it, so she could return to her natural milky newborn state. Down in the sitting room, Tara could see Violet's mother sitting next to her own mother on the Louis XV set, the set that no one sat on. Joanie was crying. It was rare that Tara saw Joanie cry, and she marvelled at how pretty it was, how her long nose became a rich pink and her eyes flooded crystal tears. Tara puffed up like a blowfish when she cried. Her face swallowed her eyes.

'It can't be all that bad,' Vi's mother was saying.

'It is. Oh, it is. Believe me. If this doesn't fix it, I don't know what in god's name will.'

'Tell me,' the other woman crooned, gathering Joanie's hand in both of her own.

'They call her . . .' her mother paused, swallowed. 'They call her Nuggy.'

Vi's mother sat back in her chair, clasped her handkerchief at her chest. She gave a little jolt that could have been a suppressed laugh, a cough, a shudder. Anything. A quake of recognition that rippled through her bony frame, made her white hair shimmer like a mirror.

'They what?'

'They call her Nuggy, Marcey,' Joanie said. 'They've always done it. It's shortened from Nugget. She's short, square. Thick. Like a nugget.'

Marcey laughed, just once, and then swallowed the sound under Joanie's glare.

'Oh, Joanie. There are worse things, surely. Nuggy? Well, it's sort of . . . cute, isn't it? It sounds snuggly. It sounds sort of –'

'It is not cute,' Joanie snarled. 'It's not snuggly. It's not cute. It's humiliating. It's like a knife in my heart.' She beat her chest with a fist, once, twice, squeezed her lips shut.

'Oh, Joanie.'

'Look at you, Marcey. Jesus Christ. You don't understand. How could you? You and David, you've got a beautiful, graceful swan and I've got . . . a nugget. A fucking nugget for a child.'

Her mother bit down and growled angry tears, buried her face in her hands.

Tara retreated quietly to the bedroom.

Here's the problem. A lot of people watch crime shows. Not only are they rigidly formulaic, but they're fast. In minutes one to three you get the crime. Minutes four to five, the detectives are called onto the job. They express shock and horror and a heartfelt pledge to catch the guy – alongside hints at their intoxicating secret lust for each other. Then you get a parade of standard possible suspects: cheerful doormen, menacing drug dealers, local eccentrics, cherry-cheeked school teachers. A detective gets a seemingly innocuous phone call or tip-off or something, remembers another minor piece of information from the beginning of the episode and – whammo! They nail the victim's boss, mother, boyfriend. The sandwich shop guy. It's that easy.

So people are used to crimes being solved before it's time for bed. In almost every scene, something is being done towards finding the perpetrator. Samples are being taken. Suspects are being hassled or chased through rainy alleyways. No one eats or sleeps. They don't take toilet or smoke breaks. Or call their girlfriends and apologise for calling them 'needy' or have make-up sex. They certainly don't stand around near the body talking with their hands in their pockets.

Unfortunately, that's precisely what Eden and I did when they found the second girl near Mrs Macquarie's Chair in the

Domain. She was sitting upright against a tree near a bike rack, in full view of anyone riding past. The victim's jacket was over her head. From a distance, an onlooker might have thought she was chilling out after a long run. The jacket, however, was hiding grievous facial injuries. A missing eye. The way her legs were stretched out, feet together, didn't suggest trauma. Whoever found her would have got a nasty surprise after pulling the hood back. The crime-scene techs had erected a tent around the victim, but Eden and I had taken a quick peek and stepped out to confer, to let the five people inside the tent do their thing. There was no phone this time but headphone jacks had been left behind, indicating that there had been one at some point. A good crowd of morning joggers and a few members of the press were gathered around the police tape, staring at us. I've got so used to their presence that I simply forgot they were there.

'Jacket over the head this time,' Eden said quietly. 'Some shame still there but we're rapidly growing out of it.'

'Bit of a confused kind of display,' I nodded. 'Wants the body to be found now. Clearly. But the killer's not particularly happy for everyone to know what's been done to the face.'

'I don't think she can help what she does to their faces. I think that's the pure rage part. I think she just goes at the face before she knows what's she's done.'

'She?' I frowned.

'I'd say it's a woman.' Eden looked at the crowd. 'Wouldn't you?'

'Statistical probability would suggest otherwise,' I said. 'But I'll hear your theory.'

'Clothes on this one aren't tussled, the way they would be if they were removed and then put back on. I'm betting the rape kit will confirm no sexual assault again. And then there's the facial injury. That's very feminine to me. Men go for the hair, the breasts, the wrists. The thin parts. They're objects for men. This –' she gestured to the tent '– this was personal.'

'But we know it's not personal. We've pretty much ruled out anyone in Ivana Lyon's life, and now –'

'Maybe it's personal by proxy,' Eden said. She took a packet of cigarettes from her back pocket and slid one out, put it between her lips, patted her pockets for her lighter. 'Hence the face. She can't get at the person she's imagining her victims to be. They might be beyond her reach somehow. So she plays the fantasy out on random women. Once the face is messed up, she can imagine the victim to be whoever she's imagining she's killing. It's pure Bundy.'

Some bystanders at the tape near us bristled with excitement at the mention of Bundy. We took a step or two away from them and turned our backs.

'That's the second time you've dropped the old Bundy stick,' I said.

It's always difficult to bring Ted Bundy into discussions about cases. The 'poster boy' of serial killing is a perfect model to teach young homicide detectives about serial murder, so Bundy is drilled into you from the moment you transfer up from patrol. Bundy was responsible for the deaths of at least thirty-six young women in the mid-1970s, from schoolgirls as young as twelve to college students on the brink of starting their professional lives. He had a 'type' – they all had long dark hair parted in the middle. Clever and beautiful girls who showed academic promise, women he lured into a Volkswagen Beetle with his charm and good looks. It was never revealed why Bundy was so taken with long dark hair parted in the middle – but some speculate that he was trying to symbolically kill an ex-girlfriend, Stephanie Brooks, who had humiliated him by rejecting him. Bundy was driven to murder her 'by proxy', to rape and mutilate and bludgeon and strangle women who looked like her as a way of enacting that same violence on Stephanie over and over.

I wasn't sure we had a Bundy killer on our hands here – as a homicide detective I'd heard the term mentioned plenty of times. It was thrown around a bit whenever violent crimes showed any kind of pattern. We had a second victim. I thought it was too early to bring out Ted.

Eden waved at me for my lighter.

'What are you doing?' I lit her cigarette. 'You don't smoke.'

'I'd argue to the contrary.' She eased smoke through her teeth.

'You're acting weird lately. The tattoo.'

'I got a tattoo, Frank. Big whoop. The press are over there if you want to make an announcement.'

'This thing with Imogen.'

'I don't have a thing with Imogen.'

'It's just not like you to let someone piss you off like that.'

'She doesn't piss me off.' Eden gave one of her old half-grins, showed me a canine. 'I just think she's a loser. I've got bigger fish in my life.'

'Who?' I asked. 'Is someone bothering you?'

'No.'

'Well,' I shrugged again, 'I'm here if you need me.'

'I neither need nor want you.' She finished her cigarette and threw it on the ground, pushed it into the wet grass.

'Hey!' someone shouted from the crowd. Eden and I turned. It was hard to know who'd spoken at first. All the faces, the eyes, were examining us. A couple of people turned towards a man in his thirties in a full running skin-suit, black lycra, slippery looking like a seal. He had a belt strapped to his waist with tiny bottles of water on it, a set of keys, some kind of step-tracker device.

'Yes?' I frowned.

'What the fuck are you two doing?' He put his gloved hands out. 'You going to catch this guy or what?'

'Excuse me?' I looked around, tried to determine if I knew the man. Eden was playing with her phone.

'I asked if you two are going to catch this guy,' the man said, folding his arms. 'You're standing there soaking up the morning like you're at a fucking picnic. People are scared out here, mate.'

I laughed. I guess I was surprised and outraged and didn't know what else to do. I checked again to see if Eden was getting this, but she just looked bored. She took my lighter out of my hand and used it to light another cigarette. The man in the seal suit pointed at her first cigarette on the ground.

'You're contaminating the crime scene.'

Crime-show fan.

'The crime scene's in there, you idiot.' I jerked a thumb towards the tent. 'Who the fuck are you?'

A couple of the press cameras had turned towards us. I heard clicks, realised my jaw was out and my shoulders were up. Eden waved her cigarette in my face and brought me back around to her.

'I'm going to get onto the CCTV and get the tech heads after that phone. If you're done cavorting with the locals, you can join me.'

I glanced at her, but my mind was elsewhere – over the shoulder of the dickhead I'd spotted something odd at the edge of the police tape. It took me a few seconds to put together what I was seeing. There was a camera crew and a reporter taking an interview from a woman just beyond the back of the crowd. I recognised the sharp ponytail, the muscled profile. It was the apocalyptic woman I'd seen at Malabar Indian. Immediately, the fight with Imogen came to mind and my stomach flipped. I ducked under the tape and worked my way through the crowd, then stood behind the cameraman and watched the woman giving the interview. She was wearing full running gear – the same kind of body suit the dickhead was wearing but without, somehow, managing to look like a seal. She looked ready to rappel down into a bank vault and steal a diamond. There was no belt, no nylon cap. She thumbed the straps of a high-tech little camel pack with a water hose. There wasn't a bead of sweat on her. She was wearing thick bronze make-up and dark gold eyeliner. I couldn't decide if she was going to a charity ball or setting out to run to Parramatta.

'What we really need to do is recognise the message behind these killings,' the woman said, swishing her ponytail. 'And that is that strong, athletic, assertive women taking charge of their own health and wellbeing are threatening the dominant masculine archetype that's so much a part of Australian history.'

'The what?' I looked at the cameraman. He was focused on the machine in his hands.

'Both these women were runners,' the woman continued. 'They were both targeted on their daily run while they were out there trying to better themselves, better their health and their lives. They were taking time for themselves. They were being selfish, which is a misunderstood and demonised word applied by ignorant people to the women they want to serve them. I think we need to take the message that this guy is giving us – that these women need to be punished for their self-empowerment, for their rejection of the simpering, weak, subordinate female mould – and we need to stick it where the sun don't shine.'

'Who is that?' I asked the cameraman. The microphone guy emerged from behind him, leaning back as he lifted the furry mic hovering above the journalist's head.

'That's Caroline Eckhart.'

'Who?'

'Caroline Eckhart.' He frowned at me like I'd asked him who Jimmy Barnes was. I shrugged helplessly. He went back to his mic with a shake of his head.

'So what you're saying is that these killings are a distinctly feminist issue?' the journalist said.

'Oh yes. There's a deep misogyny at work here, one that all Australians need to recognise, not just those horrified by these brutal murders. Domestic violence is a frightening epidemic in this country, and whoever this man is, he's –'

'Who said the killer is a man?' I scoffed. Several people turned to look at me. The crew, the journalist herself. Everyone but Caroline. She was on a rant, and nothing was stopping her. Her eyes were on the skyline, the glass windows of the distant CBD. 'What the hell is going on here?'

'Mate, you're messing up my bite,' the mic guy snapped at me.

I felt Eden's hand on my shoulder. She was pulling me towards the tent. 'Stop wasting time.'

'Who is this chick?' I yelled as Eden tugged me away. 'Woman, you have no idea what you're talking about.'

The crowd at the tape turned to look at me. Almost all of them with hateful glares.

Hooky was haunted. But she didn't mind. To be haunted was never to be alone. From the moment they had come and taken her from her classroom to the principal's office, sat her down and told her that her parents were dead, she had almost never been without her mother and father's presence, or the presence of something she believed in the beginning had been them. They hung on her, weighing heavy and hard in her chest like a rock on a chain, a lump at the base of her oesophagus. Never satisfied, as they had been in life – but unlike in life it was those around her who they were never satisfied with. She became a kind of voice for them. A puppet. She became the advocate of angry ghosts.

In the beginning it had made her silent. Drew her back from the cuddling and the crying and the sweets that had come when her parents had died, the inevitable flooding of love. She felt choked, suffocated by the smells that erupted all around her – flowers, fresh and then rotting and then dead in brown water, the food, the cakes, the pickled things. It had made her explode at those who tried to help her. Her teachers. Her friends. The awkward scruffy-haired cop named Frank who didn't quite know how to be around her, who couldn't decide if he should treat her as a victim, a child, a woman, a survivor, an oppressed ethnic minority, a toxic entity.

The hurt in her chest had receded around him for some reason, the way it did when she managed to fight her way into her father's office, into his hard leather chair – the only place where she could get the true smell of him, the feel of him, onto her skin. That haunting hurt had pulled and pulled her there, and she hadn't known why. Then she overheard the three officers at the computers arguing about who had blown their cover in the teen chat room, who didn't know anything about teen language, whether Miley Cyrus was still cool or not, what LOL meant and when to use it. She'd felt tugged forward on that chain again, a slave to the dark desire that no longer had a face or a name, that she wasn't sure really was her parents anymore, but a thing that had grown like a tumour in her, a hateful and vengeful thing. When she began lying online, she felt in control for the first time since their deaths. She felt alright with being haunted.

It was a strange sort of desire that drove the thing in Hooky. Sometimes it wasn't exactly right, if rightness could be drawn out and separated from everything that was wrong, from everything that would earn her a mark against her name – bad girl, girl on the wire. In the early days, cast out of the North Sydney Metro offices and put on a train back to her aunt's, she found herself wandering aimlessly through Chinatown towards Paddy's Markets, feeling the twisted justice pulse in her. An elderly woman had stopped at the McDonald's attached to the Entertainment Centre, shook off a leopard print umbrella and set the pretty item on the bricks outside the restaurant before going in and joining the queue. Hooky was watching with her hands in her pockets, coming up the street behind a group of girls about her age, when she saw one of the girls – a thin, lean creature with pink streaks in her hair – dart out and snatch up the umbrella and continue walking, her pace never slowing, the theft so seamless and natural it was almost expected. Hooky followed the girl into the public bathrooms inside the Market City shopping centre, waited for her to emerge from the stall, and punched her, just once, square in the nose. The blow had been right on target, crushing the hard, narrow bones there and launching a rush of blood right down the front of the girl's sparkly top. Hooky turned and left. Returning the umbrella to the old woman didn't even crossed her mind. She didn't know if what she'd done had been justified, had been 'right'. She didn't know if justice was a real thing, anyway. All she knew was that the burning in her chest was eased.

Sometimes Hooky felt compelled to cheat people. To make them believe things about her that were not true. She told herself sometimes that she did these things to hone her skills for her games with the perverted souls who lurked online – the men who wanted to be daddies pushed too far by teasing stepdaughters, the women who wanted to teach boys how to make love. But she was also aware, on some level, that she cheated and lied just because it was fun. She would strike up a conversation on a bus with an older man and build a Hooky that was not real, a twenty-one-year-old Hooky with a boyfriend named Ted who worked in graphic design, a Hooky who lived in a trashy little apartment in Erskineville and who couldn't get enough of this vegan café there. Hooky wasn't vegan. She'd only been to Erskineville once. The lies weren't even particularly extravagant. But the way the older man nodded, accepted, didn't question – that was what thrilled Hooky. No one questioned her. People trusted. Hooky could be anyone she wanted.

She began to buy costumes for her fantasy lives. Snappy suits and ragged jeans and an old stained chef's uniform, silk-lined party dresses and demure librarians' dresses, ankle-length and olive green. Money wasn't a problem. Her parents, ever practical, had left her everything and not bothered with conditions, because they knew their family wasn't the kind to waste their fortune in clubs and bars, to spend it on stupid cars and leave her and her sister high and dry for the rest of their lives. She made the necessary arrangements to have her sister's share of the inheritance ordered over to her through Victims of Crime, to continue her parents' investments, to take over their share portfolio, and she signed her name on the deed to her home. Hooky sold the house in which they had been killed for a quarter of what it was worth just weeks after the murders faded from the headlines.

Sometimes Hooky trawled the nightclubs, made men buy her drinks, played the naïve Japanese tourist dumped by her friends, curious and a little frightened by white guys and their loudness. Japanese, Vietnamese, Chinese – these guys didn't know the difference, didn't care, as long as she played to their expectations, was cowed and grateful and a little surprised by her own passion after a couple of vodkas. Naughty oriental girl. Sometimes she indulged the fantasies of older business-men, sometimes women, sitting at the bar at the Union Hotel with her expensive heels hanging off her toes, writing gibberish on napkins as she listened to a call from some director on USA time who didn't exist. She never went home with them. That was the cheat. That was the point of it all. It was all lies. When their backs were turned, she vaporised.

Hooky knew, deep down, that she was in training for something. That the thing inside her wasn't only pulling her through these little fantasies idly but was also growing, escalating, becoming hungrier. She was evolving into a skilled con woman. Soon cheating people with her chimera games wouldn't be enough. She'd begin robbing them. She'd begin hurting them, making them cry. Emptying bank accounts and ruining lives maybe. It was something she could see looming on the horizon like a wave, but there was no running to the shore before it crashed over her. Her legs were stuck, sinking, being drawn out from beneath her.

Maybe one day she would start killing them. Luring them to their deaths. The thought that there was a killer inside her was terrifying. Was that inside her the way it had been in her sister, a killer genome cooking away chemicals in her brain, building a desire to inflict pain? Would the ghosts that had once been her parents haunt her so long that only blood would sate them?

Hooky was getting her morning fix of illusory online games at Sydney Metro police station when a woman came to the counter and rapped on the surface. Hooky leaned back in her chair and saw glossy painted nails, acrylics, and went back to her conversation with Badteacher69, her fingers darting over the keys. It wasn't Hooky's job to go to the counter. As a matter of fact it wasn't officially Hooky's job to be anywhere near the Sydney Metro Homicide Department at Parramatta, but she'd been hanging out hoping Frank and Eden would come in with news about the case, and so far she'd bluffed confidence about her computer access well enough that no one questioned her presence or activities. When the woman tapped again and called out a friendly hello, Hooky looked around and saw no one was near. She unhooked her headphones and went to the counter. The woman was small and blonde and pretty, with a neat, blunt-cut strawberry fringe on a freckled, uncreased brow. The woman glanced at Hooky's outfit and the younger girl straightened her camouflage-pattern singlet, pulled up her baggy black pants full of items she'd never carry in a handbag.

'Can I help you?'

'I'm looking for Detective Frank Bennett,' the woman said. 'I'm his girlfriend, Imogen.'

'Oh.' Hooky laughed. She wasn't sure why she did, at first. Maybe it was the fact that the woman was so small and neat and stylish – hardly Frank's type. Hooky had never considered what Frank's type might be, but this woman looked like something best handled with care. She thought of Frank's big callused hands, the way he was always knocking things and crushing things, like every room was slightly too small for him, like everything was slightly too delicate. 'Oh, right.'

'I've brought him lunch,' Imogen said, setting a plastic Tupperware container on the counter. Hooky nodded and took the container, tried to determine what its contents might be. She saw raw carrot. Tried not to smile.

'Well, Frank's out, Imogen. So . . .'

'When will he be back?'

'There's no telling,' Hooky said. She felt her eyebrows dart together. 'Like, he could be anywhere.'

Hooky knew her tone was patronising, but couldn't help it. It was just the funniest thing she'd seen in a long time, some wifely figure right out of Pleasantville with her perky heels and her gold bracelets, dropping off lunch for her Frankie-bear. Hooky had once seen Frank eat a muffin with the paper still attached to it. Starving and brain dead and filthy from crawling beneath some drug dealer's house all day digging for a dead newborn baby, his hair stained black with some kind of muck and sticking out in spikes from behind his ears. Her amusement really had nothing to do with the woman at all, but Hooky watched as a coldness came over Imogen's face.

'So you're Hooker, are you?'

'Hooky,' she said.

'Right,' Imogen nodded. Her features reassembled into the smile. 'I get it now.'

'He's spoken about me?'

'Yeah, some,' Imogen smirked, looking at Hooky's shirt again. 'I feel so stupid.'

'Why?'

'Oh, I was worried. It's silly. I didn't realise you really are just a child.'

Hooky's face darkened. Imogen turned on her heel, and Hooky watched her breeze through the automatic doors into the street.

Eden was on the edge. There was no doubt about that now. At first, when Merri had told her of the woman trying to get a picture of her birthmark, Eden had been able to control her inner 'flight' reflex, the whispering voice that made her want to drop everything and run, as she had imagined doing so many times before. Hades had always made sure she had a plan in place. Money, a bag, a new identity. Going to ground, being reborn as someone new – these things didn't concern Eden. Usually.

Going undercover had taught her how to shed herself completely, like taking off a suit. Eden herself was a construction, after all. A mask she had been wearing since the morning she and Eric had become Hades' 'children', since they adopted their new names, settled into their new life with the Lord of the Underworld playing Daddy. Eden wondered, sometimes, what sort of person she might have become if Morgan Tanner, the girl she had once been, hadn't had to be snuffed out. Who was Morgan Tanner? Who would be born when Eden Archer was dead? Eden wandered, head down, up the hill to the little shack at the centre of the Utulla tip, towards the warm golden lights of her home.

Whenever she visited now something was changed, moved slightly, upgraded to allow for Hades' slow decline, the back that wouldn't hold under the weight of certain tools, the old knees that cracked when walking down steps. Everything was closer to the little house to eliminate the need to walk over uneven ground for long distances – the letterbox shifted up nearer the front door, the sun bench where the old man liked to sit and watch the workers now beside the steps, under the awning. Eden was glad. Hades insisted on living by himself out here, beyond the reach of anyone who might change a light bulb for him, who might lift a heavy pot out of the oven. But there she went again – fantasising, dreaming of lives that were not real. He was not a vulnerable old man. His hands were worn, but hard. His mind was dark, but quick. He was going to die one of these days as lethal and as malignant as he always had been. There would be no spoonfeeding in a nursing home. No adult nappies. He would meet a bloody end one of these nights with one of his clients willingly, or he would push someone into it – an end in war was Hades' only end.

Eden did not find Hades in the house. She walked over the hill towards the work shed. She passed beneath huge structures lining what had once been a rocky stone path but was now a set of immaculate steps cut into the hillside and laid with terra-cotta tiles to save the old man's ankles. A giant grizzly bear made from hundreds of bottles towered over her, the glass warped and melted together, the chest of the beast pocked and holed with open glass mouths strapped down against a ribcage of old wood wrapped with hunks of wire. A mouth roared at the sky, the innards of the skull pipes and tubes welded and tied together, the gaping eyes of microwave doors tilted, sad, one burned through from an inner explosion. Across from the bear, a lion was frozen mid-pounce; the claws reaching over Eden's head were polished brass parts from a series of ancient machines – clocks and printing presses, and the dozens and dozens of typewriters chucked into the tip each month. Down the lion's back, a rippling curve, thousands of typewriter keys spelled gibberish, the letters glimmering in the growing dark, black and white and yellowed with age. She stepped through the open door of the shed, no barriers between her and the old man, nothing stopping some stranger from wandering in here and seeing him at his dark work, as always. Hades had never been one to hide. He was too ancient to bother with precautions.

Hades was bent over a workbench. A body lay on the table before him, the thick head turned away. An old handsaw rocked in his fist, back and forth. Eden walked around the table in time to see the corpse's left knee crack off heavily, flopping wetly to the table.

'What seems to be the problem, officer?' Hades said. He put down the saw and wiped his hands on the cloth apron he would later burn, smearing black blood down his chest like war paint. Hades had always liked getting bloody. He didn't wear gloves or a mask. Tiny blood droplets had spattered his left cheek. Eden took out a handkerchief, sighed, swiped at her father's temple.

'What is this? You said you were done.'

'I am done.'

'Well, who's dropped this on you then?'

'Oh, that idiot Jesse Jeep. It was a favour returned. That's it, now. I really am done.'

'Uh-huh.' Eden glanced into a huge duffel bag lined with black garbage bags sitting behind the table. 'And you've got to do his chop work?'

'The chop work was sort of half done.' Hades shrugged one shoulder. 'Arms, at least. You know these kids, Eden. They have no stomach.'

Eden sighed again and began rolling up her sleeves. Hades handed her a long-toothed hacksaw and she set it to the man's right knee. She was about to begin cutting when she noticed a basket on the other side of Hades' feet, overflowing with old blankets.

'What is that?' She nodded. As she spoke, the creature in the basket seemed to awaken from its slumber. A pink nose on a caramel snout emerged from the blankets, snuffled the air for a moment and then sunk away.

'Is that a roo?'

'No. It's a dog.'

'You got a dog?'

'I don't go out and get things, Eden.' Hades smiled a little. 'You know that.'

For a while, they sawed the body apart in silence, Hades stopping now and then to sip from a blood-covered mug. Eden stood to the side so that the spray of fluids from the backward motion of the saw didn't stain her trousers. As she was laying the leg in the duffel bag, she paused.

'Hades, there's another leg in here.'

'What?'

'You heard me.'

'I just put a leg in there.'

'Yeah,' Eden said, holding up the leg she'd cut by the calf. 'So there's two in the bag and one in my hand.'

Hades put his saw down and limped over. He looked into the bag, looked at the leg in Eden's hand.

'Well then.'

'Yes. Well then.'

'That's a tricky sort of business,' Hades sniffed.

'Someone's mixed up the distribution. Looks like a woman's. Calf is shaved.'

'That's two grand right there, that extra leg.' Hades pointed to the bag with a stubby finger. 'The price I gave was for one body. One. Not a body and a . . . a tenth.'

'You better call him up then.'

'Oh, I will,' Hades blustered, muttered to himself as he set the saw to the corpse's throat, took a handful of hair and began to swing the blade. 'The cheek of these young people. The absolute cheek.'

'Could have been an honest mistake.'

'These young pricks.'

'Hades, I want to talk about my parents.'

The old man stopped sawing. Leaned on the head on the table, his forearm mashing the face into the bruised wood. The saw made wet patterns against his trouser leg as he hung it there.

'I'm almost certain I've told you everything I know, girl.'

'No one ever knew?' Eden shifted the leg in her hands, looked down at the toes against her forearm. The toenails were sharp. Yellow. 'Even Maggie? You never told her where we came from?'

'All I told Maggie was that if anyone ever came asking, her daughter had dropped two brats off on me, just before she necked herself. Eden, a girl, and Eric, a boy. Daughter had only been dead a week at that time, so Maggie welcomed the money. It was a simple lie. Two grandchildren she never saw, given back to their deadbeat dad. Didn't know nothing about them, didn't know where they were.'

'What if someone approached Maggie?' Eden said. 'What if someone asked to see pictures of the children?'

'Maybe there never were none. Jesus. I don't know. It's been, what . . . twenty years? More?'

'There was a Western Australian kid that went missing. Bainbridge. Ten years ago, almost exactly. You seen the news?'

'Redheaded kid. I saw it. Didn't know the name.'

'The Stronghearts Foundation has been running with it. The anniversary. They've been getting the government behind all these old cases.'

'So?'

'So people don't forget, Hades. Not ten years later, not twenty years later. They're still writing books about Mr Cruel. That's twenty-six years ago, the first one.'

'And?'

'And I looked at our case. Eric's and mine. They're bumping the reward money up by a hundred thousand dollars. The Stronghearts Foundation has recommended the government increase the reward money on a bunch of old cases to get them all solved. Us, the Evans girl, the Beaumont children. The redheaded kid, Bainbridge. There's a big push right now.'

'The reward money has always been big, Eden.'

'Maybe it'll be big enough now for someone to act on a hunch. Maybe someone's decided to just . . . go for it. I don't know.'

'Eden.'

'Maggie. You gave her our birth certificates, didn't you?' Eden chewed her nails. 'Some . . . school records?'

'I made it real, Eden. I've done it before.' Hades adjusted the grip on his saw, prepared to begin. 'You're not the first human beings I reinvented. If you'll stop biting your hands off and think for a moment, you'll remember that reinventing people is a bit of a talent of mine. I've never failed.'

'What if you failed this time?'

'Eden.'

'What if someone found out we weren't real? What if someone connected us to the Tanners?'

Hades put down his saw. He walked forward and took the leg from Eden's hand, dropped it into the bag.

'My fucking birthmark was in the paper.'

Hades cocked his head.

'This.' Eden touched her side. 'It was in all the news reports at the time we went missing. My only unique distinguishing feature. Twenty years ago it was all over the news. And now hundreds of thousands of people must have seen it on the front page of the fucking *Herald* when Frank carried me out of that farm.'

'You look at the case files for your parents' murders, Eden, and it'll say bikies,' Hades said. 'It's stamped unsolved, but there's a good four or five leads that all end with bikies. Some pieces of shit skinheads in the Dugart gang or someone or other found out about your father's research money and blasted the two of them, came up empty-handed. Botch job. Sold you or buried you or something. No one asks these questions, Eden, not anymore. No one's going to come after you because of a birthmark. The lead officer on your case is dead. He'd be the only person on earth who would remember something as tiny as that.'

'I think you're wrong. I think someone is looking for us.'

'You're being paranoid.' The old man tucked a strip of her dark hair behind her ear, remembered how hard it was for her to accept the touch of another human being and stopped. 'There have been times, over the years, that you've –'

'Someone visited Maggie. Asked her about her grandkids. Someone approached my massage therapist looking for a photo of my body.'

'What?'

'Yeah. This is serious,' Eden said.

Hades' jaw twitched, just once. A tiny tic in the muscle beside his ear.

'I feel it,' Eden said. 'Someone knows.'

The old man paused, looked at his work on the table, one of thousands of ended lives he had hidden over the years. Since he retired, his life had been all about hiding things, burying things, making things clean. Tying up loose ends and folding down corners, making murder not only clean and neat but easy, economical. Out in the grounds of his tip only the souls of those buried there remained, the leachate acid built up between the layers of landfill dissolving rapists, murderers, standover men, con victims and gamblers who'd pushed the grace of their bookies too far. Sometimes Hades heard screams in the night, but there was no telling if they were from those lost and frightened out there in the dark, or if they were echoes of his own past, memories tucked around corners and thrust into shadows, people who'd deserved his wrath, people who hadn't. He reached out and took his daughter's hand, squeezed the fingers, stained them with blood, and it was as he had done the night she came to him, a tiny child newly orphaned, a problem he had to fix. He had stained her. He had made her the monster she was.

'If it surfaces, we'll bury it,' Hades said. 'That's what we do.'

'I think something terrible happened at my house,' Ruben said. Donato sat beside him in the back row of the small, bare classroom, texting his new Australian girlfriend, a tall, leggy blonde who'd come to the hostel to complain about the music. Ruben could see the edges of picture messages on his friend's phone and tried not to lean too far sideways in his chair in case his snooping was revealed. He sighed when he couldn't see more than elbows and knees. He looked at the posters on the classroom walls instead. *G'day, mate!* cried a cartoon kangaroo. Ruben hadn't heard anyone say 'G'day' since he arrived in Australia, nor had he seen a single kangaroo. But then he spent most of his time at the house, being followed from room to room by the creaks and whispers of the ancient building.

'Something terrible like what?' Donato whispered in Italian.

Ruben told him about the watch by the bed, the inconsistent amounts of dust on the books there. He told him about the pill packet on the living-room floor, the footsteps in the attic bedroom that was always locked, the television that played the same phrases over and over.

Reach out and take what you've always wanted.

You deserve it. You deserve it. You deserve it.

Donato brushed him off.

'Why don't you just go up there? Why don't you just knock and say hello?'

'You'd understand if you were there. The house is a nightmare.'

'Come work with me then.' Donato finally put down his phone. 'I can get you a job at The Argyle. It's pumping there, brother. The chicks, oh. The chicks.' He smiled at the ceiling.

'What time did you finish up last night?'

'Three.' Donato shrugged.

'That's why I don't come and work with you.' Ruben tapped his friend's chest.

'Are you guys listening back there?' the teacher called.

'Yes,' the boys answered in English. Ruben spread a stack of old newspaper clippings before him.

'What are these?' Donato asked.

'The translation assignment, idiot. You had to bring something in.'

'Oh, shit!'

'Yeah, I brought extra for you. You'd forget your own mother.'

'What are these? They're so old.'

'They're not that old. They've just been lying in the sun. I found them at the house, in one of the bedrooms. You're going to help me figure out what they say.'

'You're like Scooby-Doo,' Donato sniggered. 'Solving mysteries. Getting to the bottom of things.'

'Shut up and translate.' Ruben shoved a dictionary into Donato's hands. 'I don't want to hear any more of your shit.'

'Are you guys working back there?'

'Yes,' they answered.

There's a feeling very much like defeat that overtakes me whenever I open a flat pack from Ikea. I would have been very good as a Neanderthal – rolling rocks together and covering them with lumps of wood. Setting things on fire and breaking things down from their natural height into smaller chunks. But when it comes to tiny screws and pieces of plastic and stickers and things that you pop out of perforated sheets, I'm incapable. There's no other word for it.

I stared at the instructions for my new kitchen for a while and then decided I'd figure everything out when I got all the pieces out of their boxes and onto the floor. Bad idea. I sat in the middle of my mess and opened fake beer and went to the instructions again. The cartoon handyman with his oversized allen key was grinning at his construction like a fool. It was midnight. I couldn't sleep. Whenever I closed my eyes I started running and there was a darkness behind me, bodiless, trying to catch up.

Sweaty nights usually accompany the beginnings of a big case. Particularly when the media get hold of it. The watchfulness, the expectation of a country, sometimes the world, flutters at the back of your mind, lingering behind everything – the look on the guy across the train carriage, the tone in the waitress' words. Desperation. Solve this. Solve this fast. If the murders keep happening or the rapist isn't caught or a body lies unidentified beyond a reasonable time, you're almost committing the crimes yourself. Why didn't you stop him? Why didn't you save her? Why don't you do something? What are you? How can you sleep at night?

You never sleep at night. Right from the beginning.

The front door opened and closed just as I finished needlessly categorising all the different screws and nails and things by size. Eden walked in and chucked her keys onto the floor beside the door, looked at the catastrophe around me.

'Can't sleep either?'

'What are you – ?' she said. She blinked at some marble countertops leaning against the wall. 'Never mind. Get out of the way.'

I took my beer and shuffled to the side of the room, grabbed a chair and put it in the corner. She sat sighing and reading the instructions as if what I'd done had been a personal insult to her. When she'd perused the diagrams for a minute or so she set them aside and started grabbing pieces from around her, fitting and locking things together with satisfying clicks. Things that looked like they fit together, things that so obviously fit together that it was beyond reason why I hadn't fitted them together myself. I didn't thank her. She wouldn't have responded if I had. She started fixing things to the wall with a wood-handled screwdriver my father had owned, her hair hanging in her face. In minutes, it seemed, a frame was assembling, the bottoms of drawers and cupboards were being slotted into place. She was such a capable person. I was jealous of her. I had been, a lot of our time together. It's not hard to feel like a loser around Eden.

Eventually she took a break and sat with her legs crossed sipping a fake beer, looking through diagrams of drawers.

'It's 2 am. We've got to brief Captain James in four hours,' she said after a time.

'You want to lead with similar crime analysis?'

'No. The tranquilliser,' she said, setting the pamphlet aside. 'It's our best lead so far. Let's face it. We've got shit all otherwise.'

Images retrieved from CCTV around Centennial Park on the evening of Ivana Lyon's murder were fairly useless, which greatly surprised us. There were cameras around the gates of the park, but few inside the 189 hectares of parkland itself. The park's cameras were designed to capture thieves or vandals targeting the café or equine centre, so were not directed towards joggers on the tracks. Crime in the park was rare. A serial rapist targeted a woman walking there at night in 1989 and was nabbed for it in a DNA sweep in 2005. In 2010 a woman was abducted and taken to Queens Park, a smaller park off the side of Centennial, and sexually assaulted. There were the odd cases of bashings and robberies in and around the park, but not enough to erect a twenty thousand dollar surveillance system, put together a command centre or hire security guards. The park was unpopular at night and too populated during the day for any real drama.

Our killer hadn't brought the van into the park itself, so we couldn't get a number plate. There were three clips of Ivana running laps, her hands flat and open and her lips pursed as she passed the gates. No sign of anyone watching or following her. No one was keeping pace with her – she was being lapped and lapping others at irregular intervals, so for long stretches she would have been on her own. On the third lap, we caught a glimpse of a shadow moving along the tree line in the bottom left-hand corner of the image, but there was no telling if it was in any way related to Ivana. We didn't capture any footage of her being shot, stumbling, perhaps being helped through the bush towards a gap in the fence, to a car waiting, while she fought for consciousness.

Plenty of people had seen others getting into vans around the time Ivana was taken. After-work traffic already clogged Anzac Parade, Oxford Street and Alison Road. The athletics field and Queens Park were flooded with corporate soccer and running teams as kids were being picked up from Little Athletics groups – there were cars whizzing in and out of the same spots, horns blasting as people squeezed into tiny gaps or waited for young ones dashing across the grass. Apologetic waves and sheepish grins in the fading orange sunlight. Dogs barking from open car windows. The killer had used the cover of crowds and noise to snatch Ivana Lyon away from the pack like a crocodile at the edge of a thundering herd of buffalo crossing a river. Nobody saw anything. A thousand people all in their own little worlds. This was how kids like Jamie Bulger got walked right out of a crowded shopping centre without anyone batting an eyelid. Crowd blindness.

It looked like Minerva Hall had been snatched at around the same time of day as Ivana. By all accounts, she'd done a couple of laps of the Botanic Gardens and Mrs Mac's Chair and then disappeared. She didn't look like Ivana – but we couldn't rely on that to differentiate the cases, because after both women's faces were beaten in they were both just female runners to the perp. Minerva's phone turned up on the rocks beside the running path where it led to the headland, washed down a crack between the oyster-laden stones. She had carpet print on her shoulders, just like Ivana, and her heels and the backs of her calves showed bloodless drag marks, suggesting her body had been moved post-mortem.

There were plenty of homeless people in the Domain at night. Far more than in Centennial. It was closer to the CBD, more opportunities for cashed-up lawyers walking home to toss some change on the grass. Even as I realised this, I was already dismissing it as a possible source of leads. Homeless people wouldn't speak to us.

Eden and I sat with our empty beer bottles, looking at the floor of my half-finished kitchen.

'The Domain footage might be better,' I said.

'Hmm,' Eden said.

'So where does a person get a tranquilliser gun? You tell me.'

'It's not the gun we're concerned about,' she said. 'You could get that anywhere.'

'I doubt you'd get one just anywhere.'

'Well, you might get one as a black market import. Go to a big game company. I mean, we might spend the next three weeks going through stolen gun reports. Any farm from here to Kalgoorlie's got the right to have one. We don't want to end up doing background checks on every big game worker from Taronga Zoo to Alice Springs. If it was me, I'd make the thing myself. Cheaper and easier to do it that way.'

'And how exactly would you set about doing that?'

'Well, I don't know exactly. I haven't really thought it through. But it doesn't sound hard. It's probably just some sort of gas compression job. You could take apart a .50 cal. paint-ball gun and –'

'Never mind,' I waved. I forgot, more frequently than was probably safe, what Eden surely did in her spare time. What she had been responsible for. It was easy to think of her as harmless when she was sitting on my kitchen floor braiding her hair. A news report I'd seen that morning on the TV in Imogen's kitchen returned to me, made my chest prickle with anxiety. It was about the same incident I'd heard reported on the radio the day Ivana was found. Four dead in mystery slaying south of Byron Bay. Police likely hunting 'expert assassin'.

'So the gun's probably a dead end.'

'The drugs aren't, though. There are only three families of drugs that would suit an uptake like that – through the muscle tissue, into the bloodstream,' Eden said. 'Sedatives, anesthetics and paralytics. Each family's got its own characteristics. Some are faster than others, last longer, work on different parts of the body. If toxicology can tell us what type of drug we're looking for, that'd be great. But I suspect it'll be difficult. The elevated heart rate of the victims, the tiny amount that would have been delivered. We might need footage to understand how the thing worked on the victim. How long the take-down took.'

'The take-down, huh?' I licked my bottom lip. 'Is that what you guys would call it? You and Eric?'

I hadn't meant the question to sound nasty, particularly as she had just about finished putting my kitchen together. I was genuinely interested. I was fairly certain that Eric and Eden had killed six men. Around the time my girlfriend was murdered, I witnessed the two stalking a man, Benjamin Annous, who subsequently disappeared. I was able to connect five other missing men with Annous. Eric coming after me had been admission enough that I'd overstepped my bounds in digging around in their night-time activities. He'd tried to kill me and Eden had stopped him.

While this was all I had, I suspected Eden and Eric had killed more people than the ones I'd discovered. I didn't know if they limited themselves to thieves and dangerous scumbags, as these men seemed to be. But if the utter lack of leads in their cases – to a body, to a suspect, to anything – was any indication of their skill level, it was possible the two had been killing for most of their lives.

Had she and her brother developed a language for what they did? Had they talked about it at all? Did they have rituals, a routine, a trophy collection, like most serial killers? It was a purely academic interest. I'd detached the deed from Eden herself, as I always did, in order to function beside her. But the way the question registered across her face, I could see that the effect of my words had been malignant. She smirked a little and went back to her work, turning the screwdriver around and around in her skilled fingers as she fitted rails to the side of a drawer. Whatever it was between us, the unspoken under-standing that we would leave her killer nature undisturbed, seemed to be thinning. The knowledge was like a black dog that followed us everywhere. Somehow I knew it wasn't going to stay quiet forever. Eventually it would insist on us acknow-ledging it, dealing with it. It would lick at my hands and nudge at my legs and feet until my remarks and questions became more frequent, until I couldn't be Eden's partner anymore, until I couldn't hunt killers in the company of a killer and find sanity in that.

Had Eden killed those four people up in Byron Bay on the weekend? Had she made a day trip of it – bought a pie at a roadside 7-Eleven and sipped iced coffee as she drove, her gun on the seat beside her? What was making me think this way? Eden was a killer and she knew about guns. That's all I was confident about. Maybe I was being paranoid.

When I asked myself if I really wanted to know if Eden was still killing, I found the answer was no.

Tara thought about killing for the first time when she was sixteen. She was standing on the sports field at the edge of the cricket match, the sun blazing on her classmates' uniforms, making them sting in her vision. Mr Willoughby was yelling instructions from the side of the field, but Tara couldn't hear them. To her right, a group of girls had given up covering their section of the field and sat in a group stringing pieces of grass, some lying with their heads in the laps of others having their hair braided.

Tara watched their easy physical intimacy and wondered about them, the popular girls, why they felt the need to constantly touch, what message that was supposed to convey. Because everything that came from them had a message. Nothing was said explicitly. Looks pierced her, words jabbed at her, turned backs left her cast out. The popular girls were always hugging and holding hands. They announced their morning greeting hugs with gleeful cheers, outstretched fingers. They shamelessly caressed and groomed each other, rubbed lipstick smears from the corners of gaping mouths. Now and then they would fall on a boy, all of them at once brushing his hair and massaging his shoulders, gripping the impossibly hard muscle through the fabric. Peter Anderson was always among them, whenever the teacher's back was turned, guiding their hands towards the hardness of his thighs, laughing when they squealed. Girls he had known since primary school, who he watched blossom slowly. Tara felt hot, seeing them there.

No one ever touched Tara. In the second grade the girls and boys in her class had developed a terror of her 'germs'. If any of them touched Tara, they would have 'Tara germs'. Anyone who touched the infected child would also have them. Tara was infectious. The game made the boys and girls squeal and run and slap at each other with their dirty, infected hands. Touching Tara meant social rejection, so when it came to grabbing a partner, getting in a group, forming a circle, Tara always found herself isolated in metres of space. The game had ended finally, worn off, over the summer holidays. But the symbolic infectiousness seemed to linger, even now that all of them were older, no one came near her.

They seemed to touch each other all the more when they knew she was near.

She watched the ball bounce heavily nearby, walked after it as the class howled, and it was then the thought came to her.

Kill all of them.

The words in her head shocked her. They were almost spoken. She was almost tempted to look around, to see if they'd been whispered from a body outside her own. But she was alone, of course. Always alone. She squinted in the sun and heard the voice again as the bell rang and the popular girls sprang to their feet.

Kill all of them, she thought. *Make them touch each other, if that's what they want. Make the boys force their fingers into the girls until they scream. Make the girls strangle each other. Make them beg. Make them grip at each other. Make them writhe together like worms, naked, flushed with blood.*

By the pile of equipment, Mr Willoughby was teaching a group of boys about the seam on the ball while Steven Korin wanked a cricket stump, holding it against his crotch, jerking the softly sanded wood. His eyes rolled up in his head. The boy directed the stump at Mr Willoughby's back, then turned on Tara as she got close and jabbed the dirt-clotted tip of the stump into her thigh.

'Oh Nuggy, baby,' the boy groaned. 'Gimme some of dat sweaty lurve!'

The boys turned and howled with laughter. Tara jammed her hands into the wet patches beneath her arms, started to run. They called after her, loud enough so that she could hear them as she ducked into the girls' bathrooms. The second bell rang for the younger kids and a crowd swelled under the awning, tiny Year Sevens with their immaculate hats and bags and huge folders bursting with books. Tara watched them pass beyond the door. She thought about their little necks in her fingers, their knobbly little knees struggling and bumping on the ground as she took them.

One day every week, Imogen took time away from her commitments at the clinic to work on her superhero life. Her pursuit of Eden Archer. Or Morgan Tanner, as Imogen was now sure was her real name. The anniversary of little Genny Bainbridge's disappearance was a month away and Imogen knew increases to the reward money for missing children nationwide would be generous, especially for a double tragedy like the Tanner children. She was confident she would have enough on Eden to scoop up the reward money almost immediately after it was announced. With the bump to the reward for any information on the disappearance of Morgan and Marcus Tanner rumoured at a hundred thousand dollars, she had to make sure she kept her investigations quiet. There would be other armchair detectives and cybersleuths out there with search engine traps who would happily hack her once they realised she was picking around the case. She'd run into some hardcore players in her time on the job, professionals who travelled the globe picking up reward money for missing kids, rich dead husbands and wives. Some were so established they handed out business cards at candlelight vigils and hounded victims' families on their doorsteps, shoulder to shoulder with the press. Imogen couldn't dream of that sort of commitment, not yet. Her clinic kept her low-level obsession with police officers under control, kept her interested in her side games with the missing children. Imogen needed multiple forms of entertainment. She'd always been a restless girl.

In her mind there was a future growing and developing slowly of her and Frank as a partnership, using his police skills and her investigative drive to make a real living out of being armchair detectives, or 'web sleuths', as the young people called them. She twirled the bracelet he had given her, a guilt token he'd come home with after the scene at Malabar. He could be bossed around. That was the first tick on Imogen's list. He had access to things she usually had to beg her way into – criminal records, driving records, family medical records, cop-shop talk and lawyer buzz. If Imogen could bring down Eden Archer, right in front of Frank, it would show him how clever she was, how blind he'd been to the possibilities of using his skills outside his dismal job with its dismal salary. It would show him that if he followed, she could take him places. She could train him up, show him the ropes, give him a taste of investigative work beyond the badge. Open his eyes to his true potential. What she was doing was sometimes rougher, sometimes harder, than being a boy in blue – but she would show him he was capable, let him be her sidekick. The hunky meathead hero rescued from the force and put to real work – it would make a great story for her girlfriends. Imogen's uni buddies had all married psychologists. She liked being the wildcard among them.

Imogen ordered a latte from the young waitress and spread her things out over the table. She pushed her glasses up her nose and prepared to make a summary of what she had on Eden. From the moment she spotted the birthmark on Eden's side in the newspaper coverage of Rye Farm, Imogen's information had grown substantially. Sunlight filtered through the trees lining Macleay Street, making patterns across her papers. The barista, a Brazilian girl, juggled the orders of the men and women around her, designers and architects and the bored housewives of Potts Point beginning their day with newspapers and little biscotti on organic pottery saucers. Imogen always came here, to Marcelle's. It was close enough to the Strip that she often saw junkies walking past the huge double doors, hearing them before they appeared, their cat-calling and grumbling as they shuffled quickly between hits. A troupe of detectives from the Kings Cross police station across the road frequented the café, so she got to eavesdrop on their conversations as she worked, live their adventures on the drug beat vicariously. The staff at Marcelle's let her work without hassling her for the table after an hour and only two coffees. Imogen was settled and ready to make some real progress. She felt warm and happy with purpose.

Her first assumption was that Eden Archer was an adult Morgan Tanner. This raised a few markers for confirmation. The birthmarks seemed the same – she'd tried for a photograph of the mark on Eden's side but hadn't managed one yet. Eden was the right age, according to her service record. She looked very much like the child in the missing posters – the same sharp features, Daddy's black hair and iceberg blue eyes. If Eden Archer was Morgan Tanner that meant there was a good chance that her deceased brother, Eric Archer, had been Marcus, the other Tanner child. He was the right age. Three very good coincidences, if that's what they were – the brother, the ages, the birthmark.

The first thing Imogen had done was investigate Eden's supposed parents. The mother, Sue Harold, had been a junkie and a dropout – a wild woman who surfed through life quickly and carelessly and who, it was reasonable to believe, departed this earth with only a box of odds and ends left at her mother Maggie's house ever suggesting she'd lived at all, her children long passed over to her ex-boyfriend and her bank accounts empty. Oddly, however, when Imogen visited Maggie Harold, asked politely to see the box of worldly possessions that Sue had bequested to her, she found not a single sentimental trace of the woman's supposed two children in it. Not a photograph. Not a card, a drawing, a teddy, not a child's blankie or a pair of old knitted booties, the kind of keepsake every mother, no matter how irresponsible, kept. There was a report card from Eric's first year at school and two copies of birth certificates. These were folded neatly and sitting in a single envelope, together, pristine, as though they'd barely been glanced at on receipt and then tucked away forever.

Imogen inferred two things from this. One, that Sue Harold did not own any mementos of Eden and Eric's early life because she had not, in fact, been there to experience it. Two, the records Maggie had were pristine and contained in the same envelope because they'd never been removed from said envelope, because they were fakes. There was no proving either of these things beyond reasonable doubt, however. Imogen had thanked the old woman, sweetly enjoyed a cup of tea beneath the stained-glass windows of her little house in Scone, fondling the plastic tablecloth, avoiding eye contact. Why didn't Maggie have any mementos of her grandchildren? she asked. Any photographs? Any children's books she'd read to them before Sue handed them off to their father? They'd not been close, the old woman said. Her daughter had always been unstable. Flighty. All over the country chasing men. The ancient woman's eyes wandered the walls, evasive, a little nervous. Imogen thanked her and left.

Imogen spread out the photographs she had of Eden Archer – one leaving her huge boutique apartment and studio in Balmain, one of the beautiful detective getting her nails done at a local salon, one of her standing outside the Parramatta headquarters smoking a cigarette. Eden hadn't been a smoker when Imogen began tailing her – had something rattled her? Did she feel herself being watched? Eden had slipped away over the weekend, out from under Imogen's watchful eye. Did something happen? Did she know, in fact, who she was – was she willing to protect her secret, if that's what it was?

As the story went, Sue Harold had dumped Eden and Eric off on their biological father, Heinrich 'Hades' Archer, when the girl was seven and the boy was nine – the exact ages that Morgan and Marcus Tanner were when they were abducted. The two grew up in the care of the decidedly older parent at the Utulla tip, surrounded by mountains of the city's discarded household waste – and, it was rumoured, the city's discarded souls. Eden's father was an interesting character. An underworld figure seemingly retired when the two children arrived, living the quiet life in his garbage wonderland. If he had been the one responsible for organising the Tanner murders, why on earth did he keep the children?

Imogen unfolded all the news reports she had on the Tanner case and spread them over the top of the photographs of Eden, a layer of black and grey sadness. The joyous faces of the Tanner parents on their wedding day, his hand on the belly of her pristine satin dress, lips by her ear. A whisper, a laugh. Had Marcus, or Eric, been in there, already conceived? A cheeky secret, the doctor and the artist knocking boots before the formalities, before the families approved of the union. The faces of the children in close-cropped pictures beneath the heavy headlines: BROKEN GLASS, SHATTERED LIVES – INSIDE THE TANNER FAMILY MURDERS.

Theories swirled through the papers, of Dr Tanner's academic rivals worldwide, his incredibly flush research funds, Mrs Tanner's questionable friends during her youth. Some were sure the two children had been snatched up to be sold into international sex rings – they'd appeared with their father in a photograph in *Scientist Weekly*, looking like beautiful, vulnerable porcelain dolls. Had someone fallen in love with the two of them there on the cover beside Daddy? Morgan's shy, downturned eyes, Marcus' devilish grin at the camera.

There had been four to six men involved in the incident at the Long Jetty house, when the children's parents had been slain and the children disappeared off the face of the earth. Bikies, the police insinuated, had been the ones who did it – smash-and-grab kidnappings were decidedly their style. But how did this connect to Hades Archer? The old man had never been involved with bikies. And using hired muscle to do his dirty work wasn't him either. He'd always been a sort of gentleman overlord, a fixer of problems and mediator of disputes, too high up, too detached, to hire people to go after the petty cash of a civilian couple staying with their kidlets at their overly extravagant, barely used holiday house. The whole thing made no sense.

WHERE ARE THE CHILDREN? the headlines roared.

Bikies were the scapegoats, Imogen decided. An international sex ring was a long shot. But so was Imogen's growing sense that the two had been adopted by Hades Archer, raised as his own to be police officers, unaware – or perhaps tight-lipped – about the lives they had lived before. The Tanner family fortune had remained untouched. If it was an unsuccessful murderous kidnapping, why would Eden and Eric remain quiet about it? Is that why Eric had been killed? Had he been on the cusp of revealing everything?

Senseless. Senseless. Imogen stared at her untouched coffee, at the foam top adhering to the edge of her cup in caramel clouds. The whole thing was senseless – but she had faith that the right clue would fit all the pieces together. Imogen had always loved puzzles. She never let one defeat her.

No matter how little you have to present in a crime report to the captain, you always present it passionately. That's the rule. If all you've got going from a twenty-person train carriage massacre is a toothpick maybe or maybe not chewed by the guy sitting next to the alleged killer, you present that toothpick like it contains the secrets not only to the crime you're trying to solve but possibly the missing link in evolution, the world food shortage and next week's Lotto numbers. If you come up bare and you're not too confident about alleviating that bareness anytime soon, you're asking to be removed from the case, hurled headfirst into the drug squad or something equally thankless, and usurped by someone younger, someone with a bit more hunger for that mystical cup of justice. It's all politics and public relations. You've got to look mean and keen or they're going to throw the bone to another dog.

Eden seemed to forget this. She sat beside me in Captain James' office staring at the floor while I squirmed around trying to talk about stuff I knew nothing about – barbiturates and gas-powered guns and running apps.

We had four seconds of footage of the Domain victim, Minerva Hall. She was stumbling and falling, righting herself just as she left the frame. There was no indication of whether she'd simply tripped or if this was the moment she'd been hit with the dart. We had a witness saying she might have seen a white van at the Ashfield crime scene, and that possibly there was some yelling or screaming coming from inside the van, but she wasn't entirely sure it hadn't been a blue van playing music. She'd only ventured into the area in the first place because it was a nice secluded spot to shoot up heroin.

I nipped at Eden for assistance during the briefing but she didn't react. Just sat there thinking. I grabbed her in the corridor outside the captain's office when he finally – reluctantly – let us get on with it. Sometimes physically touching Eden is the only way to get her to acknowledge you. She goes into these reveries which you couldn't get her out of with less than the blow of a mallet.

'What the hell is wrong with you?'

'Nothing,' she shrugged. 'I'm tired. Jesus. Lay off.'

'No, you're not right.' I held on when she tried to wrestle her bicep free of my grip. 'You haven't been right since you got out of the hospital. You're limping around without your crutches and you're staring at walls. Is there something we need to talk about?'

'No.'

'Are you hooked on something?'

'No.'

'You know I got hooked on Endone. It was easy. Ridiculously easy.'

'I know. I was there.' She peeled my fingers off her. 'I don't need you mothering me.' She began walking. I followed her, keeping close, to shut our words out of the ears of the beat cops who were all around us. Beat cops love rumours. They feed off them, like parasites.

'I reckon I remember saying the very same thing to you when I got hooked and you tried to mother me.'

'I wasn't mothering you, Frank. I was trying to get you in touch with reality. It still hasn't worked.'

'This isn't a reflection on you. On your . . . I don't know. The whole ice queen thing you carry on with.'

'Frank, if you don't –'

'Eden –'

'If you don't drop this I'm going to hurt you.' She whirled around and shoved a finger in my face, her back teeth locked. 'I'm going to punch you, hard, right in your fucking head. I'm not hooked on anything. I'm not hiding anything and I don't need your help. Back. Off. Frank.'

I let her walk on a couple of steps ahead of me. Felt better. The flashing in her eyes had definitely been the old Eden. The deadly Eden I knew. Well, sort of knew. Was familiar with. I was pleased to know she was still in there, inside the strange storm-cloudy exterior she had adopted. She went to her desk and started pushing things around assertively. I slowly, carefully, perched on the edge of the desk, out of the range of her swing.

'Let's run with the tranquilliser thing then,' I said.

'I'm waiting to hear back from my source.'

'You've got a tranquilliser source?' I scoffed. Eden ignored me, did some things on her computer.

I looked up and saw Hooky walking towards us with a manila folder in her hands. She dragged a chair up from an adjacent desk and sat right beside Eden, a funny little lizard sidling up next to a lion. Her outfit was right in line with the strange rock-punk Japanese goth thing she'd been doing since I met her – leather pants I'd never have let my seventeen-year-old walk out the door in, a floppy waist-length shimmering green shirt covered in beads and spangles and little pieces of mirror. A bone through one ear and a cross on a chain. Black fingerless gloves. Her nail polish was chipped where she'd chewed. She'd been a chewer since the early days after her parents were slaughtered. She used to sit by my desk while I worked on the case and chew my pens into fragments. Little slivers of blue and white.

Eden barely gave her a glance.

'Want some pictures?' Hooky said.

'How did you get in here?' Eden asked, typing something, frowning at her screen.

'I've got connections.'

'Eden, this is Amy Hoo–'

'I know who the girl is.' Eden gave me a warning glance.

'What pictures?' I asked, trying to defuse something I was sure was about to erupt. Women and their little seismic trembles and twitches. I didn't know what might go wrong here, but I didn't need Eden and Imogen both going after Amy, especially if she was going to be this helpful. Hooky opened the folder and finally drew Eden's attention. They were screenshots from Hooky's personal computer. I recognised the minimised windows at the bottom of the screen. Chat rooms for under-sixteens. 'Tweener Talk' and 'LolChat13+'. I hadn't known the department was letting Hooky fish for predators on her personal computer. That seemed a bit much. Was she going out on her own? Was she freelancing? I opened my mouth to ask, but she cut me off.

'I crowdsourced photos from around Centennial Park the evening Ivana Lyon was grabbed,' Hooky said, spreading pages over the desk. 'There were a total of forty-seven pictures uploaded to various social media sites in the hour before she was taken. Mostly selfies. But some shots of kids on the field at Queens Park.'

Eden took the picture nearest to her. I leaned over to see it. It was a selfie of two South American girls in matching white running shirts with WeWill! printed on the chest.

'WeWill! is a cancer research foundation. They raise money and awareness training people to be competitive runners,' Hooky said. 'They were having a training run there that evening. Lots of photos for the promo page.'

'How did you get all these?' I asked.

'I did a geographical and time-based search of image files in the deep web.'

I stared.

'The deep web,' Eden said to me. 'The web behind the web. It's like the backstage of a theatre production. Where the code that drives the surface internet lives.'

I had nothing.

'Never mind.' Hooky grabbed the page from me. 'Look here. See?'

There was a white van parked behind a bush near the girls in the picture. The edges of the image were dark. I could see a slim figure dressed in black, blurred as it moved towards the front of the van. I picked up another image from the pile. Runners in the matching white shirts coming down the footpath beneath the trees. A shape crouching in the brush near them, still murky and pixilated, barely more than a smudge.

'This is the best one,' Hooky said. She showed me a photograph, another selfie, taken by a couple sitting on a park bench. The photo had been edited, lots of little love hearts spattered around their heads, the image tone cast in sepia. But behind them, passing between the trees, there was a figure walking. A black tracksuit. A hood pulled up over a bent head. The figure was right beside a 'Do not feed the wildlife' sign. If we could find the sign, the techs could use the photograph to calculate a bunch of things about the suspect. Height, stride distance, even gender maybe. They did some groundbreaking stuff with those types of calculations in pinning Bradley John Murdoch to the murder of Peter Falconio in the outback, using only a single streak of CCTV footage of Murdoch walking from his truck into a petrol station. It was tricky business, but in a single move Hooky had doubled what we had on the killer.

'Good work, Hookleberry Hound.' I grabbed her by the neck, rattled her skull. 'Oh, she's ruthless. Nothing slips by her.'

Hooky clawed me off and shoved me hard. I wrestled with her a little. I know very well that Hooky hates being treated like a seventeen-year-old but sometimes I can't help myself. She's exactly as I'd have liked my own daughter to be. Feisty. Smart. I'd almost had a daughter once. If you play with Hooky long enough she gives in and wrestles you back, puts an elbow into your stomach and a foot in your hip. There's still a kid in there. I take a sort of pride in being able to get it out.

'Stop fucking around, the both of you.' Eden gathered up the photographs and gave them back to Hooky, who was breathless, her clothes askew. 'Get these to the tech department. See if you can get an original of the couple on the park bench. Frank and I'll be out all day today, but you've got his number, haven't you?'

'I have.' Hooky tucked the folder under her arm and left us, knocking my arm with hers as she went.

'Where are we going?' I asked Eden, gathering up my stuff. I patted my backside and found my phone was missing. I wondered if I'd left it in the coffee room.

'To see a friend,' she said. 'I just got a text. He can see us.'

'A friend? You've got a friend?'

She didn't answer, turned on me and left. Something twisted strangely in my stomach, some animalistic alert that made the hairs on the back of my neck stand up. Eden had never mentioned having a girlfriend, a boyfriend, an acquaintance, a confidante. Anything. I might rightfully have assumed once that her brother and her father and I were the only human beings she'd ever consensually interacted with. I jogged back to the coffee room to get my phone and felt oddly light-headed, and the sensation carried on as I followed Eden out through the huge double doors in the foyer.

It was a shock to run into Caroline Eckhart on the steps. She was dressed in immaculate running gear. I wondered if she owned anything else. Eden passed her without so much as an upward glance.

'Mr Bennett,' Caroline said. I offered my hand instinctively and she crushed it in hers so hard I was sure she meant to hurt me, to tell me something about my manhood. 'I was hoping we could have a chat. I'm Caroline Eckhart.'

'It's Detective Inspector Bennett,' I said, watching journalists jogging up the stairs behind her. 'And I can't imagine what we have to chat about.'

'You men and your titles, huh?' she quipped before the cameras arrived. I licked my teeth, made a sort of clicking sound. It was as close to a 'fuck you' as I thought I had time for.

'I was at the Minerva Hall crime scene yesterday in the Domain.'

'I know.'

'I want to assist your investigation in any way I can.' Caroline glanced at the cameras as they surrounded her, flipped her ponytail through her fingers and did a little head shake to assert herself. Shoulders back, chest out, chin up, ladies. 'I believe the Sydney Park Strangler is targeting women interested in fitness. Women with agency. I've got a broad influence with these women. I like to think of myself as their spokeswoman. Their voice. I want to make sure they have a say in the hunt for –'

'Ms Eckhart.' I struggled for words, looked around for Eden but could find only the black eyes of cameras burning down on me, exposing my masculinity, my selfish, brutish repressive male spirit. 'You're a fitness professional. I don't know why you see yourself as having the . . . the need, or the right, or even the training, to interfere in an active police investigation.'

Caroline drew a breath, her turn to speak again finally at hand. I saw the bones in her chest flex beneath the muscle.

'Women have been scorned for interfering where they are not wanted for centuries, *Mr* Bennett, and only the strongest of them have ignored the command.'

'Uh-huh.' I started walking down the steps. The journalists around me gasped at the action. Cameras clicked. I frowned at them all, couldn't comprehend the drama and intrigue that they obviously saw in the incredibly annoying Caroline Eckhart being incredibly annoying to someone. I was sure it happened all the time. She was still carrying on when I stepped onto the street.

'This guy, whoever he is, is targeting –'

'That's where we stop.' I put a finger up. The cameras whizzed and flashed. 'You're perpetuating unfounded rumours about the crime in the media. I don't know why. I wouldn't have thought women's fitness and murder had anything to do with each other. But when you want publicity, I guess you'll jump on any wagon.'

Caroline herself gasped now.

'What you're doing is irresponsible. It's basically fear-mongering. There's nothing at this stage to suggest that a man is responsible for these murders, or that the cases themselves are even related. This man, and his targeting, are your invention, Ms Eckhart. Not mine.' I turned the finger on her. The journalists around me shuffled, forcing their tiny microphones at my chest. 'Now look, honey, I've got to go.'

'Honey?' Caroline snapped.

I walked away from her, heard her fire her defence at her press cronies.

The radio was filled with speculation about the park murders. Eden hardly listened, nor did she pay much more attention than the necessary nods and noises to Frank's complaining about the fitness woman. She thought dimly about the girl, Hooky, who'd texted Frank to tell him that she had found a better image of the lovers on the park bench and sent the file on to be analysed by the forensics department. A strange creature, that one. There was something faintly predatory about her, like a newborn crocodile, all cute except for the teeth. Losing her parents had changed Eden, darkened something inside her. Perhaps it had done the same to this young woman. What was she now, this gifted little liar? A threat? Or just a curious natural-born police officer following her instincts? Plenty of officers Eden knew had joined the crime war because of loss, violence. The mother beaten to death by the cheating stepfather. The brother killed by a king hit in the Cross. The favourite school teacher stabbed after a mugging gone wrong. Tragedy changed lots of people. Inspired them to be cops, nurses, firemen, lawyers.

Frank fell asleep beside her as she wound the car slowly out of the city and into the Western suburbs, clapboard houses sailing unnoticed past his eyes, his arms folded and tucked into his grey woollen jumper. Given a spare minute anywhere, anytime, Frank would sleep. He slept in the locker rooms, in the tea room, in the car while she grabbed coffee at a service station. It wasn't even an exhausted sleeping – he wasn't a sleepy person. It was almost like his body went on standby when he couldn't do anything or think anything about the case for a minute or more, like a computer left unattended. The fingers of the right hand, now and then, softly twitched with an angry nerve damaged when her brother had shot him.

Eden still thought about what might have happened if she'd let Eric kill Frank, if it were him beside her now riding the M4 between wooded mountain ranges. When would Eric have stopped? When he was still alive, sometimes she wondered if their night-time killing games together hadn't been his only nocturnal activity, if killing the innocent as well as the murderers, rapists, gangsters and pedophiles they selected for their toys hadn't quietened his addiction. Was he responsible for other deaths? Had she turned a blind eye to the very same evil that they hunted together, brought onto the undeserving by her very own brother? Had killing Eric been the right thing?

Did Frank deserve to be here beside her, softly sleeping, any more than Eric did? Her night-time games had been halved since she lost her hunting partner. If she'd let him live, she would have made the world much safer, predator after predator after predator, than she was able to now. How many more could she have caught with Eric assisting her and Frank dead? How many lives could they have saved? Who was dead now, who was running free, so that Frank could live?

She shook these thoughts out of her head as they entered the Vulcan State Forest. The eucalypts towered here, reaching blackened fingertips towards the sky, burned mouths gaping, shoulder to shoulder, jealously crowding the view of their shadowed depths. Something large and reptilian streaked into the undergrowth as she rolled through the unmanned boom gates and onto the dirt road. From here, it was an upward climb through the mountains towards Bood's house.

Morris Alexander Bood had been one of Eden's first solitary hunts, when Eric was away for two months on a murder case up north. The itch had become unbearable after six weeks, and with her brother uncertain about when he'd get back, she gathered up all the information she had on the freelance assassin, caught a plane to Hobart and went after him.

She was twenty-three, violent and lustful for blood, much less controlled in her pursuits than she was now. She'd hunted down police surveillance photographs of Bood and shuffled them in her fingers on the plane, thought about his body, about the fight he'd probably put up when he discovered she planned to kill him. At 195 centimetres tall, broad and thick-limbed like a draft horse on its hind legs, he made an unlikely assassin. Most dial-a-death guys she'd encountered were small wiry types, the kind who could flit up stairwells and peek over roofs with their scopes aimed at politicians or husbands or jurymen targets, the kind who could disappear among crowds, sail through airport checkpoints unnoticed. Bood was distinctive for his sheer size alone. Cramming into passenger seats and holding cups of tea in his huge fingers, ducking under signs in airports and blocking out windows as he tracked his targets, he would draw eyes. Eden had heard whispers in the criminal community that, despite his bulk, Bood was very good. Efficient, and so cold, so callous, he was said to be the man to hire no matter the morality of the situation. He took out wives for insurance money. He knocked off grandparents for inheritances. Morris Bood was a killer without a compass, they said. He took or passed up jobs as randomly as the results of a coin toss. Sometimes he backed out of jobs for no apparent reason. Sometimes he turned and killed his client. He was unpredictable, accurate and left little evidence behind that would suggest to police that he was anything but a myth among the bottom-dwellers of the world.

Eden looked forward to killing him.

Unlike most assassins she'd known, Bood didn't stick around to fight when she cornered him in his car on the outskirts of wet, sleepy Orford one night in June. She waited in the back seat for him, felt the whole vehicle rock as he swung his legs into the cavity beneath the wheel. She slipped the wire over his head and yanked it tight, put her lips right beside his ear, blessedly warm and soft, just as she'd imagined.

'Don't move,' she said.

'Forget that,' he answered, reaching up and grabbing the wire with one hand, tugging it right out of her fingers as though it were dental floss. He turned, quick as a snake, and shoved her hard in the chest, the blow turning from a balled-fist punch to a flat-palm push at the very last second, the second he recognised her silhouette against the orange lights as that of a woman. Eden was just recovering from the surprise of the blow when Bood took off across the car park, running upright, confident, like a competition sprinter. He was at the tree line before Eden could scramble out of the car. She ran for the trees.

This is wrong, she thought as she entered the dark forest. *You're on his game board now.*

She barrelled headlong into his territory, telling herself all the while to turn back, remembering the crime-scene photographs of men and women on the bush floor, heads blown off, arms and legs splayed in the moist undergrowth. He liked to catch and release them, let them get ahead of him, relax, walk through the valleys like deer, crying and calling out. The night air was painful in Eden's lungs as she ran. She wove and ducked between the eucalypts, tiny slices of moonlight through the canopy her only guide, the only thing stopping her from slamming headfirst into a tree. She stopped, whirled, ran again at the faintest movement, a shimmer of black ahead, the grind of a leather boot. A line of white dotted against the undergrowth slowly emerged, widened, a frozen lake lit by the moon, a kilometre wide. She saw the big man run out onto the ice and followed in a direct line behind him, sure that if the ice could take his monstrous weight it could also take hers. Then she felt the ice give and heard a gut-deep yelp escape her lips. A pop noise, like a gunshot, the squeaks of dry ice rubbing. She put a foot into slush, then another into water, and she plunged. Eden screamed as the pain rushed around her, into her ears and mouth and eyes – not water but raw red hurt.

She rose up, scrambled and grabbed at the slush and chunks, her fingers and hands and now wrists numb. Eden heard her own cries and gasps and coughs as though through cotton-stuffed ears. The edge. She found it, climbed up it, felt it crack and tip and slide beneath her. She found another edge and gripped at it with her fingernails. Her coat dragging her down into the darkness. Her boots kicking at nothing.

In the chaos, she saw him out there on the ice, watching her. Between her sinking, drowning, hauling herself up and sliding back, he approached her, slowly crouched just out of reach. He was watching her die. Crouching there and watching the end of her, as she'd planned to watch his death, coldly and emotionlessly. She wouldn't beg him. Eden kicked and grabbed the surface, dug in, watched the ice curl and powder as her nails scratched lines back towards the sucking depths.

Nine or ten times she hauled herself up and slid back. Each time, it took longer. Bood watched. The moon glowed above.

Eden kicked, one last time, groped at the ice, and felt his hand on her wrists. He was lying on his belly on the surface of the lake. He pulled her and she gripped his coat, let him drag her onto the surface, drag her to the edge and dump her in the wet grass. Sounds came out of her she could not control, gasps and howls of agony. Everything was limp, useless, pulsing with her thundering heartbeat. She lay on her stomach like a doll while he pulled her coat off her arms, replaced it with his own, lifted and rolled her so that the wool brushed her numb face and her eyes took in the black sky.

'What a fighter,' she heard him laugh, somewhere above her in the haze of impending unconsciousness.

She lay there on the edge of the lake for what seemed like hours listening to the sound of ambulance officers coming down the embankment, torches sweeping. Bood was long gone. She hadn't seen him again for years.

And then one night, coming to the end of a glass of merlot at a bar in Wynyard, another arrived before she could catch the waiter's attention. Sent from the man sitting at the bar with his back to her. The blond giant turned his face just slightly and she saw his cheek lift with a devious smile.

Now here she was in the driveway of his Vulcan home. She

parked the car beside the spotless Hilux under the second-floor verandah. Frank snuffled and stretched awake, took in his surroundings with a yawn. A strong wind gusted up the hill and shook the trees at the edge of the clearing, rattled glass panels in the verandah doors above. Eden sent a text informing Bood of their arrival. There was no telling where on the property he might be.

'So this guy's our tranquilliser expert,' Frank said, popping his door and sliding out. He looked at the tree line, shielded his eyes against the bright overcast sky. 'Man's got a hell of a view.'

Eden led her partner up the stairs to the great sweeping porch, the huge redwood doors inlaid with glass. The big house was open, as she expected. Frank stood in the entrance and gaped at the massive black buffalo head hanging above the wall table across from the door. He reached out and seemed to want to touch the nose of a glassy-eyed fox mounted on a slab of polished oak next to the buffalo's right shoulder. The room was done up log-cabin style, with woolly tapestries hanging between the mounted heads of deer, bison, big cats and a variety of small, handsome forest creatures.

'Did you say you knew this guy, or . . .' Frank spied the billiard table in the sitting room off to the left of the foyer. The bar.

'I've known him for some years, yes.'

'And you've never once considered that I might like to know this guy? That we might in fact make excellent best friends?' Frank wandered to the sitting room door, noted the gigantic flat-screen television above the fireplace, the sprawling cashmere couches. 'He's got a bar.'

'You're a recovering alcoholic.'

'A bar!'

'He's not your kind of guy, Frank.'

'Oh Eden, really,' Bood said from across the dining room to their right. His boots clunked on the polished floorboards. 'I'm everyone's kind of guy.'

She'd forgotten Bood's almost supernatural sense of hearing. He could hear a sugar glider taking flight from five hundred metres. The huge man fitted his oversized surroundings, traversing the twelve-seater dining-room table in a couple of strides, thrusting his callused palm in Frank's direction. For once, Frank seemed happy to be the less impressive specimen of masculinity in the room. He shook Bood's hand enthusiastically.

'Morris. Or Bood, as my friends have it.'

'Frank. Great, great place, mate.'

'Well, thank you.' The big hunter smiled, folded his sheep's leg arms over his chest. 'When you've been a bachelor as long as I have, you can afford to dress your castle as a real man should. I'd love to take you on a tour.'

'We don't have time for tours,' Eden said. 'We're here on business.'

'Ever the pragmatist. My dear, dear Detective Archer.' Bood put an arm out and Eden leaned into it, her arms still crossed, and let him kiss her cheek. He swept her into an unexpected squeeze and Frank laughed as she wriggled free. 'I insist, though. Frank here seems like a guy who really appreciates a homeowner's efforts. Come on.'

Eden broke away, having seen it all before. The hot tub. The study with its chart tables and battered maps on the walls, the cabinets full of shimmering butterflies, thorned grass-dwellers, beetles of impossible colours and patterns.

The wine cellar, and the door down there, chipped and blue she recalled, salvaged from some crumbling church somewhere or some ancient library burned to ruins. She'd seen what lay beyond the door, where Bood kept his real trophies, the trophies he certainly would not be including in Frank's tour. Eden went into the kitchen, took a beer from the double-door stainless steel fridge and leaned against the kitchen bench sipping it. She looked at the mountains through the glass wall to the verandah. A change was coming through. Rain. She could see its slanted grey fingers on the distant white horizon.

Frank's voice could be heard all over the house. Bood's booming laughter. When Frank returned, his eyes were wide.

'Did you see the moose?'

'I've seen the moose, yes,' Eden replied.

'There's a bear in the living room.'

'And a chair as well?' she sighed.

'Now now, my love,' Bood laughed, touched her shoulder. 'We'll get to the business end of things in just a moment. You've had a long journey. Can I get you a beer, Frank? A snack?'

Frank balked. Masculinity in peril.

'One of us has got to be zero. Cop thing. No beer for you, shithead.' She jabbed Frank in the ribs. He gave her a relieved look. 'He'll take the snacks though.'

Frank followed her into the huge eastern room, stopped only to take in its high ceilings, the windows above the shelves crammed with books slowly darkening with the coming rain.

'What does this guy even do that he can live like this? What is it? Old money?'

'Probably something like that.' Eden flipped her laptop open on a coffee table set between two red, oily leather wingback chairs. 'Don't get distracted. We're here to get information and then we're leaving.'

Frank was looking through a brass telescope at nothing, fiddling with the dials. He touched a huge open notebook and Eden watched him slowly realise the instrument had likely been microscopically tuned to follow particular comets and stars. Her partner went stiff all over, shuffled guiltily to the seat beside her.

'You've been warned about touching things you're not supposed to.'

'Look at the guns, Eden.' He pointed to a rack of twelve ornate rifles wedged between two pillars of books. 'There are guns all over the goddamn house. There's a cabinet of semi-automatics near the laundry chute. We don't have this many guns in our armoury at HQ.'

'Mmm.'

Bood entered with a plate of nibbles and set them beside the laptop. He pulled one of the wingback chairs into the semicircle made by Eden and Frank's chairs. Frank set upon the crackers and cheese like he hadn't eaten in days, collecting crumbs on his knees and the floor around his feet.

'So, Frank, you'll have caught on by now, I'm sure, that Bood here's an enthusiastic big game hunter,' Eden began. She drew up her email account and extracted images of Ivana Lyon and Minerva Hall's puncture wounds that the pathologist had sent through. She set these beside each other on the screen. She turned to the big man. 'I hoped maybe you could tell us something about the tranquilliser used in capturing these two victims. I've got a toxicity report from the coroner, but we're not even close to being able to identify the brand of chemical used from the distribution alone.'

Eden sat back and let Bood take charge of the laptop. His brow was heavy, dusted with strawberry blond eyebrows that met over a long, wide nose. There was grey creeping into the sides of his short beard and spotted through the fur at the back of his neck. Eden turned away, and as she did caught Frank examining the big man with the same idle curiosity. He was a fascinating man to look at, not only in his scale, but in the objects and images that surrounded him and how they played about his features and movements. Bood lived among decorated corpses, big cats, deer, silky buffalo, large animals, small animals, predators and prey alike. Comparing his own shape and movements with the animals that surrounded him was unavoidable. His hands came together and he rested his chin upon them, careful to think through his response before he gave it.

'Well, it's a smaller dart,' Bood began. 'I can tell from the wounds. Darts of around 1.5cc won't break the skin when they're extracted. Most tranquilliser darts have a rubber stopper on the needle so the animal can't pull or knock the dart out when it falls. It goes in, and the rubber stopper stops it coming back out before all the chemical can be released into the animal's system. This dart didn't have a stopper. So it was a small quick-acting dart rather than a large slow-release dart.'

Frank took a notepad from his pocket and began writing.

'Whoever's using the darts must have some idea what they're doing,' Eden said. 'Or they would have gone over the top. Shot for an overdose, rather than have their victim limp away on an underdose. Am I right?'

'Right,' Bood said. 'It's a tricky thing to calculate. You've got to understand the nature of the animal itself. How its blood flows. Its epidermis. You can't hit a crocodile and a human with the same dart. Some darts will penetrate tough skin, like reptile skin. Some darts will penetrate softer skin. Some darts are good for animals with fur, feathers – some are better for hairless creatures. Something delicate was needed for human skin, and a delicate dart was used here. If you're going to do this, you've also got to consider dosage. How fast does the heart beat? Was the animal resting or running? Was it frightened or calm? The rate of uptake will be affected by how quickly the chemical is absorbed into the bloodstream. You don't want to hit a resting tiger with a slow-uptake tranquilliser or the thing will come around and have you for dinner.'

'It sounds as though if you're wanting the thing to survive, you've almost got to have the level of knowledge of an anesthetist,' Frank said.

'Even if you don't want the animal to survive, using the right tranquilliser is fairly standard practice.' Bood leaned back in his chair. 'Despite what you might think, most professional hunters aren't very big on animals suffering unnecessarily. Or on wasting expensive chemicals with overkill.'

'Can you speculate about a weapon?'

'Probably something gun-fired. If your victim was on the move, a jab stick or a blow pipe would have been out of the question. Particularly for a beginner. With the gun, you've got the scope and with some models the possibility of a quick re-fire. Have you got the toxicology report?'

Eden handed over a wad of papers she'd wrestled from the depths of her laptop bag. Bood sat back and read them quietly.

In time he stood up and went over to one of the pillars of books beside the fireplace. He pulled the shelf towards him to reveal a small neat cabinet of handguns. Frank and Eden followed. Frank nestled in beside the bigger man, looked at the lit shelves of tiny colourful syringes, the bottles and the screw-on feather stabilisers attached to each individual dart.

With both men blocking the cabinet, Eden looked at her hands. She had time to think about that night in Tasmania, the moment she rose from the water for what was certainly the last time and saw Bood's hand reaching, the cold resolution on his face. For a long time afterwards she thought about why he'd saved her, and decided, in the end, it was because there was no sport in watching her die that way. Most psychopaths Eden had known were forever considering how best to maximise their own entertainment, their own pleasure. Bood had watched her until he failed to be entertained, and then drew her out from her predicament, seduced by the idea of a future playmate perhaps. Maybe even a lover. The big man had to know now that Frank admired him. The thoughtful hand to his chin and theatrical snap of his fingers as decisions were made were all part of the show. He turned and in his hands he had a number of tiny capped syringes. Frank watched him select a gun from the upper shelves, a narrow long-nosed pistol with a wooden handle.

'So,' Bood said, 'I know what it isn't. It isn't anything else I've got here, and I've got a fair sample of the Australian market in this cabinet. There's a chance, a good chance, that the dart you're looking for is one of these.'

The trio returned to the chairs by the laptop, Frank and Bood beside each other this time. Bood laid the syringes out neatly, twelve in all. They were all various shades of pink or yellow.

'These are all paralysers,' Bood said. 'They're low calibre and they're low dose. From the levels in the report and the wounds in the photos, I think we're getting close to the mark here.'

'Great,' Frank said, picking up the syringe closest to him and examining it in the light of the windows. 'Can we get any closer?'

'You said you had footage of the strike?'

'Maybe,' Eden said, going back to her email. 'We've got this.'

She opened the file from the Domain security team and selected the video of Minerva Hall stumbling, almost falling, righting herself, and running on across the scope of the camera focused on a path that led to the back of the Art Gallery. Bood reached over and ran the video again, then twice more, intent on the screen. Eden brushed his fingers as she took back the laptop keyboard. She accessed the settings to slow the video down. Bood watched the woman on the screen running, seeming to trip, stumbling, pushing herself off the wet asphalt with her right hand, her fingertips, settling back into her run. At the very edge of the frame, Eden saw the same hand that had righted the runner reach down towards the back of her right thigh. Then she was gone.

'We don't even know if this is the moment.'

'Oh, it's the moment,' Bood said. He sat quietly for a few seconds considering the syringes before him. Then he selected one of the fainter pink vials, uncapped it, and stuck it into the side of Frank's neck.

'Morris.' Eden grabbed at the big man as he and Frank rose together, but it was too late. Frank stumbled backwards, grabbed at the dart in his neck, his eyes moving frantically from Bood to Eden.

'Shit!' Frank pulled out the dart. Looked at the thing in his fingers. He swayed. 'Shiiiit.'

Then he fell.

'You fucking arsehole, Morris,' Eden snarled. She pushed Bood out of the way and pulled back the coffee table. Frank had flopped onto a Persian rug in front of the fireplace, his top button popped and ankles crossed from twisting sideways to try to catch the shelves to stop his fall. Eden put her hands on his chest. As she did his left leg gave four sharp twitches, rocking his whole body. Then he was still. Her partner's eyes were locked on the ceiling.

'He's fine,' Bood said. He stood over Frank, his hands in the pockets of his trousers. 'It'll be two, three minutes maximum.'

'That was completely inappropriate.'

'Did you want answers, or guesses?'

'Tell me, then, for Christ's sake.'

'You saw those three or four little jolts of the leg there?'

'Yes.'

'That's what you call a tell,' Bood said. 'It's like a signature. It makes the brand distinct. There are complex chemical reasons why some drugs have signatures, but I couldn't begin to tell you what they are. Some brands of morphine make people nauseated. Some influenza medicines make people drowsy. Maduline makes your legs twitch.'

'Maduline?'

'I'm almost certain,' Bood said. He lowered himself back into the chair, pushed the cursor of the video back to its original place. 'Her heartbeat is elevated because she's running. So absorption, and therefore side effects, are much faster. You see here? Her right leg. Twitch twitch. She doesn't reach down to feel what hit her – so the dart probably has an anesthetic tip. She reaches more towards the knee, the top of the thigh, because her leg suddenly twitches against her will. It's Maduline. I'm sure of it.'

Eden watched the video. Watched Minerva Hall's right leg give two tiny kicks as she shifted to her left, pushed off, righted herself. Like she was shaking water from her shoe. Trying to kick off fingers suddenly gripping at her heel. Frank gave a groan beside her. She uncrossed his legs for him.

'Maduline is a fast-acting, fast-absorbing tranquilliser,' Bood said. 'It is burned out and gone in mere minutes. Animal handlers use it when they want to subdue an animal instantly, but not have that animal lying around anesthetised for hours afterwards. The occasions for use of this drug are fairly small, so you'll only find a couple of stockists in Australia. You might use Maduline if you had a deer tangled in a wire fence, for example. You subdue the animal, free it and it moves on. If you were to use something else, the animal might suffer. Might become prey. It's also good for health checks for migrating stock.'

Frank rolled onto his side and clawed his way into a sitting position. There was drool on his lip. He wiped it off and shook his head.

'Christ. Fuck me.'

'You'll feel absolutely fine in a minute, my friend.' Bood grinned at Frank, who could return only a tired stare. 'What you've had is almost like an oversized jellyfish sting. You'll be up and moving before I finish this beer.'

'I think I'd have liked a bit of warning,' Frank slurred, licked his lips. 'Shit. Jesus. Jee-sus. That was terrifying.'

Eden watched her partner righting himself uncertainly, gripping the back of the chair nearest to him, unsure about his new friend and his propensity to unexpectedly hit people with paralysing drugs. He gripped his way around the chair and sat down, rubbing the sides of his skull.

'It was like my whole body dropped from underneath me.'

'My sincerest apologies.' Bood reached over and patted Frank's hand a couple of times, the way a man might reassure his elderly father. 'But given the choice, I thought it more gentlemanly to let you take the hit than to impose such an experience on our dear Eden here.'

'Those girls,' Frank said. He covered his eyes. Eden and Bood waited in silence. Frank ran his fingers through his short shaggy hair. 'The killer wanted to stun them. Wanted them mobile in a few moments so they could . . . so they could experience it.'

'It sounds like you're after a very nasty kind of hunter,' Bood said. He glanced at Eden.

'A real prick,' Frank laughed gently.

Eden felt grateful for a moment for Frank's ever-trusting spirit. Frank was like that. Forgiving. Easily led into the darkness, into pacts he never knew were forming around him until it was too late, until he had bad choices to make and only the least worst to choose. It was why, she knew, Imogen would use him. Because he bore the kind of basic good-heartedness that begged to be used. He would have done well to be raised in the country, Eden thought, where people were like him. Trusting and uncomplicated. But he'd migrated from the Western suburbs to the city and taken with him the tragic ill-fit of an honest heart in an evil world. The two men were talking again, the homicide detective and the killer. Frank explaining the horrifying yet thrilling sensation of being tranquillised like it was a skydiving adventure he'd signed up and paid for. A once-in-a-lifetime plunge. Almost proud that he'd survived it.

They enjoyed a light lunch, then Bood shepherded them to the car, holding an umbrella for Eden as the rain began to fall. Frank shook the hunter's hand. Again Bood opened his arm and Eden reluctantly let herself be enveloped, submitted to his hairy kiss on her cheek. She thought Frank had slipped into the passenger seat, but as Bood spoke, she turned and saw the words register on her partner's face.

'So, shall I expect a visit in another fortnight?'

Eden patted the big man coldly on the shoulder and got into the car, felt her stomach slowly falling as an uncomfortable silence permeated the vehicle. She backed the car around and began driving, glancing once at Frank's face as he sat frowning at the dashboard.

'You visited Bood two weeks ago,' he said.

'I did.'

Frank nodded gently. She knew what had suddenly darkened him. His fingers pressed against the dart wound in his neck, which was slowly becoming a tiny blue bruise. She could almost see the news headlines of the last few days flickering across her partner's eyes, hidden midway through papers dominated by the park stalker killings.

FOUR DEAD IN MYSTERY SLAYING SOUTH OF BYRON.

POLICE LIKELY HUNTING 'EXPERT ASSASSIN'.

'We need to talk about this one day,' Frank said suddenly. 'About you. About your people, your friends. About all of it,

Eden. Sometime we're going to have to do something about us. About what I know.'

She opened her mouth to give him one of her usual nasty responses, the short and sharp denials that pushed his dark curiosity back into its corner, back and away from the present as it always did. But she said nothing this time.

She was beginning to wonder if something might have to be done about Frank.

Unlike her classmates, Tara did not count the days until the Year Twelve formal. Now and then she noticed signs and markings hanging about the school, like the cave paintings of a colourful and violent tribe, explosions of stars and hearts on the chalkboards sighed at and swiped away when teachers arrived. Twenty-eight days. Twenty-six days. Twenty-one. The day was coming, but the numbers meant nothing to her.

Every night was the same for Tara. Joanie came for her at sunset. Tara was hunted.

Tara thought of it very much as a hunting. A long, excruciating pursuit, a surrender, a devouring. She would run, her hips and knees immediately springing into pain, and her mother would shuffle behind her, prodding three fingers into the tender flesh beneath her right shoulder blade like a lion's claw swiping at a zebra. When the prodding stopped, the yelling began. Joanie was never out of breath. She sometimes ran sideways, like a strange, lanky crab, her joggers scraping on the wet asphalt. *Come on. Come on. Come on, Tara. Come on.*

Sometimes it was begging. Sometimes it was snarling. But the come on, come on, never stopped. When Tara stopped, as she always did, and submitted to walking, the come ons rose in pitch. *You fucking failure. You selfish failure of a girl. You're not stopping, Tara. Get moving. Get moving. Come on.*

Rocks in Tara's chest, sharp and heavy, just beneath the lowest of her ribs. The pathetic sounds that came out of her. People stared as they passed, or refused to look at all. Tara stopped and crawled and vomited in the grass, once pissed herself, dissolved into panicked, breathless tears. Nothing worked. The humiliation of one session bled into the next, until the nights flowed together in one long, sunless sentence in hell. She would crawl into her bed at night and unwrap treats she had snuck home from the school canteen, hold the wrappers beside her ear as she pulled them open, listened to the tweak of the plastic. Sucking like an infant on a chocolate breast, her teeth coated. She would gorge until she felt sick and couldn't breathe, hyperventilated into half-consciousness, fell asleep, the voice of her mother still pounding in her head like a song she couldn't dismiss, a chanting between her ears.

Those photos, Tara. Embarrass me in those photos and I'll fucking kill you.

Why didn't Tara think of her mother? Think of those final-year photographs framed and sitting on the mantelpieces of governors and their wives, sitting in the yearbook in the family library of the Prices and the Bucklands and the Lancasters. Jesus Christ, the Lancasters. They'd put it in the paper. St Ellis High Class of 2003 and their charming killer whale mascot Tara. *Save the Whales, Harpoon a Harper!* She brought a dress home for Tara, slimming black silk, sparkling, heavy with jewels. It reminded Tara of the bats that squabbled and squeaked above them in the park as they hobbled along. The dress was a twelve. Tara lifted the long skirt, watched it drip from her white fingers like ink sliding through water.

You'll fit into this or you'll go naked. I will drop you there myself, in front of everyone. You stupid thing.

Tara sat in the chair in the hairdresser on the windy, rainy afternoon of the formal and looked at the thing that she was as the old Greek woman crimped and curled her hair above the black silken smock jutting beneath her double chin, velcro pulled tight at the top of her curved spine. It was the first time her mother had called her a 'thing'. Before that, for a long time, there had been human tones to the words. *Idiot. Bitch.* But Tara was more struck with 'thing', with what it did to the way she saw her own face. If Tara was a 'thing' she was not like the others. Never had been, never had the potential of being. She watched the old hairdresser circling her, brutally stripping foils from pins holding rolls of curls, dumping them in a canister. Knowing that whatever was done, Tara wouldn't look good. Wouldn't look human. Like a frustrated painter, dabbing and stabbing at lifeless eyes. Tara would never be alive. She had been born a thing.

But 'things' had purpose. Every thing. She reached out beneath the smock and pulled a brush from the shelf beside her, turned it in her fingers. Things were created to serve. To perform.

What kind of thing was she? Her natural desire seemed to be to destroy, to consume, to stifle. Was she born a killing thing?

It was kind of a relief, realising herself as an object. She felt almost free. Free of the guilt of all her little ill-fitting parts, all the missed inferences, all the invitations refused and withheld and all the sideways glances. She felt free of the hatred of the other boys and girls. They were only doing what was natural to them. Recognising the imposter in their midst. The cuckoo in the nest. Tara had never been a girl. She'd never been a student, a friend, a teammate.

At the hall, she stood in the corner at the back as the teachers gave their speeches and awards were handed out. She listened, her slippered feet just beyond the reach of the gold downlights, as Rachael Jennings gave an acoustic rendition of Green Day's 'Good Riddance (Time of Your Life)' and a group of boys that included Peter Anderson howled a joyful 'Graduation (Friends Forever)' by Vitamin C. The boys had all come in suit jackets and bow ties over colourful board shorts and thongs, a strange defiant mismatch that caused the teachers some concern as the first drinks began and the first glass was shattered on the floorboards. Awkward dancing, and an interlude for a PowerPoint montage, showing the same five or six popular boys and girls between group shots of the goths and the nerds and the ugly girls, popular girls in primary school, high school, at the cinema, mouths full of partly digested popcorn, boys sneaking arms along backs. Tara did not appear in the montage. She thought she saw herself once in the background of one of the goth shots, sitting at the top of the stairs by the C Block science labs, but it could easily have been anyone else. Shadows fell over her figure. But she didn't mind the omission. Didn't know how to mind anymore.

As she stood by the toilet doors, Mrs Foy came and spoke to her in the colourful light. Tara liked Mrs Foy and the devoted biology teacher liked her. Biology was the only class Tara thrived in, the only time she was allowed to work alone no matter the task – the class was split on day one into five 'research teams', each a pair, with one left over, Tara. If a member of a research team was ever absent, Tara was not forced to make up the pair, because their workbooks would not match. Entering the sticky, sterile biology classroom was one of the only times in every day that Tara felt invisible. Safe from those unexpected and devastating words: 'Alright everyone, form a group.'

She sat at the back of the classroom in her little bubble of security and read. She dissected frogs and mice, toyed with their rubbery blue and red organs with her scalpel. Sometimes she ignored the class if it was too basic and simply read the textbook.

Mrs Foy told her at the formal that she'd be a great scientist, if she just 'got out of herself'. With her extraordinary precision and skill in the study of animals, she could make a very accomplished vet. She just needed confidence. Didn't she know that? Tara stared at the floor, not answering, until the woman gave up on her.

She left the formal at eleven, when it was revealed someone had brought a couple of cases of Cruisers to the back of the hall and teens were sneaking out there to smoke and pash and drink while others distracted the teachers on the dance floor. She watched the group from the basketball courts, watched Mr Tolson berating them for their irresponsibility while Mrs Emmonds looked on.

Tara was headed to the car park to seek out her driver when she ran into Louise Macken and Sam Cruitt pashing against a car.

'Oh, Nuggy.' Louise broke away from Sam stiffly, brushed down her hair. 'Hey, sorry. We didn't see you there.'

'Sorry,' Tara said, backing up to find another way between the cars.

'Hey, wait.'

'Louise!' Sam whined.

'No wait, Tara.' Louise, nimble and spritely and pretty Louise, prefect Louise who always did the right thing but never dobbed on anyone for being bad. All the boys loved Louise. She had the seductive naivety of all virgins written plainly on her face. Inexperience and freshness, bits of skin unbroken, never tested. Unviolated lips. 'Sam, I'll meet you back at the door.'

Sam trundled off towards the group behind the hall. Tara kept walking. She found herself in the familiar situation of animal being pursued, tried to keep her breathing regular as she headed towards the limo. Greg the driver in the distance, reading a newspaper in the yellow light of the car. She liked Greg. He never spoke.

'Nuggy,' Louise said. 'I wanted to tell you how pretty you look tonight.'

Both their dresses were blue. Louise's mother had made hers, made some for the popular girls too. Sketched designs cooed over in art class. Tara gathered up her skirts, a dress she'd been forced to hire in secret, the black silk gown her mother had bought her hanging in plastic in her cupboard. Louise's eyes were wide with determination to say the thing that would absolve her for the years she'd known Tara. For all the silent passages in the school hallways, eyes averted, pleas ignored. For all the stifled giggles and all the sleepover whispers and all the team exercises uncomfortably endured. For that time, in Year Two, when everyone decided that touching Tara meant that you had her germs, and someone had passed them on to Louise and she'd looked at Tara and grimaced.

It was a lot of responsibility. But Louise liked responsibility. She'd always been the one to take charge, and she'd say something to absolve everyone. Absolve the team.

'Nuggy, you look really –'

Tara was surprised at how small Louise's neck was in her fingers. She could encircle the whole thing with two hands despite the stubbiness and shortness of her fingers, the thumbs overlapping over the ribbed windpipe slippery with glittery foundation. Tara squeezed, squeezed, squeezed, in long hard pulses, each bringing Louise a little closer to the ground, until the two struggled, twisted, Louise falling back into Tara's embrace as her arm wound around the girl's neck. Tara put her hand into the complicated mess of curls and pins and sparkles at the back of Louise's head and pushed down, pulled up with her arm, felt bones grind in the girl's neck as the chokehold tightened. This was what it was like to wring the life out of a bird. Tara had always wondered about it. Kind of hoped, one day, to find herself in the position of being responsible for the mercy killing of a bird. How pretty and swift and alive they were. Tara felt Louise's feet kicking. Didn't even notice as Greg the driver stepped over them, began clawing at her bare arms, his shouts like a siren in the night.

Eden and I had our feet on the boardroom table when Captain James walked in, papers and CCTV images and reports spread around us, little evidence bags of cigarette butts and coins and hair elastics and other park debris making a mountain at the end of the table. We'd become so comfortable in the boardroom that when our boss arrived neither of us acknowledged him with anything more than a casual glance. Workplaces can be like that. Like home. I once took a piss in the upstairs station toilet with the door wide open, I was so comfortable there. A thoughtlessness infects everything. You begin to ignore other people and their belongings. The techs shuffling about. Our owl-faced colleagues in the Homicide Department flinching and shying away from Eden. The occasional collection of troubled-looking teenage boys doing a tour for high school work experience, peering in the glass panelling at the bull pit, dreaming of chasing trench-coated men down rain-soaked alleyways. I'd been put on the spot and asked to talk to a rabble of these youths once as they toured the break room. I declined. I didn't have anything promising to say to a lot like them. The bullies would find new opportunities to heave around their fragile masculinity on the job, and the bullied would find new ways to feel humiliated and degraded by criminals and their colleagues alike. It wouldn't be any different to high school. Bigger tank, same fish.

I acknowledged Captain James only when he nudged my chair.

'Morning, Cap.'

'Captain' wasn't Captain James' actual police rank, but more of a nickname, an endearing nod to the inspirational and fatherly sort of figure he represented to us. There's little you can do to make 'Chief Superintendent' sound friendly and loving, so we'd abandoned it altogether for Captain. Like most police traditions, it made little logical sense to outsiders.

'What do you know, Bennett?'

'Tranquillisers,' Eden answered for me, shifting the papers she was reading. 'We're after tranquillisers. A source confirmed a brand for me, so we're hunting down a sales list from a major distributor. Should be here within the hour.'

'I got tranquillised,' I boasted, looking gleefully at the captain. 'In the neck. I went down like a bag of shit. Bit my tongue. It was great.'

'We've also got clean CCTV shots of both the killer and the van on their way to news outlets,' Eden continued. 'We think the van's a Mitsubishi Express, 2008 or round about. We're going back now and looking for the van in the CCTV and some social media shots we've been given. I'm getting a team out on vans of that type in the area shortly.'

'We've got two bloody prints on the Lyon body,' I said. 'No matches. We're running them international.'

'And this, Bennett,' Captain James said. 'What do you know about this?'

He slapped a newspaper on top of the paperwork in front

of me. I stared, not recognising, for a few seconds, the side of my own head. My open mouth and pointing finger. I appeared to be chastising a very indignant-looking Caroline Eckhart on the steps of the Parramatta headquarters. I read the caption and my voice broke over the words.

'Get off my wagon, honey.'

'Get off my wagon, honey?' Captain James raised his eyebrows at me.

Eden reached over and snatched the paper from me, began to read. I snatched it back.

'This is not what I said.' My voice came out higher than I'd anticipated. Like a teenage girl denying she'd kissed another girl's boyfriend. I cleared my throat. 'Jesus Christ, these people will print anything.'

'Well, I don't know about anything. You must have said something about a wagon,' Captain James said.

'I said . . . I don't know. Shit. I said she'd jumped on the bandwagon.'

'What bandwagon?'

'Homicide Detective Francis Bennett joined lifestyle coach Caroline Eckhart in a heated row on the steps of Parramatta Police Headquarters yesterday morning,' Eden read. She'd taken the paper back again. 'Bennett, who is known for spearheading both the Jason Beck and Camden Runaway murder investigations, accused Eckhart of interfering in an official police investigation when the respected public health champion offered her assistance in the Sydney Parks Strangler murders.'

'Public health champion?' I scoffed.

'You didn't spearhead either of those investigations, before you get ahead of yourself,' Eden sniffed, ruffled the paper. 'You had your head in your own arse for at least 80 per cent of the Camden Runaways.'

'This doesn't look good for us, Frank.'

'I know that, Cap. I'm being set up here. This is not me. I didn't say it like that. I just brushed her off, the same way I would brush off any creep who tried to get their name in the true crime novel that'll come out of this. Caroline Eckhart is a fucking . . . she's standing on a soap box.'

'Caroline Eckhart released a statement saying she is troubled by the Sydney Metro Homicide Department's unwillingness to accept public assistance in the case,' Eden read. 'Eckhart, a renowned feminist spokesperson, called on the women of Sydney to unite in a –'

'Oh, for the love of god,' I wailed. 'A lifestyle coach, public health champion and feminist spokesperson? What else is she? A fucking brain surgeon?'

'Typical of you,' Eden said. 'Demanding that she only be one thing. Mother or career woman. Lifestyle coach or feminist. Passive or aggressive. That's a very 1950s attitude you've got there, Francis.'

'Don't start fucking with me, Eden. Just don't.'

'Did she offer you help?' Captain James asked.

'Her idea of help and mine are not the same.'

'Well look, Frank,' the old man sighed. 'We can't have the people of Sydney thinking we're chauvinists.'

'I am not a chauvinist. I have a girlfriend.'

'Chauvinists have girlfriends.' Eden flipped down a corner of the paper to frown at me. 'Why wouldn't they have girlfriends?'

'Eden, I'm not a chauvinist. Back me up.'

Eden flipped the corner of the newspaper up again.

'Frank, have Eden deal with any communication you get from this Eckhart woman or her office from now on.' Captain James pointed at me. When he pointed, you knew he was being serious. Disappointment was being threatened. The hurt, detached disappointment of the father who'd believed in you. 'Got it?'

'She doesn't have an office,' I sneered. 'She'll have a closet in a gym somewhere that reeks of rubber and ball sweat.'

'She probably just works from her kitchen,' Eden said. 'Where she belongs.'

I tried to answer, but Gina from reception was rushing past and stopped to swing in the doorway.

'Bennett, phone.'

She tossed me a cordless receiver, which I barely caught.

'Female Oppression Enterprises. Frank speaking.'

'It's Anthony.'

'Tone! What can we do you for?'

'I wondered if you'd like to come over and pick up your murderer,' he said. The smugness in his tone was dripping, even over the phone. 'We don't have the space for him here.'

I didn't realise that Eden's strange reputation for being terrifying for no obvious reason had reached all the way across the bridge to the North Sydney Metro Homicide Department, but from the look on Anthony's face as we entered, I realised it had. People had always been more scared of Eric than Eden, but since her brother's death, Eden still seemed able to command that wary, cornered-dog look from people, the quick scooting into empty offices away from her, the clearing of the tea room whenever she entered. No one but me knows what it is about Eden that's so frightening. Anthony shook my hand as we entered the bull pit. His palm was clammy.

'Frank.'

'Anthony, Eden Archer, my partner. Eden, Anthony Charters.'

'Hi,' Eden said. Shook hands. Anthony grunted in return, his eyes on my shoes, stuffed his hands in his pockets like a little kid reluctant to concede an apology.

'Those were some big words on the phone, young man.' I followed Tony as he turned across the loud, sunny bull pit towards Interrogation Row. 'You're pretty confident you've got my guy?'

'I'm confident it's him,' Tony said, rubbing his bald head. 'But I didn't get him. Come in here and meet the mother. She'll tell you what happened.'

'The mother?' Eden said.

Tony opened the door on a woman in the largest of the interrogation rooms, the ones we used for scumbags with multiple lawyers or child offenders with parents in tow. She was sitting at the steel table with her hands around a Styrofoam cup of coffee, a curvy woman with a golden tan, sun lines from smiles and ocean glare, a mother who'd spent decades chasing children in the outdoors. Long brown hair in a high ponytail fell shiny and light over one shoulder, combed back from a deep widow's peak. I knew the face: Ivana's mother.

Beside her, a stocky pitbullish thing, chocolate brown and black-snouted. A studded collar with a big name tag. Nitro. The dog sniffed as I entered, got up on its back legs and pawed at the air in my general direction as though inviting me to dance, revealing a smooth pink belly of tiny nubbed nipples. Dogs like me, for some reason. I've never owned one. On the table in front of Ivana's mother lay a shining Drummond five-iron golf club, slightly bent. Eden picked up the club and gripped either end, looked at me for explanation. I sat down.

'Charmaine here nabbed the killer.' Anthony smiled, puffed his chest out.

'I'm Charmaine Lyon.' The woman reached out and took my hand. Her skin was warm and soft. I squeezed it. 'Ivana's mum.'

'I know.' I licked my lips. 'Charmaine, I'm so sorry we haven't met. I'm Detective Inspector Frank Bennett and this is Detective Inspector Eden Archer. We were scheduled to meet you the morning Minerva Hall was found. You've met our secondary –'

'You don't have to apologise.' She held up a hand. 'I preferred that you guys were out there trying to find the killer rather than sitting around talking to the families.'

I breathed out. 'I'm very sorry for your loss.'

'So am I.'

'We all are,' Eden said stiffly. 'So let's add the mother, the dog and the golf club together and get this story moving, shall we?'

'It's a little bit Agatha Christie, isn't it?' Anthony laughed nervously, glanced at Eden. 'When you, uh, when you put it like that.'

'I found my daughter's killer,' Charmaine said, giving a loud high sniff. 'And I whacked him.'

'She knocked him out cold. Cracked his skull,' Tony said. 'What do you call that? A hole in one?'

'What are you?' Eden squinted at Anthony. 'The comic relief?'

'How do you know you've got our killer?' I asked.

'I've been at Sydney Harbour National Park two nights now. All night,' Charmaine said. 'I knew it was where he'd strike next. It's Sydney's next biggest park after Centennial and the Domain. See?' She unfolded a large battered map and spread it out before us on the table. Eden was tapping the five-iron on my chair. More of her weird nerves. Eden had always been compassionless but rarely stiff like this, fidgety, short-tempered. I'd wondered after we left Bood's if she'd been touchy because she couldn't find a way around taking me to meet one of her serial-killer friends (which I assumed was pretty nerve-racking). But she was still off-kilter. It was strange.

Charmaine pointed out the park, a big solid patch of green curving like gnarled fingers around the mouth of Sydney Harbour, some of it off Mosman, some off Balgowlah Heights and the biggest chunk right off Manly. Probably frequented by cool, beachy business types. Weekend dads and yummy mummies with blogs they ran from home. Joggers, hundreds of them, to hunt between the tall pines.

'I started just by wandering around after Ivana was found,' Charmaine said. 'I just . . . I couldn't stand by at home with everyone crying and consoling each other and making fucking phone calls. The journalists. Fuck. I wanted to do something. So I took a shot at it and I went out there. Walking around and around the paths was too obvious. I started taking cover. Watching. Watching. Watching. I saw some pretty sick stuff up there. Especially in the early morning.'

'You lay out there all night?' I couldn't believe this woman. She looked like she ought to be running a bake sale. When

I looked at the club in Eden's hands I saw blood in the grooves of the titanium. Her daughter's body wasn't even cold and here she was sniper-stalking possible suspects in a national park in the dead of the night, like something out of a Arnold Schwarzenegger movie. I was half-convinced the whole thing was some joke Tony was playing on me, but the admiration in his eyes as he looked upon Charmaine made me doubt it. I'd seen families of victims do some odd stuff over the years. Some of them pick up and go straight back to work the next day like nothing ever happened. Make their sandwiches and put them in their lunch boxes and run for the bus. I suppose something like that is denial. Maybe Charmaine was in the denial stage. Maybe she thought if she caught the killer she'd put things right again. Bring Ivana back from wherever in the universe she was.

'What'd you see?'

'Oh, there were guys rooting in the public toilets.' Charmaine curled her lip. 'People dumping rubbish. Drug deals. One guy trapping possums and taking them away in his truck. I don't know why. You name it, mate, they were doing it out there. Place is a friggen circus at night.'

'You were by yourself?'

'I had the dog.' Charmaine nudged the animal with her knee and it jumped up again, barked at me, wet eyes searching mine. I must have smelt like food. I usually do.

'Alright, so –' I released a chest full of air, shook my head. 'Jesus. Alright. So you get the idea you might lie in wait for the killer. You decide you'll do it at Sydney Harbour National Park. You go trekking around in the middle of the night spying on creepy-crawlies in the bushes. And then . . . what? You reckon you found our killer?'

'Not just found him, mate,' Charmaine smiled. 'I fucking whacked him.'

'This is incredible,' Eden said, sitting back in her chair. I think she meant 'incredible' in the true sense of the word. Not to be believed.

'George Hacker is in custody. He's on his way here. He's been treated and released to us.'

'And it looks good?' I said.

'From what we found on the video camera, it looks pretty good.'

'Video camera?'

'The suspect was found videotaping joggers. Women only. Navy blue hoodie, black tracksuit pants, crouching in the bushes videoing women coming up the path and back down again. Lots of close-ups. From a raid on his apartment, there are plenty of tapes. Edited tapes. Compilations of women's breasts, arses, their . . . their front . . . parts,' Tony coughed.

'Navy blue hoodie, was it?' I asked.

'Yep.'

'And no weapons? No guns or anything?' Eden asked.

'No, nothing like that.'

'And this occurred just now?'

'Four o'clock this morning,' Charmaine said. 'On the dot. I never believed people got up that bloody early. But the place was full of people doing yoga and running and stretching and doing that . . . what's that one they do?' She waved her arms, hands flat.

'Tai chi.'

'Tai chi,' she confirmed. She drew a long breath, eased it out slowly. She was wavering between talking about her daughter's murder like she was talking about someone she didn't know and approaching the edge of that terrifying reality in her mind. I could almost see her back away from the emotion like it was a seizure that was threatening to come over her.

Keep talking. Keep talking and you won't have to think.

Eden and I looked at each other for a beat. She turned the golf club over and over on the tabletop.

'Okay. Well, look, Charmaine,' I sighed, 'I'm sure my colleagues here will agree with me in saying that, speaking for the New South Wales Police Force, we never encourage vigilantism. What you did was reckless and dangerous. You acted without authority, without sufficient evidence, and you might have gotten yourself killed or worse out there. I mean, that was mad, lady. It was a mad, mad thing you did, and I hope you never do anything like it ever again.'

Charmaine sat and looked at me. The dog beside her started panting, its tongue slicked with foamy saliva. It swallowed loudly.

'Speaking as myself, though,' I shrugged, 'I think you're pretty fucking awesome.'

Eden sighed.

'I agree,' Tony laughed. 'What a tiger. Pow.' He gave an imaginary golf swing, shielded his eyes as he followed an imaginary decapitated head across an imaginary skyline. 'Do you even play golf?'

'I'm going to try to maintain the integrity in the room and bid you farewell,' Eden said as Tony and I continued miming golf-themed assaults. 'Frank and I will keep you up to date with the case as it progresses, Ms Lyon. Thank you for your assistance.'

Eden shook Charmaine's hand and left.

'You two better punish this fucking guy.' Charmaine pointed at me, chewing her lips. I thought I saw a shimmer of emotion in her eyes, but before I could lock on it, it was gone. 'I'm serious.'

We had the paramedic team turn around and deliver George Hacker right to his apartment on the upper level of a colourful row of terraces in Redfern. The street smelled of beer and rotting vegetables, and Otto bins stood sentry in all positions – behind buildings, on the kerb, in bushes, on landings – like faceless bottle-green robots in colourful hats. Everything smelled pissed on, both by stray dogs and drunks. The light rain that had recently passed seemed to enliven the smell. This was a place where people knew cops, uniformed or not. A group of teenagers split from the front of the house next door as we arrived, heads down and hands in pockets. They took up residence on the opposite corner and loitered, as kids do, kicking stones and glancing at us over each other's shoulders.

There was blood on the yellow front door of George's place and an army of ants trailing under the rubber liner at its bottom, fat-bellied ants grown lazy on a gluttony of leftover pizza boxes within. The government had allotted George the upper floor and given the ground floor to a family of five – a single mother who used the back door of the building, minded her own business, and didn't seem to know George had been living above her at all, let alone whether he drove a van. She didn't know when she'd seen George last or what her birth date was or whether or not she'd been arrested in the last six months. She slammed the door in my face in a mixture of disdain and relief when I bid her goodbye. Her kids were milling around her skirt as we spoke, grubby-faced and grey-toothed like little trolls under a tree, kids who spent their whole day with a baby-bottle of Coke or chin-staining strawberry cordial between their jaws. Kids who slept through fistfights and sirens, budding versions of the loiterers across the street. There was a surprising number of children visible from the front of George's row, looking out the windows of upper floors and peeking through mail slots. Dirty hands, faces that wouldn't smile back at you no matter what you were offering.

We hadn't let Anthony know how far from likely it was that George Hacker was our man. Anthony had been so smugly excited about Charmaine Lyon's find that I couldn't let him down by telling him that the hoodie was the wrong colour, the guy had been stalking joggers at the wrong time of day, there was no weaponry or abduction material found on or near him and he'd taken a little red Hyundai, rather than a van, to the park that morning. George Hacker dropped out of school in Year Nine to take up an apprenticeship as a mechanic, a qualification he proved incapable of completing due to literacy skills so poor that even TAFE exams were too much for him. He was likely too dumb to know what a tranquilliser was, let alone their different chemical nuances. He had one sexual assault charge dating back to age seventeen when he'd groped a teenage girl in the surf, making out like he was trying to break his fall from a dumper. He'd been warned about his busy hands in the white wash before, but didn't heed the caution. He only served a month, being a teen and all. He'd steered clear of much trouble after that.

Like most degenerates, George was an emaciated character, short with a big forehead like something in his skull had swelled and stretched the cranium out, pushed the parietal bone back so that it shadowed the nape of his neck. Collarbones like external plumbing popped out almost on top of the skin. He emerged handcuffed from the cab of the ambulance and stood squinting on the street, looking up at the windows of the adjacent terrace house and spying the children there watching the drama. The back of his head was bandaged, two spots of dark red blood seeping through the patch like little eyes.

'Fark off, ya little farkers,' George sneered at the kids in the windows and kicked the front gate. 'Go find something else to watch, ya nosey farken mongrels.'

'Right-o.' Eden strode forward and took George's arm. 'That's enough. We're all very impressed.'

'This here is harassment.' George spat on the ground, barely missing Eden's brown leather boot. 'You cops've had it out for me since I was farken born. This is the third time I been picked up this month. I ain't done nothing. You been watching. You been waiting. But I wasn't doing nothing but –'

'This is a Redfern street, not the State Theatre,' I said. 'Let's save the dramatics for the official statement.'

He continued unabated, spat again. 'I ain't done noth–'

'No one's listening,' I said. 'No one cares. And you spit near my partner again and I'll put your head through that fucking mail slot.'

That really set him off. Eden unlocked his cuffs and glanced at me, weary. She knew now that I was going to be the antagoniser, which made her the empathiser. Classic good cop, bad cop. The system was traditional because it worked, but I knew that Eden liked being the bad cop. She got bored being nice to crims. Was hardly convincing at it. That's why I liked to snatch it off her early. I didn't like good cop either.

I told George Hacker that no one cared for a reason. It's as effective as a sucker punch, without all the police brutality charges. Telling members of the lower socio-economic rungs of Australia that no one cares about them really gives them the shits and, I'll admit, I find that amusing. I know. It's a lowly and cruel kind of amusement. I'm always entertained by how shocked they are about it. They never expect it. If you listen to them in Centrelink queues, in police station waiting rooms, on the corners and in the shopping-centre car parks of Redfern, Kings Cross, Punchbowl, Campbelltown, all they talk about is how no one cares about them. No one gives a shit about them. The government. The police. The child welfare people. So when you tell them that actually, yes, you really don't care about them, it confirms everything they're been telling their friends and colleagues and drug dealers all their adult years. They're simultaneously infuriated that you admitted it and horrified that none of their friends, colleagues or drug dealers was around to hear the admission, hear them vindicated. I took George by the back of his neck and pushed him into the house. Eden followed us, half-heartedly trying to talk me down from being too rough.

I tossed George onto his sagging grey couch and looked around the little flat in disgust. There were a couple of centimetres of brown city dust on everything, blown in from a dozen construction sites between his apartment and the CBD. The place felt damp and cramped, like most drug hovels do, something mildly sexual about it, like regret felt after a cheap affair, sweaty sheets and head-impressed pillows. I brushed crumbs off a plastic outdoor chair that was waiting in the entrance to the kitchen like a neglected child. Sat down, looked at George.

'I want all the tapes. Everything you've got,' I said. 'And I don't want to have to get it by rummaging through your filthy drawers.'

'I'm not –' George snivelled, already looking to Eden for help. 'This ain't something I do, alright? Alright? I was just out there, this one time, just trying out me new camera. Some bitch whacks me right in the fucking head while I'm playing with a camera in a park. I'm innocent, mate. I ought to sue that farken bitch, get me some compo for this shit. I ain't got no farken tapes, so you can –'

'People like you always keep tapes, George.'

'The fuck you mean, people like me?'

'George,' I sighed. 'The tapes.'

'Tell us where the tapes are, George,' Eden said.

'I don't –'

'Tell us where you keep them.'

'I ain't got no farken tapes,' George screamed and bounced once on the couch like something had bitten him. A frustrated half-leap. 'Jesus farken Christ you coppers, you don't listen, you –'

I stood up and went into the kitchen. Grabbed a tall water glass from the sink, cloudy with fingerprints. Came back. Eden watched me walk over to a small rectangular fish tank on a wooden stand beside the television set, a sad little orange and white goldfish bobbing weakly around the surface of the water, hunting for rainbow flakes. I looked at George, waited, but he

191

didn't speak. I lifted my arm and swung my elbow into the front of the fish tank. The glass popped, and with a satisfying glubbing sound the contents began to empty onto the carpet at my feet, splashing up against the glass front of the television stand.

'Fark!' George screamed, rising up off the couch. Eden pushed him down, one-handed, bored. 'You stupid prick. Look what you've done.'

'Detective Bennett,' Eden sighed. 'Is that really necessary?'

I waited calmly as the tank emptied, the water slapping on the carpet, making a large dark blue stain that reached almost to the couch. The goldfish, strangely serene, circled the tank until the flow of the water took him through the hole in the tank and into the glass in my hand. I set the full glass, goldfish bobbing on its surface, on top of the television set.

Now the room smelled of algae and fish turds. I tried to decide if it was an improvement.

'Listen, you piece of shit. I don't have anything to give you.' George's bottom lip quivered. 'I'm not some crazy sicko out filming women. This whole thing, this is a fucking . . . misunderstanding. It's a mistake. Don't break any more of my shit, or I swear to god, I'll farken kill you!'

'Oh. Is that a threat?'

'Detective Bennett.'

I pushed over a CD rack. It crashed to the floor.

'Detective Bennett!'

'Let's see where a casual search takes us,' I said. I walked to the bookshelf under the window and selected a DVD from the extensive collection there. Scumbags always have huge collections of DVDs displayed in racks like books. I wondered idly if they emulated the bookshelves of more learned environments, the offices of lawyers who handled their compensation claims, the libraries where they conducted their job and rental searches. This was an idiot's depository of knowledge. *Wild Wild West. Die Hard III. The 40-Year-Old Virgin.* I popped open the plastic case in my hands. *Titanic.* I looked at the disc. It looked legitimately made but I doubted it had been legitimately paid for.

'Nope,' I said. I closed the case and flung it casually out the open window, over the balcony and onto the street.

'No. Stop. Stop.'

I popped open *Terminator II*. Clipped it closed, sent it spinning into the air.

'Not here either.'

'Please, please, tell him to stop.'

'I suggest if you want him to stop, you give him what he wants, George.' Eden was sitting on the back of the couch, her arms folded over her chest. I flipped *The Godfather* and *Alien* off the balcony. The teenagers from the corner sprinted across the asphalt and started scooping up the DVDs as they clattered onto the road. They'd spend the next few days getting stoned and watching them, then take them straight to Cash Converters.

'Please.'

'Not here. Not here. Not here.'

I flipped DVDs, put a good spin on them as they flew through the air like playing cards. The wind caught them and they curved away from the teenagers' hands. They laughed. It's always good to see teens laughing. It's not an easy thing to achieve.

'George, give Detective Inspector Bennett what he wants. Right now we can sting you for public nuisance at best,' Eden said gently. 'Tell us where we can find your collection, or we'll get more creative. Detective Bennett will start pulling apart your furniture and I'll start thinking of interesting ways to fuck up your world. I'm thinking use of surveillance devices to record a private activity without consent. I'm thinking filming for indecent purposes, or maybe committing indecent or offensive acts in a public place. I mean, are you absolutely certain all the runners you were filming were adults, George? I'm wondering if making indecent visual images of a child under the age of sixteen might be on the cards.'

Eden was very good with verbatim material on offences, their minimum and maximum terms. I'd always thought it was very impressive, imagined her sometimes lounging in the bath reading law manuals and shaving her legs. I flipped *Dodgeball* out the window and one of the teen boys jumped and caught it one-handed like a cricketer.

I broke three plates, kicked over a pot plant and spilt a bag of rice all over the countertops and the floor before George finally submitted. Eden had bargained and begged and bribed him as much as her black heart would allow for a good hour and a half, but I think it was the rice that finally did it. No matter how much you try, you'll never recover all the grains after a major spill. You'll still be finding them when you do your final bond clean before moving, years from now, a marriage had and failed, the entire apartment painted three times over and the kids next door grown up and moved away.

Rice. It's a bastard.

Underneath the sink, behind a row of greasy cleaning liquid bottles, a plastic Tupperware container of George's homemade DVDs lay waiting for us. We left George crying on the couch and complaining of a migraine and took the discs back to the station for analysis. Five officers on ten computers gave the recordings a quick play, so we could get a feel for George's tastes, whether they were violent or not. Eden and I stood at the front of the computer room, allowing it some distance, considering the collection of windows before us, the women huffing their way from one side to another, their dogs and prams and children out in front.

There was no overtly violent material present on any of the discs.

Now some people would say that in a way the tapes were violent, that George's predatory gaze symbolically assaulted the women he filmed for his own gratification while they frolicked freely, as they rightly should be able to, in the assumed privacy of what should be an ungendered, totally 'equal' public environment. That the penetrative lens of the camera reduced these women to sexual objects with the same type of aggressive and oppressive sentiment that a rapist might using his body, and that the non-consensual filming, or 'upskirting', of women, should in no way be considered harmless sexually themed play.

Frank Bennett: not a chauvinist.

But there was no physical violence here, and that was what Eden and I were interested in. George had mainly collected and compiled shots of female runners, particularly the curvier variety, their breasts and backsides. He seemed very interested in the women's motion, the way their bodies reacted to the impact of their gait as they ran, the rise and fall of flesh. All my feminist teachings aside, I understood George's fetish. There wasn't a man my age who hadn't been captivated at one time by Pamela Anderson's long-legged stride along Los Angeles

County beaches every Sunday evening at 7.30 on Channel Ten back in the 1990s, hormones making mush of our brains. I remembered as a teen rewinding and playing and rewinding and playing Yasmine Bleeth's beach run in the show's title sequence. The way her delicate foot hit the sand, the way that landing seemed to ripple up through her body, her powerful thighs, her taut belly, her immaculate breasts. Pam underwater, pearl white, lips taut. The reflections of the water, lightening white fingers, shimmering up the muscle of her arms, super-slow motion.

George Hacker had created his own personal *Best of Baywatch* compilation out of female runners. It wasn't right. But that didn't mean I didn't get it. It was only when I noticed Eden staring at me that I realised I was humming.

'Is that the *Baywatch* theme song?' she asked.

'It is.'

She gave me that look.

'I note your revulsion. And yet,' I raised a finger, 'it would have been impossible for you to recognise my humming as the *Baywatch* theme song without you yourself having watched *Baywatch* enough times to recognise the tune.'

'Can we do some police work?'

'Am I wrong?'

'Pull any and all images of suspicious characters,' she told the tech nearest to us. 'Email them straight through to me.'

We left. I was disappointed. The day felt long already. We left five men sitting in a computer room watching some Redfern idiot's softcore porn. There was nothing except the minor sparkle of hope that George Hacker, while he had been stalking Sydney's parks fuelling nothing but his erotic interests, might have caught something on his camera that would assist us. My shoes smelled like fish-tank water, and they were my favourite pair and it was entirely my fault. I tried to fill my mind with glittering beaches and Pamela Anderson as we headed back out into the day.

Ruben sat in the kitchen of the house near the park and read over his translations of the newspaper stories he'd found in the upstairs bedroom. Donato had been fairly uninterested in the stories Ruben pored over, texting beneath the table and sighing at the ceiling as the teacher took them through sentence structure and résumé writing in English. Donato put Ruben's interest in the attic room and the strange dark presence in the house down to nothing but childish fantasy, a Scooby-Doo mystery. But Ruben felt in his gut, somehow, that he was very close to something he needed to unravel, something he had been charged to put to rest. His father believed in callings and life missions, small tests set by God or whatever was in charge up there, tests that if Ruben failed he would be presented with at the end, whenever that came. Ruben didn't shy away from adventure. He let his curiosity lead him. It had taken him to wonderful and terrifying places.

It had been some time since he'd heard any noise from the attic room. The television behind the door was silent, and when he looked up at the window facing out across the park from the street he saw that the curtain was drawn. He had a feeling that whoever was up there had sated whatever restless desire drove him or her, that the pacing and whispering he sometimes heard before had come to a peak. Something had happened, something had been tamed or driven away as tangibly as a vicious stray dog. Ruben also had the idea that whoever it was there left the attic when he wasn't around. He found food missing from the meagre rations a mysterious someone stocked the kitchen with, and a white van parked at the garage at the back of the property showed signs of being driven – there were spider webs on everything else in the garage, and its tyres weren't flat-bottomed the way his had been when he left his little Hyundai outside his girlfriend's place to tour Germany the summer before. Whoever it was, it was the same person who left an envelope of cash under the coffee pot for him every Tuesday.

Ruben hadn't seen another staff member on the property, but he assumed someone other than the person in the attic trimmed the tiny garden beneath the sitting-room windows, kept the dust off the porch and the vines off the side of the house. He wondered sometimes about trying to track down the gardener. Ruben had even gone so far as to drive by on Thursdays and Fridays to see if he might catch the person in action so he could ask about the house's owner. But he wasn't sure he could make himself understood in English yet. His spoken English was pathetic.

Donato told him he was becoming obsessed. Ruben doubted Donato had ever thought about anything long enough to become obsessed with it.

Ruben put the articles in chronological order. He smoothed out the first, a page from the social section of a newspaper that mainly dealt with the married lives of American celebrities. There was a small column on the right side of one page devoted to Sydney socialites and their divorces, parties and drug habits. At the top of the column was a photograph of a broad-shouldered man with a beautiful but fierce-looking blonde woman on his arm, both dressed in party fineries: 'Australia's corporate elite gathered today to pay tribute to Michael Harper, celebrated CEO of Vota Media and chairman of TrueCare Research Foundation, who died last Sunday after a long battle with pancreatic cancer. In attendance were members of Mr Harper's favourite NRL team, the Manly Sea Eagles, as well as news identity Daniel Sutherland and Victoria's Secret model Saskia Kehz. Harper is survived by his wife Joan and daughter Tara, who was unable to return from studies abroad to attend the ceremony. "It'll be lonely in the house without him," Mrs Harper commented, before a family representative asked the press for privacy.'

There was another article, this one from a cheaply printed glossy magazine, the pages littered with yellow stars and collages of local celebrities pouring themselves out of limousines and cheering in the front rows of sporting events. A panel at the bottom of the page featured a shot of Joan Harper with her head in one hand, sitting with a girlfriend at a golden-lit restaurant.

Celeb-watchers in Sydney are chomping at the bit to get a look inside the Casa De Harper after the death of globe-trotting Vota Media CEO and all-round philanthropist Michael Harper, who passed away in November. Sources tell *The Talk* that Harper's daughter was conspicuously absent from his funeral, and it was not because the millionaire heiress was living it up in Amsterdam as some have suggested. A very public stoush at this year's Melbourne Cup between Joan Harper and Marcey Sage, mother of *prima ballerina assoluta*-in-the-making Violet Sage, has bolstered claims all is not right with the mysterious Tara Harper. Oh my!

'The Harper kid is a psycho. She was an ugly, violent kid in high school and she's out of control now,' says a source. 'She's basically a recluse. Mummy Harper keeps her locked away from prying eyes.' Principal of the prestigious St Ellis High School in Mosman, Richard Morris, would not confirm or deny rumours Harper Junior had engaged in self-harm throughout her troubled childhood years, or if she had launched a Carrie-style attack on another student on the evening of their Year Twelve formal. Court documents are sealed, but whispers on the grapevine tell us that the Harpers settled out of court with a St Ellis student in 2003 after her daughter was involved in a 'serious assault'! Meow!

Is there any truth to these tall tales? It's unlikely we'll find out soon. Joanie Harper has cancelled upcoming social commitments and battened down the hatches at Harper Manor. If there's more to know, *The Talk* will know it first! Stay tuned!

The final piece was a small news report wedged between two articles, one about the drowning of a young surf competitor and one, Ruben guessed, about the opening of a new hospital. There were no pictures to accompany the article. The headline read 'New laws sought after high-profile surgery mishap'.

The state government has called upon federal leaders to impose regulations to curb the growing number of young Australians seeking cheap cosmetic surgery overseas. The move comes as reports arise that Tara Harper, daughter of the late philanthropist and socialite Michael Harper, was medevaced to a hospital in Darwin last week suffering from a grievously botched surgical procedure in Bangkok.

While details of the case are yet to emerge, police allege Harper, 29, travelled to Thailand to seek multiple elective surgeries and may have fallen victim to one of the many unqualified or under-qualified cost-effective surgeons operating in the foreign city. 'They call Bangkok "The Butcher's Shop" for a reason. Young people without the financial backing to seek the services of qualified dentists and plastic surgeons here in Australia go overseas thinking they've found the cheap way out,' Deputy Police Commissioner Ryan Hennah commented. 'It seems in this case, a great number of procedures were elected at once – a number and type our experts have told us would never have been approved here. Ms Harper also had the misfortune of choosing a company with a terrible history of major surgery complications. She's lucky to be alive, if you ask me.'

In 2014, more than 700 young Australians travelled to South-East Asia to seek elective surgery and dental procedures. For those figures, it's understood at least 25 per cent were for breast augmentation. Dr Elliot Taket of the University of New South Wales Medical Research Department revealed the growing popularity of surgical tourism. 'You can get stuff done over there that you can't get done here,' he said. 'These guys will go ahead and give you breast augmentation without taking the time to decide whether or not your body can support the size and weight you're asking for. Their work is popular with models and porn stars who want to stand out in an already overcrowded industry. There are places you can go over there to get novelty work done that no one in this country would touch. Facial implants and bone grafts. You'd be surprised what people want. Most of my work here is spent dealing with the clean-up – the physical and psychological fallout from bad choices and bad practices.'

Member for Windsor Rooney Dennis will address the Senate this week with proposed restrictions on travel for surgical purposes.

As the sun began to set, Ruben took his articles up the stairs and crept to the door of the attic room. All was silent within. Holding his breath, he closed his eyes and knocked on the door three times, the third soft enough not to be heard – his courage already failing him. No answer came from within, not a whisper or a footstep. Ruben slid silently down against the door and kneeled beside it, looked at the crumpled and sun-dried papers in his hands. Somehow he felt sad for whatever being was beyond the door, its part in the terrible history he held in his fingers. After some moments, he cleared his throat.

'Are you Tara Harper?' he asked. There was a moment of silence, and then a terrible thundering on the door, so sudden and so loud Ruben fell back against the stair banister, his heart in his throat. The person behind the door was bashing on it, kicking on it, and when the noise diminished, he heard a low whisper on the other side of the wood.

'Stay away.'

Ruben struggled to breathe.

He ran down the stairs and out of the house.

There were two things Ian Buvette didn't see a lot of in or anywhere near Skytree Industries – swearing and beautiful women. But one average Thursday night, with Kent Street crowded with late-night shoppers on their way to cool their heels down by the harbour, Ian stepped out of his office building, letting the door close behind him, and found a beautiful young woman standing on the street swearing. Ian hitched his shoulder bag and paused, watching her rummage through her expensive little briefcase-style leather handbag, then stare up mournfully at the windows above him, her hands falling dejectedly at her sides. Ian was puzzled. He even turned and looked at the windows himself.

'Shit,' she said. She seemed to consider her predicament for a moment, find that it was in fact even worse than she'd realised, and then seethed again. 'Shit!'

The woman stepped into the light of the sign beneath the windows, a gigantic '103', for 103 Kent Street. She was a strange-looking woman, now that Ian could see her clearly. Smooth, caramel-skinned – Vietnamese, he guessed – but with hair cropped short, almost buzz-cut, and peroxide blonde. Heavy-framed red glasses rimmed her eyes. The dress was expensive looking, although Ian didn't know anything much about fashion. His mother had dressed him until he was twenty-five, and there was nothing so much as could be called 'style' going on upstairs at Skytree. Pear-shaped, middle-aged, single technology consultants – the entire staff of Skytree – stuck to grey trousers and business shirts. The woman set her bag down on the ground and started rummaging through it in the light of the sign. Ian swallowed twice before he spoke.

'Can I help you?'

The girl looked up at him. From down there, she looked like a beautiful, helpless child.

'Oh god, I'm sorry,' she sighed, laughed. 'I didn't even see you. I'm just. Urgh, I can't believe it. I've left my pass up there.'

She gestured towards the windows. Ian looked up.

'Up there?'

'Wilkins and Co. Seventh floor.'

'You work here?' Ian hadn't seen anyone exit the lifts at the Wilkins and Co law firm on the seventh floor who was under the age of seventy. Ever.

'As of today, and maybe only for today.' The girl gave another tired little sigh-laugh, an uneasy noise, like someone trying to find the humour in a cancer diagnosis. 'I've left my pass and the new client reports I'm supposed to have done tonight up there on my desk. It's alright. It's fine. I'll just . . . I can call security. Maybe.'

The girl flipped out her phone. Ian felt his stomach shift.

'Oh, um. I'm the last man out. They have private security here. First round isn't until midnight. I know, because I'm always the last man out. And often it's at midnight.'

Ian thought that was a pretty good line, stuffed his hands in his pockets and leaned back on his heels to prove it. Made him sound like a hard worker – and knowledgeable, too, about the building and its security, the nuances of his workplace. Her new workplace.

'Shit,' she said.

'Yeah. Shit.'

'You couldn't –' She looked at him, pressed her painted lips together until they disappeared, a humble, inside-out smile. Ian felt himself smiling. He wasn't a man who ever held power. So when the tiniest tastes and whispers of it nudged his life, he felt them as keenly as sexual release.

'I couldn't lend you my pass?'

'You couldn't, could you?'

'Well,' he smiled smugly, 'I don't know, lady. I've never seen you before.'

'Oh please.' She was really laughing now. He made her laugh. 'Do I look like a thief?'

'A cat burglar, maybe.' Where was this incredible charm and wit coming from? This was not Ian. Pudgy, video game–obsessed, mother-worshipping Ian. Something about her inspired him. It was like he was role-playing on a stage he'd been performing on for years. He knew the lines already. They were just . . . natural.

'I'll be three minutes.' She held up three perfectly manicured fingers. Her palm looked soft but firm, like satin over brick. 'Three.'

'I'll make you a deal,' Ian said. He had no idea where this confidence was coming from. She seemed to draw it out of him on a string. 'You're three minutes or less, or you have to buy me a drink down the road at the Stanton.'

'The Stanton?' She cringed. 'I'll have to rush then.'

She swiped the pass out of his hands and beeped herself through the foyer doors with all the familiarity of someone who had worked at 103 Kent Street for a decade. Ian glanced at his watch once every five seconds, cold and uncertain somehow in the wake of her, the funny little firecracker who'd turned up in his life suddenly. His face felt hot, but a chill was growing in his spine. He hoped he wasn't sweating through his shirt. At two minutes and fifty-one seconds, she burst through the doors to the elevator and ran across the dark foyer, pushing the large green exit button frantically.

'Ha!' she grinned. 'Made it.'

'Aww, too bad for me,' Ian said, without an inch of false sentiment. The girl was laughing to herself, tucking a manila folder into her briefcase bag.

'Maybe I'll lock myself out tomorrow.' The girl winked and Ian felt the gesture stab him right in the sternum. The sincerity in her words. The joke that Ian knew, somehow, felt deep in his heart, was not a joke. 'See ya.'

'See ya,' Ian said.

He stood in the street and watched her walking away. His heart aching, Ian turned towards the Stanton, glancing at his watch. There was no need to be disappointed, he told himself. A drink on the first night of meeting would have ruined it. Yes, they'd meet again. She'd deliberately lock herself out. It was perfect. A romantic little game he could think about all that night, all the next day. Who was she? He hadn't even caught her name. But wasn't that perfect too? He'd try to guess it. Wonder at it. Try to fit different sounds to her face. Where had she come from? She'd just been there – perfect woman, perfect scenario, like a tailor-made dream. Cliché almost. A wonderful cliché.

She needed the card that he possessed, and at the very moment he'd walked out the doors. Minutes earlier and she'd have caught someone else. Minutes later and he'd have been gone. It was a little Jane Austen, if he was honest with himself. It was very Jane Austen. Ian looked at the starless sky between the buildings above him, marvelled at the world and its symmetry.

Hooky walked up the block to Town Hall, stood looking at the huge ornate building lit electric pink and yellow from floodlights in its filthy gardens. On the corner, a preacher asked crowds waiting at the huge intersection whether they were ready for God to return, because he was returning, and when he did he'd be merciless on the unprepared. A group of youths ebbed around her suddenly, then continued down George Street towards the cinema, slightly too loud and slightly too deliberate, carrying shopping bags. The lights changed and a hundred people flooded the great intersection, passed each other wordlessly like trained soldiers on the march, eyes averted.

She counted off some minutes on her sensible little gold and leather-band watch, her 'office girl' watch, as she called it, and then walked back down the hill and turned right into the laneway behind Kent Street. She kept her head bowed against the security cameras hanging above the loading zone adjacent to the fire escape belonging to 103 Kent Street. It was not likely her presence would be noted and the cameras searched for images of her, as she intended to take nothing from the building that would arouse suspicion. But Hooky never shied away from extra precautions. The proactive con artist was the successful con artist. She opened the fire escape door she had left propped open when she dashed through the building with Ian's swipe card, and entered the stairwell.

Being overly cautious was only one of the many natural behaviours that made a successful con artist. Amy had discovered each in turn the hard way, because people like her – liars, cheats, shadow people – were impossible to find and were sole operators when they did reveal themselves. Tandem teams of con artists, Amy had discovered, were an invention of Hollywood. It took a being of broken, malfunctioning or completely absent morality to do what she did, and the chances of two of them collaborating successfully required each member of the team to be incapable of loyalty yet be helplessly enslaved by it. No, real con artists were loners. They were meticulous, overprepared, adaptive and artful. They didn't look back.

Amy was in no way ignorant of the fact that Ian, master deadender of Skytree Industries, would stay up all night thinking about her. That he'd dress dangerously tomorrow – the salmon shirt he'd bought on a whim at Big'n'Tall which had looked striking and bold on the mannequin in all the ways that Ian was not. That he'd think the encounter on the street had meant something, had been the zingy pesto he'd been waiting for in the iceberg lettuce salad of his life. But Hooky didn't feel anything about this other than satisfaction, a sense of equilibrium, now that she'd gained access to Imogen's building. Checkpoint: passed. If there was one thing Hooky understood, it was balance.

As she moved through the building, Hooky thought smugly about Imogen at the counter of the police station with her stupid lunch for Frank. Hooky would show her what this 'child' could do, just how much Imogen should have held onto that worry she had about Hooky's place in Frank's life. No, she wasn't after Frank. The suggestion was ridiculous. But that didn't mean she was someone who could be spoken down to. Imogen had no idea what power she held. The woman had tried to strip that hard-earned power away with a single word. Well, no one got to do that to her.

Hooky could fuck up people's entire worlds. She was not a child and she wasn't going to let anyone think she was.

There are plenty of things on a personal laptop can ruin a person. Even the most measured of people. For women she found erotic photographs, letters to the ex-boyfriend, secret bank accounts, fake dating profiles. For men, unconventional porn, party photos, gambling accounts. Amy headed straight for the laptop and brought up Imogen's email account, flipped through the recent correspondence. A lot of it was client mail about appointments and referrals, mental health care plans. Some reports back to the department about police officers who had completed programs or still had outstanding sessions keeping them off duty. Amy wondered if Imogen had ever been Frank's psychologist – if in fact that's how the two had met. It made sense. She glanced at the darkened door to the hall and then searched the computer for documents with 'Bennett' in the title. To her surprise, she came upon a file named 'BennettArcher.doc'.

Monday 17 September: Frank stonewalling but clearly in trouble. Takes time to go on the nod whenever Eden's queried. Endone? Check prescription frequency. Weight loss. Outwardly aggressive at mention of Ducote.

Of course. Martina Ducote, Frank's girlfriend, the one whose heart was cut out by Jason Beck. They never found the heart. Not at the scene. Not outside, where he was spotted by a garbage collector – leading to the chase that finally ended him. Amy wondered idly what happened to the woman's heart. Wondered if Frank wondered about it too. Beck was clearly off the rails at that point. It's possible he ate it. Fed it to the cat. Flushed it. Burned it. The hardest things about murder were the unanswered questions. Was she afraid? Did she fight? Did she say anything? What did he do with the heart? Confessions and forensic analysis and criminal profiles could answer some things, but not many, about murder. Amy had plenty of unanswered questions about her parents' murder. Questions that popped and popped into her mind all the time, sometimes triggered, sometimes not, coming at the strangest times, when she was eating lunch, when she was falling asleep.

What had their faces looked like in those last seconds?

There was no porn on Imogen's computer. No dating profiles in her internet history. Amy wandered through the cookie files in Imogen's browser and settled on one that piqued her curiosity – sandersinvestigations.com.au. Amy glanced at the contact email address, then went back to Imogen's email account and found a correspondence stream in the Sent folder.

imogenstone77@gmail.com: Brent, long time no see! Can I call on that favour you owe me for the Harrowe case?

brent@sandersinvestigations.com: Nothing slips by you, Imo. Tell me what you need and we'll call it square.

imogenstone77@gmail.com: Really need registry files on Archer, Eden. No middle name, apparently. Weird. Particularly interested in Daddy, if you can make it happen.

brent@sandersinvestigations.com: You know I love a challenge. See attached.

Amy sat back in Imogen's chair, rapped the tabletop with her fingernails. There were five files attached: birth certificates belonging to Eden, her brother Eric, her father Heinrich and her mother Sue, plus there was a conviction report for Heinrich Archer – no middle name either – beginning with thefts, assaults and loitering charges in 1970. In the pale white light of the laptop, Amy drew her legs up beneath her on the chair and leaned forward, digging deeper into Imogen's search history.

I got home at nine. I'd started calling Imogen's place 'home' about a month after we began dating, around the time I got my own drawer in her bedroom closet and started keeping a toothbrush in her bathroom. The moment you have your own toothbrush at your lover's place you live there too. The personal toothbrush is the key that opens the door to finding a spot for your underwear and dirty clothes on their bedroom floor, to reserving a favourite mug from their collection. It's the key to adding things to the fridge – the milk you like or the chocolate bar in the freezer or your brand of beer. Imogen-home wasn't the favourite of my two homes. That would always be where Greycat was, and right now that was at my burned-out terrace. Greycat was a complete arsehole, but he had that quiet kind of stability a cop needs in his permanent dwelling. Every now and then I would return to my Imogen-home and find my psychologist in a bad mood and her hair all crazy or the place smelling of bleach and her clothes all stained with it and all my stuff in a pile on the laundry floor. Greycat was never frazzled. If he was a person, he'd have been a total stoner.

There are rough days on Homicide, of course there are. But they're not the kind of rough days people imagine. Again, Hollywood misinterprets things, or reinterprets them in more socially acceptable ways. On television, a bad day in Homicide is finding a woman hanging by her neck in her apartment with her guts on the floor and her mother crying in the hall. As a matter of fact, the finding of a body is a good day in homicide. Things are fresh. Exciting. Hopeful. You've got a case. You haven't interviewed anyone yet. The scene is laid out in all its intricacies and curiosities. You'll get to know this gutted woman better than you know some of your family members. You'll become a weird and mismatched and not wholly welcome part of her family. You'll have beers with her brother and listen to her father's war stories. You'll play with her dog. You'll watch her be buried, mourned, forgotten. Watch someone else take over her job and pack up her desk. The first day is the best day. It's like a very successful date. You've got it locked in. You haven't fucked it up yet. Missed something. Underestimated the importance of a vital piece of information. It's all downhill after the first day, until the day you land the killer. That's the second best day.

The bad days are the days when nothing happens. There's nothing to look at. No one to talk to. Everyone with something to say about the case has said it. All the photographs and CCTV of the area have been reviewed and set aside. All the witnesses have been interviewed, all the ex-boyfriends leaned on, all the photographs and fingerprints and mouth swabs collected and sent off. The measurements taken and the powder spread and wiped back up. The case falls from the news and journalists stop calling you.

It's day four. Five. Fifty-seven. The parents stop calling you, except at Christmas and on the victim's birthday. A new case comes along.

It was only day four of Ivana Lyon's murder but I had that feeling of dread that starts accumulating at the pit of my stomach like heavy black bile when more leads are dismissed than present themselves in a day. The ratio tips, slowly, slowly, until the end of the seesaw bangs on the ground and you feel its painful shudder through your legs. I could feel myself falling.

I'd spent the afternoon going back over the autopsy reports on Ivana and Minerva, looking for inconsistencies and trying to understand what they meant. Eden and I had argued with each other for forty minutes over knuckle size and spread. We could measure the size of the perpetrator's hand from knuckle-print bruises on Ivana's collarbone. The hands were small. I thought there was a ring indentation on one. Eden disagreed, said it was a scratch. I'd yelled at her that she needed to get her eyes checked, she was going blind as well as deaf. That had been the catalyst for me going home. It had been a cheap shot. Eden had come away from the last case with deafness in the left ear from gunshot damage and I knew she was supposed to wear a hearing aid but didn't, probably out of pride. We had got nothing done on the case and I'd been mean to my partner. I wondered how early I could get through the daily pleasantries with Imogen and then get into bed.

When I walked in the door, I found all the apartment lights on and the hall smelling of grilled haloumi. Ed Sheeran was playing. Female laughter erupted somewhere to the left of the hall and I froze with my hand on the knob and one foot in the stairwell.

'Baby!' Imogen said. She walked down the hall towards me. I closed the door.

'Have you got friends over?'

'I have,' she said. 'Sorry. I forgot to tell you. Come in – there's plenty of food.'

She ran her fingernails over my scalp and ruffled my hair. I was being pulled in two directions by a magnetic force right in the centre of my chest, one beckoning me back out into the stairwell, whispering warnings embedded in the male psyche about the age-old danger of women with wine, the other pulling me forward with promises of food. I was biologically befuddled for a second. When a tall woman passed the hall with a packet of Smith's Original chips in her hands it was settled. I can spot Smith's from a mile away.

I bypassed the living room and went straight for the kitchen, the fridge. Plucked a cold fake beer from the box on the top shelf.

'Oh baby,' I said, and took the first painfully cold sip. Imogen was standing behind me. I turned and drank at the same time, peered at her with one eye, surveyed her temperature.

'Something amiss?'

'I'm just waiting for you to come and say hello,' she said. Not cheerlessly. Not warmly either. I sucked air between my teeth, tasted imitation beer on the vapour of my breath. Dismissed the word 'just' from what she'd said, connected 'I'm' with the inherently dangerous 'waiting for you', and noted the hands on the hips. A performance was in order. I kissed her forehead.

'I just need a minute,' I said. I rolled my shoulders, cracked my neck. 'I've had a really rough –'

'Frank,' a woman in the doorway chirped. She was a beautiful little Indian woman in a bright yellow dress. Red necklace of polished wooden beads and red pleather heels. A bit dressy for wine and bickies with the girls. The others would talk about it while she was out of the room. Her colours. Her eagerness. 'You must be Frank. We've heard so much about you.'

'Frank, this is Deepa.'

'Deepa,' I grabbed her hand and pumped it.

'We're all so interested to hear about your job. Imogen's given us a taste but there's so much she can't answer.'

Suddenly, the kitchen was full of women. My dad had taken me to a battery farm once and it was very much like this. Smelly and loud. I looked down and found my beer was empty.

'Frank, this is Shauna. This is Erica. This is Kim.'

I was turning to get another beer at the exact same moment Kim was plunging in for a kiss on my cheek. The fridge door got trapped between us and she planted her kiss right on the corner of my mouth. Her breath tasted of wine.

'Oh, hi.' I laughed, put an arm around her narrow shoulders, hugged her into the fridge door. She laughed uncomfortably. My face burned.

The place swelled with chatter. I found myself holding my beer bottle against my temple.

'She did say he was handsome.'

'Very handsome.'

'He's got that Joel Edgerton, outback Australiana flavour to him.'

'Joel Edgerton. Oh god. Now that's a flavour I wouldn't mind getting a taste of.'

'Oh Jesus. Save it, Shauna.'

'Don't mind them, Frank. They're drunk.' Kim stroked my arm.

'What are you doing?' Imogen pulled my beer down from my head. My temple was ice cold, deliciously wet. 'Stop being weird.'

'Let's go back to the living room,' someone suggested. 'I'll be the first interrogator. Are you ready for your interrogation, Frank?'

'I'm really not,' I murmured to Imogen. 'I'm really not ready for rooms full of women and noise and interrogations. I'm not. At all.'

'Don't be difficult.' Imogen glanced at the hall, the women retreating. 'It's just a bit of fun. Just give us five minutes.'

'I've had a really rough day,' I said again.

'I would have told you about the dinner,' she smoothed my hair back from my temple, 'I just forgot. Okay? I forgot. Just come and say hello for five minutes and then you can make an excuse and leave.'

'I don't want to be interrogated. I've spent my week thus far actually interrogating people. I don't want to be the centre of attention. Keep them off me, Imogen.'

'Or what?' she laughed humourlessly.

'Frank. Come on!'

'Immy, please,' I said.

'Frankie, please,' she imitated me, slipped into my arms, rubbed my chest. 'Don't be a baby. Come on. I've got plenty of treats. Bring a couple of beers with you.'

She pulled my arm, never giving me a chance to grab the beers. I was led into the living room. There was a huge platter of antipasto on the coffee table, barely touched. The olives glistened black and wet like droplets of mercury. I gathered up six olives and a handful of salami and sunk into the couch. Pulled a bowl of chips towards me. If I was going to do this, I was going to do it surrounded by my faithful brothers – meat, salt and imitation alcohol. The lights were hot.

'So Imogen tells us you're on the Sydney Parks Strangler case, Frank?'

'I'm one of the members of a task force charged with that, yes.'

'How intriguing.' Kim sat back in the armchair nearest to me, adjusted her stockings at the knee. 'You've got to give us the lowdown. What are the major leads?'

'I read in the paper you don't think it's a man. Is that right?'

'Well, there's no evidence thus far to suggest –'

'I don't think it's a man either,' Deepa said, barely managing to swallow her wine before the words were out of her mouth. 'The faces. It's very personal. Identity-driven, not power-driven. Sociopathic, rather than psychosexual, if you ask me.'

'Oh, here we go. She'll be quoting Wilhelm Reich in a minute. It's always Reich with her.'

'You're a psychologist too?' I asked. Where was all my beer going? I glanced at Imogen helplessly but she ignored me.

'We're all psychologists,' Deepa smiled.

'Oh. Excellent.'

'Imogen's the only law enforcement specialist among us,' Kim said, letting one of her navy blue velvet slip-ons slide off one heel. 'The only one with murderous interests.'

'When we heard she'd snagged you off the client list we were so excited,' Deepa grinned.

'Yes, off the client list,' Shauna tutted at Imogen. 'Naughty, naughty.'

'We'd love to hear about some of your cases.'

'Yeah,' Erica breathed. 'The really bad ones.'

'Tell them about the chainsaw guy,' Imogen said. A low moan of excitement rose around me. I felt Imogen's hands on my shoulders, trying to massage them but only succeeding in making them tighter. 'I love that one.'

I wasn't sure exactly what was happening here, and felt strangely wary that it was some sort of test. In a room full of psychologists, I was being asked to rank my case history from 'best' to 'worst'. It was a bizarre request. Yes, indeed, there were good days and bad days. Exciting days and boring days. But that there could be a 'best' among my cases, a story that could be 'loved', was beyond my understanding. Murder simply was to me. As meat was to a butcher. It came and it went. Some of it was easy to manage, some of it was more difficult. It was the material that I worked with. There was no value system attached to it. Especially the kind of value system that would rank the 'really bad ones' as the 'best'. I'd seen the aftermath when a mother drowned her three kids in the family bathtub, one at a time, like kittens, while her husband was up the street getting milk. That was bad. Really bad. My ex-girlfriend had been found disembowelled centre stage in a room painted with her blood. The attending officer had actually used the word 'painted' in the police report. That was bad. Really bad. Were these my 'best'?

Sometimes I wondered about Imogen and her propensity to burst out with a sick kind of enthusiasm for homicide detection, like it was some fantasy job she'd always wanted. Did she want to be a cop? Sometimes I could tell she was pretending not to be interested in details about some of my past cases, and sometimes she overtly tried to squeeze them out of me, the way she was doing now. It was strange.

Everyone was staring at me.

'Uh,' I scratched my head. 'The chainsaw one?'

'A bunch of twenty-year-olds are holding a work party at Palmer & Co. You know Palmer & Co?' Imogen spread her hands theatrically.

'Oh, I know that one.'

'I love that place.'

'Well, these kids are having a party there. A dress-up party. There's, like, fifteen of them, all went to uni together, all work for the same company. They're mostly film buffs, so they decide the party'll have a theme. Favourite horror flick.'

I looked around. All eyes were on Imogen. I wondered if I could slip away to get another beer. I looked past Kim into the kitchen. The lovely beers. She caught my eye and slow-winked.

'This idiot kid turns up with a real chainsaw.'

'Oh Jesus, no way.'

'What horror film is that?'

'*Texas Chainsaw Massacre*. God you're slow, Deepa.'

'When was this?'

'Last year.'

'Oh man, I think I read about that.'

I squeezed out from between the couch cushions, almost tripped on Kim's legs. Grabbed a handful of chips on my way to the kitchen. Imogen's voice was everywhere, inescapable.

'The bar staff doesn't even notice it's the real thing. They just think it's a convincing prop. Next thing you know, half the guys at the party are on ecstasy and someone grabs hold of the chainsaw and fires it up, like it's a joke, swings it around. He's high as a kite, doesn't know what he's doing, and some kid gets his fucking arm lopped off. Chainsaw goes in at the armpit, comes out at the neck, hacks the whole thing off like a chicken wing. Kid bleeds to death on the floor before anyone's even called it in.'

There were collective squeals of horror and delight. I went to the fridge and stood in the cool, looking at the beers. The fingers of my right hand had started twitching. Something had awakened the old gunshot wound in my shoulder, got it toying with the nerves down my arm. I reached for the beer, then suddenly didn't feel like it. It felt good to be in the light and the chill. I closed my eyes and just stood there, bathed in the gentle hum of the machine. Things had quietened in the other room.

'I mean, how do you say conclusively if that's murder or not?'

'Sounds like an accident to me.'

'Ah, but the plot thickens. Sounds like an accident – until you take into account the guy's long-standing grudge against the victim. His history of mental illness. Rumours around the office that he'd said he was going to "get" the victim. That his "days were numbered".'

More sighs and groans of intrigue.

I left quietly through the front door.

When I arrived at my terrace home, all the lights were on. I stood in the street and asked myself whether or not I could be bothered going into defensive mode, whether I had the strength to round the back of the house, come through the gate to the small yard. Make sure I knew who was in my house before whoever it was knew that I knew, in case some harm was being planned for me. Then I realised that I was standing crookedly, the weight of the day heavy in my shoulders and that, in this state, if someone meant to harm me they were probably going to succeed whether I surprised them or not. I spotted Greycat on the roof at the same time that he spotted me, and watched him trundle down the railings and gutters and sills that marked his path to the first floor, then the ground floor. He didn't seem concerned with the state of the house. I decided the builders had left the lights on.

The front door was unlocked and Rachmaninoff was playing somewhere. I only knew it because my father had been a big fan. The hall walls were also a soft mustard yellow. I stood looking at them, at the cream trim and skirting boards. A great hole that had been punched in the wall directly opposite the front bedroom door had been patched and filled. The ceiling wasn't painted, but holes it in had been filled also.

'Eden?' I called.

'Yuh,' she said.

I found her on the living-room floor, following the ornate skirting board along with that glossy cream paint from the hall. She'd done these walls yellow too. Though she was wearing old jeans and a man's shirt, there wasn't a fleck of paint on her. Not one. I'd never met anyone who could paint like that. When I painted, I was still picking it out of my hair three weeks later.

'This was all supposed to be blue,' I said.

'I know,' she said. I sat down near her and watched her paint. She was right about the colours. Women are usually right about colours. The room was warmer than it had been. It was a soft green when I bought it, and I picked pale blue simply because it seemed like the safest colour for the place. The yellow would have been too bold for me. But the lamps the builders had set up lit it gold. It was very homey, but it felt somehow expensive, seemed to fit the period architecture. The ceiling mouldings popped out of the yellow like well-kept teeth. They were walls that wanted art now. Yearned for classy oils. Greycat slipped through the front door and brushed against Eden's side, flopped down on the bare hard boards and started grooming himself.

I didn't know what Eden was doing in my house painting the walls while I wasn't there, making sure I didn't choose the wrong colours. I didn't know why she'd come that first day and helped me put my kitchen cupboards together. There were plenty of reasons she might. She might be genuinely worried that I'd mis-wire something, burn the place down and kill myself, thereby leaving her to catch the Sydney Parks Strangler by herself. Leave her to answer questions about why two of her detective partners and her brother had all met the same fate in a matter of months. Then again, she might just have been bored, lonely, unable to sleep – her own apartment already perfect and crammed with art she'd never sell. She might have been drawn to broken things, things in need of rescue, the way her father was. My house might have stirred the desire for some of that old Hades-style resurrection in her.

It was also possible she was trying to be close to me. Not sexually, or even emotionally, just proximity-wise. Because she couldn't ignore the fact that we needed to talk seriously and openly about her being a monster, about how long I was expected to sit by with the knowledge that she took lives, had taken lives, had taken one right in front of me, exchanging it for mine. I wasn't over that. I wasn't over the moment I let myself go and murdered Jason Beck for what he did to my girlfriend. I had given things up in those heated few milliseconds – my career, my freedom, my sanity. And then Eden had scooped all those things up from the ash and handed them back to me. I owed her. But I couldn't live like this forever. Trusting my life to her all day long and then dreaming of her coming after me all night. Eden reminded me of those trashy American documentaries I sometimes caught on weekends about people living in the Midwest who kept adult chimpanzees as pets. Hugging them and feeding them junk food and dressing them up in clothes, calling them members of the family. Denying, but knowing, deep inside somewhere, it's more than likely that one day they will turn on you. That they will surrender to the animal inside.

You can only play human for so long, and though she was very convincing, I was sure I saw flashes of something inhuman in Eden sometimes. Something cruel.

But watching her paint, so serene, so detached, I felt reluctant to ruin things right at that moment. She shifted carefully along the floor, painted the trim to the corner, sat stroking the brush along with her back to me, tendrils of hair falling from a knot at the top of her head down and around her slender neck.

When I couldn't stay awake any longer, I followed the cat to my bed.

The wake was the first time Tara thought about killing her mother. She realised one night lying on her side in the bed, her hands slippery around the marshmallow rice bar packet, that mothers were things other things came out of. The pod that released seeds into the wind. The vessel that carried small, warm, wet circular balls of life. But Joanie wasn't a vessel or a pod – she wasn't hollow. She didn't look hollow. Tara examined her on one of their hellish treks through the darkened park as she waited in the light of a street lamp, her hard ribs and flat stomach, the bellybutton stretched taut into a horizontal line over the abdominal muscles. Nothing but thin layers of skin between the surface of her and the sinew beneath. When she breathed, nothing moved – the skin didn't slide up and down the ribs like it did with other skeleton people Tara had observed, the ribs expanding and contracting around air. She didn't sweat. There was no reservoir of fluid inside her to tap. She was a stone woman. There wasn't room inside her for air, or blood or life. Or weakness. Tara didn't know where she had come from but she was sure she hadn't come from inside Joanie. There was no inside Joanie.

The wake was an uproarious affair, as far as she could tell. She lay on the floor and listened to the noise beyond the stairwell, the shrill laughter and occasional singing, the low bubbly hum like the noises of a busy kitchen, clattering and hissing. At some point, the household was called together and a silence fell over them all.

Tara strained to hear what was said about her father. It was mostly men who spoke about him. The distinct absence of female voices struck Tara. She had only been to one funeral before as a small child and the one thing she remembered about it was the women. All their talking and crying. But that night it was men who held the floor. Tara lay down on the carpet and put her ear to the crack in the wood beneath and listened. She only heard snippets, but snippets were all she had ever known of her own father. Glimpses of him around doorways, flashes of him at the bottom of the stairs as he headed out to the radio station at night, as he wheeled his bags to the airport taxi in the pale blue of early dawn. His voice, low and heavy, on the phone in the yard. Tara closed her eyes and collected the words of the men downstairs.

Quiet. Heart. Big. Shadow. Drifting. Drifting man.

A drifting man. He had been to them what he had been to Tara, a dark, half-captured spectre forever on the way to somewhere or on the way from somewhere but never here, never settled, tangible.

Time.

A man inside time. Constantly pushed forward or pulled back by it, the time remaining to do something, get somewhere. Joanie had always talked to Tara about her father in terms of time and what time did to him, and it seemed somehow that it was Tara's fault – she had taken the time from her father, that whatever there was of it left was squeezed out by her bulk, so that the man had moments, only moments. The edge around the life he might have lived here. There was too much Tara for him to really find a place in the big house. He spent his life in hotels in the city rather than here in the brightly lit rooms. When he came home he would take off his huge watch first and put it somewhere, on the edge of the dining-room table or next to the bed so that the time was never far away.

He doesn't have time for . . .

He can't waste his time with . . .

Every time he looks at you.

Every time.

There had never been a time in Michael Harper's life that Tara wasn't what she was. She wondered if there had been more of it left, if there could have been a moment one day, after Joanie perhaps, that Tara and her father could have had time. But it was all gone, and only the drifting had punctuated it, the ghostly big man laying eyes on her for a second, mumbling, while the driver lifted his luggage out to the car.

'Tar.' He'd nodded, the last time she had seen him. She didn't know when. 'Didn't catch you. You're looking –'

He'd gazed at her feet and left. You're looking. He'd always spoken, whenever she saw him, about how she looked, because that was all he knew about her. That's all there was to know really, in the end. Joanie always made sure she knew that. She was only her body and her body could squeeze men from their very homes.

Every time he looks at you.

She went down into the kitchen when darkness had descended over the house, crept over to the back windows and gazed at the yard, the glasses lying in the bushes and the possums dancing in the trees, gleeful. The huge kitchen island was cluttered with platters half-heartedly covered with aluminium foil. Pancetta-wrapped prawns spotted with pieces of black char, dripping oil. Wedges of fruit on wilted fingers of rocket. Tara peeled back the foil on one of the platters and found a group of cold meat pies in a corner like magic stones, a golden pyramid. She put one in her mouth without realising it, until the salty taste of it was at the back of her teeth, mush on her gums. Sucking. Sucking. Daddy's wake pies. This was what a dead father tasted like, salty and slightly warm like a bed only recently left and then returned to. Safe. Yes, there was a safety in his death. The haunting shadow was now gone. His eyes on her feet. Tara put another pie into her mouth and closed her lips around it, closed her eyes.

She didn't know him but she could taste him. His ashes.

Tara didn't notice the woman in the doorway until she spoke. Tara opened her eyes, and took in the lanky figure leaning there, the nimble folded arms swathed in black satin, the dramatically painted eyes. She was an unfamiliar but beautiful creature, a ginger cat-woman who'd wandered in from the lightly falling rain.

'You must be her,' the woman said. Tara felt the same strange infatuation she felt the time she laid eyes on Violet all those years ago, the loving revulsion that had swelled in her stomach when she realised, almost in the same instant, that to love someone was to lose them. Tara didn't have friends. Joanie made sure of it.

'Come here,' the mystery woman said, smiling. Tara did as she was told, following the cat-woman into the hall. She put a hand on Tara's shoulder and the girl shivered with pleasure. *Touch me. Touch me again*, she thought.

'I used to work with your mother,' the woman said. 'Before Michael. Before the money.'

'Work?' Tara trembled. 'What do you mean? She's never –'

'Yeah,' the woman laughed. 'Never. That's where all the details of Joanie's life before Michael live. In the never-never. You've got it exactly right, my love.'

Tara followed the woman to the sideboard where the collection of photographs lived. Twenty frames of different shapes and sizes. Joanie and Michael in Barcelona. Joanie and Michael in Nigeria. Joanie and Michael in Paris. And then there were others. His family. His mother. His grandmother. His father staring out the windows of his first office building.

The mystery woman smiled at Tara, then began to rearrange the photographs. She collected them all up into her arms, and started to set them on the table in a single line.

Gregory Harper. Tall. Thin. Blond.

Marilyn Harper. Short. Thin. Blonde.

Jessica and Steven Harper. Tall. Thin. Blond.

Joanie Harper. Tall. Thin. Blonde.

Michael Harper. Tall. Thin. Blond.

Tara Harper. Short. Fat. Raven-haired.

The girl in the hallway trembled, looked at the woman with the dark eyes whose name she would never learn.

'It's not about your body, baby girl,' the woman said. 'It's about your blood.'

The girl and the woman turned as they heard an exhalation. Beyond the door where Joanie stood seething, the wake raged on, people laughing and singing and glasses breaking, the occasional wail of surprise at a story told or a secret shared. But Joanie marked the door to a bubble of hatred that encapsulated Tara and the woman with the photographs. Tara watched the woman set the rest of the photographs down, smiling smugly, and head towards the huge front doors.

Before she left, she turned back and winked.

When I woke, Eden was gone and Hooky was there, standing on my porch in a long black T-shirt with 'Jumping Croc Tours' emblazoned on it and the right shoulder poetically ripped. There was a black-and-white croc on her chest reaching for a slab of chicken dangled off the side of a crowded boat. I realised that I was standing dumbly holding the door open and looking at her chest and that I was shirtless. I felt uncomfortable. Yes, uncomfortable. Strange and weird and out of sorts with a teenage girl who I'd never had anything but a healthy and wholesome sibling-like relationship with. For a second I hated Imogen for threatening to ruin what Hooky and I had. It was a weird way to be, that early in the morning. Luckily, Hooky didn't catch on to any of it.

'Want to go to the morgue with me?' she asked, like a kid asking another kid to go down to the river and play. I almost felt like turning and asking my mother's permission.

'What do I want to go to the morgue for?'

'Ah, because it's awesome there?' Hooky frowned quizzically, as though I'd asked where the sky was.

'I've got homework,' I said.

'This'll help with the homework.' She smiled.

I shrugged and went back into the house to get my shirt.

*

I drove Hooky to the Glebe Morgue, past the huge cheese-grater shaped University of Technology and its towering sister apartment building dripping with greenery and hanging vines. The two buildings hugging Broadway made for strange partners, one lush and alive, one decidedly lethal looking. Students flooded the intersections as we stopped at the lights, shrouded in touches of the absurd – fluffy penguin hats and bell-bottoms, the occasional sequined dress. One or two were barefoot. Hooky's peers. She looked at them in a kind of bemused way. It seemed to me that Hooky stood apart from them as she had her high-school mates, apart and above, bored by assessment tasks and exams and apparent social pressures – stuck between the nerdy union kids in suits and the dope smokers on the verge of dropping out and flopping out. I hoped they didn't bully her the way she'd been bullied as a kid. When her sister did what she did, Hooky ceased to be the Hooky she'd been to her classmates. All the joy and irresponsibility was dead. I'd seen it happen to kids before, seen them become ghosts in young bodies. The others don't like it. They start pecking at the strange birds in their nest, instinctively, trying to weed out the different.

'Does Imogen know Eden?' Hooky asked suddenly. I was fiddling with the radio station. I'd just missed the news.

'Ah, yes. Vaguely. Eden and I were in tandem therapy with Imogen. I know. It's weird.'

'They call that transference.'

'What?'

'Psychology patients falling in love with their doctors,' Hooky said. 'In the discipline they call it transference.'

'In my discipline, we call it "punching above your weight",' I laughed. She didn't.

'The patients redirect their feelings away from what they're dealing with and onto to the psychologist during psychotherapy,' she continued. 'They get all wrapped up in the care and consideration they get from their psychologist and they emotionally attach. Try to take it beyond the professional setting. Psychologists are supposed to keep an eye out for it. Make sure they don't take advantage of their patients while they're vulnerable.'

'I quite enjoy being taken advantage of.'

'So the two of them only know each other through therapy.'

'Yes, Eden and Imogen are certainly not friends,' I said. I remembered the evening at Malabar and cringed, turning off Parramatta Road and onto Ross Street. 'Why?'

'I was just wondering how it all fits together,' Hooky shrugged.

People assume morgues are gloomy places, full of the reservation and reflection people associate with death. But they're not. Sure, the building is stuffed with dead people in various states of assembly, but being depressed about it all day long makes for a fairly unsustainable workplace for the administration officers, pathologists, forensic scientists and nurses who work there. The first time I entered a morgue as a young police officer I was struck by the presence of a vending machine just inside the automatic doors. A vending machine? The idea that people would casually munch a Mars bar standing over the mangled body of a stranger, or grab a Coke before they go in to carve out semi-decayed livers and weigh them on scales, just boggled my mind. But they do. People do eat Mars bars at work, even when their work is with cadavers. They also gossip, laugh, play pranks on each other and decorate their little workspaces with happy pictures and fuzzy pens. They play music. They text and take smoke breaks. It's just like any other workplace.

Just outside the automatic doors, I stopped Amy on the stairs. 'Now look. You'll probably want to make a lot of hilarious puns in here,' I gestured towards the doors. 'But there are tons of them, and I know them all, and they can take a long time. So we ought to get them out of the way before we go in so that we don't waste time.' I rolled my shoulders. 'Gee, this is the dead centre of town, isn't it?' I said. 'Well, this is anything but a dead-end job. Oh dear, my back's feeling a bit stiff. This is a great place, people must be just dying to get in here. Care for a drink after work? Maybe some spirits?'

Amy looked at me.

'If you wanted to contribute,' I informed her, 'you could say something like "Oh stop, Frank, you're killing me!"'

She went inside.

I've known Carrie, the receptionist, for years, but I was surprised when she put the sign-in clipboard on the counter and smiled at my young partner with recognition.

'How you going, Amy?'

'No complaints.'

'Well, aren't you full of surprises?' I squinted at Hooky. 'What have you been doing hanging around my morgue?'

'Your morgue?' Carrie laughed.

'Research,' Amy said.

'She's dead serious about her research, Frank.' Carrie struggled to keep a straight face.

'Oh, nice delivery on that one, Carrie. Absolutely deadpan.'

'Excuse me, won't you?' Amy sighed. 'I'm going down to Lab 16, Carrie.'

Amy turned and walked down the wide hall. I followed her, soaking up the hospital disinfectant stink. People don't like that smell, but I've never minded it. It reminds me of when my dad was dying. All the treats and attention I got, the sense of newness in the air that surrounded his passing. He wasn't a nice guy.

'How long have you been coming here?' I asked.

'I drop in and out,' she said.

'And what exactly have you been telling them that has convinced them to let you in here?' I asked.

'This and that,' she said.

'You're creeping farther and farther into murder police territory, Hooky bird,' I said, after quietly considering whether I would raise the issue. 'It's a long way from what you're approved for with the department.'

'So I'm allowed to let creeps show me porn all night long but I'm not allowed to look at stiffs? That makes sense.'

'It depends on the porn.'

'Officially, I'm not approved to do that either, I'll remind you.'

'I was going to ask you about that. The chiefs know you're doing that sort of work in the offices. But was that screenshot I saw yesterday from your personal computer? Because it had some very questionable chat group names on the bottom of the screen.'

Hooky walked. She said nothing.

'You're not going off on your own to chase these guys down, are you?'

'So what if I am? It's the same thing I do in the office with a bunch of cops gawking at me. I still hand the guys in to the chiefs. I just don't do all the bullshit reporting and filling out of forms.'

'Oh Jesus, Hooky,' I moaned. 'You're too big for your own boots.'

'My mother used to say that.'

I bit my tongue. I let a minute of silence pass, in which I tried to remember that Hooky was not my child and if she got her privileges at the department stripped for overstepping her bounds, there was nothing I could do to stop it. She was as stubborn as an ox.

'Homicide is different. Very different. And if you think you can mess around and play games with your sex crimes resources, you cannot do that here.'

'You and Eden are the only ones really aware of what I'm doing, Frank,' she said. 'No one's going to kick up a stink.'

'What if I kick up a stink?' I said.

'You won't.'

'Look.' I took her arm. 'I know you can get yourself anywhere you want to go. You've proven it, to everyone. No one can stop you going after what you want, and that's fine – you've earned that. You're brilliant at what you do, so people bend the rules and look the other way for you sometimes. But that doesn't mean some of us shouldn't try to stop you when you wander into dangerous territory. I'm worried about you messing around over here.'

'Where? In the morgue?'

'In the morgue. At crime scenes. In the evidence files. Over here, over in homicide.'

She stopped walking and looked up at me. Ran a hand over her prickles and laughed, incredulous.

'You're quite happy to accept my assistance when I'm right, when it helps your case. But then I stray too far –'

'I'm not saying you're straying too far. I'm just saying that one of these days, you might. You might get in too deep. And I don't care how old you think you are. At the end of the day, you're seventeen years old. No amount of pretending is going to change that.'

'Do you think I'm going to be traumatised, Frank?'

'I'm traumatised.' I tapped my chest.

'Please.' She waved her hand at me, snuck me a dirty look. 'Don't play Daddy. You're no good at it.'

I couldn't control any of these women. Eden. Hooky. Imogen. None of them listened to me. I followed Amy towards Lab 16 and thought about getting angry. Sometimes getting angry with them works. Sometimes it blows up right in your face. It didn't work with Imogen. I hadn't been game to try it on Eden in case I woke up in a hole somewhere, startled by the pattering of the first shovel full of dirt on my chest. I gathered a lungful of air and put on my most determined face.

'You –' I started, as we got to the freezer doors.

'This is Jill Noble,' Hooky said, popping open one of the narrow compartments. Mist swirled around a blue tarpaulin body bag. Amy drew out the body rack and unzipped the thick black zipper on the side of the bag. 'She came in on 4 August, thirty-six days ago.'

I looked down at the passive face of Jill Noble. There was little I could tell about her from her shoulders up, other than that she'd been allowed to decompose indoors or sheltered from the elements somewhere for about a week before being snap-frozen in the state she was now. Her body had swelled and deflated again, the way it does in the first three days. One of her ears was black as coal from lividity and the cheek on that side was swollen, cloudy and dark purple. I glanced into the bag at her breasts, her left arm. She'd been lying on her side for quite a while. Her tricep was pressed flat.

'Hi, Jill,' I sighed.

'Jill Noble was the Sydney Parks Strangler's first victim,' Amy said.

'I wish everybody would stop calling him the fucking "Strangler". He sounds like a monster from a kid's movie. Watch out. It's the Strangler! It's the worst of the serial killer names.'

'How many are there?' She frowned.

'Are you kidding? There are heaps. Butcher. Slayer. Ripper. Slasher. Stalker. Werewolf.'

'Werewolf?'

'Albert Fish. The Werewolf of Wisteria.'

'Oh, right.'

'Jack Owen Spillman was the Werewolf Butcher,' I said. 'Now there's a cool name.'

Hooky sighed at me, gestured to the body, trying to get me focused. I was only playing games, I knew, because I didn't want to look at the body. I didn't want her to tell me what she was about to tell me. To make my world that much messier. I bit the bullet and took Jill's report, which was lying in a slot on the freezer door. On average, unexplained death reports are about thirty pages long, but if you know where to look you can skip all the bullshit and get right to the business of things. I checked the listed abrasions, lesions, respiratory conditions and stomach contents. Advanced ecchymosis of the left side and left hip. Lots of bruising in distinct patterns and laceration of the right kidney. No post-mortem trauma.

'Beaten to death,' I said. 'Probably a lump of wood. Our park girls were beaten and then strangled.'

'She was severely beaten. But she was beaten too bad, so there wasn't any fight left in her for the strangling.' Amy pushed Jill's matted brown hair back off her neck. There were tiny dried leaves in it. 'See here? Report says this mark is from her silver necklace lying on the right side of the neck while the body lay decomposing. A post-mortem weight trauma. But I don't think so. You look at the thickness of the necklace. Its weight. It was eight grams and very thin. I think this is ante-mortem. I think it's a light abrasion from a drawstring, a hood placed over the head.'

I looked at the mark on Jill's neck. To me, it was consistent with an abrasion rather than a weight. The first layer of skin was papery and the mark was a light pink rather than a deep purple or blue. It cut across her neck and disappeared around the front of the throat. I pulled Jill's hair up further and searched for a knot mark but there was none. If it was a drawstring it would have been loose, hastily tied.

'See here?'

'Mmm.' I ran my fingers over a dent in Jill's throat, a distinct dip in the taut skin over her jugular. 'Indentation. Could suggest post-mortem strangulation.'

'The killer tried to strangle Jill, but Jill was already dead. Her heart had stopped beating. So there's no bruising. She died too quickly.'

'So she was kidnapped, hooded, beaten with a stick. Maybe a bit of experimental strangling. Maybe. It's a bit of a stretch, Hooky.'

'Look at the date of death, though. This is the Park Strangler's first victim,' Amy said. 'If you look at the whole picture, it fits with what we know of the killer's tactics now, now that she's further along in her training. I think she hooded Jill's face for the same reason she now beats the face beyond recognition. Because she's trying to disguise the victim from herself, allow the victim to be whoever she is fantasising she's killing.'

Again, the visualisation of the killer as female. The recognition of the facial injuries as a type of revenge fantasy. Both Eden and Amy had marked the killings as the work of a woman on a woman, a living out of some attack that could, for whatever reason, not take place in reality.

'This is what I reckon. She started with an instrument to inflict her wounds,' Amy said. 'But it didn't suit the fantasy. It didn't feel right, and it killed the victim before she had a chance to get really personal – to strangle her. The hood wasn't right either. It interrupted the original fantasy. It was distracting. So when she got to Ivana Lyon she dumped the weapon and the hood and she was going at it bare handed.'

It made sense. There's plenty of research into violent fantasies that become realities. As homicide detectives, it's our job to keep updated on it all, to read the thick intellectual bile that comes out of university psychology departments trying to tell us in too many words why murderers do what they do. Violent fantasies can come from plenty of places, but most often they're the result of some kind of trauma. A person experiences a terrible trauma, either sudden or prolonged, and begins to relive the trauma over and over as a symptom of post-traumatic stress disorder. The trauma goes around and around and around in her mind, becoming more and more tangible every time it's revisited. Sometimes it can be the result of something as innocuous as living through an earthquake. The re-visualising of the earthquake becomes so real that sufferers swear they feel the ground shaking beneath them. Kids who were sexually abused can feel their abuser's hands on them. War vets have auditory hallucinations of gunfire, mates crying for help. It takes a lot of therapy to get yourself out of it. It took fast and hard therapy to make sure I didn't become gun-shy when Eden's brother Eric shot me. If you recognise the potential of a trauma when it happens, and immediately treat it, you can sometimes stave off the effects of PTSD.

Very rarely, sufferers of a traumatic event begin to add on to the revisualisation of the traumatic event. The child abusers see themselves being abused, and they extend the abuse out, turn and twist the fantasy until they become abusers themselves. The victim of workplace bullying revisits the bullying and adds himself calmly taking an AK-47 out from under his desk to the fantasy, blowing his colleagues away one by one. The fantasy, an involuntary thing, starts becoming voluntary. Enjoyable.

Ted Bundy mused in one of his last interviews before his execution that it was violent pornography, viewed very young, that had made him what he was. He hadn't realised it at the time, but his young, innocent mind had been violated by what he'd seen, and the reliving of the violence through the torture and killing of his victims was just the natural progression of his childhood trauma. I don't know about that. Bundy was an arrogant man, full of excuses. But the theory was popular. Violence breeding violence.

What had happened to the Sydney Parks Strangler? Who was she killing when she killed these girls?

'Where'd we find this victim?'

'Bradfield Park, Kirribilli,' Hooky said. 'She was under an old blanket, up against one of the bridge walls. People thought she was just a homeless person. Curled on her side, foetal position. It was three days before the smell was enough to start bothering people. Night-time boot camp groups had been exercising and jogging around the park, not a hundred metres from where she lay.'

'Completely covered up?'

'Yeah.'

It went with the theory that this was the killer's first victim. Ivana had been partly covered and hidden near bushes. Minerva had been more obvious again. The killer was getting bolder. Starting to 'come out' to us. Reveal herself to her audience.

'Was she in exercise gear?'

'Tracksuit.'

'Shit.' I felt the muscles gather at the base of my skull, preparing for the headache of a lifetime. 'Shit. Fuck. Balls.'

The difference between three victims and two in a homicide case might not seem like much on the surface of it, but in the public eye, it's huge. The first murder stirs people. The second unsettles them further. It's at this point that people can hang on to the hope that there isn't a serial killer on the loose – that in fact there's no connection between the two victims and any link police might be pointing to could be a fluke. They don't alter their behaviour. Sometimes, it doesn't even make front-page news – particularly if there's an election or a terrorist attack or some other major event. But whenever a link can be made between three homicide victims, killed separately, that's the signal for a media firestorm. For the public panic. For the condemnation of the lead detectives and their lack of progress, no matter how much progress has been made. The fact that Jill Noble was victim number one and we hadn't been right onto it was equally bad news.

I zipped up Jill's body bag and closed the freezer as though by containing Jill's body I could contain what it meant. 'This is on the down-low until further notice, Hook.' I pointed at her face so she knew I was serious. She shrugged.

'Good luck keeping this under wraps,' Hooky said. 'You know. I know. Carrie at the desk knows. The victim's family will talk to the media, and they'll know.'

'We can try,' I said. I took out my phone and called Eden.

As I was putting my keys into the door of my car I heard Caroline Eckhart's voice behind me. For a moment, I had to take stock of where I was. Turning and seeing her there, outside the low brown brick building that housed the morgue, was bizarre. There were no cameras in tow, but she was still wearing that running gear – the midnight-black Catwoman suit and blazing lime-green shoes. She had her hands in the front pockets of a shimmering black windcheater and I could see the outline of her knuckles and a phone. I wondered if she was recording me.

'Frank,' she said. 'Can we talk?'

'No,' I said. 'No, thanks. I think I've had enough front pages.'

I unlocked the car and gestured to Amy. She didn't get in. Unlike kids to want to be right where the drama is.

'I just want to talk.'

'There'll be no talking, witch. Begone!' I waved my arm. 'You have no power here!'

Hooky sniggered and got into the car.

'Why has George Hacker been released from custody?'

'Who?'

'George Hacker.' Caroline widened her eyes, scoffed theatrically, as though working up a crowd that hadn't arrived yet. 'The one and only lead your people have had on the Strangler so far.'

'Try to keep up. George Hacker is nothing but a creep. He's not the . . . Strangler. God, it even hurts me to say the word. George can barely tie his own shoelaces. But speaking of being a creep, did you know that the legal definition of stalking in New South Wales includes one or more acts of unwanted following, or a similar intimidatory behaviour, such as the unwanted loitering near, watching or approaching a person? I looked that up last night, in case this happened again.' I pointed to her, to myself. 'Impressive, aren't I?'

I could see Caroline's camera crew getting out of their cars on the corner. They'd struggled to find parking spaces, and she'd taken the opportunity to snag me before I drove away. I got into the car and started it up.

'Why are you visiting the morgue today, Frank?' She tapped on my window. 'Are Ivana and Minerva here?'

As I drove away, I felt my stomach sinking. Ivana and Minerva were still at the police morgue. If Caroline went and started hassling Carrie at the reception desk, her journalist buddies might be able to wrangle out of the woman which lab we'd visited and who was there. There was nothing I could legally do to stop them. News of a third victim would be on the television by the evening.

'Who is that chick?' Amy sneered.

'Nobody,' I said. 'She's a dead-set nobody.'

Hades thought the dog would probably die. He wasn't sure, with dogs. As a child, living in a brothel in the backstreets of Darlinghurst, he'd had plenty of birds die in his hands from running into windows, being buffeted by cars, being shoved out of nests too young. A bird got a funny look to it when its organs began to slowly shut down – seemed dazed, somehow, as though its quick little mind was elsewhere. When he lifted the tiny heads by the beak and they began to slowly sink down into their feathered chests, that's when he knew it was over. The child Hades had always consoled himself that he at least gave them warm and pleasant deaths in small boxes in the greenhouse, tucked under the work bench, where the wild cats that roamed Darlinghurst couldn't get them.

But he hadn't been close with dogs, not since he'd been pushed into a pit with two of them as a ten- or eleven-year-old and had his forearms stripped near to the bone by their ravenous teeth. He'd ended up killing the two huge beasts with his bare hands, a public feat that would strike almost supernatural fear into the city during his reign as criminal king of Sydney. Lord of the Underworld. Hades wasn't afraid of dogs, far from it. But now and then when he saw one in the tip's wilder parts, he remembered that night in the pit.

Dingo-dog hybrids had provided a natural alarm system at Utulla for many years and kept the stray cat and fox numbers down. But Hades didn't tempt them towards the house, as he sometimes did with the possums that clambered around his sculptures. It was better that the hounds stayed out there, in the dark.

Those night creatures were a far cry from the dog in Hades' kitchen. It was a cross also, but had some more prestigious breeds in it. It had the burned gold colour of a Weimaraner, with the sad, delicate look of a whippet. The pink nose was a mystery. It was an expensive dog, probably had a stupid 'innovation' breed name. Whipparaner. Weimarippet. The expense, the youth of the thing. There were the bills and notes in the trash – the garbage had come from an expensive area. The callousness had stunned the vengeful tip workers who discovered the thing in the bag.

Hades could understand rich people starving a dog. Rich or poor, he'd seen people do all kinds of things in his time. Cruelty had nothing to do with money, and lots to do with selfishness, carelessness, irresponsibility. The dog had probably been forgotten a series of times, accidentally at first, and then half-deliberately out of sheer laziness, spite, punishment for the chewed-up shoes or the pissed-on couch. The thing was probably very cute as a newborn but in time failed to naturally assume the behaviour of dogs that were professionally trained. Refused to sit. Didn't answer to its name. It was punished, left behind while its owners worked, took drugs, travelled, stayed over with friends. Three days turned into four. Bored and looking for sustenance, the thing had probably trashed the house a few too many times, had its living areas reduced to a small laundry room where the sound system drowned out its wailing. And then suddenly, one day, without any real warning, the dog went from skinny to dying. Visibly, undeniably, shockingly dying – beyond what a vet could fix without having to report the animal's condition. The dog was binned. A broken toy.

Hades sat looking at the thing in the basket at the foot of the couch – or what he could see of it, the snout jutting from the wicker rim in case any more slices of soft red roast beef came floating by as they sometimes did. He also fed it with syringes full of water or milk with honey. The dog was still eating, but that meant nothing. Birds ate right up until the moment the light faded from their eyes. Hades was certain that activity was a good predictor of the animal's chances, and the dog hadn't moved in two days, not so much as shifted its position in the basket. Hades hadn't seen its full body, in fact, since the moment he first picked it up. That wasn't good. If the thing had been a horse, he'd have shot it by now. When horses lie down, they stay down.

Hades knew his tip workers had the address of the people who owned the dog. He knew there was nothing he could do to stop them enacting their vengeance. Whoever they were, they would probably venture out to a nightclub or a restaurant over the weekend, and a couple of big dirty men smelling faintly of garbage would bash them up. There would be no reason given. No words said.

Hades could warn his workers against it. Tell them vengeance was hardly ever worth the trouble taken to apply it. It was a lesson he'd learned with difficulty as a young man.

But they wouldn't listen, so he wouldn't bother. Young, angry men listened to no one.

The old man turned at the sound of the fire alarm bell above the front door. A car had entered the tip grounds. He glanced at the collection of clocks at the entrance to the hall. There were fifteen clocks of differing sizes and styles, cuckoo clocks and stainless-steel postmodern clocks, plastic clocks and an old bedside alarm clock hung by a string. Averaging their times, Hades guessed it was about seven. He hoped his evening visitor wasn't Eden. She only came unannounced these days when something was wrong.

It was a woman approaching. Hades could hear that much from the difficulty of her heels on the gravel. He didn't get up. Beside him on the tabletop, as always, lay a pistol, concealed in the glossy fold of some magazine or another. Hades shifted the magazine a little closer and turned his coffee cup handle towards himself, sloshing the cooling brown liquid in its base.

A short silhouette appeared against the diamond wire of the screen door. Hades took his glasses from beside his cup. The visitor rapped.

'It's open,' he called.

The woman approached with a smile. This puzzled Hades. Unexpected clients were usually shaking and blood-spattered, still wired from the drug pick-up gone wrong or long-awaited gang hit or botched robbery that had brought them there. Unexpected clients came to him in every variety of panic, some crying and begging for advice, some with a mere clenched jaw to indicate the turmoil within. The woman came down the hall and stood behind the chair opposite Hades, not offering her hand, which was also odd, her eyes half-hidden in the shadow of thick chocolate brown bangs, concealed further by black-rimmed glasses. Hades smiled. Was this Eden's hunter?

'Heinrich Archer.' The woman finally offered her hand. 'I'm Bridget Faulkner.'

The name was fake. She was too heavy on the 'd' in Bridget and the 'l' in Faulkner to have said it a hundred thousand times over the span of a life. Fake names were best kept phonetically simple. She wasn't a practised liar, or if she was, she was nervous – had overthought her moves. Hades felt the first tingles of apprehension, and not a little excitement, on the nape of his leathery old neck, the hackles rising on an ageing wolf.

'I'm so sorry about the hour.'

'Please, Ms Faulkner,' Hades smiled, 'it's been years since I've been able to boast of lady visitors in the night hours. How can I help you?'

She laughed, wiggled uncomfortably a little at not having been offered a chair. Hades gestured to the seat across from him, and she took it with a sigh of relief.

'I'm a journalist with the *Herald*,' she said. 'I'm trying to round up a few sources for a feature on Kings Cross in the late 1970s. I was wondering if you could help? I understand you sometimes speak to journalists . . . about your time there.'

This woman was a very poor impersonator, Hades thought. He'd met enough journalists to know their tics, their little insecurities. Where was the notebook? Where was the recorder? Every journalist Hades had met had an elaborate title that set them apart from the other guppies in the crowded tank. Head Crime Correspondent. Assistant Lifestyle Features Editor. Government Policies Analyst. Where was all the pomp and ceremony? Hades reminded himself not to be too disarmed. It was possible Ms Faulkner, whoever she was, was a fool, or took Hades himself for a fool. Her glance towards the folded magazine beside him suggested the latter. How long would it be before this half-baked imposter got to her real purpose? Hades thought that now she'd spied the gun under the magazine, the pretty little woman would want to work fast.

'Oh dear, ancient history,' Hades smiled. 'Aren't you *Herald* people done with that yet? I thought there was a Cross piece just last year around this time.'

'Well, you know. It never loses its interest. We're trying to bolster intrigue for a couple of upcoming TV series.'

'Yes, I've seen snippets of some of those shows. Very drama-tic. I only wish the times themselves had been so exciting. So effortlessly profitable.'

She laughed, put her hands on the table, seemed in need of something. Hades took his coffee cup.

'Can I offer you a drink, Ms Faulkner? Coffee? Tea?'

'Oh no, thank you.'

'Mind if I get myself one?'

'Go ahead.' She had a pleasant, if crooked, smile. Her mouth was dry, the painted lips sticking to her teeth, making noises as they came unstuck. Lying either took a lot of practice, or it was natural – came with the biology of sociopaths and psychopaths and babies born with enough violence-induced chemicals in their systems to have that ability ingrained in their survival mechanisms. Hades went to the counter, turned his back to the woman, almost felt her eyeing the gun before her. He took another weapon from inside a ceramic pot marked 'Tea'. Flicked the switch on the kettle.

'It must have been a long road from what we know about your time as a crime lord to suburban family man,' Ms Faulkner said gently. Hades poured the water into his cup, watched the black grounds shrink and dissolve.

'People grow. They change,' Hades said.

'You're in your twilight years, if you don't mind me saying,' the woman continued. 'When you were the age your daughter is now, you had a stranglehold on Sydney. You had bikies and drug dealers and hitmen in terror of you. Eden, on the other hand, is a police officer. Her brother was too. What an interesting turn of events.'

'Indeed,' Hades said.

'She must have been a very different child to the one you were.'

'Oh, I wouldn't say that.'

'What was Eden like as a child?' Ms Faulkner asked.

Hades turned. Put a hand on the counter near the gun. In the other, he held his coffee. The woman calling herself Bridget Faulkner had turned in her chair, one foot out as though ready to spring to her feet. One hand was on the table. Did she know that Hades knew who she was, what she was – a threat to his child, to himself, to everything he had built? Could she see in his eyes now that, if it came down to it, he would never let anything destroy that, that he was prepared to make his front door the last door this woman would ever step through alive? Did she see the fierce paternal fury of a lion in him? Or did she just figure him for a tired old man, someone whose befuddlement at questions about Eden's first false years would tick boxes on her stupid little quest for the truth. Hades looked at his coffee.

'It was very stupid of you to come here alone, Ms Faulkner,' he said. Out of the corner of his eye, he registered the slightest twitch in her body, a sort of electric pulse as his words coursed through her. The veils were dropped.

'What if I'm not alone?'

'Oh, you are,' Hades said gently. 'We both know you are.'

'I just want answers.'

'You want money.'

'Why did you kill the Tanners?' Bridget said. Her jaw twitched repetitively as her back teeth ground with terror. 'Why did you take their children?'

Hades licked his lower lip. Gripping the edge of the counter, he put his coffee down.

'Does Eden know who she is?' Bridget asked.

The man and the woman paused, looked at each other across the yawning silence. The howl of one of the tip dogs seemed to mark the abandoning of civilities. Hades reached for his gun. As he did, Bridget's hand slipped beneath the magazine and clumsily brought the pistol's aim around to him.

Hades fired with his eyes open. The woman fired with her eyes closed, an accidental gesture, her terror at the sound of Hades' blast making her entire body clench. Her gun blasted out the window behind him. Her sharp, squinting cower at the sound turned her head away from his aim, caused his bullet to shunt into the wall by her ear. She gathered her resolve and tried to fire again without drawing the hammer back, clicked helplessly, then dropped the gun. She tried to run and he lunged, his weapon slipping from his fingers. He heard his own yelp of agony as old wounds awakened, his ancient body unused to panicked action. They struggled for the pistol on the counter, sent it clattering into the sink. She grabbed the coffee cup, broke it over him, splashed boiling water on his arms, hands, chest, her own hands. She growled. Frightened. Angry with herself.

Hades swiped at her with one arm as he went down and knocked her away from the sink. On his hands and knees, a figure shifted past him, bright and fast like a flicker of light.

The old man had never heard such a noise. The high, squealing bark of an animal giving itself over to the violence in its heart. The dog flew at the woman in the kitchen, frenzied, jaws snapping with rage. Hades turned and watched it back the woman into the wall, watched it chase her into the darkness before the door.

He barely heard the door open and close, the car beyond. The woman gone, the dog gave her a few warning barks from behind the screen, then erupted into terrified squealing, skittering back to Hades, cowering with its head tucked completely between its front legs and tail almost invisible between its hind quarters, wagging against its belly. The dog's eyes were remorseful slits, its ears flat against its skull, bracing for a blow. Have I done the right thing? The dog squealed its strange apologies, fell dramatically on its front paws beside him, surrendered.

'Good dog,' Hades panted, trying to unlock his clenched fists. The animal licked his arm, shoulder, ear, whimpering with delight at his words. 'Good dog.'

Eden didn't spend a lot of time imagining herself as a victim. It wasn't really in her nature. She assumed that when her parents had been murdered was the time to form her childish conception of victimhood. The moment to discover the benefits so many lifelong victims became addicted to – the attention, the comfort, the slow, heroic climb of recovery, little encouragements treasured along the way. But something had gone wrong that night as she sat on the table in Hades' kitchen and let him wash the blood from her face. Something had failed to connect. Psychiatrists would say that her neurological pathways leading that way, towards victimhood, were damaged or non-existent. A priest would say she had half a soul. But whatever the case, Eden had picked up her life again the next day, mildly afraid of the man who had become her new guardian, concerned whether her brother would survive, whether she would have to face this strange new life alone. She was nothing of the victim. She wondered if, even then, there'd been too much of the natural predator in her to really know how victimhood worked.

Had the night her parents died made Eden what she was? Or had the malevolent thing that made her kill always curled inside her, sleeping, until the sound of the guns shook it awake?

Had it been Hades who made her what she was? Or if, by some twist of fate, she and Eric had survived the night of their parents' murders but ended up in the care of a regular person, might they have ever killed? Did her parents' murders open the door on who Eden was, or close it?

Over the birthmark that connected her to the child she had been, Eden asked for an ornate door to be tattooed, a big oak thing with a stained-glass panel in its top depicting birds fluttering between tree branches. It was a door she knew well.

Her lack of victimhood made her job as a detective interesting. Empathy was something she tried hard at. Often she had to distinguish exactly what victims in their many varieties were feeling, what their dying faces expressed, what the escapees of dungeons and bedrooms and long rides into dark bushland were experiencing when they made it back to safety. She deeply admired Frank when he connected so instantly and completely with his now-dead girlfriend Martina after her initial escape from Jason Beck. Frank had been able to feel what she felt. He felt moved to protect her. He loved her, and then he grieved for her. He was probably still grieving now, Eden imagined, but she couldn't be sure. Why else did he bury his head so firmly in the sand in terms of his current squeeze? Imogen was so completely wrong for him. He needed someone pretty and simple and gentle, like Martina. Was he afraid of being alone? Eden had heard it was difficult to sleep when a partner you'd got used to was suddenly gone from the bed, that even washing the sheets didn't stem the desire for their presence, their warmth, the roll and tumble of them on the mattress as they twisted in the night. Their snores. Was Imogen a bed-filler to Frank?

If she was, Eden suspected she was not the first.

She sat on the bench by the water and thought about victims. She tightened the laces of her runners, drew them tight, down over her now soft, pampered feet, gone to custard through her recovery. She'd enjoyed running once. Liked looking down at the hard yellow calluses that formed at the tops of her toes, her heel, runner's feet, feet that could count kilometres, swollen and aching beautifully. Eden had not run in the street since Rye Farm. She stood and rolled her shoulders, looked at the gently jostling yachts in the harbour. She imagined herself as the Sydney Parks Strangler's next victim. Anonymous female runner catching a couple of quick Ks before dinner. She opened a run-keeper app on her phone, hooked up her earphones as she watched the tennis court café bubbling and writhing, and parents with kids on the green. The evening night wind was slowly stirring. Eden stretched her calves and began to trot. Immediately the pain swelled in her hips, her abdominals. She pushed it aside. Think victim.

There was something so blinding about running, she thought as she fell into an awkward rhythm, trying not to favour her left hip where the muscles wanted to bunch. The rhythm of her body locked her head forward, shook everything in her periphery. The motion seemed to want to dissolve all threats but that which was directly ahead. When she turned to look at families strolling the sandstone blocks by the water's edge and couples taking pictures before the glittering city across the bay, her body wanted to slow, wanted to turn, like a horse being pulled sideways by reins. Running required concentration, self-focus. She listened to her breathing, her steps, her mental commentary of aches. This hurts, this hurts, this hurts, her ankle said.

Stop, stop, stop, her shoulder pleaded. She forgot about the path ahead and ducked between two walkers. She only knew when a faster runner approached a second before they passed, a sudden colourful presence and then their calves in front pumping as they pulled away. It wouldn't be hard, she realised, for someone to creep up on you like this. Mindlessly chugging along, slipping down a dirt path between the roadways and feeling a dull tap in your thigh. The sudden presence of another being behind her, and the glorious exhaustion of a run almost completed, suddenly and shockingly increasing, gravity turned up, legs buckling. The guiding arm of the stranger directing the drunken runner to the nearby roadside, to the open van doors. Keeping vertical would be struggle enough.

She lifted her head and sucked in the cooling night air. Rushcutters Bay Park was not a likely candidate for the killer's next hit – it was expansive and bare in parts, heavily populated by fitness groups, bordered on one side by dozens of yachts with their hundreds of gaping eyes. What trees there were mainly huddled at the roadside, the city sparkling between then, lighting hidey-holes between which possums crept and shuffled, babies gripping at their shoulders. Eden didn't see herself accidentally running smack bang into the parks killer on the hunt, didn't hold out Charmaine Lyon's naïve hope. She just wanted to run. To get into the parklands. To try to understand the hunting grounds.

She wondered at the brazenness of the attacks. What kind of hunter risked parks bathed in twilight for their playground? Eden understood parks as the wonderland of rapists – they were usually drunk or high when they committed the acts, and half the time were homeless, so the parks were where they got their food, shelter, rest. Why not their sex? Eden listened to the growing evening. It was quiet out. Children's squeals of delight echoed across the water. A truck in the distant after-work rush for home shifted gear as it headed into the Cross City Tunnel. Lights came on in the pastel-coloured apartment blocks, one by one.

As she trotted along, she reviewed the evidence over and over in time to her footfalls, hoping to see a pattern, a beat, like the tempo of her soles on the concrete.

Black tracksuit. CCTV. Female runners. Bludgeoned faces. Lost identities. Strangulation. Revenge. Tranquilliser. White van.

The white van might not have caught her attention, might have been lost in the mess of thoughts, had it not crossed right in front of her as Eden turned onto the long stretch of path between the water and New Beach Road, heading towards the dead end at the lip of the bay. Eden fell victim to her curiosity immediately. She lowered her head and sprinted across grass to the road, knowing the van would have to turn and head back at her before it could escape the loop. As she teetered in the uneven gravel near the roadside, she saw the van making a three-point turn in the cul-de-sac. Two joggers stopped and watched her as she leaped out onto the asphalt, speeding up to a bone-grinding pace as the van turned around a small round-about and headed up the hill onto Yarranabbe Road.

She stopped, her hips screaming. Eden gripped at her abdomen, at the ridges of pain that throbbed and felt splintered. She closed her eyes and briefly remembered the knife inside her, the blood running up her neck. It took a moment to realise the pair of joggers had crossed the road and were standing near her, nibbling at her attention with their presence. They were laughing. Eden tugged the headphones from her ears.

'Thought you spotted the Sydney Parks Strangler?' the man said. They were a couple. The shoes were his and hers versions of the same fluorescent green, scored in a two-for-one deal. The young man grinned at her, his glasses fogged with perspiration.

'Couldn't help myself,' Eden said. The girl was delightfully curvy but painfully aware of it, tugging at her sweat-patched top now and then, trying to pull it down over the brown slit of flesh above her tights. Pixie ears and a sheepish smile. Eden licked sweat off her upper lip.

'I thought you might have been onto a winner,' the girl said. 'Every time I see a van around near the park now I fucking freak. Are you a police officer?'

'A watchful citizen.' Eden started walking. 'Bye.'

'Wasn't him.' The male of the pair held up his phone. 'He was just spotted ten minutes ago in Trumper. That's why we're here. We thought, they'll chase him away. It'll be safe. We haven't been out since it all started. Jenny used to go alone, but no more. No more, Jenny.'

Eden watched the boy shake his finger teasingly at the girl. Tried to recall if she had indeed just said goodbye aloud, and if so, figure out why they were still talking to her.

'He's like a shark,' the girl commented. Looked to her partner for approval. 'A shark going up and down the coast. Once you know which beach he's at, you can go play at one of the other ones.' She giggled at her cleverness.

People liked to talk about things that scared them, Eden mused. Talk too much about them. She shook the fog from her head suddenly. The endorphins from the run were pumping through her, old friends missed. 'Wait, did you say ten minutes ago?'

'Yeah. Trumper Park.'

Eden snatched the man's phone, flashed her eyes over the crowdsourced news site. Her mobile rang in her sleeve.

Frank was standing by the bonnet of one of the station cars, a map spread out before him, directing two uniformed officers. Eden parked in the mess of vehicles blocking Royalson Street and glanced at neighbours in the apartment buildings beside the oval. They were standing sentry on their stairs and balconies, arms folded, sceptical. A couple with a dog had taken a seat on a bench as close to the busy police officers as they could get. They sat transfixed, listening to the radio calls. The oval was empty. On the other side, the tree line was impenetrable. Trumper Park was perfect for the killer's next hunt. Eden knew it well. The leafy tracks behind the residential buildings, dug in by the feet of hundreds of joggers. The shady ponds and wooden stairs leading deep into the undergrowth. She came up behind Frank and looked over his shoulder at the cordons he was trying to impose – an impossible gesture given the limited manpower – encompassing two dozen streets or more.

'Lock up the CCTV for Ocean Street, Craigend, Glenmore, Hargrave and Jersey,' he said into his radio. 'If he's gone to ground he'll be in that ring. Secondary cordon from O'Sullivan to the Eastern Distributor.' Frank looked at her for a second, hardly seeing. 'Get someone down to Oxford Street in case he went that way.'

'Copy that.'

'What was it?' Eden asked as the officers went to work. Frank had changed his shirt since she'd seen him at the office. He'd been buried in paperwork and phone calls, now and then lifting his head to moan about how much he hated Caroline Eckhart. She'd hardly spoken to him all day. When she saw him on the smoker's balcony he'd been listening intensely to a phone call from Imogen, who was doing most of the talking.

'Could be a false alarm,' he sighed. 'Dog walker saw a person lingering on this side of the oval, in the trees over there. Black trackies, black hoodie. Doesn't know what he was looking at. When he found himself being watched he fled to a van.'

'Fled?'

'Walked quickly, head down.'

'What's she doing on this side of the park?' Eden squinted at the tree line, two hundred metres away. 'The hunting ground's over there.'

Eden puzzled at it. The stars were emerging slowly from the burnt orange hue above the city. It was the right time of day. A good place to hunt. The description was accurate. Were people becoming hysterical? Or was the killer really here? Was this a reconnaissance trip? She realised after some time that Frank was staring at her. Her lips were still salty with sweat.

'Where have you been?'

'Me?' Eden swiped a stray hair from her brow. 'Jogging.'

'Where? Here?'

'No, Rushcutters Bay. I came in the car.'

Frank looked past her, followed her gesture to her car. He averted his eyes quickly, cleared his throat as a uniformed officer came for more directions. Eden watched him. His hand fluttered restlessly by his eyes, scratching at nothing. The eyes did not come back to her.

'What?'

'What?' Frank sniffed.

'You're acting weird.'

'Oh. Finally,' he smiled crookedly. 'My turn to act weird.'

Eden watched him. He looked around at the officers busy working on maps, radioing in colleagues, following the progress of checkpoints. Nearby a woman with a dog was talking animatedly to a group of young female officers, pointing to a tree by the public toilets. Frank looked stressed. He tugged at the shirt. Eden only realised, as he touched it, how ridiculous it was on him. Too tight, salmon pink with a collar liner of little cross-hatches, peach, apricot, baby blue. He must have been on his way out to dinner with Imogen. No idea he'd be seen by his colleagues in it. He kept closing it at the throat to hide the colourful lining. Something twitched on the edge of his lips. Unspoken words.

'Look at what you're wearing,' he finally said. Eden glanced at her tracksuit pants. Her hoodie. Black. She smirked, tried to meet his eyes, but they were locked on the trees.

'Look at what you're wearing.'

'I'm just saying,' he shrugged stiffly.

Eden narrowed her eyes. Then she laughed.

'You think I'm the Sydney Parks Strangler.'

'Well, for fuck's sake. Is it that much of a stretch? You're *some* kind of killer, Eden,' he snapped, his grey-blue eyes on her at last. His words were low, barely audible. 'I don't know what. I've never known what. I know you killed six men, at least. Benjamin Annous. Jake DeLaney. The others, their cellmates. I can't prove it, but Eric trying to kill me for confronting him about it made it pretty clear that I was right. So then this murder happens up near Byron, while you're away for the weekend, and the cops up there are saying the killer used a very sophisticated gun. Your best friend's a hunting expert.' He shrugged. 'What do you want me to think?'

'Whoa!'

'Yeah. Whoa.'

'Frank, I want you to think straight, that's what I want. Think straight, and not like a fucking idiot for once.'

'I called you, what? Three minutes ago? You're saying you got from Rushcutters Bay to here in three minutes?'

'Yes, actually. I'm sorry. Should I have stopped to pick up some milk along the way?'

'You're wearing a black tracksuit. I hear about murders in the news and I wonder if you did them.' He shrugged again. Stiff and angry. 'I can't watch the news anymore. You know that? I sit there and it's like, kid's body found in a creek. And I think, was that Eden? Old man bludgeoned in an apparent home invasion. Was that Eden? Four bodies found in a van in Byron. Was that Eden? You disappeared six guys off the face of the earth without so much as a hair left behind. Am I supposed to think that was your first time?'

'Frank.'

'You're the only killer I know.'

'And that's the key, the thing you're forgetting,' Eden snapped. 'You know me, you fucking arsehole.'

'I can't even begin −' He paused as one of the area chiefs walked by them swiftly, speaking into a radio. 'I can't even begin to list the things I don't know about you, Eden.'

'Okay, we're going to stop this now.' Eden walked back to her car and got in. She put her face in her palms. Her hands were shaking. Waves of prickles rolled up and down her back. In the airless warmth of the car, she hid in her hands and flattened her tongue against the roof of her mouth and growled. She had a strange surge of emotion when she heard the door beside her pop open and the familiar groan and sigh of her partner as he eased himself into the car. Emotion was not her friend in any form, but this brief and paralysing spark was not terror or rage. It was comforting, somehow. She felt comforted. Frank sat in the passenger's seat, his usual place beside her, and looked at the mess of people moving before them, a sea of blue.

'I'm trapped here,' he said. Eden gripped the wheel and waited, but nothing more came. Frank stared at the dashboard.

'What do you mean?'

'I mean I'm trapped here, between Martina and Jason, and what he did to her and what I did to him, and you. Whenever I try to turn away from what happened between those two people, when I try to forget what happened to her, I open my eyes and there's you. Sometimes I feel like I can move on, maybe pretend she never existed. It never happened. But it did happen, and it happened because I left her there. I left her there because I was chasing you.'

Eden watched him. He stared down at his hands, lying open in his lap.

'Martina is dead, and I killed someone, because of you. And every time you've killed someone since, I've been complicit in it.'

'No you haven't,' Eden said. 'Most of the time you don't even know it's happened.'

'Did you kill those kids in Byron Bay? Those guys and those kids?'

'What did I just say?'

'There's no denying it.' Frank waved his hand, dismissed

264

her. 'I'm complicit because I know what you are and I haven't stopped you. I mean, I'm not stopping you even now.' He ran his fingers through his hair, made a mess of it. 'For some fucked-up reason, I've never stopped you.'

'You can't stop me,' she said. 'We both know that.'

He was silent. The restless hand fluttered at his eyes again, left a red mark on his brow when he scratched.

'Why don't you stop yourself?' Frank turned in his seat and finally looked at her. 'Give it up. You can turn away from it, you know. Maybe. You can leave it behind you. We both can.'

Eden felt again that wave of something, of familiarity perhaps. Of home.

She opened her mouth to answer. How to explain it all to him, a normal human man, someone with all his faculties, someone with all his emotions and neurological connections in order, someone with a soul. How to explain that at the core of her being, Eden killed people the way she breathed, the way she slept, that when she was hungry for blood it was as all-consuming as exhaustion for sleep, or the need for water to quench a thirst. Without the monsters that she hunted and caught and vanquished, she would suffocate. Flicker and extinguish. She ran on no other fuel. She was a consuming thing, and consume she must. To decide not to kill was to decide to die.

I don't want to die, she thought. *I'll kill you before I let that happen, Frank. Because I'm a predator. That's the core of it. There's a beast in me, and it only knows how to kill and how to live.*

A uniformed officer tapped on Frank's window. He rolled it down and Eden's comfort was lost.

Ruben lay in bed in the dorm past midday, which wasn't like him at all. When people came into the room to retrieve things from bags, to change, to cuddle, he turned and pretended he was sleeping. At some point Donato came and went, and for an hour or so he heard the rhythmic smacking of his basketball on the court outside, the rumble of the loose hoop hanging below the windows. Thursday at the big house by the park was coming. He had begun to dread the day. Terrified all night before he went, yet unable to pull away from the work – strangely drawn forward into the house, pulled within the orbit of the attic door.

As the sun began setting, he heard televisions come on throughout the building, the French girls upstairs with their reality television shows and the British boys catching episodes of *Neighbours* in the large living area off the bedroom in which he lay. On the edge of further frightening dreams, in which an unseen presence followed him from room to room around the big house as he furiously cleaned dirt and grime that would not shift, he heard a familiar voice. He wandered to the living-room door wrapped in his sweat-damp comforter, his hair mussed and eyes aching. The television sat like a blazing white campfire in a ring of couples, some of them sipping colourful bottles of alcoholic cola, some of them passing a joint slowly. An athletic-looking woman filled the screen, standing on the steps of a building that was out of sight, grey concrete her only backdrop. Her sunflower hair swished in a high ponytail as she talked. This was, without a doubt, the woman from the tapes in the attic room, the tapes that kept being stopped and re-started, certain words and phrases captured and replayed. The subtitles were in German. Ruben had excelled in German at high school and could follow along as the letters flashed and flickered across the screen.

'We won't stand idly by and let our voices go unheard,' the woman said. 'If all goes well, this will be the biggest gathering of like-minded souls fighting for recognition in the daily struggle against domestic violence in this country. You need to escape the you that you've become, Sydney. It's easy!'

Hooky was distracted from the laptop on her knees by her aunt jabbering away in the kitchen, the low bubbling of her voice rising to a simmer as she walked into the large, immaculate living room, setting cutlery on the table. She was complaining about the 'sickos' Hooky was chatting to on the internet. Something about her doing it at home, rather than at the station, made her aunt Ada think Hooky did it because she enjoyed it and not because she wanted to see the men she wrote to cornered, dragged into prison cells, given back some of the pain they perpetuated on their victims.

How can they let you do that at home, unsupervised? Ada asked, her Vietnamese so fast and perfect Hooky had trouble following. Who are these people? What kind of cowboys do they have running this city?

Hooky ignored her aunt. As long as her university grades didn't slip, Ada had never made good on her promise to confront her bosses at the department about just how much danger she was in and just how much freedom she had to hunt pedophiles online. Hooky made sure her grades were as near perfect as they could be. If the chiefs found out she was messing around with the perps they were watching in her own time, she'd be kicked out of the office for good.

Her fingers flashed over the keys, her eyes following as the words pumped into the small chat box at the bottom of the screen. The chatter, StanSmiles33, had already filled the screen with text in the moments Hooky was distracted. He was hooked, this one.

Hooky thought of the pedophiles she hunted in 'levels', so this was the way she reported on them to her boss when she was working alongside officers at the station. Every interaction she made, no matter how casual, had to be reported, the conversations screenshotted and logged in files labelled with screen names for each individual target. Hooky had a small database of images she was allowed to use at the very end of her interactions with her prey – in the days and hours before their proposed first meeting. More often than not, just before meeting in person, one of her chatters would ask her for a racy photograph, a 'commitment', something to show that she was 'real' and serious about meeting up. Hooky had naked photographs of twelve boys and twelve girls of varying ages and ethnicities, the faces cheekily hidden or obscured, as final bait for her chatters. Hooky knew these children well – the grinning twelve-year-old girl taking a selfie in the mirror, the taut-skinned, serious-looking fourteen-year-old boy posing on a bed. These were for the level-five chatters only. She only ever used them once.

At level one, the target approached Hooky online, or she approached him, for casual chit-chat. School, weather, parents, the latest movies at the box office. Generally, ages weren't discussed, or if they were the men chatting to Hooky told her they were close to her age range. If she told the target that she was twelve, they often pretended to be fifteen. If she was fifteen, they would say they were seventeen. Sometimes,

Hooky had five level-one chatters to report on by the end of a chat session. Level ones often progressed to nothing. There was nothing criminal about an older man lying so he could chat to a younger person online as long as the chat was fairly pedestrian, and there was any number of excuses available to the outed online predator at level one – he wanted to reconnect with his own daughter who'd become moody and detached, so he chatted to young people, tried to get a feel for their worries, their interests. He was curious, maybe, about how young people interacted these days. He was living a fantasy, perhaps. Having an age crisis in his forties and pretending he was young. Didn't everyone think like that sometimes? What if I could go back? Start again? It was harmless.

For a chatter to progress to Hooky's level-two file, chat had to be sustained for more than one conversation, and innocuous photographs were exchanged. The chatter would 'add' Hooky, or who she was pretending to be – send her a request to be her 'friend' or to 'link up', to 'follow', depending on the site. A flurry of smiley faces celebrated the newly officiated, though still virtual, relationship. At this point, the more experienced online child-groomer backed off a little. Tried to make Hooky comfortable – didn't want to come on too strong. Connections were sometimes encouraged between Hooky and his other online friends, which often involved just the same chatter using different profiles, trying to make Hooky feel like she was part of a group instead of interacting with an individual. If the guy had friends, he had to be alright, right? Groups and clubs formed. The target sometimes asked where Hooky lived towards the end of this level.

To progress to level three, at which point Hooky flagged the interactions with her chief at North Sydney Police headquarters, the talk had to turn romantic. Sometimes this was within mere hours of the chat being initiated for the first time. Sometimes it was only after months of association. It would begin with the odd love-song dedication or a 'caring' message. *I was thinking about you today.* Invariably the target would search for an opportunity to assert himself as a strong, brave, masculine hero-type. If Hooky's character had a fight with his or her parents, the target would understand. The target would have experienced the same thing, or worse, from his own parents. If Hooky's character was being bullied at school, the target would reveal his evil plans for the perpetrators of the harassment. He'd progressively reveal his real age, either in stages, or all at once, confessing that although he'd lied – he was really forty-one – he felt such a connection with Hooky's character that he didn't feel it mattered. Age is just a number, right? Often at this point he would want to send money or a gift to cheer Hooky's character up. To show he cared. So he would obtain Hooky's address.

At level four, a second 'location indicator' was exchanged. The target would ask where the girl or boy went to school or worked, maybe do a drive by of either location, or make a comment to the kid about the location. At level five, plans for a real-life meeting would be discussed. At this time, Hooky would consolidate her file, print out all the information she had, tag it and give it to her boss. And that was the end of her involvement.

There were many benefits to chatting to the perpetrators on her own, away from the office, although Hooky risked losing her job doing it. She could say what she wanted to the perps without having to get approval from the cops sitting with her. She could be more graphic. More intense. The department strictly forbade her from talking to perps on the phone or in video chat at the offices. But when a target requested phone contact, and Hooky refused it, the perps usually got spooked and slipped away.

Hooky didn't like it when they got away.

When her reports were handed in, the department would link up with the Australian Federal Police and brief them for a joint operation. Sometimes Hooky saw her targets in the newspaper two or three months after she handed over their cases. The Feds never moved until they had everything. Computer files. Polaroids. Videos. Friends. Family. Co-workers. All picked over to within an inch of their lives.

Today, Hooky's target was ready to take it to level five. She sighed, bored, and drew up a picture she'd used many times before, something from the depths of the police files, something only she had access to. An image with a hundred legal documents attached to it somewhere, marking its confiscation from the girl who'd taken it and the man she'd shared it with – a girl with no idea how much trouble she was getting herself into – and permission from her parents signed away for its use in baiting monsters like the one who had lured their baby. Hooky posted the picture and yawned, wriggled her toes, making the laptop wobble on her knees.

StanSmiles33: Dats nice baby. Really sweet ;)

HelloKitty14: U like? ;) xx

StanSmiles33: Your a beautiful girl. No . . . your a beautiful woman! No matter what your parents tell you babe I can see the incredible woman you have already become. I cant wait to see more!

HelloKitty14: You always say that lol

StanSmiles33: Stanny wantz ur fanny! :) :) :)

HelloKitty14: Oh har har har real mature

StanSmiles33: You know I'm just joking bae

HelloKitty14: lol

StanSmiles33: Meeting up 4real is my ultimate dream. I can't lie! One day well do it babe. As soon as you stop being a fraidy cat!! lol

HelloKitty14: haha maybe

StanSmiles33: Just say the word and well run away 2getha :):) Ill treat you like the princess u really are!!!! I cant wait to hold you. Just hold you and make you feel safe. <3

Hooky noticed a small icon flashing in the corner of her screen and sent smiling Stan a quick message telling him her mother had come into the room, which halted chat immediately. She flicked over to another window and drew up a long column of boxes. The software she'd used to hack Imogen's phone told her she was texting again. Hooky stretched out on the couch and balanced the laptop on her stomach, folded her hands over her chest and half-watched the television as boxes began to fill the screen slowly, one by one.

Imogen: Hey you got those bloods yet?

0447392***: Might as well go after the Hope Diamond than get Eden Archer's DNA.

Imogen: Any luck with the brother?

0447392***: That was easier. Managed to swipe the shirt he died in from evidence for a couple of hours. Emailing you now. I better get paid quick smart this time!

Imogen: Yeah yeah. Show me the goods!

Hooky tapped her short fingernails on the edge of the laptop, felt half-thoughts zinging and crashing into each other. She drew up a quick news report on Eric Archer's accidental shooting by Eden Archer in a raid in a church in Randwick. Frank at the edge of the frame, his head in his hands, a paramedic trying to lead him away. Blood all over him. His girlfriend had been murdered only hours before. Hooky took the number from the interaction on Imogen's phone and ran it through a search engine. Peter Bryson was a low-level administration worker at Surry Hills police station. Hooky watched an email come through to Imogen's inbox from his work email address. She opened the file and glanced at the DNA profile of Eric Archer.

'Interesting,' she said aloud.

A blonde woman was ranting on the television about domestic violence and a charity run in the city. Hooky looked back when the screen began flashing again.

Imogen: Any luck?

A different recipient this time. Hooky waited. Knowing Imogen was waiting somewhere, probably in her office, about to leave work for the day. The text message from the new number came back promptly, like Peter's.

0415333***: Indeed. The renowned Heinrich 'Hades' Archer submitted to a DNA swab over a missing drug dealer in 2011. I'll email it across when I see payment in my account.

Imogen: You're a star, Lisa. Sending payment now.

Hooky drew up her online banking surveillance on Imogen and watched seven hundred dollars shift out of her savings account into the ether, heading for the account of a woman named Lisa Louise Gilbert. A quick Google search told Hooky that Lisa Gilbert was an administrator at a small Western Sydney police forensics office.

'You've got little birdies everywhere, haven't you, wifey,' Hooky murmured.

Hooky opened the DNA profiles of Eric Archer and Heinrich Archer. A mere glance, to the trained eye, told her they were not father and son. Her face felt hot. She shifted up on the couch and watched more text messages begin to dart back and forth.

0447392***: Interesting little tidbit about that Eric Archer's profile . . . :)

Imogen: Don't leave me hangin', Peter.

0447392***: Seems it showed up unexpectedly at a crime scene. Well, not a crime scene . . . exactly. Got a weird little note in the case file. Never followed up.

Imogen: Which crime scene?

0447392***: I said it WASN'T a crime scene.

Imogen: Would you get to the damn point?

0447392***: Whoops! Looks like my good will has run out. Anything further is going to cost you.

Imogen: Oh come on.

0447392***: $500

Imogen: Ok.

0447392***: Transferring now?

Imogen: Alright alright alright alright. It's done. Now just tell me.

0447392***: Ok. Spot of Eric Archer's blood turned up at a missing person's house a week before Eric was killed. Inquiry puts it down to forensic team cross-contamination – Eric wasn't on the missing persons but one of his offsiders was. They dropped it after he was dead anyway. Never found missing guy. Might be interesting for whatever you're working on. Missing guy was Benjamin Annous. MPR 446193. Google him.

Imogen: One spot of blood?

0447392***: Yeah.

Imogen: Probably cross contamination. Nice to know, though!

0447392***: Happy to help in any way I can, baby cakes haha.

Hooky waited for Imogen to give an answer, staring at the boxes on the screen. None came.

Tara remembered those frantic moments before boarding, when her excitement and terror were so tangible, so real, it felt as if a cloak of electricity was brushing against her arms, searing at her neck, twisting down her legs. She went to the bathroom six or seven times in the hour she waited at the crowded airport gate, drawing stares every time she moved, a lumbering force of nature. She'd never been on an airplane before. She had almost flown once for a Year Ten science trip to Cairns – ninety students on the Barrier Reef locating, cataloguing and photographing marine life for their end-of-year portfolios.

Photographing marine life? Joanie snorted.

Tara would need two seats, and something like that was just too much for Joanie to take. Tara had looked at the skies through the trees outside the attic windows, hoping she would spot the plane trailing across the depthless blue. She imagined it suddenly combusting, a bright white spark breaking into shimmering speckles like glitter spilt across blue icing. The screams and gasps from below.

It had been around this time that Tara encountered the boy in the park. She was on one of her hunting trips with Joanie. Tara running in the dark. Gasping. Crying. Joanie coming after her, a shadow floating between the huge Moreton Bay figs. Tara swerved at the sight of the long black pole in the trees, suppressed a scream, thinking perhaps that her fantasies about Joanie the stick-insect woman had come true, that the tall black pole moving through the trees was one of Joanie's arms about to come around and spear her. She stumbled to a stop, mouth open, gasping. The pole swayed, dipped and ducked behind a tree. A boy emerged, carrying it over his shoulder. A boy and a man. They crossed the wide path in front of Tara and walked into the trees.

She looked back along the road. Joanie was nowhere to be seen. She sometimes stopped and tightened her shoelaces. Tighter and tighter as the night wore on, until the cotton laces groaned.

The man and the boy were looking up at the trees. Tara followed at a distance, her heart still hammering, sweat rolling down her chin. She swallowed the sobs that had punctuated her running breaths, stuck close to a tree to observe them.

In the darkness, they spoke softly to each other, the old man setting down his equipment, the small plastic animal cages, the cloth bags. They stood and looked into the tree canopy, pointed, murmured. The boy fiddled with the end of the pole, then turned it, aimed it carefully in the mess of leaves above. In one swift, upward thrust he jabbed at something. There was a squeal. A black bundle fell into the old man's gloved palms.

Tara gasped. The pair turned towards her.

'It's alright,' the boy said. Tara emerged from the shadows, chanced a step closer. The boy had Peter Anderson's litheness and solidity about him, the sturdiness of good genes and proud parenting, a spattering of boy-next-door freckles on his nose. He took the black bundle from the old man and came over to her. Tara fought the urge to flee.

'We're tagging them,' the boy said. 'You wanna see?'

The old man smiled and waited as the teenagers drew closer. Tara's heart hammered in her neck and cheeks as the boy opened his gloves. A small flying fox lay curved in his hands, the huge fingers of the glove gripping the creature by the back of its furry neck, its leathery, bony wings crumpled and folded in the fabric. The thing was swimming somewhere between sleep and wake, glossy black eyes blinking. A single bead of ruby red blood emerged from the orange fur of its chest and smeared on the boy's glove. He pulled a tiny dart from the creature's side and held it for her to see. She took it and looked at it. A tiny plastic vial, the silver spike.

'We have to knock them out or they panic. Get tangled in the nets. Sometimes they can hurt themselves,' he said.

She could smell his sweet breath. Tara wondered if she had ever stood as close to a boy as she stood now, his arm almost touching hers. Centimetres from contact. From contracting her germs. Did he know how close he was to being infected by her, the darkness and terror that rippled through her every waking moment? She glanced towards the road, slipping the vial into her pocket as she turned. Joanie was nowhere.

'Their hearts are really fragile. So we have to be careful with them,' the boy smiled.

My heart is really fragile, Tara thought. *Be careful with me.*

She followed him back to the old man, tried to give the boy space, but he seemed insistent on being near her, standing in the infectious cloud of her very being. She watched as they clipped the brass ring around the animal's tiny clawed feet. The thing was awake now, the fanged mouth opening, stretching, the pointed ears twitching madly, trying to get a sense of up and down.

'Whoa,' the boy said, as the black beast began to wriggle in his hands. It gave a squeal and thrashed its tiny head. Tara caught the boy looking at her and she felt the bile rise in her throat.

'Here, grab on,' the boy said, thrusting his hands at her. Tara put her trembling fingers around the outside of his warm gloves. She was, for the first time, separated from the touch of a boy by mere fabric. By choice. By strange and inexplicable choice. Her knees shook.

'One, two –' the boy said. Together they lifted and opened their hands, and a great flapping darkness was unleashed. The motion drew the two teenagers together. Their arms touched.

'Tara,' Joanie yelled. Tara looked back towards the road, saw shadows moving. She turned and ran.

Tara looked around the boarding-gate lounge and saw no one who reminded her of the boy in the park. There were only hollow eyes and sneering lips. She imagined her fellow passengers burning and writhing in their plane seats, blackening fingers struggling at seatbelts, holes tearing down the side of the fuselage, whipping and stirring the fire. All of them shuddering in unison as the plane plummeted down levels of the atmosphere like a wayward skateboard diving and bumping down stairs. She smiled. A little girl standing by a pram thought Tara was smiling at her and smiled back. Tara imagined the child sliding down the tipped aisle towards the pilot's cabin, fingernails gripping at the carpet.

On the plane, she boarded economy, thinking she might be less conspicuous here. But the usual sighs erupted as she manoeuvred herself slowly towards 23B, which she discovered was in the middle of a group of three only when she sat in it, the seat handles jutting into her hips as she wiggled down onto the cushion. A young man approached from the front of the plane, looked at Tara, looked at the seat numbers and hitched his bag up onto his shoulder, kept walking. Tara heard arguing at the back of the plane. She didn't pay much attention to it. The seats filled around her, the occasional glance coming her way as people shoved bags into overhead lockers and squeezed into their seats, paperbacks resting against chests, inches from reading eyes. A baby began wailing and preflight checks made things buzz and wheeze and bleep outside the window beside her. It was raining, and droplets slid down the small oval window into the curved rim. She felt her bladder ache again, looked towards the back of the plane. The man she'd seen and a woman were both speaking animatedly to the flight attendant. Eventually they were seated by the bathrooms.

Tara took the folded piece of paper from inside her bra and smoothed it out, warm and curved, against her thigh. On it, she found her own name and traced the letters with her fingernail, something she had done a number of times now, so that the letters were almost faded. 'Tara Harper: Surgical itinerary'. Because, yes, the document was hers completely, had been arranged and paid for by her alone. Daddy's inheritance, finally setting her free. She followed the points and the dates on the paper with her finger, whispered the procedures to herself.

Thursday 5 August, 5:00AM (GMT +7): SAL lipectomy prep – abdomen, pubis, flanks

Thursday 5 August, 5:45AM (GMT +7): SAL lipectomy procedure – abdomen, pubis, flanks

Friday 6 August, 5:45AM (GMT +7): SAL lipectomy
prep – arms, breasts, submental
Friday 6 August, 5:45AM (GMT +7): SAL lipectomy
procedure – arms, breasts, submental.

It would be a surgical marathon. Over six days, she would
have 60 per cent of her body fat removed. Tara had not been
able to find another organisation that would approve the procedures, but Dr Raji Benmal's 'fast-track' surgical overhaul had
been explained in detail on his website. Tara would be in a coma
for the entire ordeal, and for a week afterwards, and therefore her
body would not go into shock between the surgery rounds – the
four- to six-week recovery between procedures wasn't necessary
because she wouldn't be putting her body through the trauma
of waking between lipectomy rounds. Dr Benmal was going to
remove the weight, carve her away to the glorious muscle and
sinew she knew was beneath the ragged fat, and stitch her back
together like a broken doll.

With unique world-first binding procedures, laser skin
therapy, and all the care and consideration throughout her
recovery that a mother would give a child, Tara was going to
heal into a new being, a new soul. Tara had laughed at that
part: the mother offering the care to the child as her body
reeled in its new form. Tara was going to return to Australia
knowing what a mother's love was really like, and then she
was going to bring all the agony she had known in her former
body down upon Joanie, who waited, unsuspecting, in the
Lang Road house. Tara closed her eyes and imagined Joanie's
face as she walked in the door, the confusion as she tried to
fit the identity of this beautiful woman to the slightly familiar

face before her, the cheekbones and jawbones she had never seen before. Tara considered changing her name once Joanie was dead, drawing a name up from the blood of her fallen mother as she smoothed the warm red life liquid over her fingers, tasted it on her tongue. A name would come to her as she kneeled over Joanie, finally triumphant. Something powerful. Something borne of pain.

Tara realised, as she opened her eyes, that she was laughing in that awful, evil, snarling way she laughed, clutching the itinerary against her breasts, her tongue washing over her bottom lip as though she was with Joanie already, watching the life drain from her. People around her on the plane were staring. Tara smiled a devil's smile.

The dog had some strange behaviours. Hades didn't know much about dogs and their night-time activities, but when he got up around midnight to piss, a regular nocturnal journey, he spotted the thing in its basket, dreaming. Paws twitching in sequence, running in the land of fantasy, now and then the lips slipping upwards over the shining white teeth, exposing the fleshy pink beneath. The lips came forward again and narrowed, and the thing gave a low and drawn-out howl, barely audible, almost singing. Hades watched the dog until it fluttered out of the dream and raised its head, peered at him from beneath a hood of blanket, waiting like an old robed monk for his command. In the morning he caught the creature standing at the doorway, staring out at the workers at the bottom of the hill with the sharp, lethal stillness of a pointer, nose inches from the wire. Its bony silhouette against the white dawn was like a streak of ink. When he filled its bowl, it ate so fast it regularly choked and coughed up cubes of meat, so that before it was finished the meal had been chewed and regurgitated and re-chewed a number of times.

The dog wasn't sure of Eden at all when she arrived at the door, worn jeans, black cap pulling a long ponytail up behind her head. She was dressed as she did when she hunted – androgynously, lithely, as though prepared to run at any time. The flighty Eden. She'd always been like that in times of stress, prepared to disappear, bags packed and affairs in order. Even as a teenager, the old man had half-expected one day that she might run off on him, like a cat brought in from the wild, half-listening all the time to the call of the horizon, to the seductive darkness of the road. She opened the screen door and the dog trotted to the hall entrance, looked back at Hades, ears points, eyes wide and lips twitching.

'It's alright,' he said. The animal's face changed immediately, spread into that sheepish grin, narrow eyes. The thing gave a little grateful groan and slunk to the floor beside the old man's chair.

'Someone's put the boot into that thing,' Eden said as she sat across from him. Hades gave the dog a little scratch on its hard skull.

'I wouldn't be surprised.'

'Watch it doesn't turn on you. They can get confused, rescued things.'

'You never did.'

'No.' She smiled a little. She looked at the dog. 'Did you name it?'

'Yes. Jim.'

Eden stared at Hades.

'Slim Jim.'

'Of course.' She slapped a notepad on the table. Sighed. 'Well, it's all over now. You've named it. It's a done deal.'

'It's a dog. Not a marriage.'

'Still.' Eden looked at her notepad.

'So.' The old man nodded at the notepad. 'Where do I begin?'

'Height?'

'She was short,' Hades said. He glanced at the shattered mug on the countertop, the white lips of triangle shards in lime green. Tried to imagine the woman who had attacked him sitting where Eden sat now, her nimble frame and big eyes behind the glasses. 'She was petite. Looked like she might work out.'

'How was she dressed?'

'Classy. I don't remember specifically. Heels. Glasses. Big tinted glasses that hid her eyes. It was very fast. We got right down to business. She must have been here less than three minutes.'

'She smell like anything?'

'A woman.'

'Car?'

'Didn't see it. I fell. Sounded small.'

Eden nodded, kept writing. She tapped the pen on the paper and gazed at the windows. Hades pulled a folded piece of paper towards him from where it lay on top of an old newspaper to his left. Slid it across the table to Eden.

'She left this,' he said. Eden unfolded the piece of paper and took the hair she found in the crease between her thumb and forefinger. She lifted the hair to her nose, smelt it, held it up against the light and examined the frayed end where the follicle should have been. She hooked the hair around both her index fingers and pulled, snapped it, squinted at the curled cross-section.

'Human hair wig. Expensive.'

'How can you tell?'

'It's a Caucasian hair. Cheap human hair wigs are usually made from the hair of Indian women. You can tell they've been bleached. This hasn't been bleached.'

'Why is a white woman's hair more expensive than an Indian woman's hair?' Hades gave a little quizzical frown.

'Racism.'

'You women with your racist wigs,' the old man laughed.

'What was the style? Was it long?'

Hades put a finger up against his tricep.

'Okay, long, dark burgundy hair. So we can assume if she's going to all the trouble of wearing a wig she's wearing one that's as different from her normal style as possible. What's the opposite of long, dark hair?'

'Short blonde hair,' Hades said. 'You know any tricky blondes who might want to dig into your past?'

Eden sighed and wiped her eyes. It wasn't often that Hades saw her looking this tired. Her cheeks had hollowed, shadowed beneath the cap.

'None that I can think of,' Eden said, squeezing the bridge of her nose. 'None this cunning. It's possible Eric knew someone with a grudge. Someone he never told me about. I mean, we don't even know if it's this woman who's after us. She could easily have been someone's agent.'

'I've turned the cameras on. But I don't think she'll be back.'

'I don't think so either.' Eden shifted, lifted her phone out of her pocket and answered it. 'Yes?'

'That's how you answer the phone to me now?' Frank said. Eden heard a television. The insistent whining of a cat. 'Yes?'

'Darling of my heart. Sunshine of my day. How may I serve you, Vice-President of the National Arseholes' Association?'

'There's a problem.'

'What is it?'

'Turn on the TV. Channel Ten news.'

Eden crossed the floor in front of the dog and settled on the old green couch, flipped the television on. Hades leaned over the back of the chair, the grey hairs on his thick, scarred forearm catching all the kitchen light from wrist to elbow. Eden wiped dust off the television remote, found the channel she was looking for. A banner at the bottom of the screen read 'Take Back the Parks launched'.

'What is this bullshit?'

'Just watch,' Frank said.

Caroline Eckhart was standing before a crowd of gym junkies, nylon in every colour of the rainbow above a sea of uniform black tights. Ponytails and greasy quiffs, an army of the healthy, aluminium water bottles glimmering like guns. She raised a hand to them and they cheered. A middle-aged mother with a pram ignored her wailing child, clapped and hooted. Caroline was yelling over gym music. There were mirrors in the background. Just stepped out of a pump class to address the masses. The glossy, sweat-sheened Joan of Arc, still miked, dabbing at her impossibly flat brow with a gym chamois.

'Look, Sandra, we're working on the fly here, but that's the kind of people we are at Eckhart Energy. We're pulling in favours from all sorts of wonderful organisations – Woolworths, Kellogg's, plus the Pink Ribbon campaign and a whole host of other charities are on board. We need to demonstrate that violence against women just isn't on, and we're going to do that with a dramatic show of human strength. Take Back the Parks is going to show the people of Australia that we can change the face of this horrific social trend.'

The gym class cheered. Eden felt her stomach sinking. 'What exactly is Take Back the Parks?'

'It's a running festival. A night running festival,' Frank said. 'She's putting the whole thing together over the space of four days and she's got the Minister for Women behind her. They run on Sunday. The marathoners start at 5 pm. There are five K, nine K, twenty-one K and forty-five K distances. Each one ends up in a different Sydney park. Did I mention the marathoners start at 5-fucking-pm? Four Sydney parks are going to be absolutely flooded with people Sunday night and there's no finish time mentioned. They could be there all night, wandering around like dumb fucking chickens just begging for the killer to come out and play.'

'Jesus Christ's fucking beard.' Eden covered her eyes.

'What is it?' Hades asked.

'Registration has been open for an hour. Seven thousand people have signed up for this thing already. The site's crashed twice. This is going to be huge,' Frank said. 'If the killer doesn't take the bait at one of the four parks mentioned, I'll eat my hat. I don't own a hat. I don't even like hats. I'll buy one specially, and I'll fucking eat it.'

'Not me,' Eden said. 'If it was me, I'd take advantage of every police officer in Sydney being tied up in the four parks mentioned to hit one of the unattended ones.'

'Well, I've been trying to get through to the bitch for an hour but her people won't let me speak to her. She refuses to see this as a brazen act of public endangerment. She's painting it as a defiance thing. Like we're all going to get together and scare the killer off with our mighty show of fucking . . . communal spirit.'

'Urgh,' Eden sighed.

'I hate communal spirit,' Frank snarled. 'Communal spirit is my worst nightmare.'

'I'll see you at the station,' Eden said. 'We'll see if we can bring this thing down.'

For ten minutes, in silence, Eden and I sat on my desk and looked at a huge map of Sydney. Sometimes you've got to do that – just sit and 'be', absorb the electric potential around a crime, let the thing talk to you. It doesn't matter if it's before or after the event itself. A bank before a robbery is dripping with the ripe juices of violence. Everything smelling of the air-freshener plug-ins and unused paper, the slightly metallic scent of money. You can tell what a crime will be like with an environment that small. Vicious black boots crumpling white paper. The bank-teller ladies crying.

The potential of the Sydney streets flooded with cheering, huffing runners was accessible but the dream was faint. I could see people drinking on balconies, cheering the hordes as they shuffled through. I could see banner-bearing teens whooping on street corners, brandishing bottles of Gatorade from atop milk crates. Big fold-out tables full of paper cups of water. I'd done the City2Surf a few times as a young man so I knew how people got into it, the way they swept and let themselves be swept by the momentum of the herd. Groups of businessmen in ironic lime green tutus, faces painted, arms rocking back and forth, calves straining. Women with prams powering up Heartbreak Hill.

I knew that Eden, sitting beside me with her hands resting in her lap, was thinking along the same lines, but she'd have all the lethality I lacked powering through her killer mind as she followed the neatly marked streets and laneways with her eyes. The gaping mouth of Sydney Harbour in its peaceful, monochromatic pale blue. She'd be remembering bodies we pulled out of that harbour while I found myself thinking of my surfing days.

The four running tracks all began beside the bridge at Kirribilli, the overflow of runners stretching, exercise companies hawking merchandise and spectators waiting to cheer on friends and family all swirling around Bradfield Park, where Jill Noble's body had been found lying against one of the Harbour Bridge pylons.

Jill had been all over the news that morning, shots of the base of the pylon buried in flowers and teddies beneath maps marking the run routes, loading the pressure of finding her killer onto my shoulders like a third massive weight dropped into a pack on my back. Her family in tears. The angry public swarming around the pylon, yelling at the television cameras. The five-kilometre run started here and looped around and headed over the bridge towards the city, then turned left into the Domain. The nine-K left Kirribilli and went northeast, curling around in a question-mark shape and ending up at the park surrounding Manly Dam. The twenty-one kilometre runners would go northwest, finishing at Lane Cove National Park. The marathon runners looped and headed south through the city, along Anzac Parade towards La Perouse beach. They curved around the beach, ran up along the coast, taking in Coogee and Bondi, before finishing in Centennial Park.

There were eighty kilometres of running track to secure. Fifteen thousand people had registered for the run in the first four hours and there were plenty more to come. I couldn't help wondering if there were some people running in the hopes of catching a glimpse of the killer in action, the sick fantasy of the runner ahead suddenly disappearing off the side of the darkened road in the grip of a shadow, like an antelope snatched from a riverside by a croc. Gone in seconds, the ensuing panic of the runners nearby, the moment of delicious heroism when asked to give a police witness statement. 'I looked up, and I saw her eyes as she was being pulled towards the roadside. I'll never forget those desperate eyes –' Cue interviews with the local papers.

Captain James was on a television set in the coffee room condemning the festival and handing out warnings about personal safety. I could hear his fatherly voice above the shouting of reporters, eventually cut over by the news anchor. The government had leaped on the opportunity to support the festival – it had all the proactive feminist angles both parties liked to appear involved in (without all the fuss of actual policies and reforms). It looked good for their stance on women's health. Domestic violence. Violent crime.

Phone companies were going to decorate the start and finish lines with ridiculous foam mascots, and fitness companies had plans to slap ball caps on potential new members as they trotted by. High fives and big smiles. There was going to be a minute's silence before the starting gun to mark the victims who had inspired the run.

Caroline Eckhart and the City of Sydney had turned three brutal killings into what would probably end up an annual fitness wankfest with all the associated sweat, glory and plastic participation medals.

I sighed. This was going to be a nightmare.

Our colleagues swirled around us, distant birds fluttering, trying to stay out of Eden's orbit as they worked through the panic of police planning over the festival. She'd always frightened them. They didn't know why. Her brother had been the real terror in the hearts of the Drug Squad cops and beat cops and forensics experts in the office, but they still endured real nerves around Eden even when the shark in the tank was well dead. They weren't sure what kind of creature Eden was, but they didn't like the look of her spikes. Only I knew how poisonous she really was.

'So,' I said eventually, gesturing to the map. Eden looked at me for a moment.

'Yes?'

'You're the one with the killer instincts. How would you do it?'

'I wouldn't,' she said flatly.

'Are you still upset with me over the Trumper Park thing?'

'No,' she said.

'Yes,' I corrected.

'I have no emotions about the Trumper Park thing. Emotion right now would be a hindrance to our planning.'

'You're upset with me about the Trumper Park thing,' I nodded. 'You're upset that for a moment I suggested that you might be one type of killer, while really you're another. You've actually got your sook on about the variety of serial killer you are.'

She closed her eyes and chewed her lips. Seemed to be restraining herself from reaching over and strangling me that very second. Strangely, I didn't get the flushed cheeks and clenching stomach I usually felt when I tiptoed into dangerous territory with Eden. Maybe I was finally getting over my fear of her. Or more likely, I was being lulled into a false sense of security. I knew mixed into it somewhere was a real anger at her, an anger that was growing, a reaction to the physical and mental barrier she presented in my journey to wellness.

Jesus. I rubbed my eyes. I was being seduced by the support group bullshit.

'You'll get over this,' Eden said, still scanning the map. 'Anger is a part of grief.'

'I'm not angry You're angry!'

'You're angry. Why else would you be taking pathetic pot shots at me about my night-time activities?'

'Oh, I don't know. Because your night-time activities are what I have devoted my life to putting a stop to?'

'Devoted your life. Please. It was cop or council worker, Frank. Let's be realistic.'

'You're right. I'll just get over it.'

'If you had any idea what kind of killer I am, you'd be well over it,' she snapped suddenly, turning her blank, snake eyes on me. 'It's killers like me who keep the predator count down, you absolutely clueless fool of a man.'

I felt my cheeks flush. Ah, there it was. The old terror.

'You want to know why the Glebe morgue isn't stuffed full of more Martinas?' she asked, eyes wide. 'Because of killers like me.'

Eden tapped her chest violently, left white dots beneath her collarbone that faded before my eyes. I'd touched her. It was kind of cathartic, getting her all worked up. Sharing the ache and the upset.

'I don't understand what you're talking about,' I said.

'That's because you're an idiot,' she seethed. She yanked her cap straight. 'People like you see the world through a . . . a pinhole. You have no idea that there are so very many different types of evil. You're blind. Blind.'

'Those four up in Byron. Were they . . . ? I mean you're saying you hunt . . . evil people.'

'I'm done talking about this.'

'Were they bad people? The young couple, too? Is that why you do it? Did Benjamin Annous and his crew do someth–'

I realised that I was holding Eden's arm, trying to pin her, to force her to answer my questions. She wrenched herself free. I became aware that people were assembling all around us.

Eden slipped off the table and walked to the map. Our colleagues were reluctant to meet eyes with her. They stared at the ceiling, the map, their shoes. Eden took a blue marker from the edge of the partition on which the map was pinned.

'People will be safe in big groups.' She rolled her shoulders, shrugging off our argument, and started marking the four running paths on the map with savage gestures. 'So at the start of each run, when they're all together, there's little chance anyone will get snatched.'

She took a pink marker and coloured in the four paths running from the start line. The first few kilometres north, before the paths split. The bridge south.

'They'll also be under the watchful gaze of spectators at each finish line,' Eden continued. 'The parks will be flooded with people. They'll all be on the lookout for a white van. So we can assume the risk there is low too.'

Eden drew a big pink circle around all four parks. I felt the tightness in my chest easing as she stood back and revealed the four paths, each now slashed by pink marks.

'Along these paths, the danger zones will be unlit areas with discreet vehicle access. The runners will spread out as they go up hills and around corners. We can cross off these denser areas, where the killer won't want to be caught on CCTV in shopfronts and petrol stations. There are also the traffic cameras and bridges where spectators will assemble to watch the runners. So considering all that, these are the primary zones we should man heavily.'

Eden coloured in eight blocks of roadway, three of them on the path belonging to the marathoners.

'The marathon runners are the bulk of our concern, obviously,' she said, following the path with the butt of her pen as she looped around the beach at La Perouse. 'They've got the farthest to go. There are fewer of them. They'll be under a lot more physical strain than the other runners, so they'll be an easier target for an abduction.

'A lot of these areas out here on the marathon route, especially near the prison, are bushy. There are side roads down through Port Botany where a van could easily be lost. All this, here, behind Hillsdale, this is all industrial. Perfect place to stop and get the job done, dump the body and keep moving. The runners should be safe again by the time they head back up the coast. The backpackers in Coogee and Bondi will be out in force to cheer them on. So we'll have to have a heavy police presence all the way from Kingsford to Chifley.'

Gina from the front desk appeared in my peripheral vision, a welcome mirage in an emerald green dress ending right above her spotless knees and immaculate calves. She stood beckoning me with a single finger beside a short, scruffy Italian-looking guy. The young man was holding sheets of photocopied paper. I went over while Eden continued directing the station staff.

'Another tip for you.' Gina did a little flourish, gesturing to the Italian kid. Gina was sick of the tips – every crackpot and conspiracy theorist from Milperra to Madrid had called or visited the station to voice their thoughts on the killer, and Gina was the one cataloguing them all. Some of them genuinely offered useless tidbits – overheard boasts at the local pub, neighbours acting strangely, white vans by the handful – and some of them were just the ramblings of lonely old men who spent too much time Googling in public libraries. Gina was holding it together but her eyes were tired and her jaw muscles twitched.

I put my hand out for the Italian kid and he shuffled his papers to one hand, pumped with a callused palm. Backpacker. Fingers hardened from fruit picking, scraping scum off pots in the back of kitchens, cleaning houses. He hadn't shaved in a while and when he had it had been a half-effort. The sunglasses hanging off his neck were a three-dollar job.

'I am Ruben Esposito.'

'How you going, Mr Esposito?'

Gina left us, and the young man handed me a flier for the running festival, printed from the internet on a dodgy printer. Caroline Eckhart smiled up at me, arms folded, brandishing those carved stone biceps. I felt flabby and angry at the sight of her.

'This . . . woman,' Ruben struggled. Looked at the ceiling, licked his lips, carefully remembered what was probably dozens of boring English language lessons. 'The festival-e. My boss is . . . *ossessionato*. Errr. My boss is ob-sess.'

'This is your boss?' I pointed at the picture of Caroline, stabbed her face with my finger a little too hard so that the paper crumpled.

'No. No. No. My boss,' he spread his hands on his chest, 'is ob-sess with this woman.' He stabbed her face as well.

'Your boss is obsessed with Caroline Eckhart?'

'Yes.'

'Well, that's nice.' I shrugged sharply, looked back at the gathering around Eden, wondering what I was missing. 'I've kind of got a big serial killer case going on here though.'

'I think,' Ruben struggled, 'my boss . . . is . . . serial killer.'

I looked at the young man's eyes. Wondered if he was stoned. He looked worn. He'd snatched my words 'serial killer' right out of the air. It didn't sound to me like he knew what they meant, but that he was parroting them back to me to hold my attention. 'My boss is . . . eh, I am afraid. The girls. The running girls?'

He pointed at Caroline. I glanced at the other sheets of paper. There was a news story on the Sydney Parks Strangler and another older clipping about a high-profile surgical bungle, something right out of the gossip columns. Plastic surgery. Caroline Eckhart. Obsessions. I didn't have time for this.

I placed the papers on top of each other and folded them.

'I'll check this out when I get a minute.'

'Ehhh, she –'

'You've done great, mate.' I slapped Ruben on the shoulder. 'Really great. I'm going to take this information and add it to our run sheet. If you go back down to reception, Gina will give you an event number, and you'll be able to ring the station and check how your information is going. *Graci. Graci*, mate.'

'I –'

'Reception,' I pointed. 'Recepciano!'

I went back to the desk. Eden was just wrapping up. She turned to the crowd. Eyes all around me averted again, the way they do when someone cries in public, avoiding the humiliation, ignoring the hurt. There were no questions and the flock of frightened birds that had become my colleagues eventually dispersed. She sat down beside me, looking at the map. I sensed again that strange discomfort in her, the nervousness or the edginess that told me instinctively that something was wrong with her lately, that it wasn't just my slowly blossoming discontent with what she was, not just her slowly healing bones, but something much deeper disturbing her, keeping her up at night. I wavered between resenting her and wanting to help. Found myself bumping her shoulder with my own, the way I used to, the way she'd always hated me doing, making her sway, reach out and steady herself with a hand on the desk.

'Ready for the hunt?' I asked. She gave a little quarter-smile.

'Let the games begin,' she said.

A target on the move is the easiest to con. Hooky knew that Ella Preston left the house every evening at half past five, leaving herself a short twenty minutes to grab the 989 to Bondi, four minutes to walk down the hill, another four minutes to unload her stuff in the staff common room, wash her face, apply her make-up and get to work. Give or take a couple of minutes, she was always ready for the after-work customers to start flooding off the buses and in through the wide open doors, for the surf bums to come wandering up the hill in their bruised and warped thongs, spraying sand over the black rubber flooring like stars.

When she popped open her front door, Hooky was there in the hallway, looking at her phone, a black leather folio of printed real estate rental fliers clutched tightly against the chest of her bright red blazer. She made a delicate little noise of surprise and dropped the folio, adjusted her fine red glasses in embarrassment.

'Oh, excuse me,' she gushed. 'You scared the life out of me.'

'Oh, I'm sorry,' Ella laughed, bending down and dragging the pages into a pile.

'It's my fault. I was listening very carefully,' Hooky grinned. 'I'm trying to get in touch with Mr David? I called and I thought

I heard his phone ringing inside. God, I'm so stressed. Too much coffee. Too much coffee today.'

Finding out who owned the apartment across from Imogen's had been as easy as rifling through the mailboxes. Sometimes Hooky felt bored with the game. Wanted a challenge. She might have picked Imogen's lock. She might have lifted Frank's keys from his pocket when she lifted his phone to get Imogen's number. But tracking down Ella, hacking *her* phone, looking at her shifts, making sure she'd be in a rush out the door, putting on her real estate agent's uniform . . . It was all probably very unnecessary. But people don't play games because they're easy. They play them because they're fun.

'I'm sorry, I don't know that guy.' Ella watched as Amy tried to squash the papers back into the folder with her phone pinned between her cheek and shoulder. 'Did you have an appointment, or . . .'

'Yes, we did,' Hooky sighed dramatically. 'This is my day though. This is so *completely* my day. I had thirteen people turn up to an auction this morning – all gawkers. My printer is broken and the café next door is turning into one of those two-dollar shops with the recording playing all the time – you know the ones –'

'*Sports socks, six packs, two dollars only.* Yeah, I know. How awful.' Ella glanced at her watch.

'Well, now I'm supposed to be taking photos of Mr David's apartment and he's not here.' Hooky threw her hands up, or tried to, managing one full extension and one lopsided flap of her left hand, the gigantic folder pinned by an elbow into her hip. 'Oh, it's hopeless. Hopeless. This flat's got to go on the website tonight, for god's sake.'

'Man,' Ella looked at her watch again, 'that sucks.'

'I've got parties interested in China.' Hooky rubbed her brow. 'Urgh. God. If they go with the Mosman property instead of this one –'

'Um, I'm really sorry for you. I've got to go, though, so . . .' Ella started walking away.

'If only there was some way.' Hooky turned to the door at the end of the hall, Mr David's apartment, diagonally across from Ella's door. She watched Ella watching the door out of the corner of her eye, as though the girl expected it to fly open at any minute and reveal Mr David in all his glory, relieving the problem of the pretty real estate agent in the hall in time for Ella to catch the bus. Ella chewed her lip, continued backing away towards the mailboxes.

'Damn it.' Hooky tried to keep her tone sorrowful, to not blow her cover by letting her exasperation at Ella's retreating steps creep through. She gestured to the door across from Mr David's apartment, the door next to Ella's. 'Shit. I'm so close.'

'I'm really sorry. I hope he comes back.' Ella turned and grabbed the handle of the glass door to the foyer. Hooky bit her tongue. Hard. Ella was slipping away. It was time to bring out the big guns. She sobbed just once, loudly, her face buried in her fist. She heard Ella pop open the door, but not the creak as the glass swung open.

Hooky sobbed again.

'Oh. Um. Are you okay?'

'I'm fine,' Hooky gave a pathetic, crooked smile, shuffled the folders in her arms and searched her pockets for a tissue. 'Long day, that's all. I just wish it was over.'

'I wish I could help,' Ella said.

You can, you idiot, Hooky thought.

'Hang on,' Ella half-turned.

'Yes?' Hooky held her breath.

'Mr David's apartment and Imogen's should be mirror images of each other,' Ella said. She pointed to the door next to her own. Number five. 'You could take pictures of Imogen's apartment. It's just for like, a preview, right? You'll have the layout all correct. Just reverse the photos.'

Ella smiled at her own genius. Hooky felt the colour returning to her face.

'That's brilliant!'

'Well, you know . . .'

'Who's Imogen?' Hooky blinked.

'She's a doctor,' Ella said, walking back into the hall. 'She's my neighbour, in number five there. Is she home?'

'I don't know,' Hooky lied. She let hope saturate her voice. She rapped on the door to number five. There was silence. 'Would she have keys to number four?'

'No. Well, I don't think so. I don't know. But I've got keys to Imogen's place. She gave me one once after she locked herself out. You could –' Ella paused. Appreciated Hooky for a moment. Seemed to decide she was trustworthy. Hooky tried to look sweet. 'Yeah, I mean. We'll be quick, right?'

Ella swung her backpack off her shoulder, unzipped the front pocket.

'You've got keys?' Hooky covered her mouth, maybe too dramatically. She'd have to work on that one. 'That's fantastic.'

'All the apartments are exactly the same, so Imogen's corner apartment will be the same as David's. We'll go in and you can snap a few shots and then we'll be out.'

'That'd be perfect.' Hooky clapped her hands awkwardly, gripped the folder before it could slide again. 'Oh you're the best. You're an absolute lifesaver. You sure Imogen wouldn't mind?'

'She'll be alright,' Ella said. 'I'll go in with you and watch you. We'll be quick as a flash. She's a really nice chick. Uptight, but nice. We've got to be fast, though. I'm gonna be late in a minute.'

'Alright, quick as a flash.' Hooky made a show of prancing into the apartment, knees high, a happy elf. 'You're the absolute best for this. Thank you so much.'

Hooky went straight into the bedroom. This was Imogen and Frank's bed. She stood wondering at its hospital corners, the expensive cream coverlet, waffle-textured, the kind she'd forbid him dragging to the sofa on movie nights. There were books on her side of the bed – true crime novels – and nothing on his. Not committed enough to bring his books over yet, the permanency of them sitting there in a lopsided stack like promises, a list growing higher and higher towards a ceiling he couldn't bear reaching, couldn't believe he'd ever reach, before the inevitable fall. The room wasn't him at all. It was too clean, too bare, too orchestrated. The en suite was free of shards of his stubble, his scraggy hair on the shower walls. There wasn't so much as a toothbrush to symbolise that he even existed. The cat had been a resident for a short while, she knew, but now it was gone too, the strange imbalance of the token he had taken from his dead girlfriend living and lounging in his current girlfriend's place too much, too weird.

Hooky snapped a couple of photographs. Wandered around appreciating the ceilings.

'This is perfect. Thank you again so much. You're an absolute lifesaver. Nice apartments, aren't they? My Beijing investors are going to just snap these up, I'm telling you.'

'Well, I'm glad I could help.' Ella was hovering by the front door, checking at the time on her phone now, as though it was slower than the watch and could somehow give her more seconds before the bus pulled up outside. She itched to go. Hooky stalled.

'I'm just going to be a second.' Hooky snapped some photos of the balcony, came inside and stood by the desk in the corner. Looked at the manila folders all in a stack, their spines labelled neatly with printed surnames and dates. 'Just one sec here.'

Evans. Cherry. Bithway. Heildale. Smith.

She'd have the Tanner file tucked away somewhere. Tanner, the names Imogen kept Googling on her laptop over and over again, right after the texts and emails about the Archers started flying. Hooky didn't know what the connection between the Tanners and the Archers was yet, but she was going to find out. There had to be a reason Imogen was so hot on Eden's tail.

Hooky swiped away the camera on her phone and switched to the contacts list, pushed the dial button. Ella cocked her ear in the hallway as she heard her phone ringing inside her apartment.

'Shit. Shit! That's my landline. I'm just going to leave you for a sec –'

'I'm almost done,' Hooky shouted as the door clicked closed. She threw open the drawers one at a time, found the Tanner file in the very last one, under a stack of old newspapers. She shoved the file open on the desk and spread the papers out, went back to the camera and began to click. She was just pushing the bottom drawer closed, the file replaced, when Ella threw open the door again.

'All good?'

'Yeah, hang-up call.' Ella shuffled her backpack higher on her shoulder, annoyance edging into her tone. 'You done here?'

'All done.' Hooky smiled. She strode to the door, slipping the phone into the pocket of her blazer. 'You've been instrumental.'

If you count dreaming about work as work itself, which I do, I was on the planning for the running festival for about thirty-seven hours straight. When Imogen found me the night before Take Back the Parks I was sitting at her kitchen table with a glass of milk staring at the balcony doors, no idea that she'd even arrived home, my fingernails bitten down to stubs. I'd actually turned my phone off for an hour and was playing a sort of mental game with myself, battling back the desire to turn it on again, when she walked into the room. I knew when I turned it on, it would explode with messages from Eden, Hooky, Captain James, some journalists I'd known over the years. There were maps spread all over the floor of the kitchen, all over the bench tops, some stuck to the fridge, all representing the structure of security for the event in different colours and patterns.

Together, Eden and I had tracked down as many CCTV cameras on each of the run routes as possible. We'd directed a team to work through the registered runners, looking for participants with violent pasts, and we'd composed watch lists of their likenesses for the foot patrol teams. Four different security companies were covering the events – we'd briefed them all on what we were looking for, what codes to use for what kind of backup should they spot anything unusual on the night.

While all that was happening, I'd tried about seventeen times to get through to Caroline Eckhart to persuade her to cancel the event, despite being told to leave all the schmoozing to Eden. Caroline erected a wall of people to field any communication I tried to throw at her, whether it was email, call or message. I was fairly sure if I'd attempted to send a carrier pigeon to her massive apartment on the Finger Wharf, it would have been shot down. Probably with lasers. If she didn't hear from me, she couldn't refuse my direct appeal. As far as I knew, she was doing the same to Captain James.

The tension surrounding the festival was feverish. Journalists and the public wanted to be there when someone was killed. Everyone else wanted to prevent a killing taking place. The whole thing was like some horrific hunting expedition, the bear trap snapped open and set, teeth gaping, the trigger ready for the slightest breath of wind to whisper over it before it snapped shut. I was more afraid of what might happen if we lured and cornered the bear. I still had no idea who the Parks Strangler was. What sort of creature we were dealing with. I'd stood by Jill Noble's badly decomposed body in Glebe morgue and tried to get a feel for the killer – and all I got was malice. Pure, inhuman malice, the kind that takes over soldiers pushed too far by the intensity of war, the kind that makes them do sick things like burning villages, forgetting their humanity, forgetting their lives before that moment. Someone out there was letting go completely with these women, and what that person was surrendering to was nothing but a monster. It takes a long time to cultivate that sort of evil power in a human being. No one is born that angry – you have to be made that way.

Eden had said the victims were being punished by proxy, that the killer was living out revenge on them that she couldn't enact on the real target of her fury. The real target, it seemed, was unavailable somehow – she was dead or out of reach. The killer couldn't strangle and beat the real target the way she wanted to, so it was these runners who copped the violence. The original target was a runner then? A fitness junkie? Was her athleticism, her propensity to run, what was being punished? I spent three or four hours wasting time on the internet looking into the backgrounds of famous Australian athletes, trying to find female runners who'd been issued threats, who had violent boyfriends, sons, daughters, husbands. I looked at Caroline Eckhart's ex-boyfriend for a long time, half-heartedly inspired by Mr Esposito's weird tip. But Caroline and her bulky former beau were good friends. She was hardly unavailable to him for punishment.

I kind of knew I was wasting my time, fishing without bait, but I couldn't stop myself. I fell into an exhausted helpless pattern, trudging through one web page after another. Night fell. Takeaway containers lay everywhere, though I didn't remember ordering or eating anything.

And then suddenly Imogen was there, with her fingers working my neck on either side beneath my ears, nails reaching up over my scalp, dragging through my hair. She bent over my chair and kissed me on the cheek, put her arms around me. I sat back and let her squeeze me. The smell of her, the warmth of her lips against my neck, was a relief as potent as a drug. I was snapped awake, electrified.

'How's the dazed detective?'

'I'm wide awake now you're home.'

'I've been home for half an hour,' she laughed, pressing her nose against mine. 'I've had a shower and everything. You've just been sitting there staring at the windows.'

'Sorry, sorry. I'm just . . . I'm just tired. And starving, for some reason, although I think I've eaten.' I looked around.

'I've ordered pizza.' She sat down beside me. 'It'll be here soon.'

'Oh, you're a doll face.' I reached out, squeezed her taut cheeks so that her lips poked out. 'You're an absolute doll face. What happened to your arm?'

She had a massive bruise on her bicep. I gave it a squeeze and she slapped me.

'I ran into something. I don't know.'

'You tell those other men not to be so rough with you.'

'You're hilarious.' She rolled her eyes.

Imogen was a strange creature, an odd choice for me. I knew that much without Eden having to tell me. She could be very mild and gentle, as she was now, quiet in the way that suggested she'd ticked off all her goals for the day, whatever they had been, and she was satisfied to pass the soft decline of the evening light curiously poring over my maps, holding my hand, now and then looking at messages on her phone and tapping away replies. She wanted nothing from me, not that I'd have minded if she had. I might not have been there at all.

There were times, however, when I couldn't talk to her, when her mind was so tangled with clients and their problems that when she walked through the door she was ten people. She was the needy little girl with daddy issues, the OCD sufferer exhausted with worry about her health, the angry old man trying to push down the abuse suffered as a child, which rose and rose over again through the decades like bile. She could be manic with her own hidden desires and concerns – I knew the armchair detective thing was a flag of something, some ancient point she had to prove or dream she couldn't ignore, a childhood fascination with cops that needed some outlet other than me. She needed to unravel things. Part of the hobby was the money, which she greedily fantasised about, but some part of it was the thrill of the investigation – which also poked its head up in her ordinary work. She dug down into people, uncovered buried traumas, brought secrets out into the light and examined them. There was power in that. Control. Perhaps the unhealthy kind.

A part of me also recognised that what I liked about Imogen was what I liked about Eden. There was no wearing of the heart on the sleeve with these two. Their weaknesses, insecurities, embarrassing little joys were nowhere to be seen. Once or twice I'd seen the masks slip on both of them – once I caught Eden lose herself to some tune on her headphones in the station's locker room. When I say 'lose herself', I mean she did a smooth little wiggle of her hips, frowned and mouthed a nasty lyric or two, then went back to packing her things away in her locker, robotic. That was Eden 'losing herself'.

Imogen did it too, albeit more obviously. She tried too hard to get people to like her. Me, sometimes, when she ordered pizzas after spending all week trying to cram carrots and hummus down my throat. When she asked hidden or sidelong questions about our future together, trying to work out how I felt about it. Whether I loved her.

Her obvious, inescapable jealousy over girls she caught me looking at, over Hooky. I knew it must be a powerful kind of jealousy for it to emerge in the accusations over Amy. Imogen had never had a specific target for her jealousy before, but now I knew its intensity for the first time. Imogen was the kind of woman who wouldn't let an embarrassing emotional failing like jealousy show in anything more than the tips of waves, no matter what massive undercurrents swept the ocean floor. I could see hate in her eyes at the mere mention of the girl. For some reason, she didn't feel the same way about Eden, which was strange. I spent every working minute with Eden. It was natural, given what we faced together, that we might develop feelings for each other – plenty of cops did. Why was Imogen so sure Eden was no romantic threat to her? Did she know something that I didn't?

I watched her scrolling through the day's news on her phone, stopping now and then to examine commentary on some high-profile sex scandal or another, an old actor and his obscenely young wife. There was a story about some guys in council-worker uniforms who had beaten up a couple in Lavender Bay, five of them on two, with no apparent reason for the attack. Imogen looked soft in the dim light from above us, gold light falling on her arms, on the curves of her collarbones, on the backs of her hands. She had one word, 'payment', written on her hand. I don't know what she'd been doing that day, as I'd commandeered the apartment and she'd simply gone off to entertain herself and keep out of my way, but I hoped she hadn't spent her time paying bills. I reached out and took her hand, and without looking at me, she squeezed my palm.

'You're funny,' I said.

'You're funny.' She smiled to herself.

Of Bangkok, Tara remembered snippets. Heat. A heavy, numbing heat that made the body beg for relief outside the wall of air conditioning that halted like held breath at the automatic doors of the airport. A throbbing in her calves as she made her way through the crowds of freelance taxi drivers, all of them oldish, angry-looking men muttering prices as she passed, brown lips thin and dry as words rippled through them too fast. She remembered wild dogs by the side of the highway, slipping in and out between the long grass like snakes, tussling by the side of a brown canal. Huge wooden temples on impossibly high stands outside carpet shops, antique shops, supermarkets and coconut stands, heaped with pink and yellow flowers and bowls of rotting meat and coloured rice. The city beyond, grey sludge in the heat haze, the gaping mouths of half-finished and abandoned apartment buildings, tattered advertising fluttering in the breeze.

Tara remembered narrow halls and darkness, the smell of incense burning. Bright red carpet everywhere, flecked with pieces of white cotton, as though someone had washed clothes that still had a tissue in the pocket and then trailed the thing throughout the building. Thinking that there shouldn't have been carpet in the doctor's halls, that somehow the presence of carpet in an apparently sterile, surgical environment seemed odd, out of place, the way it might in a kitchen. A bathroom.

Smiles everywhere. Excited smiles. Smiles fading into the dark. She was signing documents in a dark room. People were whispering. The towels. Towels everywhere, stacked, different colours. Why were they different colours? Shouldn't they all be new and white? There were lapses in her memory and they were happening fast, snipping the edges of moments away. She was shivering in the cold. The lights were flickering. A machine was screaming beeps and the people around her were talking fast.

Darkness for a long time, a liquidy depth of dream Tara wasn't sure she would ever wake from, wasn't sure she wanted to wake from. She was free of her body for an instant. Weightless. Oh, for a moment those ancient aches in her hips and knees gave way and she had no hips or knees, and her chest collapsed inwards, dissolved, so that she was nothing but a floating consciousness, a bee buzzing from light to light as colours flashed before her. And then her eyelids were being pulled back and someone was shoving a tube into her newly formed throat.

Tara? Tara? Come back to us, Tara. Come back, honey. Squeeze my hand if you can hear me. Come on, girl. Come on, girl.

Australian voices. Why were they Australian voices? Tara squinted, tried to wriggle away from the words. *Come on. Come on.* She was running again in the dark. Joanie was behind her. She had to run. Had to get away. She felt a rhythmic pumping on her newly returned chest, and again the squeal of machines. Darkness fell again. And then there was stillness, the crisp firmness of starched hospital sheets beneath her fingertips. Everything aching. People laughing in the busy halls. A woman was there, one of those wrinkled, pleasant-faced people used to frowning with concern. Her navy blue scrubs were pinned with cheerful things – a fleshy pink watch and a ribbon, a pair of stickers printed with animals grinning maniacally, rows and rows of teeth. Tara had the impression that she had seen this woman before, that in her half-drugged state the woman had been talking to her, perhaps had talked to her for days, her bony hand playing with Tara's wrist, a skin-covered manacle impossible to break. Tara had bucked in the bed, tried to shift from a position she felt she might have been in for hours. The pain fluttered through her like a big red bird, razor-sharp feathers brushing the insides of her arms and legs, pulling on stitches. Hundreds and hundreds of stitches. She felt them tugging all at once like so many tiny spiders latched onto hunks of skin, curved teeth inserted.

People came and went, people in suits, people in police uniforms. All of them white. Tara hadn't known there were so many white people in all of Bangkok. Might have said so, but she couldn't hear her own voice above the rising and falling hum of the drugs.

'You're back in Sydney,' the nurse said gently. 'You've been back in Sydney for six weeks, honey.'

In time, she was sitting, and the nurse was talking gently to her, talking, talking, talking, and as the sun began to fall, Tara began to make sense of the words.

'But then,' the nurse was saying, 'people make bad choices. I know I have. It happens.'

'What happened . . . to me?' Tara asked.

The nurse looked at her.

'You fell victim to a terrible scam, Tara,' the nurse said. She reached for Tara's wrist again. 'And no matter what anyone tells you, girl, you're the victim in this. You thought you were being sold a service, and . . . god, I suppose the doctor you hired thought he might have been able to provide it. Christ, I don't know. He certainly made an attempt.' She seemed to want to give a laugh but swallowed it back. 'Tara, your surgery in Bangkok, your weight reduction surgery, went very, very badly.'

Tara looked at her hands. They seemed the same. Scarred, yes, by the savage pokes and prods of several IV tubes. She pulled back the sleeves of her gown. Bandages, from wrist to forearm. From forearm to shoulder. Her arms were half the size they were, but beneath the bandages she felt strange ripples and bulges of flesh, a seam of wide stitches that ran from the inside of her elbow to her armpit, the entire bottom half of her arm savagely cut away. Another seam ran from her armpit into her collarbone, disappearing in a mesh of grooves and dips. Tara watched the unfamiliar limbs trembling as she explored herself. She felt her ribs. Were those her ribs? Fluid moved beneath the surface of the skin, igniting with pain as she touched.

'Be gentle with yourself,' the nurse advised.

'What . . . happened?'

'Your body is very badly scarred,' the nurse murmured. 'We think that the doctor in Bangkok attempted the abdominal lipectomy on the first night you arrived. He performed what is commonly known as a tummy tuck. The next day – the next day, Tara, before your body could recover from what was, quite frankly, a savage procedure – he went ahead with the breasts, the arms, the back. You've got to understand . . . this person had little medical training. Well, little training in Western medical procedures. You've undergone an incredible physical trauma.'

'Get me up,' Tara said.

'You really can't –'

'Get me up,' she snapped.

The nurse didn't move. Tara yanked back the blankets, felt nausea stir in her stomach. She clawed at the chrome bed frame, her new, strange form shivering violently, making the plastic bracelets on her wrists flap against the bars. The woman with the kind, leathery face eventually came to her aid, slipping under her arm, a human crutch. The floor was dust-flecked, cold linoleum, the painful trek from the bed to the bathroom traversed a thousand times before by faceless ghosts, a stumble-and-a-half of agony before the blessed stability of the white plastic shelf in front of the glass. Tara stared at the unfamiliar face in the mirror. Reached up and touched the limp side, dragged the corner of her mouth up so that it aligned with the other, then let it fall. Her nose had been broken. When, in all this, had her nose been broken?

The bandaged, robed body before her was a crooked white question mark, not the round, solid hulk that she was used to. Her shoulders were high and her neck was low as she rested there, a rageful bird, both bewildered and terrified by the new world around it.

What am I? she wondered. She stared and shook. *What am I now?*

'Did you tell her?' someone whispered.

'I think she knows what's happened to her now, but not the other thing,' the nurse said. Tara looked, but the voices came from beyond the bathroom door and she couldn't travel back on her own. She leaned, saw a slice of white coat. A doctor.

'You need to tell her. Best she gets both halves at once, get it over with. Perfect timing. The shrinks can come in just in time and clean up the mess and we can all get back to what's important.'

'She's still coming round,' the nurse said. 'I think I'm only just now getting through. It's been days of mumbling. But I think she's comprehending now.'

'Good,' the voice said. 'Well, I need you back in A&E in an hour, so make it snappy, yeah? Sorry, dear, you fucked yourself. You'll be scarred for life. Oh, and your mother's done herself in. Best of luck, see you later. Right? Then back on the ward. Got me? We can't hold their hands forever, even the rich ones.'

There were footsteps, a sigh. Tara gripped the ledge before her.

Eden felt sheepishly happy, just for a moment, as she wandered across the wet green grass of Bradfield Park, passing softly through the crooked gates and pathways made by the elbows and shoulders of a thousand people. She was a fox slipping between dopey hounds, her ears pricking naturally to laughs and squeals and breathy sighs, the static excitement of a mob. It was a curious little ripple of happiness that pulsed in her. For a moment, she relished being in the crowd – because for at least one killer tonight, these were hunting grounds, and Eden never felt more comfortable than when she walked among prey.

She could understand the appeal of them to the Parks Strangler. The runners fluttered and flapped together in gaggling grounds like plump, stupid chickens, their muscles and tendons stretching as they readied themselves for flight. Taut calves hitched and strained, bulbous shoulders rolled upwards, then fell. Eden thought of blood, and there was so much blood here tonight, flushing in excited cheeks and pumping through jugulars. She yearned quietly, lifting her head and breathing in the scented air, pregnant with chemicals – deodorant, tiger balm, zinc, the sugary tang of energy drinks, tablets, gels. In the human-thick evening, the light beyond the harbour hit its deepest blue, wedged between an approaching storm and the black, still water. Then the orange street lamps along Alfred Street flickered and came to light, eliciting a long, low cheer from the crowd. Weighty anticipation, as real as the smell of the soil stirring in desire for the rain, another cheer as lightning pricked the distant suburbs. She picked her way up the hill towards the thick trunks of the old bridge, stopping to look at the birds high above swirling over the crowd, ducking for moths attracted to the lights.

Hunting grounds. Was Eden being hunted at that moment?

She looked at the crowd around her. Now and then she caught a face turned towards her, eyes on her own, catching her briefly before turning away. The lanky young man in black lycra, stretching his gangly arms above his head. The portly middle-aged woman in a trio of women laughing and chewing on her water-bottle nib. The old man sitting alone beneath the sprawling tree, one half of his face lit by the glass-front apartment buildings above Luna Park, an ancient mask as he tied the laces of his bulky running shoes. Somewhere a radio station was commentating on the runners assembled at the start line, a row of stoic Kenyans and fat-free middle-aged men huffing and swaying at the ribbon. Was the killer here tonight? Eden stood beneath a sprawling tree and tried to guess. If she'd ever been the sort of killer to garner this sort of attention, she was sure she'd take the bait. How does one stay home from such a grandiose event, organised almost in tribute to one's night-time games? Eden couldn't imagine her own work ever causing such a stir. Most of her victims were old men with long-held morbid fetishes – the public-toilet child molesters and cinema masturbators of the world. Where they were women, they were hard, loveless women. Black widows, Munchausen by proxy sufferers, the occasional corporate assassin. Clara, the baby-faced Byron Bay beauty, had been a breath of fresh air. The victims of the Parks Strangler were these fresh-faced girls, vulnerable to the crushing glimpse of love handles in shop windows, the all-too-common call of the jogger's pathway to panting redemption. They were incredibly easy to relate to, these women. They were all daughters, colleagues, girls next door. Eden's victims were shadows. That's what gave her the longevity she enjoyed as a hunter. Complete lack of public outrage.

Her trail of thoughts was broken when Frank swam into view beside her, flipping the bill of her black baseball cap in the annoying manner of a guilty brother. He stood on the hill beside her and looked at the writhing crowd. He was unshaven and mussed from sleep, the special operations shirt ill-fitting on his now-lean frame sagging at the collar. There was a police-issue leather jacket slung over one arm.

'Spotted the killer yet?'

'Not yet,' Eden said. 'Glad it's going to rain though. Plenty of hoodies around. Very helpful.'

'Are you going to jump rides?' he asked. The two hadn't discussed their own operations on the ground. It was good practice to have at least one of them stationed at the police command centre on Macquarie Street to field calls from cops out on patrol, assess what sounded promising and disregard the usual complaints that came with crowd control – men brawling, women falling, the inevitable mid-event heart attack. Frank must have assumed it would be Eden out in the crowd jumping rides from one patrol car to another as complaints came in.

'I might run some of it,' she said.

'You sure you should?'

'Thanks for the concern, Dad. But I know my own body. I'll hop a ride out to Kensington, then run some of that. Maybe run to Coogee, get another ride back. I want to spend at least some of it on the road. In amongst it.'

Frank nodded. 'Well. Be careful. You're not more than a week off that crutch.'

'I'll be fine,' she said. 'I want to be right there if we get anything.'

A low rumble of thunder over Balmain. The crowd whooped and cheered. Eden spotted the girl, Hooky, coming up the hill towards them, bright green Doc Martens gripping the wet slope, making muddy tracks between the people moving slowly to the start line. The girl had a computer tablet tucked under her arm.

Short blonde hair, Eden thought. But no, Hooky wasn't the journalist who had turned up at Hades' home. For one, the old man had said it was a woman, and Hooky was all girl. The tiny chunks of polished wood in her earlobes, the leather straps on her wrists. That hangdog troubled-teen look she gave everything and everyone, as if at any moment she would be misunderstood, under-represented, oppressed, the way so many teenagers were convinced they were.

Oh, yes, the girl was brilliant. She had potential. And her upbringing, the murders. Eden didn't know much about that, hadn't bothered to look into it, but she recognised that something had changed in the girl, that the survival instinct was alive in her. When someone close to you is murdered, it flips a switch inside. The world is no longer an inherently good place – it is full of predators and you realise, however explicitly, that you must become a predator in order to be immune from the same fate. It was all very simple to Eden. Her switch had been flipped early on. She had grown and evolved along those killer lines, and now she was more beast than she was anything else. Frank had been flipped, but he was so concerned with keeping those dark thoughts and melancholies under wraps that it was all he could do to stay sober at the same time.

Eden wasn't sure how far gone Hooky was. But she didn't have time for such meaningless curiosities.

'Alright,' the girl said in greeting, peeling off the cover on the little tablet. 'Let's talk about chip timing.'

'What on earth is chip timing?' Frank wrinkled his nose.

'I'm about to explain, Grandpa,' Hooky sighed, drawing up a map on the screen. 'Just hold onto your suspenders. We've got ten minutes until the start gun, so no stupid questions.'

'No stupid questions,' Frank murmured, waggling a finger in Eden's face. The older woman rolled her eyes.

'All the runners have a microchip embedded in a little foam pad on the back of their race bibs,' Hooky continued, pointing to the crowd. Eden looked at the numbers before her, pinned to the front of singlets and jackets. 'When they pass over an electronic mat on the ground at the start line, their chip registers and a start time is assigned. At the finish line, when the runners pass over another electronic mat, the microchip is blipped again, thereby giving an accurate digital time in which they ran the event. You keeping up?'

'I think so.' Frank nodded. Eden nodded.

'The runners take their registry number, the one written on the front of their bibs, and look up their results online. The chip timer also sets off an automatic camera which flashes pictures of the runners as they cross the line. So they can punch in their number and get pictures of themselves starting and finishing the event.'

'This would be really useful,' Eden said, 'if we knew the killer was going to register for the event. Which is about as likely as me winning the thing.'

'Well, it won't be useful for that,' Hooky said. 'But it will be useful for discovering if anyone goes missing from the race.'

'How?'

'Well.' Hooky drew up the map on the tablet, tapped and highlighted the starting point, where a blue bubble flashed, indicating the location of the device. 'There are electronic mats at the start line and finish line that'll tell us when runners start and when they finish. But if, say, you were some kind of technology whiz, some kind of absolute fucking genius, you could hack the system and get access to all the runner microchips during the race. Then you could set up GPS markers, say, every five hundred metres. Like the mats, the GPS markers would give you an electronic signal, a blip, every time a runner passes over them. A runner would start the race at the start line, and then every five hundred metres, blip, blip, blip, until they reach the finish line.'

Eden took the tablet from Hooky. Looked at the little bubbles intersecting the running paths on the map, flashing as they waited for the runners.

'Why are the markers so close together? Five hundred metres isn't very far.'

'I've rigged the system so that every runner in the entire event has ten minutes to complete each marker. You'd have to be going pretty damned slow to not make it five hundred metres in ten minutes. Every person who starts the race will show up on my system. If they don't get through all the markers in time, it'll send up an alert at the marker they missed. The alert will come right here, to this device. If, for some reason, a runner drops out of the race, we'll know. We'll know which five hundred-metre block they went missing in. We'll know who they are, and where they disappeared within ten minutes of the runner missing the checkpoint.'

'This is . . . this is amazing!' Frank took the tablet from Eden, stared incomprehensibly at the screen.

'Yes, I agree, I'm amazing. But it's an imperfect plan,' Hooky said. 'If someone sprains an ankle and stops midway through the race, you're going to get an alert. If someone stops to chat to someone on the sideline, and doesn't make it over the next marker in time, you're going to get an alert. There are thousands of people in this event. I suspect you're going to get fucking dozens of alerts.'

'It doesn't matter,' Frank said. 'We'll send someone to investigate every alert we get. You never know. One of these might be someone getting snatched off the track.'

'It doesn't help if your killer doesn't nab someone in the race.' Hooky looked at the crowd, distracted. 'There are no rules. Anyone is fair game. They might go after one of the spectators. But fuck it. I thought it might be a useful tool.'

There was howling from the start line. Eden recognised Caroline Eckhart's voice on the speakers, fronting a techno track for the radio station covering the event. The stirring of the crowd, the call and response, the stamping of feet at the ribbon.

'I said, are you ready to run?'

'She's a little star, this one,' Frank growled, looping an arm around Hooky's neck, crushing the girl's head against his chest. 'Oh, she's a genius.'

'I'll keep in contact with you on the road,' Eden said, watching, waiting for her partner to disentangle himself from the teen. She pointed to the girl. 'Get this one a radio. You can feed me alerts and see if I'm nearby.'

'Right,' Frank said. He grabbed the girl by the back of the neck, a big brother's grip. 'You're coming with me, young Einstein.'

Ruben stood on the ledge beneath the attic window and looked down at the grass underneath his feet. He'd broken into a few places in his life when things became desperate – once into his own bedroom after his parents had caught him out in the night and barred him from coming back in. A storm was brewing beyond the tree-lined park, just beginning to sprinkle the cars parked alongside the iron gates with rain. He'd spent the afternoon listening for sounds in the attic room, and when he was convinced no one was home, he began to climb. On top of the garage, he suddenly remembered the white van, and peeled back a worn sheet of corrugated iron to peer into the gloomy space. The van was gone.

He was well aware that his curiosity about the person in the attic room had crept beyond healthy interest. When he stood on the steps outside the police headquarters with his papers in his hands, he had questioned what drove him, what sick pull had hold of him and was reeling him in towards the attic room. He felt pain and terror behind the door at the top of the stairs – but it was more than that. He had told the disinterested Australian policeman he thought that whoever was in the room was the killer. The words had rolled off his tongue, and it was only as he said them that he knew he'd believed this from the moment he read the gossip articles about the Harper girl, and that this had grown and swelled in his mind when he heard the snarling beyond the door.

The Harper kid is a psycho . . . The physical and psychological fallout from bad choices . . .

Bad, bad, bad. There was no better word for what Ruben had heard centimetres from his fingertips, a person, a thing, raging at the wood, a slave to the badness infecting its own body. He couldn't see her, but Ruben could feel the black cloud swirling inside the room. He felt the chill of its wispy fingers slithering under the door in his first moments in the Harper house. There was no cleaning away that badness, no matter how hard he scrubbed.

The boy reached up, gripped the chipped railing beneath the attic windows and pulled. He flipped his elbows up onto the ledge, pushed up and shoved at the windows. Blessedly, they gave easily. He slid over the windowsill and through the curtains.

It was dark inside the attic room, and the air was thick with mould, the wet, damp mould of old bathrooms, metallic on the tongue. There was no light. He scrambled to the wall and tried the light switch by the door. A bulb, long-unused, snapped on above him, shuttering to life angrily like a child shaken awake. At once, the faces pressed in on him as though they had been waiting for him in the dark. It seemed, in the first moment of terror, that they all turned towards him. But in a moment he realised that there were too many. That the hundreds and hundreds of faces were static and not real. He realised, as he crouched by the door, that they were all the same face.

Joan Harper. The sharp blonde woman from the gossip columns, the one photographed sitting placidly at a restaurant with a friend. There were pictures of her littered over every surface, tacked to every square centimetre of wall. Photographs from the house. Young Joanie in her teenage years, squeezed into frame between two other blonde girls, her white teeth gleaming in a Cheshire cat smile. Joan Harper on the bow of a yacht, her short hair whipped across her forehead. Joan Harper on her wedding day, pulling on her snow-white heels. Leaning against one corner was a huge oil painting of Joan Harper reclining in a red leather wingback, her fingers coiled daintily around the stem of a wine glass.

All the pictures were eyeless. Where the eyes should have been were ovular black hollows, scribbled out so that the paper tore and black lines wound around and around the taut cheeks of the Joans crowding up into the corners of the room. The mouths gaped in identical black ovals, howling, hundreds of ghoul Joans screaming from the walls.

Ruben was trembling. He crawled to the table beside the window, put his hand down to steady himself and gagged as a grey puff of mould swirled around a collapsed plate of what might have been cake. Tiny flies billowed from a stack of mould-encrusted plates covered in photographs of Joan, eyes stabbed through, mouths swirling black abysses. Ruben pulled the window closed, felt rain on his cheeks.

I'm not cut out for management. There's too much standing around. Captain James has about forty-eight 'poised-but-ready' poses that he does around the office. But I'm just not that inventive.

As soon as I got to the command centre in Macquarie Street I knew I wasn't going to be there long. Four fold-out tables sliced the little tent in two, cords running over the pavement to wide computer monitors. Eden's scribbled mess of a map was pinned to the inside of the white marquee. The makeshift room was lit by a series of twenty-dollar Ikea lamps someone had run out and grabbed at the last minute, giving it the strange feel of a university dorm room. An esky at the side of the tent was packed with cans of Coke. Every now and then the blue arm of a beat cop slid through the wall and grabbed one before disappearing again, the hammer of boots or the ticking of a pushbike signalling his return to the beat.

Hooky was all over her iPad, tapping, shifting things around. I stood and watched alerts coming up on the screens in front of the cops sitting at the computers, listened to them chatter back and forth over their radios. An officer had dropped out of the other command centre over in Kensington and was in the process of being replaced. Descriptions of the killer were being passed around, and to me it sounded as though we were hunting a ghost. I shifted from foot to foot for a while and then went to the tent flap and looked out at the empty road. A flash of lightning between the buildings on Bridge Street lit up the glass façade of the Museum of Sydney.

'They're almost on us,' Hooky said.

I looked down Macquarie towards the Opera House and picked out a couple of runners, hovering silhouettes on the black asphalt. In seconds they were upon me, a tight group of leaders galloping by, faces set and cheeks sucking at cheekbones. Behind them was a steadily growing wall of humanity, the swinging arms and gaping mouths of an army of machines. The runners came up the hill and shot past, rubber soles clopping on the oily road.

A couple of officers at the edge of the tent cheered them as they went by. One or two of the runners raised their hands in the air, pumped fists in response.

Someone was going to die tonight.

I could feel it in the air. It was too jubilant. Too innocent. The runners had the look of happy sheep enclosed in the lush wet valley of the city buildings. But darkness was approaching. When I looked back down the street towards the harbour, I couldn't see the runners coming off the Cahill Expressway anymore. It was all shadow down there.

I went back inside and took Hooky's arm.

'As they say in the classics: let's get outta here.'

'Don't lose it,' she said. 'We've gotta stay level. The first alerts will come in soon.'

'And I want to be there,' I said. I walked out of the tent, knowing she would follow. Three police Honda bikes were standing in a row by the fence, helmets at the ready.

'You can't ride one of these,' Hooky smirked.

'You want to make a bet?'

I chucked her a helmet. I felt a surge of delight at the flash, however brief, of admiration on her face. Her iPad blipped as she was pushing the helmet onto her head. She grabbed it from where she'd set it on the back of the motorbike.

'It's an alert,' she said. 'One of the half-marathoners has missed a checkpoint on the Pacific Highway.'

'Jump on, kid,' I said. Maybe it was too much.

Eden ran. In her ears, snippets of police conversation rolled over each other, the whole of the festival police command buzzing frantically against the steady beat of her breath.

'Lyrebird to Central Command. Shifting units four-seven-zero and four-seven-one to Domain sector four. The five K runners are half done. Over.'

'Central Command to Lyrebird. Roger the last. Over.'

'Currawong to Command, have sighted the first marathoners. Over.'

'Command to Currawong, roger that. Waterhen, let me know when you've got the first runners down where you are, mate. Should be twenty minutes or so.'

'Waterhen. Gotcha, Command.'

The Central Command's voice was not Frank's. Eden did not pick his voice above the gentle spattering of talk and radio whistles as the marathon runners moved slowly towards Kensington. Around her on the wide road, runners bopped along, each with a distinctive shuffle – long-legged antelope people galloping ahead of her and short plump people with swift, shallow steps falling behind.

The storm was upon them now, but it was not as furious as it had appeared raging and flashing over the Blue Mountains. The rain fell in hard heavy drops, pattering on her shoulders and chest. It would be gone before it could dampen her socks, dissolving out over Coogee.

As the mass of runners around her approached the sprawling front gates of the University of New South Wales, a troupe of students wearing matching pink T-shirts began to swirl and bounce, buoyed after a gap in the crowd, their banners swaying from side to side above grinning heads.

If your partner is violent, don't be silent.

Fear is not a substitute for respect.

A young girl with electric blue hair approached Eden with a paper cup of orange liquid. She shook her head and kept trotting.

She didn't need sustenance. She needed painkillers. The old wound from sternum to pelvis was burning again, the tortured muscles beneath twisting as she loped along, tearing at hardened scar tissue. She kept her eyes on the group, slowing a little to keep herself in the middle of the stretch of two hundred or so runners. If she turned her head, Eden could see runners a kilometre or so behind her, some the same distance ahead. It was only a selection of those who were running the marathon, but it was a good chunk. She would leave them to catch a ride with a squad car somewhere before La Perouse to be with another group running up along the coast.

She couldn't be stationary. Not with so much prey around. Some little corner of Eden's mind acknowledged that the very thought of the killer being out there somewhere like a snake poised beneath a rock waiting for the perfect victim to sidle by would awaken the same deadly instinct in her. Because she knew someone else was hunting, Eden felt her own hunter instincts stirring. When a couple of runners came up behind her, hooted and cheered at her side for a second, having seen 'Police' on the back of her T-shirt, it was all she could do not to reach out, grab fabric, hair, skin.

At La Perouse, she trotted past Long Bay prison and its golden-lit towers. She watched the diamond wire bouncing with the motion of her body, saw the silhouettes of guards in the birdcage, the first intake area for new prisoners arriving in vans. Eden had put quite a lot of people into the Bay. Her parents' killers had been there together. She'd visited its dark concrete halls many times, looked out from the offices at the manicured internal gardens littered with cigarette butts. The place was so familiar she felt like waving as she passed. When she turned back to the road, she saw the face in the dark, a slice of face beyond a black hood, white in the glow of the moon. For just a second the person in the jacket looked back over its shoulder at Eden, grinned and turned. Eden felt the fine hairs all along her arms stand on end.

The hooded runner sped up. Eden pushed and felt her thighs respond immediately with a bone-deep ache at her new momentum, a ripple of electricity through her chest and shoulders as her body responded to the increase in effort. She watched in the grip of breathless fury as the runner in black began edging his way towards a female runner, drifting sideways, closer and closer to a woman in purple. The woman didn't even glance at him. She was locked in that face-forward position, the same that had blocked all Eden's senses as she ran through the park at Rushcutters. The hypnotic rhythm of feet, knees, hips, breath, arms had captured her, and all it took was one good knock from the side to send her stumbling towards the concrete gutter.

Eden looked around quickly. They were almost alone. What had been a tight pod of runners was now spread across the island in the centre of Anzac Parade, trees shielding their view of the attack. There were runners behind, but when Eden looked back at them, all she saw were blank faces, swinging arms, puckered mouths. The hooded runner grabbed the girl in purple by the back of her neck and pushed, let the momentum of the slope of the hill carry her down towards the tennis courts, her feet struggling to find traction in the wet grass.

Eden sprinted over the gutter, over the hill, launching herself down the slope towards the fence around the courts. Her numb fingers fumbled for the gun at the base of her spine. She had the weapon in her hands when the two runners hit the fence in a jangle of wires, tackling each other, the crash almost loud enough to drown out their laughs.

Eden skidded to a painful halt.

'We got her,' the boy laughed, dragging off the hood. He was an androgynous kind of creature with chocolate curls and big lips, grinning at an almost-identical girl. Brother and sister, Eden guessed. 'We fucking got her.'

'That was too easy,' the girl snickered. 'We're sorry, officer. We just couldn't help ourselves.'

Eden licked her lips. Stood waiting in the dark and the rain for more to come, but none did. The kids stood laughing against the fence, the boy hugging himself with a helpless kind of hilarity that Eden thought was reserved for childhood. When she'd heard enough she strode forward, and with one heavy swing cracked the boy's nose with the butt of her pistol.

The girl's laughter turned to screams as though a switch had been flipped. Blood gushed down the boy's face, over his lips and hands, an inky torrent.

'What did you do? What did you do?' the girl screamed.

'Sorry,' Eden said. She slipped her gun back into the belt holster. 'Couldn't help myself.'

She ran back up the hill to the road.

The first alert was on the Pacific Highway. When Hooky and I got there, and she recovered from the very impressive skid I did right where the checkpoint was marked, we found the runner being taken care of by a few spectators. She'd rolled her ankle on one of those rubber pipes that crosses the road surface to measure the frequency of cars. By the time we arrived, Hooky was dealing with two more alerts over the police radio. A runner had gone down with a dodgy knee back towards the Harbour Bridge, and an old man was being hauled off the hill over on the fifteen-kilometre course with chest pains. I drove Hooky back across the bridge towards an alert in the Domain. Glancing in my rear-view mirror, I saw her looking up at the giant ribs of the bridge as we passed.

'Pretty good, ay?' I yelled, my words muffled by the helmet. I felt her laugh against my back. A group of organisers heading back towards the Domain cheered at us from the side of the bridge. It might almost have been fun, burning across the empty bridge on the hot, humming machine, had there not been half a city under threat from a being whose work I had seen firsthand. All the while the radio crackled in our ears.

'Lyrebird to Command. We're getting reports of an assault on an individual near Little Bay Road, just after the prison. They're saying it might have been a police officer. We'll send a unit out.'

'Archer to Command. Don't bother with that one. Couple of crybabies.'

Eden's voice. I listened hard.

'Command to Lyrebird. Archer confirmed. Let the ambos clean it up.'

I swung the bike down the Cahill Expressway. There were still runners on the road, mums chattering as they pushed their sleeping children in prams down the road, groups of teenagers determined to be last, all enjoying the novelty of the empty expressway. To our left, a massive cruise ship lit up like an apartment building blocked the view of the bridge.

The crowds in the Domain parted as I slid the bike through. All the serious competitors had finished and were mingling among the market stalls set up on the oval, sweaty brows wiped and grins spread across faces, bubbles sparkling in plastic cups. I could smell curry burning. I nosed the bike through the crowd and gunned it up a short hill behind the café onto the road in front of the art gallery. The runners were faster here – trying to give it everything they had as they came down the hill towards the finish line in the bus loop before the gallery.

'What number?'

'Ends in 583,' Hooky yelled.

I started driving back through the runners, looking for a bib number that ended in 583. The runner had missed the last two checkpoints before the finish line. I'd told Hooky to tell me if the person came through, but she hadn't said a word, so I had to assume she was still stopped somewhere in the last kilometre of the race. Runners swaggered past me, hardly noticing the plainclothes cop on the bike, eyes set on the finish line. Arms once swinging rigidly in parallel arcs now flailed. Mouths howled for air. I inched up the hill and around the corner to the top of Macquarie.

Numbers flashed past me. I looked down the hill and could see the end of the crowd, the mothers with prams I'd seen ten minutes earlier.

'Where are they?' I asked. Hooky didn't hear me. I burned down the hill, my pulse steadily increasing, making the helmet shift against my throbbing skull. I looked down alleyways, swept the bushes at the edge of the park with my eyes, half-hoping, half-dreading the sight of a shadowed figure bent over a fallen runner. Hooky wriggled behind me, pulled the iPad out of her jacket. I slowed the bike, listened to its rhythmic beat.

'Still hasn't checked in,' she said. 'Must be here somewhere.'

I let the bike roll, looked at the doorways of the buildings. Runners wandered past, these ones too unfit to finish at a jog. I scanned their numbers: 671, 332, 400.

We were parallel to the row of green and yellow porta-loos when the door of one crashed open. Hooky and I swung around at the noise in time to see a huge hulk of a man emerge from the weak grey light inside a cubicle onto the wooden crate steps beneath the doors. He tugged his sweat-damp shorts up over his hips and wiped sweat from his neck onto a hairy forearm. He spotted us and shot me a sickly half-grin. I looked at the race bib pinned crookedly to his shirt. 11583.

'Whoo!' he panted. He jogged away on spotless white sneakers, more of an exaggerated walk than a jog at all.

'Shit,' I seethed.

'Yes. A very time-consuming one, apparently.' Hooky turned back to her iPad, which blipped the next alert.

Tara lingered in the dark alcove by the tunnel's fire escape door watching the pretty runners go by, little pods of them bobbing away like ducks being carried along by a river current, smiling as they huffed past, their little fists pumping. Now and then there would be a big wave of them, a hundred at once, whooping and howling at they entered the tunnel, relishing the thrill of their voices ballooning around the ceiling, echoing back to them. A group covered in glowstick bands bumped past, waving their fluorescent sticks and making dim triangles of pink and green and yellow in the air, a little flock of fireflies.

Tara understood their rapture at the night air. The metallic taste of the city's bitter fumes wafting from a hundred thousand exhaust pipes lying between the buildings and a ruddy red blanket of delicious smog perfumed everything, coating the park tree leaves with ash. The city was alive – it was breathing and humming and belching out stinks, it was crawling with humans. Every night she spent out of the attic room was a thrilling night for Tara, the ritual of the kill filled with so many more things than the hunt itself. She was unused to travelling the city streets, even when protected from its glorious nooks and crannies and shadows and wonders by a car.

It was thrilling to see the people in the tunnel. To be within

reach of them. Tara felt, in their proximity, one of them –
briefly, before someone noticed her and ruined the illusion.
Tara recognised the way she was instantly rejected. It was the
same as it had been before the surgery. Even when the mouth
forced its way into a smile and the hands came forward –
reaching, gripping, touching, soothing – the eyes always
betrayed the sense that Tara was far beyond the acceptable
limits of the human mould. Once she was grossly too large for
it, and now she was strangely too twisted. Her school teachers
had spent years kindly kneading and stretching and cramming
Tara into that rigid plastic-fantastic mould. Then there was
Joanie beating at her fleshy edges, trying to cut away the excess
with her sharp words. But there was just no fitting Tara, no
fitting her anywhere. She was the elephant in every room.

A big swell of runners filled the tunnel. Tara leaned out of
the shadow a little to see them coming up over the hill, silhouettes sloshing around the tunnel mouth, hands in the air as
their voices rose. Aussie Aussie Aussie. Oi Oi Oi. She turned
a tiny tranquilliser dart in her fingers, stroked the impossibly
thin tip with her thumb. Tonight she wouldn't bother with the
little dart gun she'd fashioned. She wanted to get close to the
runners. The sheer bulk of jostling people forced three runners
down the side of the tunnel, between the interlocking red road
barriers and the tunnel wall. Tara leaned back into the fire
escape shadows as they trotted past her, unawares. She heard
the voices of the cops leaning on the police car just outside the
fire escape and to the left, on the other side of the barrier.

'Inside the barrier, you lot,' one yelled. 'Inside.'

Tara saw just the tips of his fingers as he flailed his arm. At
the end of the tunnel, one runner tried to escape the press of

the crowd by cutting along outside the barrier, thought again when she saw the policeman gesturing, and sunk back into the group.

'Might have to go up there and shift that last barrier,' one of the cops said to the other. 'Push it back against the wall so they can't squeeze through.'

'Mmm,' the other agreed. Neither moved.

A tight group of orange-clad runners passed, determined faces and downturned mouths. A pod of teenagers and a father with a young son huffing away at his sides. Chills rippled up Tara's spine as the cheers suddenly rose from the people passing.

Run, run, boys and girls,
Try to get away,
We won't stop, can't stop,
Gonna make you pay.

Two women ran down the outside of the barrier. Tara leaned back and caught the flashing blue and red of the police car at the side of the tunnel. As they passed, she slipped back into the safety of the dark, a slick sea snail snapping shut the door of its shell. One of the officers let out a dramatic sigh.

'Idiots,' he grumbled, walking past the alcove. Tara watched him bumbling against the stream of runners who ducked and weaved out of his path. One last woman slipped through the gap between the barrier and the tunnel wall, glancing cheekily at the officer as she passed.

'Sorry, sorry, sorry,' she giggled. The officer waved a tired hand, heading towards the end of the barrier. He went to the opening and dragged the last barricade diagonally against the wall, cutting off the gap. When he looked back down the aisle, it was empty. He assumed the last runner must have jumped over the barrier and rejoined the crowd. His offsider was looking at the tunnel wall above the runners, the shadows of hundreds of people lit up red, then white, then blue, a strobe of pumping limbs against the flat grey curve.

It was a little cruel, Eden thought, to send the runners up Arden Street. She trotted along past the bus stations at Coogee Beach, listening to the rise and, crash of waves on the pale sand and watching the runners ahead of her grinding slowly up the massive slope towards Bronte. She'd caught a ride to the cemetery on Malabar Road and clopped down the long, steep hill, looking along side streets at the ornate beach houses nestled between the trees. The black horizon of the ocean cut into the grey sky beyond them, million-dollar views ruined by the occasional hulk of a brick apartment block stuffed with backpackers leaning out windows. Out on the ocean, sheet lightning flashed pale pink. As she ran, she listened to the buzz of police activity. Her long abdominal scar was as numb now as the rest of her, her legs working like machinery, pulling tendons in her feet and ankles, making her dance over the asphalt. The McDonald's on the beachfront was lit a painful white and crowded with runners waiting to use the toilets. They swirled in both directions around the roundabout at the bottom of the slope, a couple of jokers doing the full circle before powering at the hill, heads up, eyes on the clouds shifting across the skyline.

Halfway up the slope she saw the runner a few metres ahead of her waver slightly, the side of her right foot scraping the gutter. She dug in, head down and calves straining. The head down part wasn't a good idea, Eden thought. She watched the runner waver again and then stumble sideways into the bushes out the front of one of the houses on the slope, wet orange rose petals raining on the grass.

'You alright?'

Eden bent forward over the woman, grabbed her bicep. The woman rolled, looked up and squealed, her whole body tensing rock hard beneath Eden's fingers.

'Jesus!'

'Hey, what are you doing?' someone yelled. Eden straightened as two men ran towards her. When they spied the 'Police' lettering on her back they slowed.

'I'm alright, I'm alright.' The woman laughed nervously, still panting from the run. She let Eden drag her to her feet. She was a chubby little thing with the face of a young bulldog pup. All cheeks. 'The rooftop. The shadow of the rooftop made a . . . made a hood over your head.'

Eden looked across the road at the curved triangular roof of the postmodern monstrosity of a house. From the ground, the roof's silhouette must have made a perfect hood shape around her face as she bent over the woman. It was almost laughable. The spectre of the Sydney Parks Strangler was so close to the surface of the woman's mind, she was ready to pick Eden as the ghoul on the loose. More runners gathered around them to see what drama was unfolding, the squeal having drawn their focus from the hill. Their chattering was an excited mumble bubbling and sputtering in the dark.

'What is it? What happened?' someone asked.

'She thought she was the Parks Strangler,' someone else asked.

More runners arrived.

'Did you say Parks Strangler? Where's the Parks Strangler?'

'No, she thought she was the killer. But she's the police.'

'What's wrong with her? Did the killer come after her?'

'I don't know. I don't know what's going on.'

'Where is he now? Was he here? Was he around here?'

'Is she alright? Did anyone see him?'

Runners carried on past the group towards the top of the hill, catching snippets of the frightened words as they floated in the darkness. Little boats stealing cargo and carrying it on up the stream. Eden watched, stunned at how fast it was happening, the mouths jabbering all around her. She didn't like talking to groups unless it was behind the safety of a desk or near the protective proximity of a planning board. Still in hunting mode, she felt exposed, the faces all around her turned inwards, the hounds suddenly aware of the fox in their midst.

'No, he wasn't here.' She put her hands up. 'Just calm down a second, will you all?'

Someone at the top of the hill screamed. The message had been received up there. The killer was nearby, had made an attempt on a runner and fled. Eden watched the groups of runners gather in the centre of the road. The panic was thick smoke in the air.

We were heading to an alert in the Cross City Tunnel when the radio broadcast came through. Only seconds old, the alert popped up on Hooky's screen as we were stopped outside the hardware store on William Street, deciding where to go next.

A few runners trotted here and there, but the street was mostly empty, except for a couple of junkies who had wandered down from the Cross, staggering and twisting like the undead as they made their way against the flow down the middle of the street. Hooky put her iPad away and I hummed the bike up towards the mouth of the tunnel. The entire thing was manned by two porky male beat cops who leaned, side by side, against a squad car flashing the red and blue up over the tunnel walls. I stopped the bike beside them and lifted my visor.

'Any dropouts?'

'Not that we've seen.' One of the cops got off the car, picking me as a detective. He was suddenly straight-backed, looking up and down the tunnel lined with red plastic barricades to keep people off the gutters. The other cop was picking his nails.

'No one's approached us.'

'We might have a runner down in this area,' I said. I turned as I heard a dull thumping start somewhere close by, probably a car going over the top. 'I'll get one of you to run up over the top, see if you can spot anything.'

The alert cop dashed into the tunnel. The thumping continued. I felt a strange tension in my chest at the sound, like a hand was on my heart, gently squeezing, urging me. Urging me towards what, I didn't know. It was probably just the bike rattling my guts around for the first time in decades.

'Heron One to Command. We're getting multiple reports of a target sighting up here on Arden Street near Queens Park.'

'Archer to Command. Reject that call please. I started a game of Chinese whispers.'

Eden sounded tired. I sat listening, one hand on the bike, looking at Hooky. She was listening to the muffled voices through my helmet, squinting as she tried to pick out the words.

'Heron Two to Command. I've got runners panicking up here. Arden and Bronte.'

'Command to Heron One and Two. I've got backup on its way to you. Bronte and Tamarama units respond.'

There was no response from Eden. It was possible she couldn't get through the chatter with the Eastern suburbs unit radios alive on every frequency as cars rushed to the top of Arden Street. I lifted one foot off the ground, straightened the bike and felt Hooky wrap her arms around my waist.

I stopped. The thumping had stopped. Hooky jostled me around the ribs with her arms, made my stomach flip.

'Let's go, dickhead.'

'Hang on,' I said. I let her take the weight of the bike. A weird, queasy sensation had come over me, half the light-headedness that comes after too many skipped meals and half the guilty terror of a bad hangover – the sensation that something is wrong. I'd had the feeling before, running into the church to capture Jason Beck. At the time I couldn't have known that he'd just murdered my girlfriend. I'd passed it off as the usual fears a cop experienced rushing into an unfamiliar environment to confront a criminal.

I was looking at the entrance to the tunnel when the thumping started again. It was so faint I hardly heard it above the rush of cars overhead.

I ripped off my helmet and ran into the dark alcove beneath the glowing green exit sign and hit the iron crossbar with both hands. The fire door swung open ten centimetres and thumped into a figure on the ground. All my muscles tensed at once.

There was pure darkness before me. All the emergency lights were out.

'Amy! Amy! Amy!' I howled over my shoulder. I saw her drop the bike like it was made of cardboard. She leaped over it. The cop with the nail obsession stood dumbly at the bonnet of the patrol car. I shoved open the door, pushing the soft, limp thing behind it sideways and slipped into the dark. I drew my gun and peered into the murky red and blue of the stairwell. Amy slid into the stairwell with me. She fell on the body on the ground, gathering her arms and pulling the woman backwards, into the light cast by the doorway. I rushed blindly up the stairs, gun drawn, ears pricked. There was no one there. I could feel the emptiness of the space around me. No light came through from the above exit door. I sprinted back down the stairs.

'She's alive.' Hooky's voice in the dark was high, thin. 'Help me. Help me! She's alive!'

I could hear the two beat cops calling for backup. I kneeled in the dim light and looked at the crushed figure before me. A tiny plastic tube crunched under my knee. I groped in the dark and felt the spike, the wetness. A dart – still full, it seemed. I looked at the victim's swollen lips moving in a bloodied face. I wiped dampness from the woman's eyes with both hands. There was no telling how old she was. One eye was already swollen shut.

'Face,' she said. Her hands were on my hands, trying to touch her face. 'Hard face.'

'It's alright,' I said. I was stammering, almost crying with terror and anger. 'You're alright, love. Your face is alright.'

She passed out in my arms.

Eden didn't follow the victim to St Vincent's with Frank. It wasn't her scene. He was the one to do the coddling and worrying – she would direct the wind-down of the police operation. The cordons and checkpoints she set up after the victim was found in the Cross City Tunnel proved useless, of course. By the time the sound of Frank's bike had spooked the killer, he or she had run – and that kind of running was the most important of the killer's life. No amount of gall that the Strangler had struck right under their noses was going to help the police catch up. Eden knew that kind of terror, the electric flight of a hunter being pursued. Bodily limitations meant nothing. It was instinctive. Escape or perish.

At 3 am she returned home, shut her apartment door and breathed for the first time without feeling the strange tightening of her throat muscles that happened whenever she was in charge. She went straight to the bath, slipped beneath the steaming water and dragged the rack at the end of the tub towards her. For an hour or so, she clacked away at the keys of her laptop in the candlelight, sipping absent-mindedly at a single glass of cold moscato, now and then licking the beads of condensation from the side of the bulbous glass. When her officer report was finished, she got into bed and filled in her operations overview report and an advisory report to the media, and updated the case log on the police intranet. When the sun began to peek beneath the heavy red curtains across the balcony door, she shut the little silver device and fell asleep.

It was dark beneath the curtains when she woke. Having a very expensive bed, with very expensive sheets and covers, Eden always slept like the dead. The trouble with that was that waking was always difficult and she was often forced to throw off the sheets completely and let the coolness of the dark room prick at her naked skin to bring her fully to consciousness. She took the phone from the side of the bed and read through Frank's text messages one at a time.

2.22 am Victim is Fiona Ollevaris, 28. Some bad facial fracturing/broken ribs/minor strangling but no brain damage. Coma natural at this stage. Will update. FYI last thing she said to me was 'hard face'. Any ideas on that one?

6.47 am No movement yet. Family blubbering everywhere. Media.

12.12 pm Family says victim is MMA fighter. What??? Picked the wrong runner! Checking hospitals for injuries in case perp comes in.

2.00 pm Induced coma for facial surgery.

4.14 pm Hard face hard face hard face hard face I'm going nuts here. Any thoughts? U there?

Eden stretched, yawned, and rolled out of the bed. She pulled on her clothes and threw open the curtains, looked at the orange-lit night. Lovers walked along the sandstone wall across the street, arm in arm. A bus roaring past almost drowned out the sound of knocking at the front door. Eden padded to the door on the cold tiles and looked at the small monitor next to the intercom, a pinhole she'd installed beside the outer handle for those rare cases, like now, when someone slipped in the front door without buzzing. The visitor waiting there made a small wave of heat sweep over her body, the instinctive sizzle of nerves rushing to their edge. She opened the door a crack.

'Hi,' Amy said.

'Can I help you?'

'Yeah,' Amy smirked. Eden remembered all the times Frank had bugged her lately about how she greeted people, the straight-to-the-business style that had infected her since her accident out on Rye Farm. Eden came close to death that night. Lately, pleasantries seemed a waste of borrowed time.

She supposed she should let the girl in, so after a moment or two of silent contemplating, thoughts slowed by the girl's incredibly bad outfit, she let the teen wearing the dusty purple boots into the apartment and shut the door. The girl's attire had struck Eden since she first laid eyes on her as a confusing mix of 'look at me' and 'stay away'. Yet another side-effect of her near-death experience had been an aversion to confused motives. She headed to the kitchen, putting the marble island between the girl and herself. She recognised this as her first survival-mode strategy. Why had she suddenly flipped into survival mode? She found herself opening the fridge without knowing why, taking out a bottle of milk.

'Coffee? Tea?'

Eden wasn't even sure she had any tea. She heard the girl ease onto one of the stools on the other side of the island, drop her shoulder bag on the floor. There were knives in a block to the girl's right. Eden added this to the calculations hurrying through her mind.

'No, neither. Thanks.'

'Did you go to the hospital with Frank?'

Keep the conversation on your terms, until you know the motive for the visit, then decide whether you'll allow the original reason for the visit to be addressed. Everything was about control now. The conversation. The environment. The available tools. Eden opened a cupboard beneath the sink and took out a spray bottle, ran a cloth under the water as though preparing to mop up a recently noticed spill. She gave a couple of sprays, mopped at the invisible spot.

Why was she so paranoid? She paused by the sink and closed her eyes. This was all a symptom of being alone with a teenage girl again. The last teenage girl she'd trusted had tried to kill her. Amy might just be trying to hold onto the Parks Strangler case while Frank was tied up, and had got the message, however wrong, however moronic, that Eden welcomed her as a companion. Eden couldn't recall even the most subtle indication she might have given the girl over the last few days that would inspire the idea. She'd mostly ignored Frank's weird little fangirl completely. Or so she thought.

'No. No, I hung around after the ambos got there for a little while and then I went home.' The girl coughed. Eden put the kettle on. 'We need to talk though.'

Eden turned, the spray bottle and cloth in hand, and looked at the girl's short blonde prickles. It was an odd look. Amy's pale cream skin led naturally to expecting striking black Asian hair framing the high cheekbones and chocolate eyes. The style was new-recruit military but she'd bleached it hard so that it was almost snow white.

Short blonde hair.

The girl held Eden's eyes. Defiant.

'Out with it then,' Eden said.

The girl drew a breath and nibbled her bottom lip, just once, refusing to back away from the cliff edge she had crept onto. When she began to speak the words tumbled out, one after the other, a series of gunshots.

'I know that you're Morgan Tanner.'

Eden's mouth was immediately dry, denying any verbal response. She found herself smiling, licking her lips. She hadn't thought it would be this easy, the solution to the problem of the woman who attacked Hades. It was terrifyingly easy. The mouse had wandered right into the cat's basket.

'Oh,' Eden said. She looked at the floor. 'That's interesting.'

Amy opened her mouth to reply, as Eden anticipated she would, and it was in those precious microseconds that she was inhaling air to make her response that Eden lifted the spray bottle and pulled the trigger, saturating the girl in trichloromethane. Eden didn't use chloroform in any of her night-time games – she found the practice a little unfair. But a homemade cocktail of the stuff in an easy dispenser was a must for her household. She wandered around the kitchen island as the girl coughed and spluttered, wiping at her nose and eyes, the wooden stool tumbling and splitting the air as it hit the ground. A couple more puffs and the girl was on her knees.

'Wait, wait, wait!'

Eden didn't wait. She gave the girl another good spray and watched her fall, listened to the satisfying clunk of the back of her head on the tiles.

Waiting for Fiona Ollevaris was like watching one of those time-lapse documentaries when a camera is set up over the carcass of a dead rabbit and little creatures are captured rushing in, taking tiny pieces and scuttling away quicker than the eye can follow.

I sat by her in the curtained-off section of the trauma ward at St Vincent's and observed these many creatures coming and going, the doctors and nurses who monitored her vitals, poked and prodded her, put things into her and took things out while she lay swaddled in bandages from the neck up. Forensics people photographed her injuries, took swabs from her scraped knuckles, picked and bottled skin and blood cells from beneath her fingernails, measured her abrasions and marked things down on evidence forms. Patrollies and hospital staff pushed back journalists who posed as friends and relatives at the door and maybe reached the windows at the side of the ward and ogled a bit at her feet, which was all they could see from that angle.

Her real family members arrived one by one and stood around uncomfortably – the older brother first, an awkward man with the kind of gravely set face that I'm sure wouldn't have altered much if she were dead, a man who wanted to pace with his arms folded. The mother and sister came next, sobbing women who seemed to want to smother me with affection by way of coffees and baked treats from the downstairs café for my role in her rescue. Then came the father, another stern man who took up residence at my side as a kind of silent tribute, following me like a long-faced dog when I went out to make phone calls and send texts.

When they took Fiona off to surgery, the family all stood around in the empty space her bed had occupied and talked about her, as though they'd not been able to in her unconscious presence. I learned she was an amateur mixed martial arts fighter who'd had a couple of bouts with other girls her size. That probably explained the skin under the nails, the blood all over the walls of the fire escape, patterns of hands and palms I'd glimpsed briefly in the torchlight as the paramedics attended to Fiona. It probably explained the thumping I'd heard, the scuffle while Fiona was being strangled, a hold she probably knew how to get out of – and was pretty close to getting out of when I arrived with Hooky. The mother berated the father about his aversion to Fiona taking up the sport, as though she'd always known that it would come in handy one day when a serial killer struck their daughter in the middle of a public running festival. He didn't reply. I guessed they were divorced.

All the while, as I was sitting there on the stool I'd nabbed from the nurse's station, Fiona's last words before she drifted into unconsciousness plagued me. No way that I tried to interpret the words made any sense. Hard face. Was she talking about the killer's face? It was a strange message if she meant to tell me what the killer looked like so that I could identify him or her in my suspect pool. I was looking for someone stern?

Emotionless? Someone old, deeply lined and weathered, like the hard-faced captains who came to visit headquarters every now and then to confer with Captain James? Fiona's father and brother had pretty hard faces. That didn't help. I'd be better off knowing for sure if the killer was male or female. What colour his or her hair was. What ethnicity, age.

Was she talking about her own face? She was touching her face when she said it. Was she telling me the assault she'd suffered at the hands of the killer wouldn't break her, wouldn't destroy her beauty – that she had a hard face? A strange sort of thing to say to your rescuing cop on the edge of impending darkness, if that was what she meant. From the pictures her mother had shown me, tattered things she drew from the depths of her purse, Fiona didn't have a hard face at all. She was a very pretty, soft-looking girl, an oval-faced beauty with long brunette curls she swept up in a high pony when she was fighting. She had big lips and a generous smile. There was nothing hard about her, I imagined, except for her right hook. I knew that from all the skin she'd taken off her knuckles in the struggle. She'd gone right down to bone.

The day dragged on. I ate myself into a pot-bellied, languid state. I needed something to do with my hands and people kept bringing me treats, everybody's favourite cat under the table lolling on its side, snapping up sardines. It was not a good situation. About four in the afternoon I was so frustrated with the 'hard face' problem I was talking to myself, staring at the floor.

'Hard face,' I murmured. 'Hard . . . face.'

'She's got the same plastic surgeon that Renee Kelly had after the bus accident,' Fiona's mother was telling her father. 'He did such a good job. You'd never know.'

'What bus accident?'

'Bus cleaned her up off the side of the road while she was waiting on George Street. She was mincemeat, apparently.'

'Who's Renee Kelly?'

'The singer. Renee Kelly. God, you're old.'

Hard face. I turned my paper coffee cup around and around in my hands. It was stone cold. Hard face. Hard face. Fiona had had a lot of blood in her mouth. Maybe I'd only heard 'hard face'. Maybe it was something else.

I felt my heartbeat quicken. I watched the couple beside me as they argued.

Hard race. Hard pace. Hard chase.

I needed to be systematic. Fiona's mother's sigh was like a steam train. I could almost see her breath.

Ard face. Bard face. Card face. Dard face. Eard Face. Fard face. Gard face. Hard face.

I chewed my fingernails. They tasted like butter.

Quard face. Rard face. Sard face.

Scarred face.

I stood. My coffee cup fell to the floor.

The voices came first. Eden's and what sounded like that of an old man, but Hooky could not be sure she wasn't dreaming. She opened one eye and caught a glimpse of the floor she was lying on before her vision blurred. Tiles. Mismatched, laid in a complicated pattern, bathroom tiles with wave patterns and broken pieces of kitchen tile, ornate burnt gold tiles with upraised filigree. She could see a pair of legs close by. The voices came to her ears in bumbling tones, the words tripping over each other, sliding on top of each other, impossible to discern in order.

'. . . really, really stupid.'

Suddenly her hearing cleared, all at once, as though her ears had popped. She sighed through her nose, tried to moan through the duct tape on her lips. An animal came towards her – she felt the wetness of its nose in her ear, on her cheek, its hot breath against her nostrils. There were whispers brushing her eyelashes.

'Jimmy,' the old man said.

The animal disappeared. She heard Eden sigh somewhere behind her. Hooky tried to move but her fingers were numb and strangely distant from where she expected them to be. They were at the small of her back and bunched together. She shifted her cheek against the cold tiles, the panic rising.

'Asian would have been the very first thing I said,' the old man was complaining. 'When you asked me *what did she look like*, I'd have said, *she was Asian*, straight up.'

'I guess I don't think as racially as you do.'

'Don't be smart.'

'Give me a break,' Eden snapped. 'We're looking for a petite woman with short blonde hair who knows who I am. This one turns up at my place and spills her guts. What did you expect me to do? Turn her away? You're telling me I should have expected there to be two –'

'Where are her things?' the old man asked.

'Here.'

Hooky heard something slide across the floor. She was losing consciousness again. The animal, whatever it was, was near her, one golden brown paw visible, tendons straining as the animal shifted.

'Got any spare spots?' Eden asked.

'I've always got something.'

Hooky slept. The sleep was so delicious, so welcoming, that it was only the pain in her neck and shoulders as she was dragged along the ground that drew her out of it. If she'd been carried, she might have slept through the stars overhead, a thousand pinpricks of light peering between smears of cloud and gloom. When she became aware of the T-shirt bunching up at her back and her arms sliding in the dirt, she was snapped into a consciousness so complete she could feel every injury she had endured in the last few hours, from the bruises on her legs she must have got when she was being loaded into the boot of Eden's car to marks on her wrists and ankles from the duct tape. Hooky twisted, tried to look around her, but all she saw were strange black mountains too close to be real mountains, strangely shaped silhouettes with spikes, bumps, ridges. She was in some kind of wasteland. The sour smell of rotting garbage assaulted her. She looked down and saw Eden dragging her by the left cuff of her jeans.

Hooky kicked. Eden turned and grabbed both ankles and held on as the girl struggled.

'Don't be stupid,' she said.

They stopped by a hole in the earth. Hooky squirmed, caught a glimpse of the old man leaning on a cane, a squat creature with scruffy grey hair that was growing out of a short back and sides. A terrifying creature hovered by his side, like the skeleton of a dog reanimated, the eyes bulbous and black. Hooky looked at the neat edge of the hole, the pile of trash lying beside it, the great yellow excavator squatting behind the pile ready to shove the tyres, bags, pieces of lumber into the black cavern dug into the earth. Hooky felt a wave of nausea ripple through her insides and shudder in her throat. Her face was burning, damp with terror, the sweat coming from nowhere and suddenly drenching her clothes, making dirt tickle on her cheeks and neck.

'No, no, no, no, no,' she moaned. She tried to twist, to look up at Eden's face. Her moaning rose to a scream. 'No! No! No!'

Eden grabbed Hooky's shoulder and rolled her into the pit.

I called the Parramatta headquarters while I ran through the car park behind St Vincent's hospital, huffing my way down the concrete ramps. Trying to direct Gina through my desk in the bull pit was excruciating. For a receptionist at one of the biggest law enforcement establishments in the country, she's got no ability to zero in from the big picture.

'I don't know. There's stuff everywhere.'

'It's a photocopy of a newspaper article. I would have just dropped it somewhere there on the surface.'

I heard drawers opening and closing. I reached my car and got inside, my shirt clinging to my back and sides with sweat. Paper rustled on the other end of the phone.

'There's a coffee mug here with mould in it.'

'It's a forensics experiment. Part of an investigation.'

'Right.'

'Keep looking.'

'New laws sought after high-profile surgery mishap?'

'That's the one,' I gasped, my heart thundering in my neck, half the run, half pure exhilaration at the chase. 'Read it to me.'

'The state government has called upon federal leaders to impose regulations to curb the growing number of young

Australians seeking cheap cosmetic surgery overseas,' Gina read. 'The move comes as reports arise that Tara Harper –'

'Tara Harper,' I said. 'Did it say what kind of surgery she had?'

'It just says a great number at once,' she said. 'Are you onto something, Frank?'

'I'm not sure,' I said. 'Maybe. Get me everything you can on the Harper girl.'

I had a team assembled just down the street from the Harper house by the time the sun set – eight or nine Kevlar-clad specialists, two of them women, standing around a squad car tucked behind a huge fig tree. Cars took the roundabout near us slowly, heads turning, before pulling onto Lang Road, running alongside the park itself. The yawning sandstone gates to a car-lined hill were directly across the road from number 7. The house was a gigantic cream mansion that could easily have been divided into two profitable semis, the ornate front garden lined with sandstone and iron, maintaining the neighbourhood style. White block-out curtains were drawn over the French doors of all four balconies, and the only thing moving on the property was a sickly looking ginger cat that had taken up residence on the wall beside the house to watch the raid.

I directed two of my team to the rear of the property. This involved barging through other people's houses and commandeering their back porches so we could see if they had a view into the house. The few times I've done this myself I've found people to be more excited about helping the police nab the bad guy than concerned I'm going to judge them on their household mess or hassle them about the bong on their coffee table.

When the two were in place, I received a report that the rear of number 7 was all curtained as well. There was a garage behind the property, accessed by a narrow driveway down the right-hand side of the house. One of the officers reported that it was secured with a huge padlock and chain.

I sent two agents to the front of the house. They were wearing jackets over their police vests. After an initial walk-by, they reported that nothing stirred.

By now we'd garnered plenty of neighbourly attention. A woman stood on her step with a couple of children, describing our operations into a mobile phone while the little ones pointed and gaped. It was not an uncommon reaction. People who spot a police operation in their street will invariably try to get close to it, and if they can't will report it, sharing the experience with their friends, family, sometimes the media. *Sharon! You'll never believe this! There's a SWAT team outside the Calverts' house! Get over here – they're still setting up.* The kids obviously asked their mother permission to go down to the fence, and she allowed it. Their little heads poked up over the red brick fence, eager, probably wondering if I had any 'Cops are Tops' stickers in my pockets. Almost as though she'd heard my thoughts, another housewife burst out of the house next door and jogged through the front gates, up to the porch to join her neighbour watching the drama.

'Alright,' I told my team of four, 'I've going to get those two to do a knock. You two take the sides, you two go in at the front.'

They rushed off. I gave the two walkers-by the command to knock on the front door. When no one answered, I gave it a few seconds, then sent them in. I gave myself just a moment to be sad that I'd once been one of those hot-cheeked officers at the back of the raid team, wondering what was behind the closed door. Bellowing down the empty halls. Now I was too important for that. My 'forensically trained mind' was put to better use elsewhere and only the 'grunts' were allowed to do the front-line work, where they might brush up against any danger. I missed being a grunt. It was exciting.

The two housewives had a better view of the front door than I did. When the team busted through it, they clapped and the children cheered. I spotted a couple of teenagers by a tree on the other side of the park gates. One was filming the scene with her phone.

I'd learned all I could about Tara Harper while I got approval for the raid, both from what Gina phoned in over the next hour and a search on my phone. There wasn't much about the girl going around. She had no social media presence whatsoever, which was strange. There wasn't a tried and failed Twitter account, a blog, a jobseeker profile – so far as I could tell she'd never had a job. There wasn't a picture of the girl anywhere, not even on a memorial page dedicated to her father set up by the company he'd worked for. Her mother, a stunning blonde woman with perfect cheekbones, was pictured frequently on society websites. Whippet-thin and eagle-eyed, she never smiled fully – she had discovered her perfect angle to camera and worked out a half-smile that made her look both powerful and coy, and she stuck with it. She'd been a sports model in her late-teen years, and then had met her sugar daddy and settled down to being a mother – which seemed to mean acting on the board of charities, drinking champagne, shopping and going to premieres. She ran. A lot. Half the paparazzi shots of her were snapped for 'Celebrities without make-up' – cheekbones exaggerated as she inhaled, mouth a supple O, the picture itself buried low on the page. Because even free of make-up, Joanie Harper was what I would, as a young man, have called a 'honey'. She was fantasy material. A visual feast of human genes at their fittest and fairest. I didn't know what kind of surgery her daughter had sought in Thailand – all that was bottled up in media privacy laws – but I couldn't understand, if she shared even a portion of her mother's genes, why she'd sought any at all.

I was immediately struck by the smell of the house, the shut-in stink of mould and accumulated dusts, carpets that needed airing out and food that had gone off and dried. Dead flower water, perfume reaching through stink and being pressed down. The place was immaculate and gave the impression that was because nothing ever moved. A cabinet full of ornate tea sets near a sideboard that was bare except for an empty wooden bowl. The signs of life were missing – keys, newspapers, letters, pens that should have been set down where they were used, left behind to be used again. There were no magnets on the fridge and nothing in or around the sink. When I opened the kitchen cupboards, I found there to be no plates.

All the plates, it turned out, were in the attic room. The specialist team members called me straight there. I saw the top of Ruben's head from the stairs. He was lying as though a gust of wind from the windows had blown him right over, but the window was shut and the curtains were drawn. I ordered the team out of the room and stood in the doorway so as not to disturb anything.

I looked in. Ruben had been stabbed a bunch of times in the chest – for a second that made me wonder if I hadn't accidentally stumbled on an isolated murder and not found the Parks Strangler. The Parks killer had never penetrated skin, which for the novice doesn't sound like a substantial advance in technique. It is, however. There's a big difference between strangling and stabbing – the bloodlessness is the main thing, but the real distinction is in effort. It's difficult to stab someone. There are all sorts of thing in the way. Clothes and ribs and, usually, the person's arms as they grab and flail and try to stop you. And people make all sorts of awful noises when they're stabbed. They wheeze and cough and gurgle and scream – they panic and run around. Until that moment, Tara – if she was the Parks Strangler – had been dealing with half-subdued victims, and she close-fisted bashed in faces before fitting her hands around necks almost pre-made for the job. I crouched at Ruben's head, turned his face slightly with the tip of my pinky finger. The face was barely touched. She'd knocked him down and gone for it. When I peeled his wet shirt back from his chest, I saw the wounds were many and shallow. A surprise attack, meant to be over quickly.

I didn't linger on Ruben for long. I was half-listening to the specialist team commander giving an 'all units alert' for the suspect. We had her name, but the commander gave a pause when it came to description. We still didn't know what Tara looked like. Tara would be flagged if she used her credit card, any transport tickets or cars registered in her name, but from all indications she didn't have any of those things. While I listened to the team members trying to come up with points to look out for to broadcast to our colleagues, I walked into the attic room and beheld the display around me. The thousands of defaced faces, the mesmerising Joanie Harper in all her stony beauty. It was a visual punch. The crowded faces all seemed to howl at once, a noise I could hear in my brain, an angry, despairing noise, the noise animals make in final grisly moments of being eaten alive. In this room full of mouldy plates, Tara had erected an inescapable moment in which, multiplied infinitely, her mother howled at her, squealed, the hateful, accusatory pleading of a mother at a bad child.

My Googling before the raid had told me that Joanie Harper had slipped peacefully away over a couple of bottles of wine and some sleeping pills. It was so gentle, so easy, that the coroner hadn't been able to determine if it was suicide or not.

I had the feeling, standing there, that Joanie's delicate exit from life hadn't been what her daughter wanted.

Hooky hit the ground with her shoulder and rolled twice. Her body took control as the terror overcame her, flattening against the bottom of the grave, a strange carpet of damp earth and rotting detritus, now and then the hard, sharp edge of a buried toothbrush, a sliver of plastic, the rim of a can. The grave had been dug neatly into the already acidic, degrading layers of waste, and as she lay panting short breaths she heard, with bursts of bladder-clenching horror, Eden walking around the grave and mounting the huge digger. Hooky knew she should move, should make a last shot at life, but her body was paralysed at the shuddering visions of the darkness and pressure that would come in seconds, the sickening weight of the dirt and rubbish as it piled onto her.

The machine started with a hideous roar. Hooky heard the clattering and grinding of the rubbish and soil as it started to move. The initial tumble of objects onto her legs was so gentle it made her sick. This was how her death would be. Gentle and slow and smothering, an excruciating fight against rock solid limbs that would not struggle against the tape, that would not roll her, that would not shift towards the edge of the pit out of sheer animal fright at what was being done to her. She was powerless to do anything but let out a long howl through her nose, her teeth biting down against her tongue as the rubbish rolled over her.

The digger stopped. Its engine cut, neatly and clearly, leaving ringing silence in its wake. Somewhere beyond her grave, Hooky could hear dogs barking. She lay and shook against the dirt and listened to the night.

It took a long time for her limbs to respond. Only her legs were covered. She turned her face against the ground and saw that the pile at the side of the grave, the weight that would have smothered her, was still very much intact. What had happened? Had the engine stalled? She curled in a ball and wept hard, the sobs now and then breaking into panicked snuffles that racked her entire frame, awakened what were surely cracked ribs down her side.

She was feeling pain. That was good. If she could bring herself out of shock, perhaps she could push the ordeal towards whatever end was meant for it – whether it was the restarting of the engine and her smothering, choking death or, and she could not yet imagine it, her climbing out of the grave. She rolled onto her good side and groped at the ground with her fingers, picked up a square of some ancient discarded thing, poked and pricked at the tape between her wrists. When the sobbing interrupted her bid for freedom she was forced to stop. She tossed away the square when the back of her wrist brushed against something better, a sharp twist of glass. She broke the binds and tore her wrists apart.

Hooky grabbed at the gag. The sounds, when she released them, were repetitive gasps and cries. She rolled and pulled the tape from her legs, tears pouring down her filthy cheeks.

It seemed an age getting up the slope of rubbish to the top

of the three-metre-deep grave. By the time she scrambled onto the living earth again her crying had subsided into a morbidly quiet tremor in all her limbs. Her teeth chattered. There, some metres away from the grave, stood Eden and the old man, a squat, menacing creature sitting on the curve of an old tyre. The terrifying skeleton dog was there, wagging its brown tail enthusiastically. Eden looked bemused, her arms folded as she surveyed Hooky where she slumped against the ground.

'Are you sure that took long enough?' Eden drawled.

'Imogen. Imogen –'

'We know,' Eden said. 'We worked that one out by going through your things.'

Hooky scrambled to a crouch and surveyed her injuries. She was sure both wrists were at least sprained, if not fractured. Her right foot was numb. The shaking would not stop. She wondered if she would vomit in front of them both.

'You stupid bitch,' Hooky said. Her voice was a hellish rasp. 'You stupid fucking bitch.'

The old man laughed, turned his cane so it dug a hole in the ground.

'She's got you worked out,' he told Eden cheerfully.

'Why didn't you kill me?' Hooky pleaded. She looked at the hole in the ground and felt hot tears at the corners of her eyes. 'Why. Why did you –'

'You're a child,' Eden said. She jerked a thumb towards the old man. 'This one here's got a sort of . . . philosophy about it.'

'I came to warn you.'

'I realise that,' Eden said. She gestured to the grave. 'Now we're even.'

'We're not even,' Hooky snarled. 'We're not done.'

'Oh no, this isn't over, no. I completely agree,' Eden said. 'This grave will always be here waiting for you. You'll never, ever be much farther from where you were just a couple of minutes ago. No farther than a heartbeat really. You should take a moment to remember what it was like down there. Cement it in your mind. Because I'll be keeping it warm for you, little girl.'

Hooky breathed. She didn't doubt the older woman as she stood silhouetted against the orange sodium lamps that lit the tip, the trash mountain range behind her, an apocalyptic wasteland of discarded things.

'My parents were murdered too,' Hooky said. She scrunched her eyes against the childish sound of her own voice. Her trembling hand tapped, flat, against her own chest. 'I came to you because I understand you.'

Eden twitched at the words, as though startled by a whistle on the wind. Something in the woman looked hurt, Hooky thought, or frightened. It was only an instant of vulnerability, a flash of some past assault, the breeching of the walls by an enemy long defeated, put aside from concern. The woman laughed harshly to cover it, but Hooky saw a glimmer of that fear remaining in Eden's eyes. A nervous curiosity. Her lips sneered but the rest of her beheld Hooky with the interest a lion takes in the shimmer of movement in the grass near his pride.

'Stop talking shit,' Eden snapped. 'Get up and get out of here.'

'No,' Hooky said. Even the old man laughed at that one. She tried to unlock her gritted teeth. 'I said we weren't done.'

Caroline Eckhart had my number from the obscene number of times I'd tried to ring her to get her to call off the running festival. When I saw her number flash up on my mobile at the Harper house crime scene, I was sure she was calling me to offer some bullshit apology couched in a bunch of backhanded clues that it was all my fault. I was holding a coffee in one hand and the phone in the other, and Ruben Esposito's dead head was at my feet. All around me, forensics specialists snapped pictures, dabbed fingerprint powder, laid out little measurement stickers and exhibit numbers alongside interesting bits and pieces. I was waiting for Eden to get back to me, or for one of the squads to tell me they'd pulled over a white van, perhaps the one that I was hoping was missing from the empty garage. I would probably have taken a call from anyone at that moment, so tense was my entire body with longing to hear something about the monster that had obviously flown this very room only minutes before we arrived.

When Caroline called, I was overcome with distaste for her. I couldn't imagine her helping me comb my hair let alone helping me solve this case.

So I cancelled the call. It's possible I contributed to what happened to her when I pressed that button. I was lucky, when

she called a few seconds later, that curiosity overcame my preju-
dice and I answered.

'Detective Be—'

The call ended. I looked at my phone. She sounded puffed,
like she was on a run, though her one-and-a-half words were
on a higher octave than she usually spoke. I felt a little queasy
and called her back immediately. The phone was off.

I stood thinking about the voice. Running it over and over in
my mind. Detective Be. Detective Be. Why would she call me
in the middle of a run? So that I could be impressed with her?
Caroline Eckhart only has time to field calls from nobodies when she's
improving her blood-oxygen saturation capacity and when she's on
the john. Sounded about right. What hadn't sounded right was
the background. It didn't sound as if she was outside. Was she
on her treadmill? Why hadn't I heard the machine in the background, thrumming away as she plodded towards perfection?

I sucked air between my teeth, clicked my tongue against
the roof of my mouth. Was I really prepared to leave my current
crime scene to make sure Caroline Eckhart of all people hadn't
fallen down the stairs while she was on the phone to me and
was now lying in a pile of taut, cellulite-free limbs at the bottom
of a fire escape somewhere? I tried calling her three more times.
Then I gave the biggest sigh in human history, drawing the
attention of three forensics freaks nearby.

'I'm popping out for a minute. I'll be back,' I said. Of course
I didn't let anyone know where I was going.

Caroline lived near the end of the Woolloomooloo Finger
Wharf, arguably Sydney's most envied address. There was

nowhere else a creature like Caroline could live – she needed to demonstrate the success, the prestige, the perfection that her public image was all about, so it was here that she took interviews with magazine journalists, doing crunches under the gaze of the cityscape. It was here that she shot 'Caroline at Home' spreads for *Woman's Day*, lounging on her pristine white leather couches – both she and the furniture hard as stone and constructed with all the care of a master sculptor. She breakfasted here on egg white and kale omelettes with her neighbours – the few ridiculously powerful shock jocks and Hollywood actors Australia boasted of – when they were home.

I parked on Cowper Wharf Road between a Porsche 911 Turbo and a Bentley Mulsanne, with an arm over the back of the passenger seat and sweat beading in my hairline, pretending it wasn't the most important reverse park of my life. Harry's Café de Wheels hotdog stand was crowded with late-night drinkers with the munchies, a series of young, pot-bellied men who dropped their papers and cardboard boxes when they'd had their fill for the seagulls to swoop up.

Two suited goons on the door stopped me as I tried to enter the huge open cavern of the wharf, once a wool factory and a migrant processing centre. I imagined the scared refugees milling and huddling around the postmodern sculptures that adorned the glossy foyer, children in blankets, barefoot. I flashed my badge and the goons parted. I glanced back and saw the valet scrambling for his phone. The media would be on speed dial, the apartment I accessed noted for the next edition of *The Talk*.

It was eleven. When I pounded on the door of Caroline's fourth-floor apartment, a man in the flat next to hers popped out of his front door, a weathered zombie-creature kept alive on fame alone. He shouted some abuse, fluffed his wispy white hair. I glanced at him, still knocking.

'Caroline!' I smacked the door with an open palm, the sound echoing about the huge hall. 'Oi! Car-o-line!'

I stood at the door and called her phone another three times. I tried the door and found it locked. Then I turned and started to leave, the old guy glaring at me with his sagging lizard eyes and snarling with wet lips. I'd only turned on my heel when I heard a double thump from inside Caroline's apartment.

I drew my gun and the old man clambered inside his apartment.

In my policing career, I've kicked down about three doors. Two of them were very successful, dramatic knock-downs that got me plenty of cheers at the station afterward, and on the third, I went crooked at the last second and sprained my ankle.

I knew the old man was at least listening, so I didn't want him to hear me (a) having to have multiple shots at the door or (b) howling in agony on the floor after I'd snapped my Achilles tendon. Equally as threatening was the possibility that Caroline Eckhart was fine in there, that she'd simply overdosed on whey protein and was lying paralysed watching me trying to get into her apartment. I didn't want her telling *Woman's Day* what a pussy I was. In the three seconds I prepared for the shot, I reviewed all my academy training on doors and their tenuous relationship with feet. And then I gave it my best.

The door slammed open, knocking over a huge ornate vase, which shattered on the spotless cream tiles. I was overwhelmed, momentarily, with self-admiration.

All the lights were on. I stood in the doorway and dialled the

Officer Assistance number on my phone, then put it back in my pocket. My colleagues would triangulate me via GPS and send a team, probably the same team that had crawled all over Tara Harper's house at Centennial Park. I actioned my weapon and listened. A deep, gravelly voice said, 'Close the door.'

I did what I was told. A small hall led off the front door. On the left was what was probably a bathroom door, and to the right was a huge living area with a glass wall that looked out over the navy ships docked at Garden Island. A frigate was directly across from us, lit gold with a hundred yellow lights. To the left, another glass wall looked out over the black harbour. I had seconds to take in the view before I assessed the scene in front of the huge balcony.

Caroline Eckhart was flopped like a rag doll on the floor by a weight machine. I could see that she'd taken a good knock to the nose and forehead. Her lip was split in the front and her forehead was just beginning to work on a huge blue egg right near her hairline. She was lying as though on a bed with her head on a pillow that was much too high. The pillow was a set of black steel weights on the bottom of a pulley exercise machine. On either side of her face, two chrome bars kept the weights in line as they slid up and down. Above her head were suspended six weights all in a row, solid blocks of steel I guessed weighed about thirty kilos together. The line pulling the weights ran up through a pulley, down through another pulley, and up into the hand of a woman standing by the machine.

The Sydney Parks Strangler was indeed a woman, but I could only see that because I was standing seven metres from her and I'd heard her voice. From the shape in the black tracksuit, there was no telling her sex. The hood was pulled up around her face, so that I could only see two brightly twinkling eyes in a mass of black shadow and a widely stretched mouth. She stood with one hand by her side and one arm outstretched, fist gripping the rubber handle of the steel-weave line holding the weights.

'Step any closer and I'll let go,' she said.

'Okay,' I said.

'Put the gun down.'

I did. I even kicked it away a little out of good faith so that the weapon slid under a side table stacked with dozens of Caroline Eckhart's ten-week weight-loss program DVDs. The woman in the hood and I stood in silence for a minute or so, each carefully examining the options. I was trying to recall a list of poorly written checkpoints I'd seen on a white-board more than a decade earlier in an overheated classroom in Goulburn while the crisis negotiation specialist prattled on about hostages he'd rescued over the years.

Step one: Prolong the situation.

Step two: Ensure the safety of the hostages.

Step three: I couldn't remember. I was probably checking out the female recruits.

Step four: Foster a relationship between the hostage-taker and the negotiator, and the hostage-taker and the hostages.

'That weight's going to get heavy in a minute,' I said. The wide smile in the hood remained rigid. I was beginning to notice a lopsidedness to it, a kind of menacing Joker quality to its edges that seemed to curl too high, as though the skin from the top had been folded and tucked and now shadowed that on the bottom. A puppet smile. 'Why don't you put it on the hook and we can talk without me worrying about you crushing Caroline's head like a watermelon?'

The woman in the hood laughed. 'What a pretty image. The broken edges of a green skull. All that red-pink mush.'

'I wouldn't rely on there being too much mush in there.'

'Good tactic. Badmouth the victim. Try to relate to me.'

'It wasn't intentional.' I bit my tongue. There was sweat on my brow but I didn't want to make any sudden movements to wipe it away. 'She's not my favourite person in the world, but that doesn't mean I want to see her squished.'

I took a step closer. The woman took a step back. The line twanged in the pulley, a sickening sound.

'It's been a long time since I did this, but I think we're supposed to introduce ourselves first.'

'I know you.'

'Yes, good.' I opened my arms. 'That saves us time, doesn't it? I'm Detective Frank Bennett, I'll be your hostage negotiator for this evening.'

She didn't answer.

'And it's Ms Harper, I presume.'

'You found Ruben.'

'I found everything you left out for me,' I said. I was treading in dangerous territory, literally and metaphorically, so I kept my tone friendly. 'I think you meant that.'

I took a couple of sideways steps, then stepped back the way I'd come. I wanted her to get comfortable with the idea of me moving my feet, perhaps as a nervous gesture, so that eventually I might try to close some of the gap between us without her noticing. I went sideways, and back again, and she didn't shift back. I took half a step forward as I spoke. She didn't seem to care. The gap was now six-and-a-half metres, I guessed. Negotiations were always slow.

'Why don't you tell me what you were trying to say, Tara?'

'Why don't you tell me what I was trying to say?' she said. Her tone had changed suddenly, from amused to annoyed, and I felt my chest tighten at the sound of it. Such a seamless emotional change mid-conversation was not a good sign. Tara was not stable. She was not going to be an easy audience. She needed to talk more. There was too much going on in her mind and not enough going on here, now, with me.

'What do you mean?'

'You've got me all worked out. You know me. Why don't you tell me more about myself?'

'I didn't want –'

'*I think you meant for us to find what you left out, Tara. I'll be your negotiator, Tara. Let's not kill Caroline, Tara. Sweetie, honey, buddy, baby! Let's be friends, Tara!*'

Her words were snarled, spittle flying off her mismatched lips, but when she finished snarling them the snarls evolved into a wet laughter so high and full of rage it made my skin tingle. My mouth was bone dry. I tried to gather some saliva, looked at Caroline. She was really out of it. Her chest inflated and deflated in little shudders that produced soft snores through her open mouth. All she had to do was wake up and slide off the machine. But she wasn't going to do it. Consistent with every interaction we'd had so far, Caroline was going to be completely unhelpful to me.

'She's beautiful, isn't she?' Tara asked. She was back down to 25 per cent of the 100 per cent fury I'd seen in her only seconds before. Sliding up and down the rage scale the way the weights above Caroline's head slid up and down as Tara adjusted her grip on the handle. I'd been put right back in my box, so I just nodded and agreed.

'Isn't it interesting, what's beautiful?' Tara said. The big dark hood, deep enough that it had probably got the disfigured girl all the way through the foyer and up to Caroline's apartment without garnering attention, had slipped back a little, so I could see the lower half of her face. Two long scars lined her jaw on either side, perfectly, as though her face was a mask that could be lifted off and set in the palm of the hand. One cheek was bigger than the other. She was looking at Caroline. I could see the gap between Tara's nose and mouth gave an unnatural slant, like her nose was stuck on. 'Maybe that's how we're all supposed to be. Pure. Strong. We're supposed to be born like that, show all those bones and edges. Built for swimming. Sprinting. Climbing. She's mother nature's finest work.'

Tara crouched down, letting the handle of the weight go with her, the line feeding back into the bottom pulley, the top pulley, lowering the block of pure death that hung above Caroline's head. Tara stroked Caroline's temple with a single finger, found the edge of the bone in the immaculate, caramel-brown flesh and pressed down hard. I snuck a couple more steps sideways, back, and then forward. Five metres.

'If you're not beautiful, you're not natural. You weren't born right.'

'Is that what your mother used to tell you, Tara?'

'No,' Tara smirked. 'She didn't tell me anything. I had to have one of her old friends tell me, at a funeral, when I was a kid. Joanie just told me I was fat. But it wasn't that at all. Not really. All the running and the pinching and the hiding away. It wasn't about fat. It was because I wasn't born right.'

She tugged back the hood. One side of her neck was lined with scars, skin bunched directly below the ear as though a seam had torn and torn again and she'd been run over back and forth with some grisly sewing machine. She was very much a torn doll. Her black hair was tied back haphazardly in a ponytail, knotted and matted where the ribbon cut into the wavy locks, and I felt the desire to untangle it. To try to fix her. I had a biological longing to try to make her pretty, standing there, looking at her. Perhaps I was beginning to understand.

'She met him at a bucks night,' Tara said quietly. 'She and another girl were the entertainment. He wasn't into the whole thing. The show they were putting on. She got talking to him out on the porch. He liked her. He didn't know I was already growing inside her. I'm not sure she knew it herself.'

Tara wiped at her scarred lips. Curled a hand against her cheek, a doll in thought.

'I wonder what she thought when I was born. All that black hair.'

'Tara,' I said.

'I wonder if she knew which client it was.'

'Tara, what happened to you in Bangkok?' I asked.

'Caroline Eckhart says there's a beautiful person inside you. You've just got to reach in and pull her out,' Tara said. She stood, still examining the sleeping beauty on the floor. Her voice rose to a high imitation, a child's teasing. '*Take what you've always wanted! You deserve it! You deserve it! You deserve it!*'

I tried not to shake.

'I thought maybe there was something beautiful inside me. So I tried to fix myself. I tried to cut away the badness. I was trying to do Joanie's work, search for the beautiful thing in me, but I wanted to do it faster. I was going to be like a peach –

when all that useless flesh was removed there was going to be a seed in there that would grow a new life. A new me.'

'But that was never going to work,' I said.

'No. Because there's no beautiful person inside me. I'm rotten. Joanie thought maybe there was a little version of her in here.' She pointed to her chest. 'Maybe if she beat hard enough I'd come out.'

Tara laughed. That crooked smile bunched the loose flesh at the corners of her eyes.

'I'd planned to come out alright. I was going to come out and show her that she couldn't hurt me anymore.'

'But you didn't get that chance.'

'No. She slipped away from me.' Tara squeezed the handle of the weight machine. 'Isn't that just . . . perfect?'

'Tara.'

'She was wearing the pink Chanel dress,' Tara's voice dropped to a whisper. 'They said she looked just like she was sleeping.'

I heard sirens in the distance, saw flashes of red and blue between the big ships lining the distant wharf as three squad cars raced down the hill from Potts Point.

Step Five: Hear the demands, and make a deal.

'Killing Caroline isn't going to give you what you missed out on with your mother, Tara,' I said. 'You can't deface Joanie by defacing these women. The world is full of pretty women. Joan Harper is gone and she'll never feel what you wanted her to feel.'

'It might satisfy me for a while, though,' Tara let the weight slide up and down. 'I might feel full.'

I took a couple of steps forward. Tara took the zipper of her jacket with her spare hand and started unzipping. She slipped out of the jacket. Underneath, she was a mess of crooked seams and bubbled, puckered lines, the flesh mismatched and zigzagged. She had no breasts to speak of. No navel. She was a human patchwork doll. She jutted one hip and then the other. Slid out of the black pants and kicked off her shoes. Naked, I could follow all the seams, large and small, where skin grafts had patched flesh that had been cut away, had become infected, had been replaced with fresh skin from here and there. Two great long lines down her thighs marked where a fat reduction procedure had gone wrong, taking half the leg, leaving two uneven stilts with bulbous knees. Some parts of her were the purple of an old man's veins. I heard the telltale murmurs of the specialist raid team behind the apartment's front door and glanced that way.

'Look at me,' Tara said.

'I'm looking,' I said.

'This is me,' she smiled. She dropped a hip, put her hands up as though modelling in a pageant. A grotesque marionette dancing on a gold-lit stage. 'This is what ugly looks like.'

'Tara, you're not –' I took a step forward. I wanted to tell her she wasn't ugly, but that wasn't true. I'd seen what she had done to those runners, and it was as ugly as humanity gets. I'd been in the dark stairwell where Tara had tried to end Fiona Ollevaris' life, the lonely parkways where Ivana, Minerva and Jill had been dumped like trash. There was nothing but ugliness about Tara, and I realised that was what she was trying to tell me. She was an abomination. Finally, by showing herself, she was free. She nodded as she watched me realise this, accepting her message to me.

'There are plenty of ugly souls in prison,' I said. 'You must have thought about how well you'd fit in there.'

'I have thought about it,' Tara said. The arm that held the weight was trembling. 'I've dreamed about it. It would be just like high school, wouldn't it? But there'd be no cool kids. We'd all be rejects.'

'Let me take you then,' I said. I reached out towards her, took a couple more steps. 'It's over. Put the handle on the hook.'

'I'd be happy there in a safe little cage?' Tara asked.

'I'm sure you would.'

'With all my ugly little friends.'

'Tara, put the handle –'

'But I've never been much good at making friends.'

Tara let the handle of the weight machine go.

I heard the zipping of the line in the pulleys over my head. I dived forward on my knees and grabbed the handle as it flew towards the floor. The weights clanked. I fell on my chest, my fingers tangled in the handle and the wire. The team outside must have heard the calamity and rushed the door. There were feet all around me, three sets of hands gripping the wire and taking it from me. I could see them sliding an unharmed Caroline from her place on the weight guillotine. I lay and looked across the floor, out the balcony doors, where Tara was standing with her naked back against the balcony rail.

She gave me a little wave and then curled backwards over the rail, her arms and head, and then her shoulders, and then her back arching until she was a perfect curve over the edge. A backward dive into the dark night. A couple of the squad cops grabbed at her, but she'd landed three flights below before they closed their fists on air. I heard a crash, and the screaming of some rich couple down there on the first-floor balcony as Tara's body crashed through their outdoor dining table.

Outside the Finger Wharf apartments, the trauma team swooped on everyone except me. I stood in the crowd near Harry's and watched the old man from the apartment next to Caroline's being wheeled out of the building on a stretcher, an oxygen mask clamped to his face. Caroline was on another stretcher, somewhere in those lovely folds of mid-consciousness, looking lazily and silently at the crowd as she was brought to the ambulance, red and blue lights bouncing perfectly off her cheekbones for the cameras. The valet would have called the television channel that had him on their payroll, but everyone had heard somehow, and Cowper Wharf Road was blocked off, cars being redirected back past Frisco's. There were even water police doing laps alongside the navy boats – their decks were busy with curious sailors brought up from their bowels by the lights.

I expected the group of four people who'd had their dinner party rudely interrupted by Tara to be lapping up the media attention, but they stood quietly huddled in the ring of commotion, watching the police activity. Two women and two men dressed to the nines, one of the women with a little fur-lined jacket wrapped about her shoulders.

A cursory glance over the balcony rail at Tara's body had

told me she'd gone headfirst through a glass table cluttered with dinner bowls and knives and glasses and plates, candles and napkins. She ended up twisted in an unnatural shape, her head tilted up towards the sky and eyes closed, her naked body covered in food and glass. I didn't look for too long. I felt sad.

I imagined Imogen would see the news report when I didn't get home as expected. I called her as I stood there in the night. The phone rang out. When I looked up Eden was standing beside me watching the fray, still wearing that black baseball cap. I didn't know how long she'd been standing there. She hadn't said a word.

'You're like one of those people who asks if they can help just when the last plate is being dried,' I said.

'I wasn't asking to help.'

'She's dead,' I said. I realised, now that I was talking, that shock was trying to nibble at me. When you've experienced it before, shock is as tangible and predictable as the onset of a cold. Usually, my teeth started chattering first. Waves of goosebumps ran up and down my arms. 'Olympic-grade backflip off the balcony.'

Eden made a little half-interested noise. I rubbed my arms.

'Come on,' she sighed at last. 'The ants have got it.'

We walked through the crowd towards the edge of the cordon. I didn't ask where we were going or why. I was thinking about Eden's propensity to call the police, fire and ambulance crews who would deconstruct the scene and drag away all the necessary samples, victims and photographs 'ants'. It was very good. She was good like that, Eden, with the metaphors. I realised my mind was wandering.

It was a relief to get into the car. Warm in there. I drew out my phone and tried to call Imogen again. She didn't answer so I sent a text.

I'd assumed Eden was going to take us to Parramatta head-quarters, but she turned right at the end of Cowper Wharf Road and went into the tunnel. I thought she was driving to North Sydney station – maybe we'd been called there. But before I thought about it again we were on the Pacific Highway heading north. I wasn't too concerned about it. Eden was like an autopilot. You didn't have to watch her driving or question her route. She got you where you needed to go. The shock wore off and with all my adrenalin spent I slumped in the passenger seat with my phone in my lap, only concerned about when Imogen would call me back.

'I killed Beck,' I yawned at Eden. 'You killed just about everything that moved on Rye Farm, and now the Sydney Parks Strangler is dead. We're getting fired.'

'Or promoted.'

'Where are we going? Are you abducting me?' I stretched and groaned. For once, she gave a little laugh.

'Something like that.'

I fell asleep somewhere around Berowra, after making a crack about a romantic getaway. Eden drove in the dark in silence, the headlights blasting tiny white bugs and moths that flew into the windscreen. I don't know how I rationalised it. Maybe I thought she was taking me to our next case. We were going to turn up at a car park in Gosford where a kid had been found stabbed or something grisly like that. But I didn't even give it that much thought. I just trusted her, the way a little boy trusts his friend when he turns to the dense bush and beckons, 'Come and look at this.'

I was on the come-down from a major case. All the weight and worry about Tara Harper and who her next victim would be had fallen off me. I'd shelved the case, the way I had all the others in my career, for it to be dragged out in flashbacks when I was sixty, when I finally let myself be vulnerable to delayed PTSD and went nuts before having to be crammed in a nursing home by whoever I was shacked up with at the time. Maybe Imogen. An old and glamorous Imogen.

When I opened my eyes we were pulling into the driveway of a large house by a lake. The moon was finally out, lighting water as still and flat as glass between the pine trees. Distant mountains rippled over the horizon. I guessed we were some-where around The Entrance. I'd spent my childhood holidays here, throwing blow-up pool mattresses off the shore into the tumbling, bumbling surf, being dragged with my holiday friends towards the ocean at what felt to us like breakneck speed. We used to go fishing on that very lake. When I got out of the car, the wind whistling through the pine trees was something I remembered from that time, a sound I heard nowhere else. A high-pitched whisper that rose and fell like a ghoulish song.

All the lights in the house were on. I followed Eden through the pretty garden, saw beads of dew on the blue flowers by the big oak door as she unlocked it. A stained-glass panel was set at eye-level in the wood, little blue birds hopping from branch to branch. She led me inside. On the wall by the door was a row of hooks. She put the keys on the only empty one. On others there were little backpacks and little hats, a girl's pink umbrella. I looked at a family picture by the wall. Two pretty little black-haired kids and their handsome parents, he a broad-shouldered, dark-eyed man and she a whippet-thin waify type in a starched, collared white shirt. Hanging beside the photograph was a bare white canvas. I frowned at the empty canvas on the wall. Reached out and touched the unprimed material as I passed.

In the living room, more puzzles. The long dining-room table was full of glasses and plates and cutlery as if someone had just been eating there, but there was no food. A big wooden bowl was off-centre, empty. It might have held a salad. There was an empty lasagne tray on a wooden cutting board. Someone had brought a teddy bear to the make-believe dinner. It sat flopped on a chair. Two of the chairs were pushed in and two were pulled out.

Eden went to the kitchen and ran a hand over the empty bench. She looked at the couches. I followed her eyes. The long grey couches were arranged in an L-shape facing huge windows to the lake. Their cushions were awry. One was on the floor by an open colouring book and some pencils. From where I stood, I could see that half a page was coloured in, as though whoever had been working on it had only just left and was going to be back soon to finish the pink pig and the green turtle. There was a throw rug crumpled in one corner.

It felt as though a family was meant to be here. But the house didn't smell like a family. That's what was missing, I realised. There was another picture on the wall, a photograph of a woman that had been printed on regular copying paper and framed – an imitation. But the smell. A family house smells of food and toys and damp bathrooms. It smells like washing powder and farts and sour fruit left too long at the bottom of school bags. It smells like plants on the kitchen windowsill and perfume and sweet tooth-paste. Of chaos. Loving chaos. This house smelled like nothing. It was a theatre set. I knew, somehow, that no one had ever lived here – or if they had, that they were long gone. There was another blank canvas hanging by the entrance to the kitchen.

I started to feel the trembling I'd experienced back in the city beginning at my fingertips. But it wasn't shock this time. I'd forgotten all about Tara Harper.

'It took a long time to get it like this,' Eden said. She looked at the table, at the empty glasses – two water, two wine. 'I pieced it together mostly from crime-scene photographs. Some of the things I had to hunt down – the toys in the bedrooms were particularly difficult. Everything went into the trash when they died. There was no one to leave it to.'

'What . . .' I cleared my throat, 'what is this place?'

Eden wasn't listening. Her eyes were on the distant lake. The house was secluded. I couldn't see another for miles – at least not one that was lit up. Out on the water, a single boat sat still as a stone on the surface. It had all the deadness of a painting. The background of the set. A single strip of grey between layers of black.

'They came in through the French doors.' Eden nodded to a doorway behind me, which led to the side of the house. 'We were here, in the living room. Marcus was colouring. I was in my mother's lap. When they heard the glass breaking, they didn't move. You'd think they'd move. In the movies, they'd have got up and grabbed weapons or rushed us out the kitchen door. But my parents weren't heroes. They just sat and waited and watched as six men came into the house.'

My teeth were chattering. I clenched my jaw. Somehow I'd lost the ability to stand straight, some powerful thing was twisting and twisting in my stomach until my back started to hunch and my arms started to fold around my middle. I wasn't a hero either. I never had been. And as Eden spoke I found myself, just like the people she was describing, rooted to the spot in the middle of the house.

'They were still in their seats when they were murdered,' she said. She was looking at the couches as though she could see them there, the bodies of her parents. 'They'd dragged Marcus and me out to the car by then, so we didn't see it. But we heard it. It all went wrong so quickly. It was over in seconds.'

'Marcus . . . Marcus Tanner,' I remembered. 'The Tanner family murders.'

'The government repossessed the house when we were declared dead. The second inquest – they ruled that Eric and I had likely been killed. I bought the house a few years ago and I hunted down the crime-scene photographs, and piece by piece I started to put it all back together,' Eden said. Her eyes flickered over the china cabinet against the wall, the crystal glasses inside. A wind chime hanging from the roof guttering just outside the window was still, sheltered from the wind that only seemed to touch the trees. 'I got the pictures from murder sites online. The ones that gather clues. The cutlery in the kitchen is the same. The coverlets on the beds are the same. It's all perfect. It had to be perfect, or as perfect as I could make it. The one thing I couldn't replicate were her paintings. I didn't try. She was better than I am. Far better.'

'Eden,' I said. 'I –'

'This is the moment they entered,' she continued, gesturing to the room. 'Everything was just like this. Sometimes I come here and I try to imagine that moment, try to be there, somehow, to stop it. It's easy to be there, but it's impossible to stop it. I sit on the floor and I see them coming in just the way they did, a group of monsters. I see myself screaming. When you're a kid you always imagine monsters in the singular. You don't expect an army.'

I'd glimpsed things about the Tanner family murders across my career, but never really sat down to look at it in detail. People talked about the case when there was nothing to talk about, in elevators, in coffee rooms, at Christmas parties. It had fallen from memory into the back corner of cop conversation and existed nowhere else. Except here. It was perfectly present here. I felt the tangible danger in the room. Knowing what had happened here, I was being infected, drugged, with the terror of the victims. I felt in real danger of being grabbed. I was a child before her.

'You're Morgan Tanner,' I said.

'Yes.' She smiled a little sadly.

'Why now? Why are you telling me this?'

'I brought you here because you wanted us to address this thing between us,' Eden said. She went and perched on the back of the couch, her hands between her knees. 'And you were right. We needed to address it. It's been too long since you found out what I am. Part of what I am, I suppose. You're almost certain I killed Benjamin Annous. Trying to discover that cost you the woman you loved.'

'Don't.' My eyes began to sting.

'You deserve to know,' Eden said. Her own voice sounded strange. Deeper. Threatening to crack. 'I killed Benjamin

Annous because he was one of the men who murdered my parents. And yes, Eric and I, we killed the other men involved. But I'm responsible for so many more deaths. I'm a hunter. I hunt people like this.'

She gestured to the French doors as though the dead men she spoke of were standing there, frozen in her memory, hands out and reaching for her child-self and her brother. Innocent at the time, about to be ruined forever. Eden wiped at her eyes. I'd never seen her like this. She seemed broken somehow. A once-perfect machine now rattled, something loose inside, ticking and scraping against its housing as it turned, in need of tightening, replacement, repair. When she stood again the thing that was broken stopped ticking, and she was that immaculate monster again, her face hardened, eyes shadowed by the cap. Lost to me.

'I like pedophiles,' she said. 'But I'm diverse. I like the challenge of finding and capturing other skilled hunters. I've killed drug dealers and rapists and violent husbands. I've killed mothers and wives and daughters. I look for their true nature, the predator inside, and I take them down.'

I was really shaking now.

'Eden, please stop.'

'You have to know why I do what I do. It's important to me to keep the landscape thinned of monsters like the ones who took my parents. Then I feel as if I have some measure of control back from this moment, this moment here, when I lost everything.'

Absurdly, I took out my phone and dialled Imogen. I think my body knew what was happening even if my mind wasn't ready to go there yet.

'You have to understand, so one day you can accept what I've had to do.'

'Just wait,' I stammered. I fumbled with the phone to dial again when the call rang out. 'Just wait a second.'

There were tears on my face. I had to swipe at them to recognise the figure that emerged from the kitchen, looking behind her briefly to watch the door click closed. Hooky took her place beside Eden, and I looked at the two women before me, helpless for words.

'Imogen found out what I am,' Eden said. Her words burned in my ears, words I knew were coming but I wasn't ready for. 'She's been working on the Tanner case to try to get hold of the reward.'

'Please, please, please, please.' I ran my fingers through my sweaty hair, dialled and hung up and dialled. 'Please, no.'

'She didn't kill her,' Hooky said gently. I lifted my eyes to the child-woman standing before me. I didn't even ask how Hooky had been brought into this. My little friend. My damaged little genius. 'She wanted to, but I said no.'

'My new apprentice here has erased all the evidence Imogen gathered,' Eden said, looking at Hooky. 'The DNA listings have been altered. The registry files have been replaced. All the reports have been adjusted in the necessary way so that anything Imogen has is useless now.'

'God,' I was stammering. 'Oh God.'

'That should have been it. But you know me, Frank. I wanted her to die. The child convinced me that you wouldn't be able to handle it if I took Imogen away from you. You wouldn't be able to endure another Martina.'

'Please, Eden.'

'So I need assurance,' Eden said, lifting her eyes to me. 'I need to show Imogen that I'm serious.'

Eden reached into the back of her jeans, and from her waist belt drew a gun. It wasn't her service weapon.

'I told Imogen that I'd take everything she ever held dear if she whispered a word of my story to anyone,' Eden said, actioning the gun and pointing it at me. 'She needs to know I mean it.'

I felt the impact of the bullets before I heard the sound. Two sharp, hard punches in my midsection, the thumps of a metallic fist that doubled me slightly in the middle. I heard the sound next, two claps of thunder that made my eardrums pump. There was no pain in those first few seconds. I reached down and gripped at my torn T-shirt, not even wet yet. And then I realised I couldn't draw a breath. I'd exhaled hard with the impact. I struggled to pull in air, dropped down to my knees and steadied myself with a hand against the floor. A sort of a pop, and the air came, and the pain was blinding, limb-crumpling, so that I folded and thumped my head on the floor.

I heard Eden say, 'Go, go.'

And then both the women were grabbing me, turning me over, gripping me under the arms and knees. My head fell back against Eden's chest. I was looking up at her jaw, her cold predator eyes as they carried me through the doorway.

The fire alarm sounded, and Jim began to howl. Hades remembered a time, long, long ago, when he'd heard the sound of a car slowly creeping up the gravel drive, as it did now, delivering a new life to him. He hadn't known it at the time, of course. He'd thought his life was in the slow and gentle roll towards stillness. Quiet. He'd thought the twilight finally had him. And then there they were, two children for him to raise. Two beautiful little killers who needed him, needed his ancient evil wisdom to guide the chaos of their minds.

Eden and Eric had been a surprise for Hades. But this child was not. He'd been expecting her. In fact, she was early.

A storm was flashing on the red horizon, glowing in the diamonds of the screen door as he wandered down the hall. He opened the door, and Jim flew past him, stood on the crest of the hill before his shack and watched the battered little Kia gripping its way onto the flat, parking under the tree. The objects hanging in the tree swayed and jangled in the growing winds, cogs and wheels from engines polished and shining, bottles and chains, some tea cups and tin cans.

Hooky stepped from the car and slung a backpack shaped like a shark over one narrow shoulder. She looked tired. Gold sequined boots settled in the dust and the skirt of her black cotton dress was lit for a moment by the distant lightning seeping through the lace.

'Old man,' she said as she approached him. He looked at her fondly, remembered her swearing and snarling at Eden as the garbage dripped from her body. He remembered her spitting blood on the dirt.

Hades knew, the moment he had laid eyes upon the girl, that the same thing that had been twisted and broken away from the souls of Eden and Eric when they arrived on his doorstep was gone in her too. The light that twinkled in the eyes of most children, even older children like Hooky, had been extinguished. He didn't know yet if he could turn her off the dark path she was following, if he could somehow stop her progress towards being helplessly evil, the way that Eric had been, the way Eden sometimes was. Maybe there was something of her that could be redeemed yet. She was smart. She was tough. She didn't have to go bad. Maybe if he tried hard enough, he could save her.

And if he couldn't save her, he'd do the best he could to patch her up. The way he did with everything that came to him in the tip. She'd be crooked. She'd be hollow. But she'd be alive again.

Hooky smiled at Hades as she walked towards the little house, and the old man remembered seeing the same sarcastic teenage smile on Eden many, many years ago. The smile that breaks through the loneliness, that gives every day new purpose.

The two walked inside. The dog followed.

Epilogue

It wasn't so much consciousness but a series of half-formed thoughts that whistled through my drugged brain as I lay in the bed, sometimes seeing, sometimes just watching colours and shapes. The first realisation that formed with any real clarity was that I'd lost the sight in my left eye. I felt as though I'd heard this mentioned a couple of times by people in the room while I was asleep. I didn't know for certain who was speaking, but I picked up and held little pieces of what they said, repeated them over and over in dreams.

We're seeing some minor brain damage from lack of blood flow to the brain. Nothing that'll hinder him too badly. He's been talking in his sleep. Making sense. But that left optical nerve has died. That's lifelong, that one.

There's nothing we can do to save it?

Two close-range gut shots and twenty minutes or more to the hospital? This guy had a 30 per cent chance at survival. The eye is collateral damage.

My head was turned, and my vision was restricted to half the window beside my bed, the people going past, disembodied chests and shoulders and heads. Nurses in green with gentle faces. Freckles. Big smiles. Imogens, all of them, in their prettiness and simultaneous hardness, women who could care for a dying man, bring him back out of the arms of death.

I'd been out a long time. A good-size beard prickled against the pillow, felt sore against my temples. Everything ached. Not a powerful or unbearable ache, but the frighteningly deep kind you know is being held in check by blessed drugs, the kind of pain that will be all-consuming if the drugs so much as waiver, a feeling that makes you sick inside. Helpless.

Some story had been orchestrated about the shooting. I knew this because I had a sense that Eden had been in the room, more than once, while I floated between layers of dream. I'd heard her voice, confident and soft, commanding the way that only pack leaders can command, with the certainty that they'll be taken seriously. No apologies. No requests. I had the feeling she had sat for some time on the end of the bed and watched me sleep.

Thirty per cent chance. She had to have known those were the odds she was playing with when she shot me in the guts. It had to look like she'd meant to kill me. Imogen had to think my survival had been a mistake, an accident, and that if she didn't run now, Eden would come for me again when she could.

I lay and looked out the windows to the corridor with my one working eye, realising things behind the oxygen mask but not yet ready for anyone to know I was awake. I was aware that Imogen had never been in the room. I couldn't remember ever hearing anyone talk about her as I drifted in and out, fighting for my life. That didn't mean I'd heard everything. Maybe she'd called. I doubted it. If I knew Imogen, I knew she was smart, and if she was smart she was a long way from me right now. If she loved me, she was gone. She'd have left a break-up note, packed her things and moved to Perth if she had any sense. Eden had tried to kill me. And if Eden was willing to kill me, her own partner, she was willing to go further – to kill everyone Imogen had ever loved and held dear, to make her watch, and then to come for the beautiful psychologist in the night, maybe tomorrow, maybe the next day, maybe a year from now. I was an example. A demonstration of Eden's seriousness. If Imogen was smart she was already changing her name, and she would never speak of Eden Archer or Morgan Tanner ever again.

No matter how far she went, Eden would be watching. Imogen would know that.

Imogen was lost to me now, as wholly and completely as if she were dead, the way I was meant to be. She might follow my story in the paper but she would never contact me or anyone close to me ever again. I saw her poring over my story in the papers in a sunny café in Fremantle, her hair dyed and her shoulders bronzed and those damned freckles standing out everywhere like mud spatter. I hoped that's what she was doing. I hoped she was clever and she stayed alive. I hoped I never laid eyes on her.

I realised as I lay there that I would never bring anyone into my life like that again. Hooky had been right to turn Eden away from killing Imogen. She was right when she told the older woman that I wouldn't be able take it. I owed Hooky so much for that. For protecting me.

I would give my life over to her now, to protect her while she lingered, however long, under the dark wing of that deathly bird she'd chosen to sidle up to. There was no way on earth Hooky knew what she had done. How completely she'd signed her soul away, the true nature of the being who now owned it. I would never leave her now. I was locked to the two of them.

This was what I had been destined for, from the moment I walked into the Parramatta headquarters and Captain James introduced me to my beautiful new partner. Eden had me now and I'd never be free.

As I lay looking, a man came to the desk beyond the window ledge and stood there marking down things, a white-coated man with a thick black beard. I knew I knew him, but at first I didn't know from where. I realised who he was when I saw him lift his dark eyes to the clock on the wall behind the desk, almost instinctively, as though an alarm had gone off inside him, as it did every night. It was eight o'clock. Aamir looked at the clock for a long moment, and then went back to his paperwork, his jaw tightened and his brow heavy.

It's Ehan's bedtime, I saw him thinking. *I have to go say goodnight.*

What felt like years ago, I had told this man that there was nothing after the cold, consuming tragedy of murder. That when you lose someone so completely, as I had lost Martina, there was no great revelation, no meaning, no answer. I'd tried to give him realistic expectations of life after his son was lost to him.

But I wasn't sure now. When Eden lost her parents, it had been just the beginning of what she was. So much would come after that. Their murders stood forever as the sentinel over a life cluttered with darkness and evil and pain. She was the afterwards. She was the clean-up crew, the response of nature after the event that righted the balance of living and dead, of agony matched with agony. She was the seed that cracked free of its shell and grew, despite all odds, after the fire had ripped through the land, destroying everything else.

Eden was my fire. And what was growing in me now as I lay in the hospital bed was something so new, something so different, that I could feel its tendrils creeping up my insides, feel its curling sprouts fluttering open in my mind. Those seeds had been there a long time, but it was only the heat of the bullets Eden had put in me, and the child's heart she now held hostage, that had given them what they needed to sprout.

I didn't know what I was becoming. But I knew it wasn't good.

Acknowledgements

This book, like all my books, is the product of my apprenticeship under truly great minds in creative writing teaching in Australia. Most notably these include Dr Gary Crew and Dr Ross Watkins of the University of the Sunshine Coast, and James Forsyth. I also owe much to Dr Kim Wilkins and Dr Roslyn Petelin of the University of Queensland, and Dr Camilla Nelson of the University of Notre Dame, Sydney.

I am grateful to a number of cafés and restaurants who have tolerated my quiet and persistent yet hardly lucrative presence, including Marcelle on Macleay in Potts Point and The Upside Café in Chippendale.

I couldn't do what I do without my tough and brilliant agent Gaby Naher and that sweet-hearted Bev Cousins.

My thanks to my wonderful editor, Kathryn Knight.

Finally, my lovely Tim. Here is a man who endures living

with a crime writer who, among offering constant trivia about killers, can't bare to have him read her work without checking what page he's on every five minutes so that she can know if his emotional expressions are appropriate to the material. You are my rock.

If you enjoyed *Fall*, read on for an extract from the first novel in the gripping Crimson Lake series by Candice Fox.

CRIMSON LAKE

12.46:
THIRTEEN-YEAR-OLD CLAIRE BINGLEY STANDS ALONE
AT A BUS STOP.

12.47:
TED CONKAFFEY PARKS HIS CAR BESIDE HER.

12.52:
THE GIRL IS MISSING . . .

Six minutes is all it takes to ruin Ted Conkaffey's life.

Accused but not convicted of Claire's abduction, he's now living in the croc-infested wetlands of Crimson Lake.

Where a high-profile local man has just gone missing . . .

'A masterful novel.' Harlan Coben

AVAILABLE NOW IN PAPERBACK AND EBOOK

PROLOGUE

I was having some seriously dark thoughts when I found Woman. The only company I'd had in a month was my gun, and they can start to talk to you after a while, guns, if you're alone with them long enough. The weapon watched me with its black eye as I rattled around the bare house, saw when I failed to unpack the boxes in the hallway day after day. It lay on its side and judged my drinking. Halfway down a bottle of Wild Turkey one night, I started asking the gun what its fucking solution to everything was if it was so smart. A gun has only one answer.

The night before I found Woman, there'd been another brick through the front window. It was the third since I'd arrived in Crimson Lake, and I hadn't bothered to patch it up this time. I'd looked at the glass for a while and then gone out to the back porch and taken up residence there as the sun began to set, watched it blinking red across the wetlands, dancing on the grey sand. The house was falling apart anyway, which was why I rented it so cheap. The previous inhabitants had done a good job on the back porch, though. There was a nice strong rail and sturdy stairs, and the wire fence at the bottom of the yard that kept me safe from the crocs was intact.

The fence was also very familiar. I was used to looking at the world through diamond wire.

I'd sat there in the evenings wondering if the former residents had been hiding from something too, relishing in the predictability of nightfall as I did. The stickiness. The swell of insect life. The crocs beginning their barking in the dark, hidden, sliding in the wet and smelling me up here on the porch.

Between the vigilantes out the front and the crocs out the back I felt like I was in prison again, which wasn't so bad, because it was secure. I was free from the decision to run, because I couldn't run anymore from my crime. Then the gun reminded me, sitting beside me on the dry, cracked wood, that I still had an avenue out. I was just looking at the weapon and agreeing a little and swigging the last remnants of the bourbon when I heard the bird down near the fence.

I thought she was a swan at first. The sound coming out of her wasn't like anything I'd ever heard a bird make: a kind of coughing squeak, like she had a rock in her throat. I bumbled down the hill through the long grass and, incredibly, she approached me from the other side of the fence, so that I could see a mess of little grey chicks all swirling and scattering clumsily around her as she tried to walk. The goose seemed to rethink the approach and stumbled back, hissing and flapping one great white wing.

'Jesus Christ, are you nuts?' I asked.

I do that when I'm drunk. Talk to things. My gun. Birds. She was nuts though, clearly, waddling around wounded and plump on the banks of the croc-infested Cairns marshlands. I glanced out over the water and then opened the gate.

I'd never opened the gate before. When I'd moved into the rundown house thirty days earlier I'd asked the estate agent why the previous inhabitants had even installed one. Unless they had a boat, which it didn't appear they had, there was nothing out there in the water but certain death. He hadn't had an answer. I stepped out tentatively and my bare feet sank into the muddy sand, crab holes bubbling.

'Come here.' I waved at the bird, gripping the gate. The goose flapped and squeaked. Her babies gathered together, a terrified bundle of fluff. I looked out at the water again, seemed to spy a hundred black ripples that could have been croc eyes. The sun was down. It was their time now. 'Come here, you stupid bitch.'

I sucked in a gutful of air, rushed forward and lunged at the bird, missed, lunged again and gathered it upside down in a tangle of bones and limbs and claws and feathers. It snapped at my nose, ear, eyebrow, drew blood. The chicks scattered, reformed, clicking and squealing an infantile rendition of their mother's noise. I turned and threw the goose into my yard. The chicks followed, drawn along in a frantic row by some instinctive fishing line. I slammed the gate closed, ran up the yard and grabbed a towel that had been hanging on the verandah rail, leaving the gun sitting on the step.

On the way to the vet, the big bird and her chicks stuffed into a cardboard box, the squealing got to me. It was a heartbreaking distress siren. I yelled, 'Jesus, shut up, woman!'

I guess her name was Woman from that moment on.

In the sterile light of the vet's office, the bird seemed smaller somehow, peering from the bottom of the box at the man who had opened the door for me. She and the chicks were revealed united, a panting mound of crooked feathers in the dark. They were all silent now. I stood back so the vet couldn't smell my breath, but from the disdain on his face as he'd watched my hack parking job and my bare sandy feet coming up the drive I was fairly sure he had me pegged. I folded my arms and tried not to take up too much of his tiny examination room with my hulk. The vet didn't seem to have recognised me yet, so I took a chance and spoke up as he lifted the struggling Woman out of the box, wincing as she snapped at his collar.

'She can't walk on that foot there,' I said.

'Yep. Looks fractured. This wing too.'

I watched as he folded the goose into her natural shape, reassembling the barely contained terror-mess that she was until her feet were beneath her thick, round frame and her wings lay flat against her sides. The bird looked around the room, black eyes big and wild. The vet squeezed her gently all over, lifted her tail and looked at her fluffy rear.

'So I'll just leave her with you, I guess?' I clapped in summation, startling the bird.

'Well, that's up to you, Mr . . .?'

'Collins,' I lied.

'That's up to you, Mr Collins, but you're aware we don't have the resources for unpaid treatment here?'

'Uh, no. I wasn't aware.'

'No, we can't treat this animal without compensation.'

I scratched my head. 'I found her, though.'

'Yes,' the vet agreed.

'Well, I mean, she's not mine. Doesn't belong to me.'

'You've said.' The vet nodded.

'So that's not my goose.' I pointed to Woman, tried to tighten up my slurred speech in case that was why I was being misunderstood. 'Neither are they.' I pointed at the chicks. 'They're . . . dumped, I suppose. Abandoned. Don't you people rescue abandoned animals?'

'We people?'

'Vets.'

He gave me a long stare. 'This is not a native Australian goose. This is an Anser. A domesticated goose. It's an introduced species in this country. I'm afraid a wildlife rescue wouldn't treat it either.'

'Well, what will you do with her?' I asked. 'If I just leave her here with you?'

The vet stared again. I blinked under the fluorescent lights. Their gentle humming filled the room like gas.

'Christ,' I said. 'Well, okay. This is a business, I s'pose. You can't just go around rescuing everything for free.' I took out my wallet and flipped through the red and blue notes there. 'How much is it to fix a broken goose?'

'It's a lot, Mr Collins,' the vet said, squeezing Woman again around the base of her long, lean neck.

Seven hundred dollars later I drove home trembling and sick and the new owner of a family of domestic geese. It wasn't the fact that I now had exactly fifty-nine dollars to my name that gave me the shakes. The vet had noticed the name on my credit card was Conkaffey, not Collins. It's an unusual name. People don't forget it. And it had only been a month since it was all over the national news. I'd watched his face harden. Watched the lines around his mouth deepen, and then his eyes begin to lift. I grabbed the box of birds and left before I could see the look on his face.

I was sick of that look.

1

I didn't know Sean was there until his shadow fell over me. I jolted, grabbed my gun. I'd fallen asleep in my usual place on the porch, spread out against the wall on an old blanket. For a moment I thought an attack was coming.

'This is a sorry sight,' my lawyer said. The morning light was already blazing behind him.

'You look like an angel,' I said.

'What are you doing sleeping out here?'

'It's glorious,' I groaned, stretched. It was true. The hot nights on the porch behind the mosquito netting were like a dream. The roll of distant thunder. Kids laughing, lighting fires on the faraway bank. The old blanket was about as thick as the mattress I'd had in segregation.

Sean looked around for a chair on which to place his expensively fabricked backside. When he didn't see one he went to the step, put the coffees he'd been carrying and the bag on his elbow on the wood and started brushing off a spot. Even in the Cairns humidity there was some silk in his ensemble, as always. I sat up and joined him, scratched my scalp awake. I'd placed Woman and her young in the cardboard box turned on its side in a corner of the porch, a door made out of a towel. The big goose hissed at the sound of us from behind the towel and Sean whipped around.

'Don't tell me –'

'It's a goose,' I said. '*Anser domesticus.*'

'Oh, I thought it was a snake.' The lawyer gripped at his tie, flattened and consoled it with strokes. 'What the hell have you got a goose for?'

'Geese, actually. It's a long story.'

'They always are with you.'

'What are you doing up here? When did you get here?'

'Yesterday. I'm heading to Cairns, so I thought I'd stop by. Got a sexual assault defendant who's jumped bail. I'm going to try to talk him back down. Everybody flees north.'

'If you've got to hide, it's better to do it where it's warm.'

'Right.' Sean looked at me. 'Look, good news, Ted. Not only have I brought my favourite client a delightful care-package, but as of this morning your assets are officially defrosted.'

The white-haired man handed me a plastic bag of goodies. Inside were a couple of paperbacks and some food items. I didn't have the heart to tell him about my fridgeless state. There was an envelope of forms as thick as a dictionary in the bag. He took one of the coffees and handed it to me. It smelled good, but it wasn't hot. There wasn't anything at all within twenty minutes' drive of the house, certainly nowhere that made coffee. It didn't matter. The scary forms and the cold coffee couldn't possibly dampen my joy at seeing Sean. There were about twenty-one million people in Australia who believed I was guilty of my crime. And one silk-clad solicitor who didn't.

'I imagine there's something in that envelope from Kelly,' I said.

'Adjustments to the divorce settlement. Again. Semantic stuff. She's stalling.'

'It's almost as though she wants to stay married to me.'

'No. She just wants to watch you wriggle.'

I sipped the coffee and looked at the marshlands. It was flat as glass out there, the mountains on the other side blue in the morning haze.

'Any sign of . . .?' I cleared my throat.

'No, Ted. No custody inclusions. But she doesn't have to rush, she can do that any time.'

I stroked my face. 'Maybe I'll grow a beard,' I said.

We considered the horizon.

'Well, look at you. I'm proud of you,' Sean said suddenly. 'You're a single, handsome, thirty-nine-year-old man starting all over again with a rental house and a few too many pets. You're not really that much worse off than a lot of guys out there.'

I snorted. 'You're delusional.'

'Serious. This is your opportunity for a do-over. A clean slate.'

I sighed. He wasn't convincing either of us.

'So are they guard geese?' he asked, changing the subject.

I had to think for a moment what he meant.

'The Nazis used geese to guard their concentration camps,' he explained.

'That so?'

'Can I take a look?'

I waved. He approached the box cautiously, squatted and lifted the towel with manicured fingers. He wore houndstooth socks. Probably alpaca. I heard Woman squeal from the gloomy depths. Sean laughed.

'Wowsers,' he said.

'All still alive?' I asked.

'Looks like it.' Sean glanced at me. 'You looking for work?'

'Not yet. Too soon.'

The little geese pipped and shuffled around in the box. Claws on cardboard. He left them alone.

'Would you do me a favour?' Sean said.

'Probably.'

'Would you check out a girl in town named Amanda Pharrell?'

'Would I *check out a girl?*' I looked at him, incredulous.

'A woman,' Sean sighed and gave me an apologetic smile. 'Will you pay a visit to a woman in town?'

'Who is she?'

'Just a woman.' Sean shrugged.

'What do I want to visit her for?'

'You're full of questions. Stop asking questions. Just do what I tell you. She'll be good for you, that's all. Not to date. Just to meet.'

'So it's not romantic in any way.'

'No,' Sean said.

'Then what the hell is it?'

'Jesus, Ted,' he laughed, before repeating an adage he'd used many times during my trial prep. 'I'm your lawyer. Don't ask me why. Just *do* it.'

I made no commitment.

We sat for a while talking about what he was doing in Cairns and how long he'd stay. Sean was sweating through his linen trousers. His poreless nose was burned already by the sneaky tropical sun, slowly cooking the unwary Sydney man through the wet air. I'd managed a nut-brown tan just trudging around the property for a month, walking to the nearest shops to buy Wild Turkey. I hoped I'd fit in eventually. That I'd grow safely unrecognisable from the man who had graced the cover of the *Telegraph* for weeks at a time, the broad-shouldered ghoul in a suit hanging his head outside the courthouse, pale from jail. A beard might do it, I thought. And time. I'd need plenty of time.

2

Here's what I remember. And it's a lie. It's a composite memory, built from things I actually remember, stuff I heard during my trial, what I read in the paper and things whispered to me in my jail cell while I was on remand. Some bits and pieces I'm sure come from my nightmares – it's possible that the storm wasn't so foreboding, or her eyes so big and pretty. But the memory of those fatal moments is impossibly clear. More fabrication than history. The narrative is woven from many colourful strings. It cannot be snapped now, even if small fibres over the years will part and coil away. I believe it. Even if I know it isn't true.

She was standing by the side of the road, exactly in line with the road barrier markers, which weren't that much shorter than her. She was thirteen. She looked ten. The girl was so pale, and her hair was so doused in flaming afternoon sunlight coming through the clouds that she almost became one of those markers; a white sentry beside the isolated highway, still as stone. I didn't see her at first. I saw the bus stop and the well-worn tracks of the great vehicles in the dry mud. I slowed, turned off the highway and pulled in to the bus stop area, parking my car somewhere between ten and fifteen metres from the girl.

A blue Hyundai Getz drove past on the highway going south,

carrying Marilyn Hope, 37, and her daughter Sally, 14. They would testify to witnessing my car pull off the highway 'suddenly' and park 'close' to the girl. It was 12.47 pm. Sally Hope testified to the exact time I pulled off the road because she glanced at the clock in the car as they went by, and she remembered calculating that they had thirteen minutes to get to her dance lesson.

I got out of the car and spotted the pale girl standing there for the first time. She was looking at me, her pink Pokémon backpack sitting on the ground beside her.

My first thought was: *Where did she come from?*

My second thought was: *Fix the noise.*

The fishing rod had been tapping against the back window of my Corolla. I opened the back left-hand door of the car, climbed halfway in, and pulled the rod and the tackle box towards me across the seat so that the handle of the fishing rod slid down into the gap behind the front passenger seat, pulling the tip of the rod away from the window.

A red Commodore drove past on the highway going north, carrying Gary Fisher, 51. Gary was the third witness. He would testify to seeing my car parked by the girl, the back passenger-side door open. The door closest to the girl.

I spotted my car insurance renewal notice, open and crumpled, in the mess of papers and takeaway containers on the floor behind the driver's seat. I picked up the pale green paper and examined it, still half-in, half-out of the door.

Truck driver Michael Lee-Reynolds, 48, drove past on the highway going south. Witness number four. He'd back up Gary's claim of seeing me parked by the girl, the back passenger door open. A tall, broad-shouldered man fitting my description, halfway in, halfway out of the back seat.

I leaned out of the vehicle, righted myself, and tucked the insurance notice into the pocket of my jeans. I looked at the girl. She was still watching me. A light rain had begun to fall and it was caught by the gentle breeze, tiny droplets misting all around her in the sunlight like tiny golden insects. She kicked the dirt with her shoe and played with the belt loops of her jeans, then turned away. She was a thin girl. That's about all I would genuinely remember about her, all I would tell the police I remembered in my initial interrogations. She'd been thin, bony, and white. The rest of my recollections of the girl who would ruin my life I would fill in from photographs at the trial. I'd see her big teeth in 'before the attack' pictures. The way her nose crinkled when she smiled.

I stood beside the highway on that terrible day and glanced at the dark purple horizon beyond the trees as I closed the car door.

'Some pretty heavy rain coming,' I said.

A red Kia drove past going south, carrying sisters Jessica and Diana Harper, 34 and 36 respectively. Witnesses five and six testified that they'd seen me talking to the girl. They were unable to agree whether my back left door was open or shut. It was 12.49 pm.

'Yeah,' the girl said.

'Your bus coming soon?' I asked.

'In a minute,' she said and smiled. Crinkled her nose. Or maybe she didn't. I don't know anymore.

'All right,' I said. Two more cars full of witnesses drove past, uncertain, between them, if when I waved at the girl it was with my right hand, palm flat, facing towards her, in a 'goodbye' type of gesture, or if in fact I was beckoning her, left hand up, palm open and turned towards me, in a 'come here' type gesture. Testimony about the exact nature of the 'goodbye'/'come here' gesture would last three days.

All of them would agree, in the end, that I made some sort of gesture while I was standing by the back passenger door of my car. The door closest to the girl.

I walked around the front of my car, got into the driver's seat, started it, and drove away. I didn't look back.

At 12.52 pm, the girl's bus drove past. The exact time would be recorded on the vehicle's GPS. The Pokémon backpack was on the ground, the driver and passengers all agreed.

But there was no girl.

Claire Bingley was abducted from the bus stop at Mount Annan, on the edge of the highway, that Sunday afternoon. She was driven to a patch of bush about five minutes away along dusty back roads dividing cattle farms and vacant lots. In the dark of the woods, she was beaten, brutally raped and then strangled until she lost consciousness. Her attacker must have thought she was dead. But with the unexplainable tenacity and physical resilience possessed by some children, the girl, against all odds, didn't die. Claire lay in the dark listening to the sounds of the bush around her for several hours, terrified that her attacker was nearby. Night fell and then the horizon lit again. The girl wandered out of the bush and walked in a zombie-like daze to the highway, reappearing some ten kilometres south of where she'd vanished. It was about six o'clock the next morning. Claire had been missing for seventeen hours.

An old man driving to Razorback to help his son move house spotted her crouched at the roadside, nude. Her face was so bloody he'd thought at first she was wearing a red mask. Her throat was so damaged she couldn't explain what had happened to her.

Social media, by this time, was well into a frenzy that had begun the previous evening, about three hours after the girl disappeared. The eight o'clock news updates picked it up, right between *The Project* and *MasterChef*. The whole country saw it. Her parents whipped up the panic until it was on all news networks, and a quickly designed missing poster of Claire was shared online eight hundred thousand times, in places as far away as San Francisco. Claire had been abducted. They knew it. The disappearance was totally uncharacteristic of their daughter. Claire's parents knew in their hearts that something terrible had happened. They were right.

The first time a suspect was ever mentioned was in the comments section of one of the social media posts. Under a picture of Claire, plastered with pleas to share the image of the missing child around, one of the drivers who had been on the highway that day wrote 'I think I saw the guy.'

That guy was me.

Redemption

An abducted girl. An innocent man caught in the crossfire.

When former detective Ted Conkaffey is wrongly accused of abducting a teenage girl, he hopes the Queensland town of Crimson Lake will be the perfect place to disappear. But nowhere is safe from the girl's devastated father.

Meanwhile in a nearby roadside hovel, the bodies of two young bartenders lie on the beer-sodden floor. As a homicide investigation unravels, Ted and his unlikely ally private detective Amanda Pharrell are brought in to assist on the case.

While Ted fights to clear his own name, their hunt for the killer will draw them into a violent dance with evil . . .

Steeped in tension, REDEMPTION is an absorbing crime thriller from an award-winning writer which will hold you in its grip to the final page.

Available now in paperback and eBook

arrow books